EXONERATED WITH LOVE

Skye McNeil

Exonerated with Love © 2018 by Skye McNeil

Exonerated with Love is a work of fiction. All names, characters, events and places found therein are either from the author's imagination or used fictitiously. Any similarity to persons alive or dead, actual events, locations, or organizations is entirely coincidental and not intended by the author.

For information, contact the publisher, Hot Tree Publishing.

WWW.HOTTREEPUBLISHING.COM

EDITING: Hot Tree Editing

COVER DESIGNER: Claire Smith

FORMATTING: RMGraphX

ISBN: 978-1-925655-63-6

10 9 8 7 6 5 4 3 2 1

For the paralegals, legal assistants, and court attendants who keep the courts/law firms afloat.

PROLOGUE

The group of police officers gathered beneath a cloudless sky. A cheerful summer breeze drifted through the towering trees while children skipped rocks on Gray's Lake. Songbirds twittered joyous tunes in the exact park where destruction had reigned in the cooler months.

Squad cars lined the beaten paths, silent after the honorary ceremony. The annual police department luncheon was sprawled on picnic tables while the soft strains of dueling guitars played under a sycamore tree.

Never had Joci Dorous felt more Zen as she sat up against a tree trunk, her hands weaving between the clipped waves of Officer Cameron Shearer's hair. Her eyes surveyed the happy troops of families while charcoal grills sputtered flames. "Did you ever imagine anything like this for your life?" she asked.

The man with his head on her lap shifted to face her, but his view was obstructed by her slightly swollen waist. Peeking over, Cameron pressed a kiss to the baby bump as he replied, "No, my mind could never conjure anything so glorious."

Joci's face broke into a smile, and he leaned up on his elbow. "Are you happy then?" he inquired, kissing the crease of her lips.

Catching his face between her hands, she nodded vigorously. "Very much so."

The instant she dropped his chin, Cameron sprang into action and crawled up beside her. Sweat lined his brow as he dug a hand into his back pocket. He knelt before her with a small black box in his grip.

Whispers scattered through the crowd around them, but neither paid heed. The sun cast perfect light through the tree's leaves, enveloping them in eternal bliss.

"How about now, Joci?" Cameron said in a loud voice. The shimmer in his brown eyes matched the one in hers. "We're not well-traveled archaeologists, and I think I'm a few years late, but I love you. If you will have me, I'll spend every day I live proving we were always meant to be together."

In stunned silence, Joci gaped at the three-carat diamond, impressive for a modest police officer. Without a doubt, his continued alliance with the Del Rossi mob assisted him in the purchase. "Will you arrest me if I say no?" she replied, with a smirk.

"Hell yeah!" a heckler who sounded a lot like Quinn called.

She swiveled her gaze from the ring back to Cameron. The brilliant colors of his ornate tattoos poked from beneath his police uniform, a perfect collision of worlds. Her eyes darkened to green and a shy grin spread across her cheeks.

"Then I better say yes before another woman does," she managed, her face blushing a shade that would put a rose to shame.

Cameron flashed a set of straight teeth and hauled her to him. "Good, because otherwise I owe Quinn five hundred bucks."

Gaping, she swatted the back of his head, but he still possessively kissed her lips. The group surrounding them clapped, a few whistled, and the women cooed over the scene.

From beneath the flowing branches of a weeping willow, the scarred onlooker had another reaction. The one emotion that looked best on Joci Dorous was love. Unfortunately for his mangled self, the same happy gleam in her ever-adapting hazel eyes had shone on him not yet seven months ago.

But now he was back. Back for his wife and unborn child. Hell would come as a welcoming embrace for Cameron Shearer when Adrian Petosa was finished with him. Taking his life for a short amount of time was one thing, but after the grueling battle Adrian fought the last few months, the mobster turned cop wouldn't get her eternal devotion too. Not while he breathed. Not while he watched their every move.

CHAPTER ONE

"Where do you want these boxes?"

Joci lifted her sights to the brawny man holding three file boxes. If she hadn't been so distracted by the fresh ink on his arms, she would've noticed him poke his head around the cardboard.

"Joce, I know you think I have superhuman strength, but I'm pretty positive there are bricks in here," Cameron complained.

Standing, she pointed to the storage closet off to the right. "Sorry. Over there is fine. And they're books, not bricks."

After dropping the boxes, Cameron leaned a palm against the doorframe. "Please tell me those were the last of them."

Meeting his mocha-colored eyes, she nodded. "Yep, don't worry." She reached over and looped her arm around his waist. Weeks of rigorous police training only accentuated his body, forming lean muscle beneath his plethora of artwork. Despite all of the academy training, Cameron's chest heaved as they stood in the empty office. They'd been at it all morning, and it almost looked homey now thanks to their efforts.

"Great, because I need food." He nuzzled his nose to her nape. "Got anything for me?"

Ignoring the sultry tone in his voice and the solid curve prodding her side, Joci pushed away and waved him toward the exit. "Come on. There's a ton of unpacking to do. I can't have any distractions." She met his devious smirk.

He took a step in her direction, pulling off his T-shirt. "It's awfully hot in this place. I should really check out that air-conditioning unit," he began, balling up the police-emblemed shirt and tossing it to the side. His fluid movement couldn't have been sexier if he tried. "I don't think it's working properly."

"Cameron," she warned, holding up her palms.

When all he did was shrug, a giggle escaped her. Unable to tear her eyes from his frame, Joci was enamored at the rippled abs and splay of colors across his skin. They were as breathtaking as when she initially saw them.

By the time he reached her, organizing the new office was the absolute last notion in her mind. "I thought you were hungry," she remarked when Cameron's lips dallied on her collarbone.

"Oh, I am. Famished, in fact," he replied, tilting her head up. "And you're the only sustenance able to quell my starvation."

Joci's heart thudded against her rib cage, the sound resonating in her ears. Even though she was six months pregnant, he wanted her, craved her more each day they were together. It was a wonder she ever got anything done at work with how often he stopped by for "lunch."

"In that case, I can't let you waste away." The second the words escaped her lips, Cameron was there, engulfing her mouth. Taken aback, Joci clung to his sweaty shoulders, eager to feel each inch of the cop fiancé consuming her heart.

He leaned her against the wall, and his hands cupped her jaw as he fervently kissed her lips. She couldn't have stopped him if she wanted to, which she didn't. Ever. He was a man with a new lease on life, and that included devouring her no matter the time or location.

Joci's breath hitched when he lifted her off the floor and set her on the edge of a stack of unpacked boxes before his hand slipped under her flowing skirt. As he lifted it, a cool rush of air scattered goose bumps on her flesh. His fingers traced her silky legs, working up to her thighs. Every sexy movement was deliberate and forced her mind away from the mundane task of moving.

"Ooh, looks like lunch *and* a show today," a friendly voice harassed from the edge of reality.

Gasping at the intrusion, Joci struggled to correct her skirt. "Rayna. Shit, I forgot you were coming in today." Her cheeks flamed, and she fanned herself as her business partner came into view.

"It's Wednesday, Joci. Normal people work on Wednesday." Rayna Alley's stilettos halted, and she reviewed the officer's shirtless torso. "I like the new tatt, by the way. I wonder why you got the justice code in Latin."

Cameron offered a cheeky smile, but didn't budge from

his hold on his fiancée. "This hot attorney inspired me. What can I say?"

Blowing bangs in desperate need of a trim from her eyes, Rayna harrumphed. "Uh-huh, whatever, lovebirds." She held up a bag from the café up the street. "I've got extras. Anyone hungry?" She pulled out a sandwich and frowned at Cameron. "But maybe put a shirt on, stud muffin. If anyone walks in here, they'll think we're hosting a *Magic Mike* audition."

"Which I would win, hands down," he replied with a cocky tilt of his head.

Rayna gave him a once-over and shrugged. "Eh, I've seen better."

Joci observed Cameron roll his eyes before he and Rayna dove into the turkey and ham concoctions. *It can't get more perfect than this.* Her stomach grumbled at the scent of sandwiches, and she chuckled when the baby started kicking. *This kiddo sure knows when food's around.*

Though the office space had been in use the last three months, she hadn't been able to leave Petosa until recently. The high-rise held too many memories, both good and bad, and shaking them wasn't easy. Now, Alley and Dorous Law Firm was officially open, thanks to the moving boxes and freshly printed business cards.

Pulling up a chair, she grabbed a pickle spear. The satisfying crunch and saltiness calmed the rambunctious baby within seconds. Cameron winked at her, then resumed his argument with Rayna about lazy law enforcement in Des Moines.

She munched silently. Maybe it was the fact of only recovering Adrian's ring and blood that had kept her at his father's firm so long. In some twisted way, she hoped he'd resurrect, if solely to tell her he was fine with the way she'd moved on. No such miracle graced her.

Joci nibbled on a potato chip and cracked her neck. Mostly, she guessed doubt had kept her from entirely shifting life from Petosa to her own firm. It was a huge step in any situation, but especially for her. Petosa was where she'd formed connections and grown to become the attorney she was today. Leaving solidified the end of her tenure there.

"Do you need help with the depositions next week?" Rayna asked, interrupting her wayward musings.

Recollecting the theft case, she shook her head. "Nah, I'm good. There are four witnesses, so it won't take long. But that reminds me, I need to call the court reporter." She dug out a notepad and scribbled a note.

Cameron plopped a sandwich in her hands. "Please eat something other than chips and pickles." He glanced to the other attorney. "It's all she eats at home. Ice cream too, I guess."

"I'm fine." She waved off the concern, but it remained etched on his brow. His protectiveness warmed her heart, but also annoyed her some days.

Rayna and Cameron exchanged knowing glances. "I have to agree with him. Little *bambino* needs more carbs and meat."

Unwrapping the ham and cheese, Joci took an exaggerated bite. "Happy now?" she muttered through a full mouth.

Cameron leaned over and kissed her nose. "Yes." He wiped off the mustard smeared on her bottom lip and popped the finger in his mouth. "You're all I need to be happy."

Joci could almost hear Rayna's gray eyes rolling. She hadn't expected the man beside her to ever reform from his criminal ways, but he proved her wrong on a daily basis. In her wildest dreams, she'd never have guessed her childhood neighbor would be the perfect man for her. He was the same carefree smartass she'd fallen in love with as a child and over the last months. Still, there was part of him that he hid from the rest of the world. Cameron's minimal Del Rossi affiliation was kept under wraps, something she was simultaneously grateful and concerned about. She trusted him, yet a part of her wouldn't turn a blind eye to the mob. Maybe it was the streak of justice running through her veins giving her pause. While she wasn't a fan of the mob, they did expedite his police officer's training, so she couldn't complain too much.

"I'd stay here all day, but I'm late for work." Cameron pressed his lips to hers briefly. As he pulled away, she wished he didn't have to go. With their hectic schedules, any time spent with him was precious. "We'll finish this later."

The rumbling of his promise urged her to close up shop then and there, but he had a full shift to get through before any shenanigans could occur. She watched the sway of his tight ass. And there'd be many shenanigans too.

"Ray, try to keep her under control, will ya?" he teased, retrieving his shirt.

Both women watched in disappointment as he yanked

the article in place, hiding the flamboyant hues and robust physique.

"I will if you tell Quinn to stop pulling me over," Rayna quipped. "It's always when I'm busy too. He knows it ruins my day, the jerk." She chomped into a chocolate walnut cookie and waved him through the door.

"Quinn giving you trouble again? Geez, I wonder why," he heckled with a faux puzzled expression.

Stretching her legs, Joci rested the sandwich on her baby bulge. "I'll call you later."

Cameron brushed his hair off his brow. It was too long by police standards, but he always used gel to keep it back enough to be within regulation. "No matter how many times you use your belly as a table, it's adorable." He pecked her lips again and softened his voice. "You're going to wait up for me, right? Or should I wake you up when I get home?"

Running a palm along his toned ass, she squeezed. "Better wake me up. I doubt I'll make it to the evening news."

Snatching his sunglasses from the top of a box, he opened the front door. "All right. Keep the cuffs by the bed, darlin'."

"Oh my God, Cameron! Too much information," Rayna complained as he shut the door with a suggestive lift of his eyebrows. "You sure you love him? He's a bit of a freak."

Joci swirled a hand on her stomach. "Yeah, Rayna, that's part of why I love him."

Her partner flicked her auburn hair and said, "Whatever you say."

Taking a deep breath, Joci reviewed the boxes that needed to be put away. For the time being, they could wait. Cameron's mild cologne lingered in the air, and she closed her eyes. The last months with him had been every girl's dream come true. He was attentive to her every whim, but was also the cocky kid she'd known in Ohio. Little by little, she found herself succumbing to the essence of their relationship. She'd rather spend time with him than pore over case law, and that was a huge change for her. Something about Cameron's love uncovered a part of her she long thought lost after her divorce and the sad deaths in her life. Sure, she still wrangled county attorneys for the best possible deals for her clients, but now she saw beyond the criminal façade to the person beneath. And it was all because of Cameron. She couldn't ask for a better man in her life.

She eyed the boxes once more then decided to focus on a few cases to keep her mind off Cameron. Joci retreated to her large office and did her best to ignore the sunny summer sky and the lingering sensation filtering through her body from time spent with her gorgeous fiancé. She bit her bottom lip as her stomach flipped in anticipation. Maybe she'd spice things up tonight and stay awake long enough to surprise him with a dessert he'd be sure to enjoy more than once.

***

Clicking his pen obnoxiously, Cameron scanned the vehicles zooming by the undercover patrol car. For the most part, brake lights lit up the night when the drivers discovered their car wasn't scouting out new places to park and make out. It was rather comical, really, when the citizens slammed on their pedals in hopes of leniency.

They'd made a good run thus far. Meeting their quota wasn't difficult when Quinn was addicted to the radar gun and Cameron was pedal happy to pull dumbasses over. Quitting time was virtually upon them, but the night seemed to drag on more than usual.

He loosened the seat belt and rehashed the call received from Jerry on his way to the station. Though his credible job as a police officer helped pay the bills, it also supplied the Del Rossi mob with priceless intel from the streets of the capital. He wasn't fond of dropping off his gang findings at Gray's Lake. It was an ironic drop point, and Cameron cringed whenever he met Jerry's goons. *Another four and a half years and I'm done.* He clicked the pen faster, his angst rising as he thought about the moonlighting that secured a future with Joci. The substantial pay didn't dampen his outlook either. The mafia was a necessary evil for the foreseeable future. He'd make it all work. Somehow.

"Okay, you need to stop," Quinn growled, snatching the writing utensil from his copilot.

"Sorry. Nerves." He reviewed the reports from their shift, nothing sticking out as activity Del Rossi would be interested in learning. Gnawing his thumbnail, he hoped something would surface soon. The recent inactivity was suspicious, and his boss was booked to visit later in the week. Giving Jerry an in-person update on his operation sounded as delightful as getting blown up. Again.

"How're things with Joci?"

Cameron eyed the man he once considered competition. "You don't want to hear my domestic life ramblings."

Shifting in his seat, Quinn changed the radio station. "I do, actually. She was a close friend of mine before you buffaloed into town. Need I remind you how close?"

A pang of envy coursed through Cameron. He'd understood the relationship Joci and Quinn shared long before he fell for her. It shouldn't bother him that his friend and the woman he loved had a long-standing bond, but it did.

"Yeah, yeah. Joci and I are good" was all Cameron could muster. He was never one to go into great detail or make friends easily, and he didn't want to mess this up. It had come as a complete shock when he and Quinn shared a kinship. He was grateful to have a seasoned officer as a partner, even if doubt filtered into his mind off and on about Joci and Quinn.

"That's all I get? Come on, Shearer. I know there's more." Quinn flipped the radio to country, Cameron's least favorite.

"We're new in our relationship." He cranked down the knob when the banjos blared a loud riff. "It's been six-ish months, she's carrying Adrian's baby, and I'm terrified I'll screw it up somehow or she'll wake up one day and realize her mistake." He thought it was best to avoid the whole mob infiltration bit at this point. Quinn was by the book, and Cameron ruffled the pages at every turn.

Mulling over the abrupt confession, Quinn took a sip

from his bright green water bottle. If he was trying to remain incognito, he'd chosen the wrong drink carrier. "Your fear is understandable. Hell, I was afraid to lose Joci, and I did after two years." He held up his hand when he saw the panic on Cameron's face. "But she told me from the start she wasn't looking for anything except a good time." He smirked, his eyes taking on a far-off look. "And boy did I help her achieve that. Many, many times."

Cameron narrowed his eyes to slits. "Not cool, asshole, not cool."

Quinn chuckled. "Ha, sorry. I forget who I'm talking to sometimes."

A call spit over the radio for a domestic disturbance, but another car responded first.

"But honestly, Cam, don't overthink this." Quinn crossed his arms, the muscles displaying dedication at the gym. "Your fiancée—" He made a face. "God, that's weird." He straightened his shoulders and continued. "She doesn't settle. She knows who she wants, and no one will sway her otherwise."

Soaking in their conversation, Cameron admitted, "I don't want to lose her again." Never had a woman gripped him by the soul like Joci. It was why he craved being near her, being with her in every sense as frequently as possible. These sensations weren't common for the semi-converted mobster. No other woman compelled him the way Joci did.

"Joci loves you." His pal shifted the car into drive when a canary-yellow sports car raced by. "No clue why, but she does. Stop worrying." He flipped on the flashing lights, his smile broad as it was each time he pulled someone over. "She doesn't love unless she means it."

Cameron patted his seat belt as the car lurched to life. He didn't need to respond. Quinn was right, of course, but his gut nagged at him. It felt as though a storm was brewing above Des Moines and he couldn't stop it.

***

An hour later, the exhausted rookie cop unlocked the front door of the three-bedroom ranch on the outskirts of the capital. Kicking off his heavy boots, Cameron's nose caught the remnants of strawberry candle wax. He breathed it in then closed his eyes as memories flooded him. Joci consistently smelled of summer, and their home was no different. He wouldn't have it any other way. Her fragrance had kept him sane while on trial for murder. Berries would forever ignite an olfactory cue back to Joci and their time spent together.

The light on the microwave blinked angrily, so he strolled into the kitchen. Popping it open, he shook his head when he spotted the cup of herbal tea Joci had left in the black box. Taking it out, he noticed it was warm. His forgetful fiancée hadn't been asleep long. The rest of the kitchen was spotless; her favorite pastime.

Yawning, he flicked off the dome light and crossed the maple hardwood floor to the master bedroom. When he stepped inside the large expanse, his breathing paused at what met him. Joci lay on her right side, hugging his pillow as she slumbered. The lightweight nightdress settled around her thighs and left little to the imagination. The messy chestnut bun atop her head made him recall how the damn thing tickled his nose each night. He noticed her glasses were lopsided, as if she'd fallen asleep unexpectedly. He'd never tire of coming home to this. To opening the front door and finding her passed out with homicide photos plastered to her cheek. Pregnancy ate at her stamina, but he was grateful it didn't hinder her in other aspects of their cohabitation.

After being alone for too many years, he'd been hesitant about living with anyone, much less a woman he loved this much. But after experiencing evenings with the attorney burrowed in his arms, sleeping without her was no longer an option.

Easing beside her, Cameron plucked the glasses from her face and rested them on the side table. Smoothing wayward hair off her brow, he took in the delicacy of her face, memorizing the creases and lines where she smiled. They'd grow deeper with age, something he was looking forward to observing in the coming years.

"You're too damn beautiful," he whispered, not anticipating a reply.

"And you're late." Slowly, her hazel eyes came into view. They engrossed him no matter the situation. The brown and green specks muddled together and cast a gaze of adoration over his frame. She was his beautiful siren, and he'd crash on the jagged rocks of Joci's love for eternity, not once regretting it.

"Sorry. Quinn got carried away with the last drunk driver. He literally made him do every test in the book plus the chicken dance. It was pretty funny to be entirely honest." He pressed a kiss to her temple. "You forgot your tea again."

Sitting up, she winced at the bright light above. "Shit. I thought I was forgetting something." She scrunched her nose. "Dammit, I forgot your dessert too." She pointed to the jar of maraschino cherries. "That was part of it."

Holding in a chuckle, Cameron picked up the jar and eyed the bright red cherries. "And what was I supposed to do with these?"

Joci's eyes lowered to the comforter. "Well, there was supposed to be whipped cream and chocolate sauce too, but I fell asleep."

He did let out a laugh this time. "And where precisely was I supposed to eat this fruit?"

Her face turned pink. It was too cute. "Um, off me."

As her adorably awry dessert plans washed over him, his heart rate picked up. Even though she was getting to the uncomfortable phase of pregnancy, Joci never failed to please him. Or attempt to satisfy his stamina. He replaced the jar to the side table. He'd never complain, though, since she was just as addicted to his body as he was to hers.

"That's okay, babe. You can surprise me with all your kinky ways another time." Cameron stole his pillow from her and fluffed it. "How was your night?"

"Well, I drafted a proof brief, then spilled pasta sauce on my pants, so not the best." She nudged into his warmth. "It's better now."

"Good." He nestled her head against his chest and ran a

hand over her belly. "And how's he?"

Joci lifted her chin defiantly. "She."

"Nah, these are strong kicks," he stated, and the baby obliged with a rapid hit to his palm. "Boy for sure."

Snuggling closer, she sighed. "We'll find out soon, won't we?"

They sat feeling the effects of the child's tumbling until Cameron broke the peace and stood. "Do you think the baby will hate me?"

"What? No. Why would you think that?" Joci turned toward him, her expression perturbed.

Cameron stood. "I don't know. It's Adrian's, and I'd think he or she would see me as a villain the older they get." He shrugged out of his uniform and pulled on a pair of gym shorts, not bothering with a shirt.

"You are this baby's dad, whether biological or not," she argued, catching his wrist.

Nodding, he moved to the bed's edge and grazed her chin with his index finger. "You're right. It's scary, is all. I don't know what I'd do if anything happened to either of you."

Understanding flooded her face, and she pulled him onto the bed. "We can't worry about what may happen." She hugged him. "Whatever comes, good or bad, we have each other and we'll get through it."

Tracing her neck with agile fingers, he agreed. It was his sole option. "I know, but promise me one thing." She nodded for him to go on. "You'll never ever wear underwear again."

Laughter bubbled up from her throat, and she slugged

his arm playfully. "You're relentless," she teased.

Kissing her soundly, Cameron unlatched his lips only after hearing her satisfied sigh. "Yes, I am. Relentlessly in love with you."

Rolling her on top of him, he stole her mouth once more. "Wanna play cops and robbers?"

Smirking, Joci grabbed his wrists and pushed them into the bedding above his head. He didn't bother resisting. Why would he when he was exactly where he wanted to be? "It depends. Which one am I?"

Relishing the way she sprung to life above him, he grinned. "The robber, obviously, because you steal my heart on a consistent basis."

No more words were needed from then on in, for Cameron was certain moans of pleasure didn't count as words.

***

"Are you sure we should be doing this? I look like a beached whale," Joci whined.

Rayna's throaty laughter fluttered from the dressing room next door. "Of course, I'm sure. You're engaged, Joci. Just because you haven't set a date, doesn't mean you can't try on a few wedding dresses." The door creaked with her exit. "Come on, don't be shy. I've got one on too."

"Ugh, I hate how much you're enjoying my torture," Joci replied, setting the straps in place. "Ready or not, here I sail." She flung the door wide and strutted toward the panel of mirrors.

"You. Look. Fabulous," Rayna enunciated, face alight with glee. "Eek! I can't believe you're getting married."

"It doesn't fit, Ray." She twirled to show the failed attempt to zip the lacy gown.

"Aw, once you pop that kid out, you'll be a size eight within a week," the attorney promised after trying the zipper herself. She flipped her bangs from her face and shrugged. "I like the material. Very sophisticated."

Joci reviewed her reflection. In honesty, the dress was gorgeous, with delicate cream flowers dotted along the entire length. She doubted anyone would find fault in it. The half sheer-half lace straps dipped into a V neckline, promising a lusty reveal for the groom to look forward to. "Cam would love it."

"Especially if he saw you in it right now. Your boobs are popping!" Rayna bopped Joci's breasts in jest.

"Oh, shut it." She laughed, but had to agree. Cameron was rather fond of the physical effects pregnancy had on her, and she wasn't complaining one bit. It was a confidence boost really to know he still found her attractive despite her changing body.

Taking in the off-white gown beside her, Joci's lips split into a broad smile. "Dang, you look ready to waltz down the aisle yourself."

Rayna snorted and fluffed the bottom of the tulle train. "Uh, no."

Joci fingered the mermaid-style strapless gown with a bedazzled belt around the other woman's tiny waist. The neckline left little to the imagination, a fact she was sure many a man would enjoy. "Would a special Des Moines cop be at the other end, by chance?"

"You're hysterical." Rayna's gray eyes dipped in annoyance with her sarcastic words. "If I ever decide to marry—" She paused and shook her index finger. "—and it's a big *if*, I won't get married in some huge event at a stained-glass-windowed church with clergymen in white robes. It'll be on a beach or something with two witnesses. End of story."

Smoothing the lace where it swelled thanks to her belly, Joci hid a grin. "That's what Adrian and I did. As romantic as it was, I don't know if I'd do it again. Friends and family were pissed we eloped, you know?" She snagged a veil and tucked it in Rayna's bright hair. "I want the big, flashy wedding with our engagement picture in the newspaper and a cheesy DJ to close out the night."

"And what does your hunky officer want?" Rayna asked.

"I don't know. We haven't talked about it much." She spread the veil's thin material over Rayna's shoulders. "I think he wants to wait until the little guy or girl is here to move forward."

She nearly added a snippet about Bernard "Jerry" Del Rossi all but insisting he attend and fund their nuptials. Rayna wouldn't approve of a mob boss amid cousins and colleagues.

Rayna spun around. Her hair floated to her shoulders when she stopped, but the veil kept going until it smacked her in the face. She giggled and tore it off. "You have time. I mean, you guys went from basically strangers to betrothed within a year. Some waiting may do you good."

"What's that supposed to mean?"

Rayna held up her hands. "What I meant was you can enjoy a lengthy engagement." She patted Joci's gut. "Your baby daddy is gone, and you've no reason to rush." She hugged her best friend tight. "Enough gabbing. I saw an incredible Vera Wang you must try on. You will melt into an anti-bridezilla puddle."

"Fine, but then can we get fried chicken?" Joci licked her lips. "Really craving it today."

Tickling Joci's side, Rayna skipped down the hallway and teased, "Remember you said that in six months when you're bitching about the stubborn love handles that won't go away."

Ignoring the playful jab, Joci followed at a slower pace. Rayna's cautionary statements gave her pause. *Are we moving too quickly?* It felt like yesterday Cameron was on trial for murder, and now she was flouncing around as any giddy bride would.

Shaking her head, she shuffled to the changing room and hoped the next dress would make her feel a tinge better about all the planning. A-class felonies she could handle; weddings weren't something she'd ever master.

CHAPTER TWO

Joci peered at the four flights of stairs in front of her then to her shoes and back again. The pink pumps were already sending warnings to her swollen ankles, but she had no choice. The elevators were on the fritz, which meant everyone in the courthouse was hoofing it.

"Of all days," she mumbled under her breath, taking the first step. Her last hearing of the morning was on the fourth floor. Other than bouncing between the first and second floors, the clients hadn't bothered her. They were easy cases, unlike the one she was headed to. Now, as she made it halfway to the second set of stairs, she regretted agreeing to this particular person. The case was open and shut for the county attorney's office, yet it was a Petosa client and she wouldn't let them down.

"What the hell are you doing, Joci?"

Turning as carefully as manageable, she caught sight of Quinn bounding up the stairs two at a time. "Walking. What're you doing, Officer Quinn?"

Quinn grabbed her left elbow to steady her when she

teetered on her heels. "We're in the same courtroom," he advised, nodding upward. "My hearing just doesn't start for a bit." His cheerful green eyes dipped to her feet. "I thought you agreed to more comfortable shoes from this month on." He clucked his tongue. "I distinctly recalling us having that conversation following a status conference, Ms. Dorous."

Offering him a disgruntled huff, Joci snapped her attention to the last few steps on the staircase. "A girl needs to look fabulous, and shoes are a big part of it." She groaned when the next set of stairs came into view. "Even if slippers would be a lot better."

Quinn's good-natured chuckle resonated down his arm and transferred to Joci. "I don't offer this very often, but I can carry you the rest of the way if you want. I don't think a piggy-back ride would work with that outfit, but I'll gladly do the bridal threshold carry."

Joci scrunched her nose. "You'd like that a wee bit too much. Plus, I'm not going to be seen as an invalid. I can't baby myself. Nope. I'm not even seven months pregnant." She gripped the thick handrail and urged her body onward. It was odd, the way her weight gain pained her some days and paled others. Chalking it up to the effects of a busy day, she trudged on.

"What's your partner up to?" Quinn asked when Joci stopped to take a drink of water from the handy bottle that'd become her best friend of late. Her intake of water increased more each week, and she felt as though some days she may just drift away in a pool of liquid.

Reviewing the courthouse, she locked her gaze to the

younger attorney on the second floor. "Looks like she's heading in for an arraignment." With a sly grin, Joci added, "Want to run into her, huh?"

"What? No, nothing like that. I'm the arresting officer in one of her cases." Quinn scratched his smooth jaw, scouring the busy building. "Thought we could catch up on a few things."

"Mm, right," she replied, the words dripping with sarcasm. She'd known Quinn long enough to catch him in a lie. It was apparent he fancied Rayna. Why he hadn't made a move yet baffled her. They were perfect for each other.

They attained the landing of the third floor, and out of breath, Joci held up her folders. "I really should work out with Cameron more. This is ridiculous."

Guiding them to a bench off to the side, Quinn's eyes twinkled with mischief. "From what he's told me, the two of you get plenty of exercise."

"Levi Quinn!" she scolded.

"What? Just the truth. I mean, hell, he's all smiley and shit almost every day." Quinn ignored the grimace on her face and crossed his ankle onto the other knee. "You were stellar before, but it's apparent, pregnancy brings out the nympho in you." He gently nudged her side. "I should've knocked you up."

"All right, you're done," she declared, removing her left shoe. Massaging her toes, she sighed and met her friend's eyes. "I meant going to the gym, smartass."

They sat in muted conversation, the myriad of voices from court-goers milling around them. Finally, Joci heard the familiar tone of the court attendant from Judge Logan's courtroom. She was by far her favorite attendant, but one no attorney should ever piss off. Joci was fairly certain the woman had a voodoo doll stashed in her desk drawer.

"There's my cue." Replacing the heel, she winced at the first lunge.

Quinn's long legs easily caught up with her. "It's been too long since we've caught up." He smiled at a passing deputy. "You're happy, right?"

"Extremely."

"And the baby is healthy?"

Joci shifted the case folder under her dominant arm. In truth, the baby was fine, save an emergency room visit shortly after Adrian's death. The doctors assured her everything was acceptable, but the substantial blood loss scared her. Since that day, she was especially careful not to push herself too hard. She needed a part of Adrian to live on for both their sakes.

"Joci?" Quinn's voice cut into her woolgathering.

"Oh, sorry." She pushed up her frames. "*Bambino* is progressing normally, so yeah, he or she is healthy." She eyed the cop in full gear. "Why? What's with all the questions? Not trying to make another play on me, are you?"

They reached the top of the massive flight and paused on the marble. "I'd be dead within hours if I even thought about stealing you back." He squeezed her hand. "But I miss you nevertheless." Joci raised her eyebrows and he quickly amended, "As friends, obviously. It's one thing to do business with you but another to scarcely see you outside the office or courtroom. We used to hang. Your fiancé gets in the way of our comradery these days. Well, and the baby. We can't exactly go bar hopping anymore."

Recalling the past months, blame nagged her. Since moving in with Cameron, she'd all but forgotten about her friendship with the police officer. Quinn had been her rock after the divorce. Ignoring him wasn't right on a number of levels. He and Cameron got along swimmingly, and she deserved friends too. Heaven knew someone had to keep a watchful eye on the attractive officer of the law. He was liable to cause all sorts of trouble if she didn't.

"You know, you're right. I'm sorry." She patted her stomach. "I've been too caught up with this little one, my new office, and yes, Cameron. I won't be receiving the 'best friend of the year' award." She clasped his hand and couldn't help but wonder how he'd fared lately. They had cases together, but nothing like the past.

"Joci Dorous, your client is here. Finally," Zaneta, the court attendant, called, her strong voice bouncing off the tall ceiling.

"Damn, I better get in there." She offered Quinn a smile. "I'll make it up to you. I promise." Her heels clopped faster, though her body wasn't moving with equal speed.

With a wiggle of his eyebrows, he asked, "Like you used to?"

Her cheeks burned and she shot him a wide-eyed glance. "I didn't know you had a pregnancy fetish, Officer Quinn," she proclaimed loud enough for a passerby to give him a funny look. "But we can go out with Rayna and Cameron one of these nights," she completed after his handsome face flushed with embarrassment.

Before ducking into the room, Joci saw his nod and faint grin. She didn't crave him sexually. She doubted she'd ever want another man after Cameron, but she did miss Quinn's easygoing attitude and humor.

Focusing on her client, she pulled back the chair and addressed the court. "Your Honor, my client is prepared to plead guilty with the following adjustments...."

***

"Keep it up and I'll accidentally put you in the back of the K-9 truck," Cameron heckled, wiping his nose with the sleeve of his shirt. The no-good scumbag in his grip had hooked him when he wasn't prepared. Needless to say, both bore substantial slashes and welts.

Eyeing the bloodstain, he wondered if roughing up the guy a little more would hurt. Pushing the temptation to the back of his mind, he shoved the woman-beater into the rear of the patrol car and slammed the door. If the guy's long nose got caught in the door, he didn't give a shit. It was one thing to hit a man, but a whole other story with a woman. If he'd been doing Jerry's bidding, the lout wouldn't live to see the sunrise, but his coworker's voice reminded him otherwise.

"Ouch. That's going to smart," Quinn commented, catching up, the other suspect and alleged victim in cuffs as well.

Checking the two over, Cameron noticed his guy was

equally battered as the woman. It made him wonder who the aggressor truly was. It didn't matter. They'd book them both and let the court figure it all out. After Quinn slid the divider down between the suspects, he whistled low and flicked Cameron's nose. "Yeah, this isn't my favorite part of the job." He studied his face in the side mirror. "But then again, I'm used to throwing punches, not taking them."

"No jail time threatening your head, so it's a better deal, even if it sucks." Quinn pulled the laptop out of the car. "Ugh, what the hell is that smell?" He opened the computer, nose scrunched.

"Probably your nasty-ass protein shake," Cameron noted, pointing to the half-full teal bottle.

Quinn shrugged and began typing. "So, I'm adding interference with official acts and assaulting a police officer to get the son of a bitch back. Justice at its finest."

The criminal smashed his head against the window, but neither cop moved to see the damage. "Sounds good." Cameron leaned up on the back of the vehicle, letting the August rays settle on his face. "Day shift sucks almost as much as last shift. At least at night, I don't miss all the fun in the sun." Grabbing his shades, he swung them between his index and middle finger. "What do normal people do in Iowa during summertime?"

Quinn peeked up from the report. "Other than the state fair?"

"Yeah. Years have come and gone since I didn't have illegal activities consuming my life," Cameron continued. "Are barbeques and picnics still in, or do I need to buy a hoverboard?"

Snickering, his partner snapped the laptop shut. "I'd hold off on the hoverboard, McFly, but yeah, grilling or going to the park is what normies do." He slugged Cameron's shoulder. "You're sounding tamer by the day." Once the words dropped from Quinn's mouth, his smile turned upside down. "Sorry, didn't mean to rub salt in there."

It was no secret Cameron wasn't accustomed to a stable lifestyle, but Quinn wasn't wrong. He did act like a typical, blue-blooded American these days. He didn't have the best role models when it came to relationships, and he wasn't positive he could enforce the normal Joci desired.

Despite the sweltering heat, his skin turned cold and clammy. He didn't want to let Joci down, but he didn't know how to move forward. He was treading water in desperate search of a lifeboat. Proposing to Joci was supposed to help him see straight. It didn't. If anything, it had sent him into a nosedive.

Quinn's voice shook him to the present. "Did you swallow a fish, because you don't look so hot."

Pulling on his sunglasses, Cameron focused on Quinn's puzzled face. "I'm good. Overthinking as usual." He grabbed the driver door. "Let's get these guys back before they melt." Before Quinn could answer, Cameron added, "Why don't you and Rayna meet us for dinner tonight at the Flying Mango? Joce keeps telling me about how awesome it is. It's high time we checked it out."

A peculiar smile crossed his partner's face. "Yeah, that'll work."

***

Pouring over the discovery discs, Joci squinted her eyes, wishing the evidence would vanish instead of convict. She'd scoured the abundance of criminal files since returning from court, and her eyes were at their limit. The notion of accepting complex cases wasn't so bad two months ago, but now she was regretting it. Doctor appointments, birthing classes, and hearings didn't mesh.

"I'm heading out. Gotta change into something less official." Rayna pointed to the navy pantsuit. "See you at the restaurant."

Joci whipped her head around in alarm. "Shit. I forgot all about dinner." Shuffling the pleadings back into the file, she stacked the folders neatly.

"You want me to lock up?" Rayna offered, her newly manicured fingers resting on the brass handle.

"Don't worry about it." Standing, Joci sighed. "I'm done for the day anyhow. I'll be there in a bit. Order me some nachos, will you?"

Without another word, Rayna ducked out of the office, the door chiming her exit.

Powering down her laptop then tablet, Joci flicked the lights off and snatched her purse from the chair across the desk. The leather felt foreign to her fingers. She should've donated the Prada piece. It was a constant reminder of Adrian. Her stomach jolted, and she shook her head. Their child was all she needed, yet her brain told her to keep remnants of her past life. She wouldn't admit it to Cameron, but she missed her ex-husband. "God, that sounds delightful," she scoffed to the empty room.

She fingered the thick ring on her necklace. She couldn't put away the last bit of Adrian, and she'd tried. Many times. No matter how much she attempted to let go of his Harvard ring, she couldn't bring herself to do it. She needed the constant reminder of him or she was afraid she'd forget him altogether.

Tucking it back under her shirt, Joci sighed. Without a doubt, it bothered Cameron, her hanging on to—quite literally—a part of Adrian. After the funeral, she'd boxed all his possessions up and stowed them in a storage unit. It wasn't something she had to do, but she needed to put Adrian's memory away. Too bad for her, the one shred of his existence around her neck was all she needed to wallow in the past.

"Any time for one more case?"

Twirling on her heels, Joci shook her mind free of the Adrian-infested cobwebs and beamed at the man on the office threshold. With all her thoughts consumed by Adrian, she hadn't heard the bell. Where was her mind? "Brett, what're you doing here?" Immediately she wrapped him in an awkward hug.

"I see my grandchild is thriving." He pulled back and dropped his eyes to her bump. "I'm not surprised in the least with you as the mother. You and Adrian would've been the best parents." His voice with a slight Irish accent dropped off, as if assaulted by bittersweet memories.

Signaling for him to take a seat, Joci flipped on the lights. It was a rare occasion when Brett Petosa stopped by anyone's office, much less hers. Despite being shorter than his son, Adrian's dad had the same lean build and dashing attributes. A pang of remorse filled her gut, and she cradled both hands over her stomach.

"I didn't mean to barge in near closing time, but I was in the neighborhood," he said.

Her phone chimed from within the blue purse, catching her attention. Choosing to ignore Cameron's personalized ringtone, she sat beside Brett. "No problem. It's good to see you. Has it been busy at the firm?"

"The hell if I know. Undoubtedly, if my bank account means anything. You know I only stop in to sign things, then jet off to get a few rounds of golf in somewhere," the older attorney teased. His face knit into a frown. "Adrian's not there to keep me updated, and neither are you. I miss it. I miss him."

Unable to resist, she patted his forearm. "Me too. I wish he could be part of his child's life."

Shaking his head, Brett cleared his throat in a gentlemanly fashion. "Yes, well, you've got other things to worry about these days. I popped by to let you know returning to Petosa is always an option for you. A partner position is yours should you want it." He stood when her phone buzzed once more. "Anytime, Joci. You're the daughter I had for a very limited time. Everything is yours when I'm gone."

Confused, she stood. "What? No, don't even talk like that."

He placed both hands on her shoulders, his blue eyes filled with tears. "I'm thankful you gave Adrian another chance. He was always a better version of himself when you two were together."

Joci's reactions sputtered to a halt. She didn't want to spill the dirty secret about her change of heart, so instead, she smiled and nodded. "Me too."

"All right, well, that man of yours is blowing up your phone, so I'll scurry out of your hair." Before Brett shuffled expensive loafers to the exit, he tentatively patted her stomach. "Let's do lunch some afternoon and catch up, okay? I want to know my grandchild before I'm senile."

Laughing, she agreed, then followed him out the door. He didn't wait for her to lock up the suite before climbing into his convertible and blazing down the street.

Hopping into her Mercedes, Joci rolled down all the windows and let the humid breeze drift through her long hair. Never in her life had she assumed Brett Petosa would name her as his heir. It was unheard of and sure to piss a lot of people off. Joci navigated the car onto the busy side street and toward the restaurant. Life was going better than she hoped. Nothing could go wrong.

***

Dipping the bright red tortilla chip in the chicken dip, Cameron did his damnedest to forget the recent conversation he'd had with Jerry. The mobster wanted to meet up the next day to discuss new issues arising in Des Moines. He shoveled another chip into his mouth and didn't hear Rayna and Quinn argue about which judge was their favorite. He was preoccupied by what to tell Joci. She was aware of his involvement with Del Rossi, yet he chose to keep certain aspects of the spiderweb to himself. It was part of the reason why he felt guilty whenever she questioned him. She deserved the truth, but it'd paint him in a green jumpsuit. He didn't want a repeat of their jail visit with her on the opposite side of a table and cameras watching when all he wanted to do was rip off her skirt and bend her over. Despite how lovely such a scenario would be, he wasn't keen on the potential prison time.

The waiter brought a platter of chicken wings and drinks to the table as he scanned the small restaurant. So far, the food was delicious yet somehow soured in his gut. If Jerry was visiting, it meant the threat was genuine and not something easily manipulated from a million-dollar Chicago condo.

The bell at the entrance caught his ear, and he craned his neck to see a slender form head in their direction. Joci looked stunning as usual, but especially with the basketball beneath her summery blouse. Seeing her made his heart rate skyrocket. No matter how many times she came into view, he'd love the sight.

"Hey, guys, sorry I'm late." Joci slid into the booth beside him and squeezed his thigh. "Brett Petosa stopped by after you left," she directed to Rayna.

"What? Really? Why?" Rayna fired off, pushing the chip bowl toward her friend.

Joci popped a tortilla morsel into her mouth. "Wow, those are good." She glanced up then giggled. "Sorry. Preggo brain. He wants to get lunch and discuss the baby's future."

Cameron chewed on his straw, not loving the new involvement from her ex's dad.

"Holy damn!" Rayna snatched a chicken wing. "Does he want you back at Petosa too?" she joked, followed by a frown when she looked at Joci. "Oh my God, he does."

Joci waved the proclamation aside. "He does, but I can't, even if the open-ending partner position is mine."

The cola in Cameron's mouth fizzled out at her remark. If she returned to the Petosa fold, her mind would dwell on Adrian even more than it already did. He'd noticed in the past months. She didn't think he heard the sniffling or seen the dried tears, but he couldn't miss them. "Are you thinking about it?" He spoke up, engaging in the discussion again.

Snatching a menu, Joci lifted her shoulders. "I did for one hot minute, but I have my own place now." She grinned at Rayna. "And we're kickass. No big boss to tell us what to do. I don't want to move backward." She gently poked his ribs. "I like where I am."

Cameron looped his arm around Joci's waist and pressed a kiss to her cheek. "Glad to hear it." The admiration in her eyes briefly calmed his apprehension. For the time being, he wouldn't fret about Del Rossi issues. He needed to focus on the ones at the table.

The waiter returned and scribbled down their orders before Joci dropped a bomb, depleting his calm in the storm. "Brett's naming me as his heir," she said in a quiet voice.

Rayna choked on her strawberry margarita, causing Quinn to slap her back until she stopped coughing. Her reaction mirrored the internal one Cameron felt.

"That's a shit ton of money," Quinn remarked, his eyes latched on Joci.

"Um, yeah, you're going to be a millionaire," Rayna added.

Joci pushed back the basket of wings. "Nah, he'll find some sexy babe to dump his money on before he dies. He's in-between girlfriends, that's all."

"So, if Adrian was alive, you don't think Brett's will would include you?" Quinn asked, a bit too involved for Cameron's liking.

"No clue. Knowing Brett, it'd probably depend on whether I was with Adrian or not." Joci glanced to him. "Which I wouldn't be."

Cameron nodded even though he didn't completely believe her. Joci was an opportunist. He'd discovered it during his criminal case. A big chunk of change might tempt her if Adrian was in the picture. The two women babbled on about work while Quinn kicked his shin under the table. "What the hell, man?"

Quinn leaned across the table and lowered his voice. "She wouldn't go back to him."

They eyed Rayna and Joci chowing down on appetizers. For ladies, their appetites were monstrous, something he didn't mind. He'd rather have a woman who loved her food than one he couldn't hug without breaking bones.

Cameron eyed the cheese dip. "It's a ton of money. She'd be set for life—"

"But she wouldn't have you," his partner cut in,

predicting where his friend was heading. "She tossed two guys aside for you. I don't get why you're paranoid."

"I have this feeling." Cameron pointed to his torso. "It won't relent."

Quinn snorted. "Damn, rookie. You already got the cop gut? Took me two years." He chuckled and jerked his thumb to Joci. "If you believe something's going to happen to her, you sure as hell better tell me. I'm not losing her anytime soon. Got it?"

Cameron observed Rayna steal a chip from Joci, who in turn stole the dip. "Yeah, I got it."

***

Stuffed full of Cajun chicken and gumbo, Joci waddled through the hallway later that night. The conversation at dinner was animated and hilarious: two things she loved about their small group. Stepping into the room recently painted light gray, she saw Cameron reading a book on unsolved criminal cases. She'd happened upon him in a similar situation almost a year ago during his homicide case. He looked better now, though his brows were knit together. Instantly, she found herself missing his piercings. The police force didn't allow them, but they were an odd craving to her hormonal mind. He was plenty bad boy without them, but they were still fun for role play. She shivered at the thought of the numerous couplings they'd had following his acquittal. She'd never forget any of them either. They were by far the best she'd ever had and the best she could ever imagine. His body was made solely for the purpose of her pleasure. Her mouth watered just recalling the connection they had then—and as recently as earlier that morning.

Crawling into the king-sized bed, she smirked when she noticed he was on the same page as when she left him. "Must be an intense dialogue if you're still on it," she said, turning off the light on the bedside table.

"Huh?" He craned his neck to her and chuckled. "No, just thinking."

Locking her arm through his, she traced her fingers along his tattooed flesh. She loved every part of him, but the creative ink designs were at the top of her list. "Anything I can help with?"

Chucking the paperback to his table, he kissed the top of her head. "Not unless you can make a few mobs disappear."

Rubbing her lips together, Joci nodded. She wasn't fond of the toll the Del Rossi network had on him. She'd never truly known him without a hammer held over his head one way or another. His strength and endurance encouraged her yet also frightened her in regard to their relationship. They were linked to a mafia, and while there were a few pros, she mostly saw the cons. "If I could, I would."

"I know, Joce. I wish I didn't involve you at all." Cameron wiggled free of her hold and stood. "I wish I could've protected you without them." He began pacing the floor.

"I'm fine." She pointed to her body as proof. "See?"

He ran fingers through his wavy hair. She made it no secret that she missed the longer curls, but with his new haircut came the honor associated with the police department, and she'd never regret that.

"Right now, yes, but Jerry's coming in soon and said he has bad news." Cameron's eyes turned a deeper hue of brown, reminding her of semisweet chocolate. "I have a hunch it may change things."

Joci moved to where he stood with hands on his hips. "Then we'll get through it." She traced his biceps. "Together."

"My past may come back to haunt me," he warned.

"Been there, done that, still waiting on the T-shirt."

Wrapping a palm around the base of her neck, Cameron cracked a weak smile. "God, I love you so much. I guarantee I didn't know what that meant before you."

Pushing further into his arms, Joci inhaled. It wasn't anything extraordinary; simple masculine energy and a hint of musk from his bodywash. It inebriated her more than any expensive cologne and soothed her no matter the struggle. This was how being with someone should've been all along. "Neither did I," she whispered, nearing his full lips. They summoned just as much havoc when she stared at them as when they met her mouth. "I trust you, and if you ask me to take a mini-vacation, I'll go visit my parents." She held his chin in place, her thumb tracing his stubble. "But I'd much rather be right here with you."

The strained expression vanished from his face. Letting out a heavy sigh, Cameron kissed her forehead. "How'd I get so lucky?"

"I don't think being arrested on murder charges is lucky."

He took her lips, beckoning a different response. "It is

when I end up with you as my attorney."

"You're cheesy."

"And you love it," he reminded her.

Giving him a comical face, Joci shrieked when he picked her up and overwhelmed her mouth. Kissing Cameron transported her to a world where mobsters didn't exist, and the only nourishment she longed for was him. "All right, I concede," she breathed when her back hit the fluffy comforter. "I do love it." She wrapped her legs around his hips. "But mostly, I love you."

Wiggling his eyebrows, Cameron nodded confidently. "Yeah, I figured as much. You can go to bed now." He reached back and swatted her ass for good measure.

"Psh, I'm not finished with you," Joci said, pulling him to her. Her eyes skimmed the toned abs lined with tattoos and scars of a past life. His body was a perfect combination of what she never knew she wanted. "Not ever."

***

"Cameroni, you made it."

Securing the door of the police car, Cameron clenched his hand into a fist and plastered a smile to his face. "Well, when you show up at my workplace, I don't exactly have a choice."

Jerry sniggered, waving aside the two beefy bodyguards. It wasn't as though he needed them with an entire law enforcement agency on all sides, even if they were unknowing.

"There's always a choice," the mobster declared with a

cheeky grin. "But yours resorts back to me no matter what you decide."

Cameron leaned against the hood of the car and checked over his shoulder. He'd purposefully arrived in between shifts so no one would recognize his benefactor. The questions that'd follow weren't friendly or ones he desired to answer. He already got the runaround from Quinn. If his captain found out who was in the parking lot, the entire force would be on them in a minute. "What's so important you left your luxurious Chi-Town abode to tell me?"

Jerry sauntered over to him then patted his thigh. "Directly to business. It's why we do well together."

The coffee in Cameron's stomach churned as the wail of sirens met his ears. Des Moines never slept, which meant neither did its cops. He should be helping his colleagues instead of plotting with Del Rossi.

"There's a hit out on you, Cameron." Jerry's words punched the air from Cameron's lungs.

Shock filtered through his mind. "What? Are you sure? Who put it out?"

Jerry cleared his throat. "It appears the Mikkelsens learned of your personal role in Joci's life. And with her being under Del Rossi protection…." He let the rest hang in the balance between them.

"I'm not supposed to be involved with her," the cop finished, sweat lining his brow. The light breeze did nothing to the sweltering heat bubbling within him. By now, his relationship with the gorgeous attorney was common knowledge. His heart pounded as the jigsaw pieces fell together to complete the cataclysmic picture. "J.J.'s alive, isn't he?"

One of the guards handed a folder to him as the question lingered on the air. His hands trembled as he opened it. Inside was the request for Cameron Shearer's death, along with J.J.'s noteworthy signature.

"But wait, there's more." Jerry flipped to the second page. "He wasn't the only person to survive the car blast."

A bead of perspiration dripped down Cameron's nose and landed on the damning evidence. Signed in red ink was Adrian Petosa's name. Snapping up his neck, he met Jerry's soulless eyes. "No, it's not possible. They're dead. Both of them. The remains that were found came back positive for Adrian's blood type. Plus, they found his class ring."

Jerry shook his index finger. "Yes, but nothing definitive to prove their deaths. Anyone can lose a bit of blood and still live, Cameroni. The ring may have been planted."

Cameron swallowed the bile rising in his throat as realization collided with reality. "Adrian's coming back for Joci, and J.J.'s set on killing me. Hell, so is Adrian. Great. Just great."

The moment the words slipped from his mouth, he regretted saying them. Obscure deaths were common in the mob scene, but these resurrections unsettled him more than the rest. All at once, his world crumbled, and he wasn't positive anyone could rebuild it. "You have to help me," he implored, pacing. "I can't lose Joci."

His employer with salt and pepper hair meshed his chubby fingers together. The telling expression on his face reverberated in Cameron's stomach. Jerry would help, but it would cost him. No longer caring about anything except the pregnant fiancée on her way to court, Cameron closed his eyes and pictured her from this morning. She was magnificent, with bright eyes and a sexy smile that turned him into putty whenever she graced him with it. He'd do whatever it took for her sake. Even if it meant being shackled to the Del Rossi mob for life.

CHAPTER THREE

Popping her head out the window, Joci scowled at the onslaught of cars involved in the traffic jam. It was a commonality for downtown commuters, but today she needed to hurry it along. "At this rate, my client will plead guilty to anything the county attorney offers her," she mumbled, toying with the radio. Finding a catchy new tune from Brett Eldridge, she tapped her fingers on the steering wheel as three lanes on the interstate lit up with taillights.

A new message from Cameron popped up on the car's navigation screen. She let the robotic woman read it aloud, but didn't bother replying. Ever since meeting with Jerry two weeks ago, Cameron's mood had been off. His typical temperament bordered on obsessively protective, but when pressed, he wouldn't explain his reasoning. It was clear something was stirring their usually tranquil pot.

Birds swooped over the cars on the four-lane bridge over the Des Moines River, chirping as if to mock their constraint. Joci patted her hand over the kicking wonder in her midsection and giggled when the babe kept up the gymnastics. Finding out the gender could've happened at her appointment a month ago, but the courage to ask the ultrasound technician never found her lips. No matter the answer, she'd love Adrian's baby.

Her face fell and her rhythmic rubbing slowed, thinking about him. He would've begged to know the gender and would adore being a father. She smirked, imagining him doing exactly that. *But he's gone.* Her eyes misted at the constant reminder. She wanted to talk to Adrian about names and hear his addictive laugh when the baby kicked his hands. "So many great memories." She sighed and frowned. "And some not so great ones."

Shaking her head, she glanced to the rearview mirror and wiped away a stream of mascara that somehow escaped along with a tear. "Get it together, Joci." She smoothed her hair next, thoughts circling the ex who once drove all over town to satisfy her pregnancy cravings. It was buffalo chicken pizza and sour cream back then. These days, Ben & Jerry's brownie batter ice cream and hot wings were among her favorites.

The minivan behind her honked, hurtling her to the present. To her relief, car speeds picked up. The wind whipped her hair straight in her face. By the time she cleared the long strands off her line of vision, it was too late and she slammed into the car ahead of her. The squeal of tires set off a domino effect of colliding vehicles on all sides. The truck beside her swerved, nailing the delivery van two cars from her location.

The airbag deployed, and Joci's head throbbed as it

struck her face. White residue filled the car's interior as her neck jerked to its correct position. It was like being struck with giant marshmallows. Hardened ones, not soft and fluffy ones. Just as she straightened, another force from behind thrust her chest against the deflated airbag, jamming the tight seat belt into her again.

Time and space extended in slow motion, the echo of crunching metal the solitary sound she could decipher. When the screeching ended, no lane of traffic was clear of an accident. She batted at the deflated bags, pain jolting through her arms. A pool of blood met her gaze when she glanced to her lower extremities.

Not seeing the cell phone in its usual spot, fear seized her when she couldn't find it. "Dammit," she huffed, catching her reflection in the side mirror. Her face was bloody, and a hint of purple bruising reflected back. Fumbling with the seat belt, she cursed when it wouldn't budge.

Distant sirens temporarily reassured her, until flames burst from under the car hood. "Shit!"

She yanked on the belt again with the same result. Frantic, she pulled until her hands burned. "Help!" she yelled, now fully aware of the possibility of burning alive. Her phone chirped from the passenger seat, and she struggled to grab it. Straining against the restriction, Joci managed to touch the device as it stopped ringing.

Letting out a string of profanities, she gasped at a sharp pain in her abdomen. Doubling over, she slid shut her eyes as it wracked her senses. "No, no, no," she moaned. "This can't happen another time."

"Hey, are you all right?" a man's voice with a slight Irish accent asked from the ajar window.

Cracking her eyelids open, Joci turned her head to see a shock of red hair. "Adrian?" she gasped, then clamped her mouth shut when her gaze lowered to the man's face. He looked nothing like Adrian, yet the warmth of his graveled voice and his concerned green eyes made her think of the man nevertheless. "No. I'm stuck," she confided, gritting her teeth at the discomfort.

The tall man pried open the door and stooped into the car. His eyes scoured her body, genuine worry lining his brow. "Okay, I think I can get you out, but we can wait for the EMTs if you'd rather."

A whoosh of flames from the front of the car made her shake her head. "Hell no. Get me out, please."

Nodding, he produced a pocket knife and cut through the seat belt. Joci couldn't help but notice the man's shaking hands as he scooped her into his arms. Slowly, he backed out of the Mercedes, his grip tightening as a low moan erupted from the sedan. Joci watched in horror as the car was quickly engulfed in red.

Reaching the side of the lane, a loud explosion set off another chain reaction. The man's hand was suddenly against her head, burrowing her further into him. Unable to do anything else, Joci marveled at how comfortable she was there. Cars were literally blowing up behind them, but the familiar scent of Ralph Lauren cologne clung to the man protecting her with his body. "I think we're clear of it," he stated, lowering her to the ground.

Slowly, she detached her arms from his neck and offered an appreciative smile. "Thank you…." She paused, hoping he would give her a name.

"Derrick."

Joci's eyebrows shot up at the irony. Just when she was thinking about Adrian, some guy with Adrian's middle name saved her from a burning car. "Well, thank you, Derrick. I'd be toast if you hadn't come along when you did."

Derrick waved aside her words, his eyes lowering to the protruding belly between them. "I saw the fire and knew I had to help where I could." He nodded to her pants now stained red. "Shit, you're bleeding."

Alarm flushed through Joci, and her hands instantly gripped the bump. She frantically looked down and sighed in relief when she realized the seat belt dug into her thigh and caused the bleeding. "I'll be okay. It's just a cut."

Worry covered his face. "I hope the little one's all right."

A long moment passed before a light kick met her palm. Relief washed over her and she smiled. "He's kicking, so I'll take it as a good thing."

Dropping to his knees beside her, her rescuer's face lit up. "A boy, huh?"

"Well, I'm not sure. That's my guess. He's as persistent as his father, so it wouldn't surprise me." Joci studied the heroic stranger who was enraptured with her bump. He reminded her of Sam Heughan in nearly all aspects of his face. A small discoloration of his left cheek made him real, otherwise, she would've sworn he was manufactured in a lab. He continued to study her abdomen as if it'd lurch to life. It appeared he'd never felt a growing child. Used to the constant slew of strangers rubbing her belly, she grabbed his large hand and placed it on the epicenter of kicks. "Here, feel for yourself." she offered.

Recognition lapsed into awe as a steady beat of feet met his touch. Gasping, Joci wondered why this particular man caused the reaction. "Wow, you have some way with kids, and this one's not even born. I've never felt so much activity."

A gloomy smile crept on his face. "Yeah, I guess so."

The wail of ambulances was closer, only to be outshone by the fire trucks following. Glancing up, Joci noticed more people stumbling from cars and assisting others. This was Iowa. No matter what happened, the residents were quick to help, stranger or no. Searching the crowd, she let out a sigh when two familiar police officers headed their direction. "Oh, thank God."

"Wait here, I'll grab a paramedic," Derrick insisted when she tried to stand. She nodded, and he slipped into the congested traffic.

Curious, Joci followed his movements with a hand shielding her eyes from the sun, befuddled at the reaction the unborn child had to the man. After she lost him in the group of emergency vehicles, Cameron was at her side.

"Oh God, Joci. Are you all right?" He hugged her tight, moderately cautious not to cause further damage. Pulling back, his eyes scoured her injuries. "You're bleeding."

"And your car is burning!" Quinn noted, kneeling as well.

Watching the firefighters at work with hoses, she sniffled. "Dammit, I just paid it off."

Cameron's brown eyes turned black at the attempt to joke. "Seriously, Joce? You're kidding around when you could've been killed in a car fire."

Joci looked up and winced at the severity of the situation. "Sorry."

Quinn coughed and stood. "Well, I'm going to see what I can do here about a paramedic." He disappeared to a nearby ambulance with a hand on his police walkie.

Brushing back her hair, Cameron studied her injuries. "Are you sure you're okay?"

"I'm fine," she noted on his second pass over her legs. "Some guy pulled me out." She pointed in the direction Derrick went, but the hero had vanished entirely.

Cameron cupped her jaw in his hands. "We were just up the road when the accident came across the radio. I couldn't breathe. I knew you were in trouble." His eyes glazed over in unshed tears, but he coughed and gruffly wiped them away. Scouring their surroundings, he pointed out, "Good, Quinn's getting some help." His voice evened out, emotions fully in check once more. "Where'd this mystery rescuer go? I'd like to thank him."

Joci shrugged and eyed the area. "No clue. He went toward the first ambulance on the scene, but I don't see him anywhere." She winced when the response team reached them and started working on her gashes.

Between the arms and gauze, she saw Cam scan the cars before he returned to her. "Well, for the time being, I'll thank my lucky stars extra tonight, since you're safe." His hands covered her swell and the baby kicked as if to solidify his words. "And little *bambino* too." After kissing the palm of her hand, he placed it over his heart. "Without you two, this would stop beating."

From the corner of her eye, Joci saw the EMT roll his eyes. "Come the fuck on, Officer Shearer. You're making normal guys look like dicks."

Cameron smirked then winked at her. "Yeah, well, once you find a girl like Joci, give me a ring, O'Brien." He squeezed her hand. "She's worth much more than mere words."

The tall first responder pasted a bandage to Joci's brow. "If you can find a girl worth the trouble, let me know."

Before Cameron could come up with a snarky reply, the paramedics hoisted Joci onto the stretcher and guided it to the waiting ambulance.

"We'll meet you at the hospital," O'Brien stated. "I don't want a lovefest in my truck," he added, shutting the doors.

Tapering off a laugh, Joci observed Cameron's deep frown through the back window. The two men exchanged more pleasantries, but the events of the morning quickly drowned out the voices until all she heard was the song of the siren.

***

Pulsing his left leg up and down, Cameron bit his thumbnail as he waited for news from a doctor. She was fine, that's what they told him when he arrived, but his distrust when it came to hospitals was worse than with the court system. He'd been in similar waiting rooms after his parents overdosed. The outcome then was never good. At least now, he wasn't a scared kid. *No, just a scared adult.* He pushed aside the thoughts of his past and stared at the double doors where Joci had disappeared through.

"Will you stop? You're going to shake the entire floor," Quinn chided from the vending machine. The man was constantly munching on something no matter where they went.

"It's been too long. I'm heading in there." He stood and strode toward the door, his keys jangling with the handcuffs.

"You sure you want to see her in stirrups quite yet?" Quinn's question paused Cameron's grip on the handle. "Her legs up in the air aren't kinky at the gynecologist." He offered the bag of peanuts. "Don't ruin it."

Deciding his friend probably spoke from experience, Cameron declined the snack and paced the floor. The prenatal wing of Des Moines largest hospital, Mercy Central, wasn't bustling but still had enough staff members roaming to maintain the constant hum.

Cameron toyed with his gun holster, flicking the locking device open and closed. Joci's accident sent his blood pressure through the roof. It couldn't have been a coincidence that two weeks after Jerry brought the kill order to light, a protected member of Del Rossi narrowly escaped death. *No, you're being ridiculous.* According to Joci's explanation, it was the very definition of a car accident. Still, the heroic and anonymous rescuer made him uneasy. She hadn't mentioned being worried about someone following her, so he did the worrying for her. With whispers of the Mikkelsens in town, he was on alert at all times.

Since obtaining a copy of the warrant for a known drug exchange in the south side of Des Moines, he'd reached out to every person he knew in gang-related activities. Across the county, his informants kept their eyes and ears out for new information. He didn't like where this was headed, and none of his underground contacts could confirm J.J. or Adrian's whereabouts or health. It was a constant gauntlet around his neck, slowly squeezing the life out of him.

The singular lead came from his guy deep in one of the Mexican gangs in Des Moines. According to Jorge, a cloud of desperados had swarmed the city streets over the last two weeks, ever since the hit became public. Well, on the underworld markets that was. Cameron couldn't believe the two weren't related. He had a bounty on his head. Criminals from surrounding states were the first to inquire about his location. Jerry had managed to run most of the men off, but with $250,000 at stake, he'd stick around too.

"Mr. Shearer, can you come in, please?" the nurse asked from the doorway.

Exchanging a glance with his friend, Cameron took a breath and followed the woman clad in yellow rubber ducky scrubs. Once inside, he was relieved to see Joci on the bed, an unusual smile on her face.

"What's going on?" He looked over to the doctor with an ultrasound wand. "Is she okay?"

"I'm Dr. Miller," the blonde stated, waving the bottle of belly jelly. "I'll be taking over Joci's files."

"Nice to meet you." He turned to Joci and hovered above her. "What's the matter?"

Clutching his hand, Joci's face brightened. "Nothing. Stop worrying. I'm fine. We're fine." She pulled up the hospital gown. "All of us."

Not certain what she meant, Cameron opened his mouth—just as the doctor squirted the liquid on Joci. Quieted for the moment, he watched the screen come to life, the steady whir music to his ears.

"Alrighty, here we go." Dr. Miller moved the wand around until she stopped on the mass of thumping. "Very strong heartbeats."

"Good." Cameron pushed aside her verbiage and squeezed Joci's shoulder.

"Both boys look fabulously healthy," the doctor stated.

Wrinkling his eyebrows together, he couldn't let that one slide. "You mean boy."

Joci and Dr. Miller traded a secret grin. "No, actually, boys, plural," the doctor emphasized. "You're having twins. Congratulations."

The circuits in Cameron's brain skidded to a halt, freezing his reaction. He opened and shut his mouth like a fish, unable to form words.

"Cameron?" Joci tugged on his belt, bringing him out of shock.

"Uh, yeah." He squinted. "Are you sure? Maybe you're hearing Joci's heartbeat too."

Dr. Miller shook her head. "Afraid not. There're two kiddos in there." She expanded the screen. "Would've seen the second guy earlier, but he kept in his brother's shadow until today. It happens now and then; the earlier sonograms don't always catch a twin. It was a good thing she came in today—despite the accident of course."

Too many emotions flooded his mind. *Two miniature Adrians. Great.* His stomach pitched at the mere thought.

"Cam, are *you* okay?" Joci grabbed his hand. "Your face is white."

Forcing a smile to his lips, he nodded. "Mhm, you bet." The room seemed to close in on him, stifling the air. "I should tell Quinn." Before either woman could stop him, Cameron rushed through the door, snagging his chum's arm on the way.

"Whoa, what's the rush?" Quinn asked, trailing behind him.

Ignoring his partner, Cameron kept his pace until they attained the outside courtyard. "Twins. She's pregnant with two Adrian lookalikes." He gripped the thick metal fence and reviewed the Des Moines skyline.

"Oh, shit," Quinn's replied, eyes wide. "Talk about rough."

"I don't know why, but I was banking on a girl. You know, one with hints of Adrian." Cameron let his shoulders sag. "But now I'll have two redheaded boys wishing he was here and not me." Running a hand over the back of his neck, he inhaled the summer breeze. A hint of freshly cut grass, sweet corn, and watermelon mixed amid the diesel and exhaust fumes.

"How's she taking it?" his friend asked after a moment of silence.

Whirling around, Cameron slapped a hand to his forehead. "Dammit! I burst out of there too fast to find out. I should go back."

Quinn gripped Cameron's upper arm, pausing the retreat. "Give her a few minutes. I'd bet she needs to adjust too."

"Yeah, adjust." He shook his head. "That's all I need." Cameron returned to brood by the fence as he took in the information. He'd never anticipated this for his life. He smirked at the sun bouncing off his badge. Whether they were his kids or not, he was a dad. And a cop. *And part of the Del Rossi mob.* The last one regurgitated sour doubt. His mafia role would continuously endanger his family, as borrowed as they may be.

"Look, I know you probably don't want to hear this from your fiancée's ex-lover," Quinn began, then coughed at Cameron's aggravated expression. "But I'd switch you places any day." He paused. "Except for amateur night at the strip club, that's downright hilariously sexy somehow."

Rolling his eyes to the sky, Cameron was thankful for the man's light nature. With the surprises this month had brought thus far, he needed a reprieve. "Thanks. You're right. Oh, and I don't want to hear about how you spend your nights as a bachelor. It's nasty."

Tucking his partner in a headlock, Quinn rubbed his fist against Cameron's head. "Yeah, yeah, now go kiss some ass or she'll name 'em both Adrian."

***

Fingering the ultrasound photo, Joci crinkled the edges. Twins had never crossed her mind when she thought about kids. During her last pregnancy, nothing had gone wrong, but this one felt different. Things that could go wrong did. She wasn't thrilled when the nurse chided her for high blood pressure either. Blaming it on the day's events, Joci hoped this wasn't a precursor for the remainder of the pregnancy. She had enough things to deal with without health issues getting in the way.

Dr. Miller explained everything once Cameron hightailed out of the room. She wasn't shocked, but his behavior puzzled her. "These aren't his. What if he doesn't want them or me?" she asked Rayna, who was on speakerphone. Since dressing and being cleared to leave, Joci was passing the time by calling her friend. "I mean, there's two of them, Ray. He never signed up for one, much less two."

"This is huge, Joci. As in, you find out Cameron has some secret family on the lowdown, huge. I would freak out too, so try not to be too hard on him," Rayna suggested.

Joci peeked into the hallway, not spotting the officer on her mind. "Yeah. I won't."

She didn't want to consider the alternative: losing Cameron. She never entertained such a thought until today. His parents were horrid examples, making any apprehension he felt feasible.

"Did you make it to the bond review hearing?"

Rayna snorted. "Of course. You're back to shop talk already."

"Well, somebody has to keep you on your toes," Joci replied, spying a familiar head. "Hey, I'm gonna go. I'll be in later."

"Sure, but make sure you and Cameron hash this out. It could turn ugly if you don't."

Heeding Rayna's advice, Joci propped the door open as she disconnected the call. "Hey, Derrick, right?"

The redhead wearing dark wash jeans and a blue polo swiveled her direction. Recognition registered on his face; he looked almost relieved to see her. "Yeah, hey." He stepped toward her, limping slightly. "I never caught your name. I've been going around asking if the pregnant lady is all right." He grinned. "I think the security guards have my photo by now."

"It's Joci." She held out her hand. "Thank you again for getting me out of the ticking time bomb. I never like to be the damsel in distress, but you really saved my ass." She rubbed her stomach. "Our asses."

Derrick's face lit up. "Happy to help a single mom."

"Oh, I'm not—" She paused when his eyes dipped to her hand. The engagement ring remained in her pocket. She'd forgotten to put it back on after the doctor examined her. Slipping it on, she studied his body language. His attitude seemed to have changed with her action. *I wonder why.*

His stature and build were comparable to Adrian's, but this meek man was his complete opposite, demeanor wise. Had it been Adrian who saved her, the news stations would've known within minutes.

"Do you want to feel them again?" she asked, noticing

he was staring at her belly.

"Su—Wait, them? There's more than one in there?" His curious green eyes clashed with hers, sending old feelings through her body. It was eerie on a number of levels.

"Um, yeah. Twins. I found out today. A few minutes ago, in fact. It was a big surprise to say the least." She pushed her glasses up. "I guess the accident was a good thing in a way."

Unhurried, Derrick slowly scanned her. On any other man, the act would appear seductive, but with him, it was almost as if he was memorizing her form for safekeeping. The hint of longing in his gaze sent wary shivers across Joci's skin.

"That's great. I'm sure your husband is thrilled."

"I'm not married." She eyed the massive diamond in the ring and saw him do the same. "Yet." Derrick scratched his brow, prompting her to continue. "But the boys' dad isn't my fiancé. He's not alive, so I have no clue how he'd react to such big news."

"I guarantee he'd be delighted." His smile turned down slightly. "What man wouldn't be?"

The way he easily said the words made Joci's stomach flutter. "You're probably right." A small smile escaped her. "Goodness, they're feisty in there. All the kicks make sense now that I know there's two of them in there. Double trouble already." The symphony of jolts thumped from the inside out.

Without asking permission, Derrick laid both hands over her shirt. The smile on his face was contagious. "Wow! It's incredible. You get to feel this all the time?"

"Believe me, it's not all shits and giggles, especially at night." She poked at one of the feet nudging. "One of these guys likes to hide under my ribs. It hurts like a bugger."

Raising her gaze, Joci swore she was staring into eyes recently departed of this earth. The tender way Derrick searched her face and captured her stomach with his hands moved her. He wasn't Adrian, but could pass for a more enlightened half-brother.

"Something going on here?" Cameron's voice broke into the intense moment, shattering it. She was grateful for the interruption. Derrick seemed a little too interested in her.

Derrick dropped his hold and retreated a step. "Uh, no. I was just feeling them kick." He met the other man's gaze. "Officer." His hand automatically shot out. "Derrick Wheeler."

"He's the one who rescued me," Joci added when she noticed the tightened jaw of her betrothed.

Cameron looked between them before nodding curtly. "I have you to thank then." He extended his hand also.

"And you're the lucky man who gets to come home to this beauty." They shook hands, and Joci didn't miss the stiff exchange. "I was at the right place at the right time. Anyone else would do the same."

Cameron nodded then moved to Joci. Gathering her into his embrace, he pressed a kiss to her cheek. "I'm glad you were. This woman is my life."

Joci's heart lifted to hear he wasn't upset at the change in their plans. Studying Cameron, she saw a hint of envy in his handsome features. Why, she wasn't certain. Strangers groped her stomach all hours and places of the day, but when this man touched her, something bothered Cameron about it.

Derrick took a breath and let it out slowly, twice, as if he were calming himself. "I should be going." His lips curled to a smile. "I trust I won't be hauling you out of burning cars anytime soon?"

Shaking her head, she reached over and squeezed his hand. The genuine care in his face demanded no other response. "Nope."

Derrick's eyebrows twitched. "Good." He backed up another few paces, scratching his elbow. "Nice to officially meet you two." He turned to leave then pointed his finger to Cameron and added, "Oh, and good luck. Taking care of two kids who aren't yours is a Goliath task. I hope you're up for it, Officer."

Cameron's muscles rippled around her. The last jab from the redheaded man haunted her. Adrian would say something along those lines to rile Cameron up. A shudder ran through her body at the not so distant memories involving the two men. They'd never like each other, and seeing this interaction made her think back to the courthouse before Adrian had been taken hostage. It felt too familiar.

"More than up for it," he bit out before Derrick ducked around a corner. His grip on her loosened as his nostrils flared.

Noticing the tension, Joci said, "He was trying to be friendly."

Cameron's sharp intake of breath forced a strained reply. "You don't know him. He could've dragged you off and held you for ransom."

"Cam, not everything turns into a kidnapping." She couldn't fault him for being protective, but he was being unreasonable.

"And I didn't like the way he was looking at you," he added.

"Seriously? He was being nice. That's it."

Taking a step back, he shook his head. "Joci, you don't—"

She interrupted, "He's gone now, okay? We'll never see him again." She lowered her voice when a male nurse raised judgmental eyebrows at them nearly yelling in the hallway. Dragging Cameron in the opposite direction would've been easier if he wasn't built like a rock. "Where were you anyway? I turned around and poof, you're gone."

"I needed to think." Cameron pointed to the bandage on his arm. "So I gave blood to pass the time."

"That's nice of you." She eyed his arm. "Odd, but nice." She didn't buy it. Clearly, he was still hung up on the recent visitor. "Can we go home, please? I need to fit in a quick catnap before heading to the office." She yawned, suddenly drained from the busy morning.

Crossing his long arms over his chest, Cameron shook his head. "No way. You're not going to work after what you've been through. You need to take it easy."

"No, I need to go to work," she argued, her face heating up.

"The hell you do." His low voice rumbled, scaring a passing orderly.

Realizing fighting through this wasn't the best course of action, Joci unclenched her fisted hands. Slanting eyes over him, she sighed at his chaotic curls, from the wind or pushing his fingers through it she wasn't sure. The holes where his nose and eyebrow rings used to sit glared at her, fleetingly making her wish they were in place once more. His jaw was set, but his lips were pouty, an irresistible sight if she ever saw one. The adamant expression in his dark brown eyes siphoned all anger from her. He was concerned for her health, but there was something else lying behind his tone. His reflection sent her back to their childhood in Ohio. He'd puckered a similar face when they disagreed as kids. *No wonder he always got his way, the ass.*

He wasn't wrong in his apprehension; however, letting him win this argument wouldn't happen. He loved her, which meant he knew she was as stubborn as him. They were a perfect match from the start. Bullheaded and ornery. Work would always be at the top of her list, and he knew it better than anyone from personal experience.

Stepping to his sulking position against the wall, Joci slipped her hands around his waist, her fingers grazing each of the devices hanging from the police utility belt. "Cam, all this excitement drained me. I need a bit of cuddle time, and I bet you know the perfect guy."

His face released its strained hold and his lips slackened. "Maybe."

Beaming up at him, she tilted her head to the right. "Maybe you know a guy, or maybe you are the guy?"

His chin lowered until she was touching noses with him. "I *am* the guy," he fiercely replied.

Joci snaked her hand up his spine to the back of his head. Compelling his neck toward her, she locked her gaze with his stormy mahogany one. "The only guy."

A tiny smile broke across his cheeks. "Then there's no place I'd rather be."

He leaned forward, imprinting his lips to her for eternity. The taste of mint clung to his breath, luring her to kiss him until she explored every facet of his mouth. His tongue tangoed with hers, causing adrenaline to spike through her body. Pressing harder against his mouth, she gasped when her back carefully hit the wall. Anyone could witness their brazen embrace, but she didn't care. She needed his lips on her right now. His teeth nipped her lower lip. And if he wasn't careful, she'd lug him to the nearest supply closet and bar the door just to show him how much she needed him.

When he finally eased away, Joci wasn't sure if she was breathing on her own. He had this effect on her when she least expected but sorely craved it.

"I'm glad you're safe," he whispered, his brown eyes etched with leftover concern. "Promise you'll never leave." His hands rubbed the protruding stomach between them. "I can't do this without you."

Kissing him hard, Joci hoped he felt a molecule of the chaos his lips caused in her. "I promise."

At Cameron's relaxed sigh, she snuggled into him. A movement behind them distracted her as he straightened.

She couldn't see who was spying, only recognized a shock of red hair as they moved to the exit.

CHAPTER FOUR

"What do you mean there's no record of him?" Cameron peered to the other half of the bed, but Joci kept snoozing. Easing out of the room, he remained mute until reaching the kitchen. "There has to be some record of a Derrick Wheeler at the hospital following the accident. He yanked Joci out of a burning car. Surely he had burns after the valiant act. Des Moines residents are nosy. Somebody had to see him."

Cameron punched the light on the coffee maker, willing Jerry to have better news. Dealing with an early morning wake-up call was easy compared to the uncertainty in his boss's voice. Del Rossi tracked people to the ends of the globe yet somehow couldn't pinpoint who a Good Samaritan was? He wasn't buying it. Someone had to be aiding Derrick, whoever he was.

"Sorry, Cameron," Jerry apologized. "My guys are pros. They've scoured the hospital and police files, but no dice. Derrick is a ghost."

"I was afraid you'd say something along those lines." Switching the cell to his opposite ear, Cameron made his way to the window overlooking the quiet neighborhood. A week had passed since the freak accident, and while Joci was business as usual, he couldn't join in. Not completely. Too much about the stranger's interference set him on edge.

"If anything pops up, you'll be the first to know." Jerry chuckled. "Well, the second, but who's keeping track?" The mob lord rattled off something in Italian, but Cameron didn't even try to translate the words.

The neighbor to the west opened his garage, lawn mower in tow. "Don't do it, motherfucker," he warned when the man scanned the yard. This particular neighbor tended to do outside work at godforsaken times of the day. It appeared today was no different. Cameron watched the neighbor's movements closely. Instead of cranking the engine, the guy flopped to the ground and pulled out a bottle of motor oil. Peace would reign, but Cameron doubted the tranquility would endure long.

Cameron hadn't grasped the mundane suburb life. He highly doubted it'd ever be easy. Staying in one place for long hadn't happened in Ohio. Between his druggie parents and gang happenings, bags were rarely unpacked and one was always in his closet ready to go. It had taken him a month before he could fall asleep on his own in the house. There wasn't enough noise for him to block out. Ultimately, it was why he was perfectly fine switching to the night shift.

Jerry started informing him of new players in Des Moines, but he couldn't concentrate on the discussion. Life in a cozy area riled his nerves. His suspicion of the surrounding houses had made Joci roll her eyes when they initially moved in. He couldn't help but wonder if Jerry had planted people nearby to keep an eye on him. The man had enough invested that he'd be a fool not to. Plus, Joci was under Del Rossi protection. A safeguard was within yelling distance. He'd bet his life on it.

Opening the window, he breathed in the midsummer air. "I don't know how much longer I can do this, Jer," he acknowledged. "I can only lie to her for so long. She'll figure it out soon."

"Then let her. What she doesn't know isn't hurting her." Jerry coughed. "It may hurt you should she decide her pendulum swings towards attorneys…." He let the rest hang in the silence. The dick.

Cameron wholeheartedly disagreed, but didn't vocalize it. Selfishly, he didn't want his fiancée to know there was a possibility Adrian lived. With his kids cooking in her oven and the keys to unlimited wealth, she'd be insane not to rush into the lawyer's lavish arms. Even considering such a thing made his skin clammy.

"And the money?" he asked.

A crack skittered across the line, whether a walnut or vertebra, Cameron didn't care to find out.

Jerry cleared his throat. "My accountant funneled the funds through various investment accounts, Shearer. Unless she goes all detective on her business, we're scot-free."

"Not reassuring, but it'll do." Another crack, this time followed by a thud. *Necks it is.*

"Good chat. Get me an update on whether the Mikkelsens have stepped into Des Moines yet. My informants will follow up on the J.J. and Adrian issues. I should've just killed both those assholes when I had the chance." The call dropped before Cameron could utter a retort.

Scratching his head, he tossed around the idea of crawling into bed once more. Sunday mornings were meant for cuddling, not collusion. *Dear God, I'm domesticated.*

Turning on the balls of his feet, his heart dropped when he spied Joci at the kitchen's entrance. An indiscernible expression covered her sleepy face, no tell in the crease of her pink lips. "Did you just wake up?" He went for a subtle question instead of direct confrontation. Hell knew he didn't want to battle the inevitable at this hour.

Shuffling to the cupboard, she retrieved a mug and filled it with the fresh brew. "Yeah." She took a sip, glancing at him over the rim, her black glasses mirroring the coffee's hue. "Everything okay?"

Cameron tossed the phone to the counter. "Yep. Standard Del Rossi shit." He nabbed a cup identical to hers and poured coffee inside. It wouldn't do a damn since it was decaf, but he needed to do something with his hands.

Joci's hazel eyes traveled down his shirtless torso and lingered over his red boxers. If his mind hadn't been stuck on the evil deeds he and Jerry discussed earlier, he would've enjoyed her perusal. "You'd tell me if anything was wrong, right?"

Swallowing the scalding liquid, he bobbed his head up and down. "Of course."

She narrowed her eyes then relaxed after a moment. "It's too early," she noted after taking in the clock's hands. "I'm going to catch a few more winks. It's not like this unleaded shit helps me wake up anyway."

"I'm right behind you," he called, watching her move toward the bedroom. She didn't buy his story. Well, good, it was part of the reason he worshiped her. She saw through all the bullshit and loved him despite it. He only hoped the same would be true about the secrets he concealed these days.

***

"And here are four guns for you to choose items with."

The two men greedily snatched the relatively harmless in-store guns used to add items to the baby list. Cameron wasn't too keen on shopping, but when the store clerk mentioned the ability to "shoot" items, he was suddenly on board.

"You guys look a little too enthralled with those things," Rayna mentioned as she listened to the young cashier's rundown of how to use the weapons of no destruction.

"Hey, we're men and you just gave us toys. What do you expect?" Quinn punched his fingers at the screen. He aimed and fired the gun toward Cameron, who in turn feigned a fatal shot.

Joci's sigh signaled her resignation of a mature afternoon at Baby Barn in West Des Moines. "Why don't you two handle the, um"—she glanced to her friend for support, but Rayna merely shrugged—"toys. Find age-appropriate toys for the boys, not you."

Cameron slung his gun on his belt and smirked at Quinn.

"I think we can handle that."

"Oh, most definitely." Quinn took off down the blue linoleum aisle, not bothering to wave.

Blowing Joci a kiss, Cameron followed at an equally jovial speed. The huff of disgust from Rayna wasn't lost to him. It wasn't his idea to spend one of his days off at a baby store. Hell, if he had his way, he'd let the women handle such a task. Shopping wasn't a favorite pastime. With all the Del Rossi and Mikkelsen shit swarming his brain, buying baby stuff was the last thing he wanted to do. In some sense, he felt out of place choosing a pair of sandals the boys would look cute in, which was why he was grateful the task of picking toys was handed to him instead.

Arriving at the infant section of the store, his face fell at the selection. "Holy hell."

"Yeah, that's what I said too." Quinn nodded to the back wall. "All rattles and chew things. How many teeth does an infant have? I mean, shit, do they just chew all day? I thought these were babies, not puppies." Chuckling, he pointed to the row of bottles. "Why are there so many types of nipples? Aren't they all the same?"

Cameron picked up one of the bottles packaged with a cartoon baby on it and studied the label. "This is all Greek to me. What does the flow level even mean?" Both shrugged. Cameron wasn't sure of anything in this store.

"I thought Joci was breastfeeding." Snapping his fingers at Quinn's statement, Cameron hustled to that area. The shelves of various merchandise didn't ease his mind. It was retail overhaul. How anyone made a decision on a brand was beyond him.

"Look, it's nipple cream." The taller man held up the small jar. "Says here, it's an ease for her nipples." His eyes lit up, a cheesy grin on his face. "Boob ease. Get it? Boobies." He snickered like a teenager with a newfound pun book.

"All right. I think you need a different section." He swiped the container from Quinn's grip and put it in its place. During this moment, his friend managed to sneak over to the interactive breast pump model. *It's like they want men to fuck around while women shop.*

"Cam, be serious. Does this make my boobs look fat?" Quinn held up the pump to his left pec and flexed.

"You're going to hell," he replied with a chortle, tossing a package of bra liners toward him.

"I'll save you a seat," Quinn replied with a cheeky smile.

Cameron jerked his chin to the assortment of teething toys. "Let's start with those. Surely we can choose a few out of the hundreds there."

Quinn ambled to the area, carefully reading the ages on each toy. After going down one row, he threw up his hands. "Screw it, I'm aiming and pulling the trigger. The girls can sort out the good ones from the crappy ones."

"Not a bad idea," Cameron commented when he noticed the items were basically the same, save a few minor details such as color and animal shape.

Twenty minutes passed before they finished at that spot and moved to the next. While Cameron filtered through crib accessories, Quinn rifled the stacks of puzzles and books that were infant-friendly.

"Check it out, I'm a baby."

Glancing around, Cameron caught sight of his usually manly partner smashed beneath a playmat sporting an assortment of zoo animals. He batted at them and adjusted the mirrors as if he was settling in for a long day of playtime. "Yeah, I don't know if 'baby' does you justice," he stated, standing above him. "You look like an idiot."

Quinn snagged a pacifier from the nearby shelf. "What? Me? Nah. I'm totally going to pick up chicks with this thing."

Scanning the area, Cameron grinned when he spotted a familiar face. "Yeah, I'm going to pretend I don't know you because a superhot woman is heading our way."

"Wait, what?" The stunned expression on the man's features was priceless when the curled auburn hair of Rayna popped into view. Her gray eyes clouded and her smile dipped when she recognized the off-duty officer lying on the ground.

"What the hell are you doing, Quinn?" Rayna asked with a scowl.

Startled, he tried to get up, but ended tangled in the web of dangling lions and monkeys. At last, he stood, wearing the playmat like a sash. "Uh, I was making sure it was safe." He patted it reassuringly. "Yep, it passed the police officer test."

"Uh-huh." Rayna pointed to the pacifier latched to his shirt. "And that?"

"Testing resilience." Quinn swiped it away just as Joci caught up to them.

"What's going on?" Her hazel eyes took in the scene. "Do I even want to know?"

Cameron grabbed a stuffed koala bear off the shelf and handed it to her, hoping to give Quinn time to correct himself. "Nope, but I think we should get this. Oh, and there's a few questions I had about bottles. I have no clue what kind to put on the registry. There's way too many."

Joci swiveled to the right and took in the selection. "Damn, that's a lot of shit. I don't remember all this the last time I was pregnant."

She fired away at bright packages with her own gun while Cameron snuck a glance over his shoulder to see Quinn's red face and the grin on Rayna's lips. The only plausible reason for the other man to come baby shopping was the hope of pleasing a woman. It was his reason, so Quinn couldn't be far behind. Since Joci was off the playing field, that left one woman. It was more than obvious the sassy attorney had snared Quinn in her net, but it seemed she wasn't ready to reel him in for the long haul yet.

Two hours and testing every baby toy in the store later, Cameron examined the long list of items the four of them had scanned into the computer. It was daunting, especially the final price tag at the bottom. Sure, it was pocket change to some, but with everything from bedding sets to bibs, he couldn't swallow paying those prices for babies who'd never remember the glamour.

"Sheesh, I think we scanned every article in the store two little boys would love," Rayna joked, taking a bite of her veggie burger. "And their mommy."

Joci pushed around the chili cheese fries on her plate with a fork. "No kidding. My back is killing me."

The drastic contrast of the in-store dining area amazed Cameron. The menu boasted snacks for the healthy and junk food aficionado alike. It was smart, since pregnant women tended to go from kale smoothie to fried onion rings within moments.

"Think you'll get a fraction of it?" Quinn inquired, cinnamon roll in hand.

"Maybe." She flipped to the outfits on the list. "Clothes are usually the big purchase, so I made sure to put plenty there. I'd bet most of these will be from the court attendants I know." Her eyes skittered along to the rest of the pages. "But my guess is Adrian's dad will buy a lot of the items. They're Brett's grandkids and the only relatives left he cares about." She glanced up

and amended, "According to him, that is."

Cameron's gut flipped at the mention of Adrian. He should tell Joci the truth about the man she mourned. His heart wouldn't allow it. Not with the storm circling the Mikkelsen puppet. Perhaps it was selfish of him to want more time alone with Joci before she uncovered the layer of his lies, but he didn't care anymore. Her return to Adrian, even if as a friend alone, was unavoidable once she digested the news. He couldn't blame her either. He'd known for far too long and refused to divulge crucial information. Any words she spewed, he rightfully deserved the wrath behind them. Sure, they had a deep connection, but could she see through the bullshit and stay with him? He wasn't sure he wanted to know the answer.

"Cameron, you still with us?" Quinn asked.

Whipping his eyes from the cold chicken quesadilla, he met Quinn's gaze. "Yeah, sorry. I was just imagining a manlier activity for us to do after all the girly stuff today. You want to hit up the shooting range?"

Quinn nodded enthusiastically. Both men needed to fire real guns with honest to God results. Him especially. It was one of his newfound favorite ways to release tension. He'd all but given up his drum set, since he didn't have one in Iowa. The pull to rock out with druggies in smoke-filled bars just wasn't in him anymore. Part of that could've been because he mainly did those gigs for Del Rossi business.

Cameron took in the sight of Joci and Rayna, chatting as though nothing else mattered in the world except choosing onesies for the twins to come home in. He didn't regret stealing time with his fiancée. From the conversation he and Jerry shared the other day about Joci's predestined legal role in the mob, she'd be safer once Adrian made his grand entrance. Despite that, a part of his heart wouldn't release her. Not entirely. Not until she shoved him from her life.

Joci fawned over a navy-colored sleeper with a blue teddy bear on the rump. She walked around all day toting a giant bowling ball on her front, all while looking like a goddess. *Damn, she's incredible.* Joci pushed the black glasses up her nose and he winced. He hoped there'd never be a day he didn't watch the adorable habit. His phone vibrated with a new taunt from the Mikkelsen crew. Ignoring it, he sat silently and watched her converse with the two friends closest to them. He'd make every second count while time permitted. With her stamina, he may be hurled to Texas once she found out his secrets.

CHAPTER FIVE

Double-clicking with the mouse, Joci did her best to wait until the phone ceased ringing to speak. She didn't want to talk to Cameron at the moment for more reasons than she cared to admit. "There's extra money showing on my investment statements and I don't know where it's coming from. Maybe I'm being paranoid because I've only done this for a month, but it just doesn't feel right." She chewed on her bottom lip.

Quinn crossed his arms over his chest. "Are you sure it isn't fluctuations with stocks and shit? I thought you had an accountant."

"I do, and maybe they are the investment proceeds, but I have this funny feeling that it's more than that. It's a sizeable amount of money."

"So why am I here again?" her friend asked, checking his phone. "I'm no digital forensic tech."

"Because I think someone is fixing the books. I spoke to Rayna about it and she had no clue. When I asked the accountant about the money, he gave me some accounting jargon and ended the conversation."

The police officer leaned forward. "Hmm, it could be something. Not all people are honest, especially when it comes to money." He nodded to her phone. "But why not tell Cam to go find out. I'm sure one of his old colleagues with the mob could help get an answer out of the accountant."

Joci grabbed the bottle of water on her desk and took a sip. "Well, I overheard a conversation the other day and…"

"You think he's lying to you about something?" Quinn's tone of voice coupled with the elevation of his eyebrows made her increasingly uncomfortable.

She nodded. "He admitted as much to the person on the other end."

"Whoa. Who was it?"

"No clue," she said, shrugging. "Probably somebody on the force."

Holding up his hand, Quinn revised, "Or one of his mafia contacts. And you're 100 percent sure they just weren't bullshitting? Men do that from time to time." He stretched his long legs out and slumped in the office chair opposite her. With his police uniform on, he was a marvelous specimen to behold. The deep hue of his green eyes popped against the dark material, and his close-cut hair sat in perfection. He was a catch for any woman in Des Moines. Despite his godlike features, she focused on the conversation.

"It had to be more than a man chat. He said something about me, but that's not what we're here to talk about. I'll deal with him on my own." She produced a thumb drive from her desk drawer. "I don't trust anyone else right now.

Which is why I'm asking you to do this off the books and not mention it to Cam. This is all the information I have on the investment account since opening."

Her friend offered an annoyed glance. "Okay and…?"

"And I want you to see if any of the money is dirty. Rayna and I pulled from our savings to open the business, and ever since then, we hired an administrator who's also an accountant to handle the investing for us. Now, I'm thinking there could be something fishy at work."

The cop sat up straight. "Fishy as in the Del Rossis are involved or fishy as in the accountant is stealing from you?"

Joci let out a breath. "I hope neither one and that I'm being paranoid, but I need to find out. Since you're the closest thing I have to a private investigator, it falls to you."

Taking the device, Quinn studied it then stuffed it in his breast pocket. "I don't like this, Joci. And I don't like the idea of Cameron keeping something from you."

"Neither do I," she said, standing. "But for now, I need to figure out why my investment numbers are off."

"Yeah, okay, I get it. I know better than to get in between the two of you." The humor in Quinn's voice was mirrored on his face.

"Yeah, yeah, you're just sore because you lost."

"I plead the Fifth." He patted his chest. "I'll see what I can uncover, but I'm not completely comfortable with this. I'm sure it's just investments gone awry with the market. We're friends, so I'll see what I can do."

"Thanks, Quinn, you're the best."

"I know." Quinn pushed up to his feet and smiled.

"But make sure you talk to Cameron. He's in love with you, and I don't want to see either of you hurt over a stupid miscommunication."

Hugging him, Joci rolled her eyes when he kissed her cheek. "Handsy, just like I remember. You better get to work before your partner comes looking for you." She pinched his side. "You wouldn't want him thinking you're making a play on his woman. He gets real possessive."

His playful eyes twinkled, and he offered a mock salute. Joci caught the subtle wink the officer tossed Rayna's direction before sailing out the building. It was rather cute the way her two friends flirted.

"What was he here for?" Rayna asked as a gush of warm air filled the entry.

Propping up against the door hinge, Joci let out a breath. "Work." She should confide in her partner, but if she was wrong, she didn't want the extra judgment. "He's looking into the investment fluctuations we talked about."

"Ah, good. But if it's a mistake and we just struck it rich, don't tell," the auburn-haired woman called, heading to the door. "I'm on my way to jail court. Wahoo. Have anyone you need me to visit while I'm there?"

Wracking her memory, she snapped her fingers. "Actually, yes." She scurried into the office and grabbed a thick folder. "Can you get this guy to sign his speedy trial waiver?"

Taking the file, the attorney reviewed the pleadings. "He's not bad looking," she said, pointing to the mug shot. "Your infamous Joci Dorous sexy scheme didn't work on him?"

Joci looked down to her belly. "Yeah, not too many inmates have pregnancy fetishes, and my alternative and very normal techniques haven't worked of late. Plus, I gave it up after Cameron's backfired."

Giggling, Rayna tucked the newest duty under her arm. "Good point. I doubt I'll be back. I'm meeting Quinn for drinks later."

"Ooh," Joci crooned in a girlish tone. "Is something happening between you two?"

A flash of red crept on her friend's cheeks. "Yeah, right. That'd be dumb. He's too much of a player."

"From what I recall, he plays very well with others," Joci teased.

"Joci!" Rayna's face turned bright red. Clearly, she wasn't the only woman with her mind in the office's gutter.

"What? Just the truth." She took a step into her office. "In case you needed a little release, I'd highly suggest Quinn. With his muscly body and tight ass, he'd definitely help you along." Joci peeked back and gave her a wicked smirk. "After all, it *has* been a while, Ray." She closed the door before one of Rayna's high heels soared through the air. The resounding thud and subsequent huff from the other side made Joci snicker. She wasn't certain if those two would amount to anything except bedmates unless one of them put the effort into a first move. "But it'd be worth a shot."

A catchy country ballad rang through the silence, indicating Cameron's call. He detested the song, but you couldn't go wrong with Tim McGraw. Walking over to it, she held her breath until his photo disappeared on the screen.

As badly as she wanted to hear his voice, she deserved the truth more. Secrets weren't far when the sexy-looking ex-convict was involved; a bad combination for her.

***

Jamming the smartphone into his pocket, Cameron let out a low snarl. His expectant fiancée hadn't returned his calls all day, which bothered him. Sure, she had court appearances here and there, but she'd always made time to call him back. Nodding to the bulky man in a tight black T-shirt, he moved through the hotel at a steady pace. He needed to find out what was so damned important. Spending copious time among the Del Rossi mob tempted his demons. It'd be too easy to fall into the past and pick up more money than his cop payload.

"What's up, Jer?" He stepped over the threshold of the room filled to the brim with computer monitors. The place was more lit up than the Pentagon, with an equally frigid atmosphere.

The leader of the brood of mobsters craned his neck from the posh twirly chair. "Good, you're here." He splayed his hand toward the screen. "There's something you should see."

Moving to the space, Cameron studied the video surveillance. "Where's this at?"

"The hospital," the computer tech filled in.

Squinting his eyes, Cameron watched a dozen people pass before he caught sight of Derrick. The redheaded wonder walked leisurely despite a mild limp. At each camera, he made a point to tilt his head up and smirk, as if he knew the recording would be reviewed. Clenching his hands on the table, the cop held in a groan when Derrick saluted the camera before exiting the building.

"He knew we'd watch," Jerry noted.

"Who is he?" Cameron asked, afraid to hear the answer.

The technician's fingers glided over the keyboards, pulling up facial recognition software. After running Derrick's face through the system, nothing popped up on the screen. "Nope, sorry. I'm not getting a hit on any ID for this guy." The computer guru clicked through another screen. "But I did find other locations this guy's been in the last twenty-four hours."

Dozens of camera feeds spit on the monitors above Cameron's head. Scanning each one, he grasped this part of the job wasn't remotely legal. It was a necessary evil, chiefly when the Derrick fellow entered the Polk County courthouse.

"He's a busy guy," Jerry stated, puffing on the cigar that somehow snapped in existence. The man was never without one vice or another. "And look, he even peered through Joci's office window."

Now fully erect, Cameron summoned his courage and studied the monitor at the end of Jerry's tubby pinky. Sure enough, a redheaded man was snooping around the one place Cameron had thought secure.

"Motherfucker," he mumbled, the tidbits of information weighing on his mind. He'd be an imbecile to ignore the connecting dots. Derrick wasn't just anyone. He was someone vital to Joci. "Can you track a fingerprint if I get you one?" he inquired of the nerdy man in front of him.

The computer tech nodded. "Yeah, no problem."

After slapping a hand on the tech's shoulder, Cameron turned to leave. One last flash of footage insisted on his return. When the loop ran out, he knew precisely where to get the required evidence of a resurrection.

***

Cameron placed the bags of Chinese takeout on the kitchen table later that night. "Joce, dinner's here." He wiped a bead of sweat off his forehead with the back of his hand. Though the temperature was near arctic in the house, he still wore his uniform. Coming from the humid outdoors, it always took him a while to cool down. Joci walked into the small dining area. *Especially, when she wears something like that.* His eyes traveled up her long legs to the barely-there shorts and spaghetti strapped tank top. She looked marvelous with the large bump under the polka-dot shirt. He'd never thought pregnant women could be sexy until he saw Joci.

"What'd you bring me?" she asked, pulling out the chair opposite him. Her distance unnerved him. Usually, she sat as close as possible to him. She hadn't been her usual self since she overheard part of his conversation with Jerry. He'd chalked it up to her condition, but maybe he was wrong to do so.

Pulling out the white boxes, he replied. "Everything a woman with a craving could want. Lo mein, egg rolls, chicken fried rice, beef and broccoli, orange chicken, and of course loads of crab rangoons." He popped open the tops and slid a pair of chopsticks to her.

Joci's stomach grumbled in response to the savory smells wafting through the air. "Yum." She grabbed the box of lo mein and dug in without another word.

He sat back, box of fried rice in hand. For a moment, Cameron merely watched as she ate. If inhaling food was a sport, she'd win every time. He held in a chuckle as she slurped a noodle. Fuck prim and proper, he'd rather have a woman comfortable enough to not care if she had sauce on her face. Which Joci did. A lot of it. "So, how was your day?" Even as he said the words, he couldn't help but cringe. It sounded so domestic.

"Fine. I was at the courthouse most of the day." She flipped open a magazine on the table and scanned the article. "What about you?"

Cameron stabbed the rice with his chopsticks. "It was okay, I guess." She nodded, but kept her attention on the magazine. "Quinn took a longer lunch than usual yesterday. Any idea why?"

Coughing on her bite of egg roll, Joci's eyes flew to his face. "What? Why?"

Now suspicious, he prodded, "Was Quinn with you?"

She grabbed a bottle of water from the refrigerator then returned to the table. "Um, yes, he was."

"Doing...?" He didn't want to sound jealous, but it came out anyway.

Joci cocked her head to the left and rolled her eyes. "We had lunch. We're friends. Friends have lunch every now and then." She wiped her mouth with a napkin and squinted her eyes. "Why? Is anything wrong with it?"

She wasn't telling him the full truth. That much was clear when she got defensive. It was one of the things he learned about her in the last months. It was difficult for her to turn the attorney façade off sometimes, and he wasn't a fan of it. "No, of course not. You and Quinn were friends long before I came around again. I want to make sure we're doing all right."

Joci switched to the box of orange chicken. "Why wouldn't we be?"

"You didn't answer any of my calls yesterday or today. We usually talk at least once."

"Sorry, I was busy. I don't expect you to answer every time I call. We both have demanding jobs." Her phone buzzed, and she set down her chopsticks to check the message.

He tossed the box of rice to the table and plunged his fingers into his hair. The gel from the morning was nearly gone and made his curls bounce to his brow. "I know, I know. I'm not trying to control you or anything, I just..." He glanced down at his uniform. "Is something wrong, Joce? You're more talkative than this."

Joci cleared her throat, bringing his eyes back to her. "I don't know, maybe."

"What do you mean? Did I do something?" The events of the last two days ran through his mind. Joci wasn't the type to play games or toy with his emotions. She said what she meant, even if it wasn't what he wanted to hear. It was why they were so good together. They didn't have secrets. He frowned. Well, she didn't. His secrets weren't optional with the mob and she knew it going in.

"Who were you talking to the other morning before we went to register at the baby store?" she asked.

The conversation with Jerry buzzed in his ears. He couldn't very well tell her the details of their chat. "Just a mob buddy."

Her hazel eyes studied his face. "You told the other person you were lying to me."

Fuck. Cameron leaned forward and pushed the white carton out of his eyesight. Tepid egg rolls were the last thing on his mind now. "Ah, that."

"Yes, that." She crossed her arms over her chest. "Want to explain?"

After scratching his forearm, he took a drink from her water bottle. "I can't."

"What do you mean you can't?" She snatched the beverage back.

"It's mob shit, babe. I don't want to get you more involved than you already are." He reached over and placed his hand over hers. "There's some stuff you can't know for your protection." Her eyebrow rose at his words, so he continued. "It's not that I don't want to tell you. I'm not allowed. Not yet, at least."

When he saw his explanation wasn't getting anywhere, Cameron scooted his chair around the table until it was directly beside Joci. The familiar scent of her coconut shampoo comforted him despite the circumstances. Gently, he cupped her jaw and tilted her eyes to meet his. "I love you, Joci, and nobody else comes close to you. Believe me when I say I wish I could share every little detail about my mafia job, but I can't."

"I know. It's difficult to remember sometimes. Mostly when it involves me." Her brows furrowed together, and she chewed on her bottom lip. "It sucks. I don't want anything between us."

He chuckled. "Yeah, I agree. Just think, only another four-ish years and I'll be all yours. You can learn every deep, dark secret about me on a daily basis." Cameron kissed her temple. "You're going to lose all interest in me when I'm not a bad boy anymore."

Joci smirked then pressed her lips to his. The tangy orange sauce from the food combined with her natural taste sent his mind spinning. When she pulled back, he was 100 percent finished with dinner. "You'll always be my bad boy," she murmured.

Her husky reply coupled with the coy grin on her face made him lose any control he'd been holding onto. Gathering her into his arms, Cameron kissed her until the sound of his police radio interrupted them. He pulled back and clicked it off. He'd been so set on seeing Joci, he didn't have the chance to do anything with his police gear yet. It wasn't too problematic since her fingers were currently unbuttoning his shirt. Gazing down at Joci, he ran his thumb across her swollen lips. "Your safety is my first and only concern. I swear I'll tell you everything I can without putting you at risk."

Her fingers threaded through his hair, pulling him closer. "I guess I can live with that," she whispered, hazel eyes shining brightly.

"Good. Now, I really need to know something."

"Anything."

Cameron nodded toward the table. "Are you going eat all the lo mein? Because I haven't gotten any yet. You were seriously hogging it."

Joci grabbed the box of Chinese and flung a noodle at him. The wayward food stuck to his cheek and resulted in boisterous laughter from the brunette. "Oops."

Flicking the noodle off his face, Cameron locked eyes with her. "You won't win at a food fight with me, sweetheart."

With a smile on her face too perfect to deny, she tossed another one his direction. This one hit his chest. "Guess we'll find out, won't we?"

"Can't wait." He gripped the water bottle and splashed it toward her, soaking the top half of the white and pink tank top. Instant gratification met his gaze when her sheer bra underneath left nothing to the imagination. Joci shrieked as droplets slid down her chin. For today, they were fine. She loved him enough to throw food at him and trusted him with her heart. Her giggle met his ears when she placed a noodle across the top of his lip. If every day ended with food and sex with Joci, he would never complain.

***

"Your Honor, my client shouldn't be reprimanded because the alleged victim snuck into the house and violated the protective order," Joci argued with a sideways glare at the blonde county attorney. She wasn't a fan of the know-it-all. Undoubtedly it was reciprocated, since the woman flicked her short hair out of her oval face.

"Judge, Mr. Hascal intentionally sent a message to the victim regarding his whereabouts through his brother," Anne Scott sputtered, her pale pink pumps clicking on the marble flooring.

Jabbing a hand over her client's raised finger, Joci shook her head violently and shot the thirty-one-year-old a glare that would otherwise silence a demon. The judge with thin spectacles shuffled a stack of pleadings on his desk and looked between the two parties. Joci felt her client's posture slacken when the courtroom's door swung open and the victim fled. She didn't care what happened in the residence Joseph Hascal stayed at the other night, but it was obvious he hadn't acted alone.

"Ms. Dorous, your client admitted to police officers at the scene of a romantic interlude between himself and Ms. Richards." Judge Dickerson dropped his small frames to the files and studied her. "Whether it was accidental or predisposed, relations imply Mr. Hascal knew what they were doing."

Joci tightened her grip on the rich client beside her when he covered up a chuckle with a cough. This lovely account was passed from the Petosa firm. It seemed the man was a tad handsy with his previous attorney, which prompted the move. Thankfully, the real estate broker failed to try anything with his new counsel. Though she was certain if she wasn't pregnant, a pinched ass cheek or two would've occurred prior to today's hearing.

The county attorney perked up and said, "Judge, the State requests ninety days in the county jail for failure to abide by the Order."

Instead of arguing with the Barbie-wannabe, Joci kept her lips closed. She didn't need to pop a blood vessel while shoving something down Anne's throat.

"Ms. Scott, I agree Mr. Hascal should be chastised, but the amount of time you suggest isn't likely to aid in this case," the judge included. "Plus, the jail is nearly to full capacity. And I'm not about to ship him to a nearby prison for such a sentence."

"Your Honor, might I suggest assaultive behavior classes and house arrest at the Petosa loft, which would include daily therapy with Dr. Mills?" Joci's feet sweated after the words slipped out. If she had to deal with Petosa's leftovers, then so would they.

Banging the gavel, Judge Dickerson nodded. "Mr. Hascal, you're to serve ninety days under house arrest at the Petosa Law Firm's secured holding facility. While in their custody, you will attend daily sessions with Dr. Mills as well as complete the assaultive behavior course. The No-Contact Order shall continue to be in effect pending the disposition of your case."

Hascal practically kissed Joci when the judge stood and shifted to the small set of stairs.

"Oh, and, Ms. Scott, please draft the proposed order for filing," the weathered judge included before disappearing into his private chambers.

Anne snapped her head toward Joci, her lipstick no longer the brightest thing on her face. "Really, Joci? You can't let me have one win?"

"Please. You were the same sore loser when I passed the Bar first." Joci swung her purse over her shoulder. "You're just mad because I even the playing field."

The county attorney scrunched her face and huffed out of the room, the door slamming at her escape. It wasn't how she liked to win, but Anne had pissed her off since day one in law school.

"Well done, Ms. Dorous." A one-man clapping crowd echoed in the open space. "I must say, I was surprised when Petosa tossed me in your direction, but I understand why now." Joseph Hascal plucked at his eyebrow, a frequent and nasty habit.

"Don't worry, your bill will reflect how good I am," she reminded him, buttoning her suit coat. She eyed his slicked-back hair and designer duds. "For now, try to keep your liaisons to a minimum. I don't need a judge yelling at me because of your dick."

Joseph's brown eyes grew, and he doubled over in laughter. "God, you're exactly what Petosa said you'd be." He wiped his hands on his shirt. "Expect a lifetime retainer if you keep this up."

Not waiting for him to hand her a golden goose, Joci swept through the empty benches and out the double doors. Hubbub from matching courtrooms on the second floor distracted her when two women chased each other up and down the split stairs, deputies attempting to catch them.

Shaking her head, she smirked. This was why she loved Des Moines. There were enough crazy-ass people here to keep her in business for years to come. Worrying about clients was foolhardy since, oftentimes, they landed at her feet.

Skimming her e-mails on her phone, she opened one from the county attorney she had court with later on. "Probation and community service, huh? Exactly what my client needs." She typed a reply, not watching as she walked down the hall.

"Didn't they recently pass a law forbidding texting while walking?" a teasing voice broke into her Internet negotiations.

Looking up, Joci held in her surprise when she spied Derrick Wheeler perched on the bench outside courtroom 204. *Hmm, weird to see him here.* She put on a smile. "Shh, don't tell. I need to close this deal."

He zipped a finger over his lips. "Your secret's safe with me."

She walked over and took a seat. After standing for the last hour, her feet were begging for a reprieve. "What're you doing at the courthouse? Not in any legal trouble, are you? Because I know an attorney who could help." Her purse slipped from her shoulder. "Pro bono of course, for my savior."

Derrick grinned. "Thanks, but no, I'm here to meet with a friend."

Numerous questions peppered Joci's mind. If he had friends at the courthouse, who was he truly? Normal people didn't hang out in the courthouse hallways while they waited for a friend. A shiver ran up her spine. *Surely he's not here for me. Is he?* She swallowed back the creepy thought. "Well, then I'll give you one of my cards in case of emergencies." She rifled through her bag and handed him a business card.

"I didn't peg you as a designer type of girl." He pointed to her satchel.

Holding it close, she pushed her hair off her collarbone. "I'm not. It was a gift from my husband at the time." The victorious mood she gained while in the courtroom dissipated at the mention of Adrian.

"Sorry, I wasn't trying to pry." Derrick tucked her card into the pocket of his jeans. "Thanks. I'll keep you in mind if I'm in a jam."

"All right, I better get to my next hearing." She glanced at her swollen ankles, and the thought of moving flew from her mind. She was comfortable, and not because of the wooden bench biting at her ass. Willing herself to get up, her body unashamedly disobeyed.

Covering her hand on the seat, Derrick's eyes dipped to her lips. Without thought, she licked them, his reaction worth the dismal rebuke she gave herself. "I hope to run into you again sometime, Joci. You make my day brighter."

Powerless to snatch her fingers or gaze from him, Joci opened her mouth then slammed it shut. His quiet words settled around her like an eerie mist. Her stomach rumbled from the twins' kicking. Their pattern, one she couldn't decipher, increased when his thumb stroked the back of her hand.

The cologne clinging to his skin reminded her of Adrian, but the lower tone of his voice didn't compute. He wasn't anything like her ex, yet something felt familiar about him. *No, snap out of it, Joci! Damn hormones.* Taken aback by his bold movement, Joci cleared her throat. Her hormones were way out of whack. "Okay, see you later." With that, she awkwardly jumped to her feet and all but jogged down the hall.

Stealing a look over her shoulder, she caught Derrick's eyes fastened to her retreating figure. "There's something about him," she muttered, ducking into her next courtroom. She couldn't pinpoint why the abundance of twitches from her womb erupted when he was near.

CHAPTER SIX

Cameron wasn't sure why he was here. Months had whizzed by since he visited, and he hadn't liked it then. This place bred death, yet when he got behind the wheel, the squad car ended up in Des Moines's largest cemetery. Attaining a fingerprint from Joci's ex was easier than he thought. She kept most of his belongings in a storage unit off Douglas Avenue and every now and then would rearrange the clutter as a coping mechanism. He understood her mourning, but not the reason behind retaining the items. She told him it was for the baby's sake, but as time went on, he doubted it was the true motive.

Putting the car in park, he rolled down the window. No one was visible through the thickly wooded area. Still, the hair on his arms stood at attention despite the early autumn weather.

"What're we doing?"

Quinn's voice brought Cameron to the present. He wasn't fond of graveyards, but who was? The last time he was here, he'd watched in muted agony as Joci wept over a man he thought of as cagey now more than ever. "I need to see it again."

"Adrian's empty grave?" The experienced cop scoffed. "Yeah, that'll give you closure." He pulled an energy bar from his pants pocket. "You have fun with the ghost of boyfriends past. I'll hold down the fort in case an actual case comes in."

Cameron swung open the door then paused. "This is crazy."

"What exactly are you expecting to find? An angel perched atop the headstone saying, 'Go for it, dude'?" his friend asked.

Cameron scratched his ear. "No, that's ridiculous."

Quinn took a chomp out of the chocolate chip bar. "All right, then tell me."

With one foot out of the vehicle, Cameron stayed in limbo, his mind wavering on his actions. "No clue, but one of my old mob contacts says J.J. is supposedly alive, so I must put my doubts to rest." He stepped out completely, closing the door with finality.

"Are you serious? They think J.J. lived through the explosion?"

"It's a possibility, yeah." Cameron rubbed his lips together. "People have a funny way of cheating death when they're in the mob."

"Great. Well, if you don't return in twenty minutes, I'll call for someone to go after you." Quinn shuddered, his face ashen. "Cemeteries creep me the hell out."

Taking a breath to bolster his nerve, Cameron trekked

in the direction of the Petosa mausoleum. Not surprisingly, it was the largest in the park and ideally located amidst a coven of ancient maple trees. Careful not to disturb those at rest, the police officer wove through the maze until he reached Adrian's final resting place.

The above-ground family burial site was magnificent. Before this year, he'd never set foot in one. The experience was surreal in more ways than he cared to elaborate on. Taking it in now, he decided he didn't want his body above the freeze line when the time came. His past was colorful, and his future appeared to gleam the same shades.

Hiking up the knoll, he tucked his sunglasses into the uniform's pocket. The expensive granite building held remnants of years of grotesque Iowa winters, but the tiny stained glass windows lining the top gave a friendly vibe.

As he took the last turn, a body met his gaze. The almost-blond red hair of the lanky man caught him off guard. Even without seeing a face, Cameron knew it was a Petosa. The Irish-born family practically cloned their male members. The funeral had been a sea of strawberry-blond hair from all in attendance, but the men were almost exact duplicates.

Reaching the large building, he wondered if he should say something or not. It wasn't *his* family buried there after all. He was simply there to pay respects. Well, respects of sorts.

"It's funny how people mourn," the man, whose voice held a chafed tone, said when Cameron's foot broke a fallen twig. "Some people lay flowers." He nodded to the graves nearby littered with daffodils. "While others choose to ignore their loss."

Cameron planted his boots ten feet from the stranger. "Everyone survives in their own way."

"And what about you?"

"He wasn't my loved one," he defended, unnerved by the way the man stayed in the sun's direct light, obscuring his face.

"But you knew him?" the man asked, his Irish accent waning the longer they spoke.

"I suppose, but not very well. He was my attorney." It sounded weird even to his own ears.

The visitor clasped his hands behind his back. "He must've won your case if you're taking time out of your day to talk to a decomposing body."

Cameron shifted his weight, not comfortable with the line of dialogue. "He did."

"And this is how you repay him, eh? By stealing his fiancée and children?"

Cameron's blood turned to ice at the directness. "Who are you?"

Finally, the man pivoted and met him face on. "Don't you recognize me?" The voice no longer held a hint of an accent. That fact alone chilled Cameron's blood.

Putting the identity together wasn't difficult. He'd been searching for this guy since the hospital fiasco. His heart pounded and his palms sweat as his subconscious connected the dots. "Yeah. You're the guy who saved Joci."

"Mm, yes, I am, but someone else too." He took a giant step over a freshly covered grave. "I'm the one she loved first."

Any chance of remaining calm flew on the breeze as Cameron digested the words. He didn't want to believe it despite the glaring evidence. "Adrian? Shit, I thought you were dead." His eyes swiveled to the name scrawled on the plaque then to the cold eyes opposite him.

"Well, I was. Sort of. It's incredible what mafia doctors can do for you." He fingered his chin. "Too bad they couldn't give me the same face, though. This one's all right, but I prefer the original."

"Holy shit!" Cameron mumbled, still wary of the meteoroid that just hit him. He wanted to believe Jerry was wrong. *I guess not.*

Adrian's lips curved into a wicked smile. "I think Joci's already fond of this mug, don't you? She seems enraptured whenever I see her." He met Cameron's eyes. "Which is quite often these days. We bump into each every now and then. Today's no exclusion."

Cameron's first instinct was to whip out his gun and fire off two rounds in the devil's skull. His fingers twitched near his belt, but he refrained. This wasn't a Del Rossi matter. Violence wasn't necessary. Plus, he wouldn't be the one to put Adrian down a second time. "Leave her out of this."

"I can't." Adrian walked a circle around him, scrutinizing every inch. "You look decent as a cop. She has a thing for men in uniform, but I'll bet Joci misses the bad boy vibe. It's the sole reason she took a liking to you. But all those gangster moves are gone, aren't they? You're on the straight and narrow." He paused. "Or are you?"

The new tattoos on Cameron's forearms ached for action. Just one swing was all it'd take to bring this rival down. "What do you want?"

Spinning on expensive shoes, Adrian cocked his head to the left. "I thought it was obvious."

Cameron bit the inside of his cheek, willing him to say the words he dreaded. The words that would turn his world topsy-turvy. The ones he deserved to hear.

"I want my life back," Adrian admitted. "I want you dead and Joci as mine. Why else would I turn a mob loose on you? They were quite enthusiastic when I gave them the name too. You have quite the reputation with the Mikkelsens. What'd you do?"

"Never happening." Not taking the bait, Cameron clenched his jaw until he was sure it would fracture.

Adrian lowered his voice and snatched a leaf from Cameron's shirt. "This time, I'll be the shoulder she cries on when your deadly past comes for you. When she discovers who I am, you won't be there to distract her a second time." He crumbled the crisp orange reminder of fall and patted Cameron's shoulder.

"No. Joci loves me." Even as he uttered the words, Cameron doubted their veracity.

"Shearer, she loves you today, sure, but only until the next guy who needs her comes around. I've seen it before. She'll want me back, don't you worry." Adrian put ten yards between them, his accent fully intact now mingling with the rustle of foliage. "You wouldn't happen to have any skeletons in your closet waiting for the perfect time to emerge, would you?"

Flashes from his bloody youth skimmed Cameron's mind. He possessed much more to hide than Adrian. The trouble was, he couldn't tell Joci any part of this.

***

Receiving a dazzling grin from Judge Bleecher, Joci grabbed her client's sentencing order and all but hauled the woman from the courtroom. She'd snagged the judge and county attorney on a good day. It didn't happen often, and she was going to escape before they changed their minds.

Once outside the room, she handed the recently filed paper to the woman in her late twenties. "Okay, Brittley, you have forty hours of community service and court costs to complete within sixty days. Think you can handle it?"

The short woman bobbed her head. "Yep. Thanks, Joci."

Without another word, she hightailed it to the elevator. Brittley would be back. It was a common occurrence with the homeless of Des Moines. Thus far, this was her fourth case with the woman who could claim public intoxication as an occupation. Somehow, Brittley always came up with the retainer money, though. Joci didn't want to think of how she came across the funds to pay an attorney. No doubt it'd be another criminal infraction to add to the long rap sheet.

Tucking the last file into her black expandable folder, she waited patiently for the aged elevator to make an arrival. She glanced over the railing to the crowd milling about below. Walking was a better choice, but she'd earned a reprieve after torturing her feet in heels all day.

Flicking her brown hair over one shoulder, Joci dug around in her purse for her phone. An e-mail about a potential client piqued her interest, so she quickly sent a reply and set up an appointment. It was a wonder she had any downtime these days. If Petosa wasn't handing off cases, the court was. The twins tumbled in her abdomen and she smirked. Getting in as many billable hours as possible before those two were born was the ultimate motivation out there. Taking a long maternity leave was the goal, and she'd get there if she hauled ass now.

The metal doors groaned open, and when Joci looked up, she was face-to-face with a black uniform sporting "Shearer" on the right pocket.

"Cameron, hey. I wasn't expecting to see you here. What's up?" Her lips curved into a smile as she met his eyes. The brown depths brewed something different this afternoon. Immediately, she wanted to know the cause behind the clouds.

Hooking his hand with hers, Cameron led them to the largest courtroom on the floor. His shoulders relaxed when it was empty upon entrance. Taping the "Quiet, Court in session" sign over the rectangular window, he turned to face her.

"You okay? I didn't think you had any court appearances today." Joci's stomach jumbled nervously. Seeing him in full cop getup was enough to send her blood pumping, but his peculiar behavior paused those thoughts.

Cameron placed his hands on his belt, the sight too damned sexy not to stare at. "I'm fine. I had to see you, that's all." He closed the distance to her and locked her in his arms.

His earthy scent calmed her on impact. "Oh, well in that case, I'm glad."

In one swift act, he picked her up and plopped her on the court reporter's desk, pinning her against the towering judge's desk. "I needed to feel you." His hands snaked her skirt up, delicately tracing his fingers up her thigh. Lips hovering above her mouth, his eyes searched hers with enough intensity to steal her breath. "Plus, I've had this fantasy since the day we were in court together." His mouth peppered down her neck, scattering chills along the satin skin.

Unable to move, Joci slid her fingers through his wavy hair. "Oh, really?" She arched her back when he popped one of the buttons clean off her turquoise blouse.

His teeth nipped her swelled breast, hands shoving the useless red bra aside. "Yeah, there's just something about this place and your tiny skirt." He lifted his eyes to her, desire laced in the chocolate rims.

Swallowing, she pulled his head closer to hers. "Then by all means. I want your every fantasy to come true."

A boyish grin covered his face. "I won't be the only one," he promised, clashing his lips to hers.

Taken aback by his possessiveness, she wrapped both legs around his waist, fingers hard at work on his belt. She wasn't certain what got into him, but she adored each shot of adrenaline his touch sent through her body.

Gripping the top of the desk, her hand nudged a wooden

object. One of them was getting pounded, and it sure as hell wasn't the gavel inches away.

***

Adjusting his shirt in the elevator's reflective doors, Cameron noticed the mess Joci had made of his hair. He let himself smile, recalling her throaty moans and sweet bite marks pressed to his neck. It was enough to make him want to hit the button and return for round two.

He didn't know what had possessed him to act like a horny teenager. Well, he did know, but he wasn't going to give Adrian any credit.

After racing from the cemetery, all he'd craved was Joci. To feel her tender skin in his arms and taste her on his tongue. He did both with enough precision to make Joci shatter not once but twice before he even unzipped his pants. The naughty images made him lick his lips, the taste of her still prevalent in his mouth.

He didn't give a shit that Quinn had heckled him when they turned into the courthouse parking lot. His partner wasn't aware of the circumstances of Cameron's urgent need to mark Joci as his. It was a primal force he couldn't dissuade if he tried. Nothing would've stopped him, much less his joking friend.

The doors sprang open and he stepped out with ease. Adrian's threat loomed over his form and spurred him forward. The possibility of his time with Joci being limited was more real than he ever hoped it would be. He'd make it count now and every new day he shared with the attorney he left with crooked glasses and a wrinkled skirt.

His phone buzzed from its confines, and after waving to the deputy on the way out of the courthouse, Cameron clicked on the message. A photo popped up of Joci's shirt, forcing him to gulp a chuckle. He'd made quick work of the buttons since they leapt off the blouse like bouncy balls. It was a wonder the shirt wasn't in tatters.

Not responding, he shoved the device away and whipped on his shades. As predicted, Quinn sat in the driver seat of the police car, his jaw munching something new and disastrously unhealthy.

"So, how'd it go?" Quinn asked when his partner climbed inside. "Did you get a little bow chicka bow wow while you were supposed to be working?" His eyebrows danced in a seductive manner, and he puckered his lips.

Buckling his seat belt, Cameron smoothed his pants. "Not that it's any of your business, but yes, I did."

Howling like a wolf, Quinn slugged him. "Atta boy." He threw the vehicle into gear and peeled out, merging with traffic.

Cameron felt the aftereffects of Joci glow over him and laughed at his friend's antics. If she experienced half what he did currently, there was no way she'd cast him aside for another man. Even if it was Adrian.

"Do you find it at all weird that we talk about the woman we've both had sex with?" Quinn asked, running a yellow light. Among other things, the veteran was a bit of an adrenaline junkie when it came to the power of being a police officer.

Scrolling through the reports on the car's laptop, Cameron shrugged. "A little bit, yeah." He clicked on a recent traffic accident. "Especially when you'd move the world to get her back if I wasn't around."

"Hey, hey, bros before—" he hesitated, searching for a fitting description. "Ex-booty calls."

Cameron rolled his eyes at the improvisation. "Good one, bro."

"Yeah, well, I'm not good at rhyming."

Dispatch crackled over the radio and both men fell silent. "A three-car collision on I-235 westbound, requesting unit 7345 and emergency response at the scene. Injuries reported. Possible 10-55 and 10-32."

Quinn flipped on the siren and lights as Cameron replied to the call. "Unit 7345 en route."

Doing a 180, the green-eyed wonder wiggled his index finger. "You'll have to catch me up on your courtroom coitus another time."

"No, I won't," Cameron replied, waving his sidepiece. "If there's a drunk wielding a gun at the accident, I get first dibs. I need an outlet."

"Damn! I bet you would've stayed with her all day rattling pencils off desks."

They zoomed through traffic, cars pulling to the side to let them pass. "You're right, I would've," Cameron said with a grin.

Laughter mingled with the blaring siren as Cameron's gut churned. Closing the laptop, he reran the day's events over and over again, trying to remember it all. The first half, he wanted to wipe from memory but couldn't. The second half was heaven on earth. He inhaled; Joci's luscious scent of raspberries hugged his skin even then and hurled him to their courtroom rendezvous. He didn't want to forget any detail.

"Cameron? Yo, earth to newbie."

Glancing to his left, Cameron drew his brows together. "Sorry, what?"

"We're here and I need you to have my back." Quinn nodded toward the accident. Taking it all in, Cameron checked his bulletproof vest. It was a hostage situation: a drunk driver who'd smashed his car on the median and had a random pedestrian in his grip with a gun to her head.

"Shit. Not a good end to the shift." Double-checking his gun, Cameron snapped it firmly in his hand.

"You go right, I'll go left. Loser has to buy drinks," Quinn said.

"Game on."

The two officers stealthily hopped out of the car, Quinn veering left and Cameron heading the opposite direction. The man waving a handgun was closer to the sidewalk, so Cameron took to the tree line in hopes of managing a surprise attack.

Hearing Quinn's stern voice address the miscreant, Cameron crept forward until he was in prime position behind the man. The babbling hostage had streaks of mascara running down her face, but otherwise looked unharmed. Noting the hold wasn't strong, Cameron's gut pitched when a flash of metal shone from the woman's back pocket. His eyes narrowed, recognizing the Beretta.

"Quinn, she has a gun too," he whispered in the radio. Glancing beyond the perp and his accomplice, Cameron snuck to a tree for cover and took the safety off his weapon.

Peeking around the trunk, he wasn't prepared for the onslaught of bullets aimed for his face. Jerking backward, he gripped the tree as bark flew around him.

"Shearer!" Quinn yelled from his position.

There was no way Cameron could leave the spot without being nailed at least three times. "I'm good," he hollered.

Quinn called for backup over the police line, but Cameron couldn't wait. If they didn't act now, the assailants would be off and running. Shaking his head free of the cobwebs on his mob tendencies, he stepped out of the haven and started firing at the couple, clipping the man in the arm and the woman's thigh; both went down within seconds.

Rushing over to them, he kicked the two guns out of reach and yanked the man's shirt, pulling his face close. "What the fuck are you doing?"

"J.J. sends his regards," the man said with a vile twist of his lips.

"How'd you even know I would answer this call?" he growled.

The man glanced to his accomplice. "You don't think you're the only one with friends in the police force do you, Shearer?"

"You were waiting for me to make the scene. Let me guess, you paid off somebody at dispatch to request our unit respond," Cameron put together and the man nodded. It made sense now. No doubt, J.J. and Adrian tag-teamed him today in hopes of ending the competition. He clenched his jaw and glared at them. "You messed with the wrong guy."

"It's a lot of money," the woman replied, holding her leg. "Shit, can I get a hospital or something? You shot me!"

Cameron kneeled, his blood hot from the altercation. "Not that you deserve one, but yes, an ambulance will be here shortly."

Quinn hustled to the scene, visually checking for injuries. "Good work." He snagged his handcuffs and placed them on the man while Cameron quickly did the same to the other half of the idiotic duo.

Once the criminals were in the back of the ambulance with two more police officers right alongside them, Quinn directed traffic away from the spectacle so the technicians could perform their duties and clean up the scene.

All Cameron could do was take his gun apart then put it back together. He counted his bullets not once but four times before shoving them into place. Car horns beeped and people shouted, but he didn't hear them. He was too busy coming to terms with his new reality. The Mikkelsen hit wasn't a farce. People were here for the reward money. He was as good as dead one way or another.

No matter where he went, he was a moving target because of the mob. It'd be easier if he severed all ties and went underground. He wasn't keen on the idea, but it would ensure Joci's safety. He was willing to go to any length for her happiness, even if it included deleting himself from her hard drive until the danger was gone. Should his past crimes come to light, she would push the detonation button herself. He'd rather get ahead of it. It's how Del Rossi trained him, but his subconscious kept fighting back. He hadn't beaten a conviction to run away. He needed Joci more than the air he breathed. Without her, he'd revert to the way things were before his court case.

"You wanna tell me why two fools tried to kill you back there?" Quinn asked, his shadow looming over Cameron.

"Not really, no."

Quinn plopped down and snatched the gun from his partner's hands. "Tell me." It wasn't a request, but a demand instead.

"There's a hit out for my life. Not one of those dead or alive ones either, just dead." Cameron eyed his friend. Shock registered on the man's face, though not as much as he predicted.

Quinn whistled low. "Shit, that's not good. Who put out the hit?"

"J.J."

"So, it's true? He escaped." Quinn's response drew attention from all around. He waved away the onlookers. "How is this possible?"

"It's the mob, anything's possible. He's keeping his identity low-key, but he's here somewhere." Cameron harshly rubbed the back of his neck.

"And Joci doesn't know," Quinn put together.

Cameron shook his head. "Nope."

"You need to tell her."

Jumping to his feet, Cameron shook his head until it hurt.

"Hell no. She needs to be as innocent to all this as possible."

"What aren't you telling me?" Quinn asked, joining him.

They watched traffic pick up speed as the response teams left, their patrol car the only one remaining. "I may ask you to take her out of town in the coming days." Cameron met the icy green eyes of the seasoned cop. "Don't ask questions, just take her, okay? She must be safe even if I'm not."

Quinn's mouth maintained the befuddled frown, but he nodded. "All right."

"Thanks." Cameron didn't feel relieved in the least. Death was knocking at his door and everyone had a key.

CHAPTER SEVEN

Sailing through the office door, Joci didn't bother to hide her good mood. Who knew screwing in a courtroom could rejuvenate a person?

"Well, aren't you easy, breezy, and beautiful?" Rayna commented, coming out of her cozy den with an iced coffee in hand.

"Court went well," Joci filled in with a sly smile. "You don't happen to have a decaf one of those lying around, do you?"

"As if you have to ask." Rayna disappeared then returned with a matching cup, decaf this time.

"Yum, thanks." Joci moved toward the massive desk in the corner, but found she wasn't alone.

"Um, slut-er-ella, you wanna tell me how your shirt ripped?"

Glancing at Cameron's handiwork, she blushed. "Oh, that." Joci pulled her seat out from under the desk and sank onto the comfortable cushion. "I had an impromptu visitor after my last hearing." She snagged her bottom lip between her teeth. "It's safe to say his old courtroom has new memories."

Rayna sputtered on her straw. "Hooking up in the courtroom, huh? Wow, aren't you the kinky couple."

"I don't know about that, but it was incredible." She jiggled the computer mouse. "I'd highly recommend it."

Rubbing her lips together, Rayna propped up her feet on the empty chair. "When I find some tatted cop for a lover, I'll be sure to send court pleadings flying."

Joci thought about bringing up the sizzle between Rayna and Quinn, but opted against it. If neither of them would start the recipe, she wouldn't stir the pot. Swirling the ice chips with the pink straw, Joci had to admit part of her silence came from another source. She loved the two separately, but she and Quinn had been intimate and some sliver of her wasn't ready to see him with another woman. It was beyond selfish, so she blamed it on the hormones. They were becoming a consistent scapegoat.

"Have any more appointments today?" Joci asked after they watched her phone ring. The flashing red light signaled a new message, which was promptly ignored. Why answer the phone when you could call the person back on your own terms?

"Just a probation revocation hearing in half an hour." Rayna eyed the clock on the wall. "Which I should be getting to." Standing, she lingered by the chair. "How about you?"

"A new client meeting whenever he shows up." She nodded and adjusted her blouse, attempting to hide the missing buttons. "Another one sent from Petosa. I swear, half my business is from them."

"Hmm, I wonder why," her friend harassed good-naturedly. "It couldn't be because you're carrying the heirs to the place."

Finding a stress ball on her desk, Joci chucked it toward the other woman. Rayna's sarcasm was one of the reasons she loved her. "No, it's because I'm a kickass lawyer."

Rayna swiped her bangs out of gray eyes sparkling with mischief. "Right, of course. How could I forget?" she called, exiting.

After checking her voice mails and clicking through e-mails, Joci was relieved when the bell above the front door jingled. Sitting for too long made her antsy, so the arrival was a blessing.

Moving through the room, Joci reviewed her reflection one last time before stepping into view of the small lobby. "Hello," she greeted the man studying the framed art on the wall. It was one of Adrian's pieces, her favorite in fact. She couldn't pack it up with the others. Not many people knew Adrian had dallied in artwork on the side. It was a secret she held close to her heart as one of the few.

"Ms. Dorous." He turned and a smile lit up his face when their eyes met.

Holy hell. This is getting a little creepy. She held out her hand and thought back to the quick conversation about the referral. All the receptionists at Petosa Law told her was it was a new case they couldn't take on. Joci hadn't bothered to get more information since the client referrals were lucrative for a small business. *I should probably start getting names when they call.* "Mr. Wheeler, I keep running into you."

"Not on purpose, is it?" he teased, shaking her hand, making her cheeks flush at the smooth tone. "And it's Derrick, please."

Accents were always a weakness for her, but she couldn't find it sexy on this man for some reason. She tugged at her skirt, suddenly wishing she wore pants. "Not that I know of, Derrick."

His gaze dipped over her languidly. "I must say I'm surprised Petosa Law sent me your way." He surveyed the open-concept office space. "They don't typically dish out cases to competing firms."

"Not usually, but I used to work for them." She studied the man dressed in cobalt-blue jeans and a lightweight button-up green shirt. "How do you know Petosa?"

Staring at the painting again, he cleared his throat. "Family connections." He nodded to the art. "This is exquisite. Where'd you get it?"

A bundle of nerves festered at Joci's core. "It was my husband's."

"Was?"

She pasted on a smile. "He died earlier this year."

"Ah, yes, you mentioned that at the hospital. I'm terribly sorry."

"Thanks, me too." Pointing to the larger of the two offices, she nodded. "If you'll follow me, we can discuss your case." Getting down to business was the safest route for the man who kept showing up in her life.

Derrick didn't answer, but lifted his brows then followed her. All of a sudden, Joci's palms began to sweat. Her eyes caught a glimpse of the thermostat. The suite was set at sixty-nine degrees, but felt ten degrees warmer. Rayna constantly complained about the frigid temperature, but at the moment, she could use ice cubes glued to her forehead.

"Can I get you anything to drink? Water? Coffee? Pop?" she offered when they passed the kitchenette.

"Thank you, but no." Derrick's eyes turned concerned when she fanned her face. "Can I get you something? You look feverish."

"I'm fine," she snapped, and then smiled guiltily. "Being pregnant with twins really sucks once you start to gain the weight to support them."

"Well, you appear to handle it brilliantly."

"Thanks." Joci sank into her faux leather chair and grabbed a yellow legal pad. "Please, sit."

The potential client ogled the two chairs opposite her desk. They were a matching set, the three chairs, from Adrian's old office. Once she had a little more money saved, she was going to buy a new set. This one reminded her too much of her ex.

As if reading her thoughts, Derrick spoke. "I like these chairs. Very chic." He settled into one and rested his right ankle on his left knee, pulling up the hem slightly.

Joci tried to forget how many times she'd witnessed Adrian do the exact thing. "Okay, so why don't you tell me about the situation, and I can decide if it's in my realm of expertise." She clicked her blue pen and sat poised for note-taking.

"Oh, it's a simple speeding ticket," he admitted. "The cop was being a bit of an asshole and added interference with official acts on top of the ticket, so I want it all to go away."

Scribbling incoherently to everyone but her, she nodded. "Uh-huh, and the officer's name?"

Derrick sat forward in his seat. "I think it was Officer Reyes. Can't remember the first name."

Joci held in a relieved sigh. The name wasn't familiar, and it wasn't Quinn or Cameron. She could take the case even though her gut tossed at the thought of spending more time with the man who set her on edge. "All right. Do you have the police report or traffic ticket?"

Derrick cracked his neck to the left, rubbing the opposite shoulder, and Joci attempted to remain stoic. Her newest client may as well be Adrian reincarnate. Too many times, her clothes disappeared after Adrian did the exact act. Her eyes lowered. And their bodies mingled on that very desk. Adrian's father insisted she take Adrian's desk when she went out on her own. Now, she wondered if keeping it was a mistake. Shaking the past to the back of her head, she fixed her gaze to Derrick.

Sensing her attention, he lifted his chin. The tumultuous haze in his blue eyes caused her pen to wobble between her fingers.

"I do." He licked his lips. "But it's at my apartment. Can I bring it by later?"

"Yeah, sure. That'll work." She set down the unstable writing utensil and placed her hand on the rolling twins in her womb. "I'll file an appearance once I get the pleadings and your retainer."

"And how much will it be?"

Even without seeing his wallet, it was clear he could afford to pay any number she threw out. What she didn't understand was why he chose not to pay the fine. "Five hundred should cover it." She smiled. "Since you're a Petosa referral, I like to give a small discount." Normally, she offered the discount because she wanted repeat business, but the way Derrick was looking at her, she wasn't certain she wanted that from him.

"No problem. I'll drop off the funds with my ticket." His eyes roamed the office, hitching on the framed photo of her and Cameron from their childhood. "That's your fiancé, right? He's a police officer, isn't he?"

"Yep. Cameron and I grew up together in Ohio." She wiped dust from the wood. "It was pure happenstance we reconnected in Iowa."

Scratching the side of his nose, Derrick kept his gaze averted. "Your deceased husband, was he a fan of your reunion?" The tinge of anger in his tone perplexed her.

"He knew what he was getting into when we were together," she defended, though she wasn't sure why. This client knew nothing of the strife her life involved when it came to the men she loved. Standing, she pushed in the chair, done with the sharp turn their interview had taken.

"Of course, I apologize." Derrick's dazzling smile spread

as he stood. His eyes slid over another photo on the desk. "Is this him? Your husband? Sorry, your late husband."

It was odd to refer to Adrian in that way. She hadn't done it until right then. Reacting instead of thinking, Joci nabbed the frame. Nobody was supposed to see the picture. "Yes." She pried it around to face forward. She'd been unpacking boxes earlier in the day and forgot to put the frame back. "It was taken right after we eloped."

"You eloped, huh? How romantic."

"To the courthouse, so not exactly Tahiti." She grinned at the distant memory.

"You must've been in love." Derrick pointed to the photo, and the stray scars on his flesh caught her attention.

Averting her eyes, she scanned the smiling faces. "We were. Very much so."

"He was a lucky guy for the short amount of time he had you."

Joci placed the frame in a box she'd compiled to send to storage. Glancing to Derrick, her heart rate picked up when she realized he was much closer to the edge of the desk than she had believed. Curiosity got the better of her and her eyes inspected his frame. *Joci, stop it!* She glanced away, but when he shifted his feet, the movement drew her back in.

He extended his hand. "Thanks for everything. I'll be back later this week with all you need."

"Sounds good." Tentatively, she clasped it and found she was quickly lost to the static of their touch. It was comfortable in a way, as if her palm knew his intimately. Raising her eyes, she opened her lips to speak, but the familiarity she saw in his baby blues stopped her.

"I'm glad our paths keep crossing, Joci." Derrick dropped his hold and moved to the door. His brow furrowed together when he caught sight of the missing buttons on her blouse. "If you wear that in court, my ticket will be gone before I even see a judge."

Self-consciously, Joci's hands rushed to her breast. Not having a spare at the office, she attempted to make the missing buttons less obvious. Evidently, her cockamamie fix hadn't worked. "It was an accident," she fibbed. She didn't know why, but she felt as though she needed to explain herself to him.

A cunning grin covered his face. "It always is when a pretty girl is involved."

Her face burned with embarrassment at his unconcealed flirting.

"Have a good evening, Miss Dorous. I look forward to seeing your next wardrobe malfunction. Maybe next time, I can help."

As he exited the building, so did the gasp from Joci's lips. The sensations this man created unnerved her. She was largely pregnant, engaged to a police officer, and yet somehow, Derrick managed to sneak a suggestive request that made her gut churn. The way he said it made her more uncomfortable than anything. *Maybe Rayna should take his case.*

Waving her hand in front of her face from the heat, Joci retreated to her office. With the day she just had, a cold bubble bath was more than deserved.

CHAPTER EIGHT

"Surprise!"

Joci stumbled backward, hand fluttering over her racing heart. "Holy shit." Her eyes flicked to the auburn beauty whose face bore a proud grin.

"Did we catch you off guard?" Rayna asked, the crowd dispersing for the moment.

Catching her breath, Joci eyed the room full of women. Green and blue streamers dangled from the ceiling and matching balloons speckled every direction. "Are you kidding? I almost gave birth to the boys!" she replied.

Rayna's airy laugh flitted through the room. "Good, sort of." Pulling on her hand, she led her among the crowd. "Come see who's here. I invited pretty much everyone in your e-mail contacts list." "Is that my dermatologist?" Joci waved at the forty-year-old woman with wide-rimmed glasses.

Rayna blushed. "Whoops, sorry. When I said 'everyone,' I may have gone overboard."

Recognizing more faces than she could remember,

Joci smiled. "Thanks, Rayna. You didn't have to do all this." She motioned to the cake covered in blue icing with tiny toy trucks driving up the side.

"Of course I did! You're my best friend." She pulled her to the center of the room. "Let's make this woman earn her presents," she called out to the ladies.

Joci wasn't prepared for the onslaught of organized games over the next hour. To her knowledge, she and Rayna had been going to have a nice lunch at their favorite restaurant. Skimming over the heads of females, she accepted that "quiet" and "calm" weren't in the near future.

For the first few games, she participated. Swaddling a baby doll was easy enough. When the next round of activities sprang up, Joci copped out. She held back gagging when the women were urged to taste melted bits of candy bars smeared in a diaper to guess the type of chocolate. Though it was chocolate, and God did she love chocolate, she couldn't muster herself to join that particular commotion.

Following "ice ice baby" where contestants tried to melt their ice cubes to see the gender of a miniature baby figurine inside, Joci was grateful when presents started to fall at her feet. She could use a rest from all the chatter.

Unfortunately for her, opening gobs of itty-bitty baby clothes did nothing to alleviate the throbbing in her head. The audible sighs at each new set of onesies was enough to make her consider early inducement. It wasn't that she was against adoring friends, it was just the women present weren't her favorite people. Sure, Rayna was among the watery eyes, but she would've been perfectly happy if the two of them went to a baby store and filled up a cart then called it a day.

When at last the guests broke off to consume the vanilla bean cake slices, Joci nabbed a glass of fruit punch and snuck out to the terrace. Somehow, the afternoon had warped into evening and streaks of orange sunlight met her eyes. Letting out a breath, she rolled her neck back and forth, the muscles in dire need of strong fingers. The scent of burning leaves made her crave hot apple cider. Fall in Iowa was glorious.

"I thought I may catch you out here."

Without turning, she knew Cameron was beside her. True to form, the muscular man wrapped her against his chest, resting his chin on the top of her head. "How are you holding up, counselor?"

"Much better now." She relaxed under his embrace.

"Good. Only another month left before we meet these little guys."

"Yeah, hey, wait, why are you here?" she asked, realizing he wasn't supposed to meet up with her until later that night.

"Quinn threw me a stag party or some shit like that. Supposed to be the guy version of a baby shower." He snickered. "Turned out being the off-duty guys and our captain drinking. It would've been weird if the bartender didn't keep the drinks fresh."

"Then you enjoyed it?" She muzzled a grin, fully aware of Quinn's crazy notion before today. She hadn't thought he'd follow through, but was glad he had. Even if Cameron didn't

father the twins, he was their dad and the person who'd

be around the rest of their lives. He deserved to be celebrated too.

"As it happens, yes, I did." He placed both hands on top of hers. "But being out here is a ton more fun than the rousing darts tournament."

Joci snuggled deeper into his sturdy chest. "I'm scared, Cam."

"Aw, why, babe?"

"The last time I went to the hospital to give birth, my family fell apart. What if it happens a second time? I don't think I can handle that." She shivered at the memory.

Tenderly twirling her to face him, Cameron pressed his warm lips to her mouth. Arms coaxing for a response, he wasn't disappointed when Joci's fingers found their way to his head and pulled him closer yet. She could kiss him for a minute or an hour and crave more. His lips were made for the act. Hell, so were hers, but only when it came to Cameron. With any other man, she'd tire of the subtle nibbles his teeth danced across her lip or the invasive advance of his tongue when she least suspected. His lips, his body, his soul was sculpted solely for her use, and she'd be damned if she didn't take advantage of the gift.

Breaking free, he didn't go far. "This time won't be like the last. I swear."

She patted his cheek then kissed it. "If you say so."

"I do." He nudged closer, but found the act difficult with the distance her belly created. "Once this barrier is gone, you better clear your schedule." He lowered his voice, tongue trailing the outer rim of her ear. "Because I'm going to lock you in our bedroom and screw you until the walls fall down."

Heart racing at his proposition, Joci met his desire-laced gaze. "Promise?"

"I give you my word."

She traced a heart over his pecs. "I've heard taking an ex-convict's word for something isn't wise."

"Then allow me to change your perception." He hoisted her off the floor, cupping her ass.

Giggling with glee, she batted at his head. "All right, inmate, you need to stop before you hike up my dress any more than you already have."

"Is that a challenge?"

Joci rolled her eyes, but couldn't dissuade him. "I better get back in there. You should too. I'll bet Quinn is lost without you." She placed a smooch on his head, and he reluctantly returned her feet to the porch.

Cameron kissed the tip of her nose. "Yeah, it happens more than you think."

Running her thumb along the ink on his hand, she added, "I know I would be."

"Good thing I'm staying put, huh?"

She nodded. "A very good thing."

"Yoo-hoo, Cameron? Where'd you go?" Quinn's voice bounced across the skyline, scaring a pigeon into flight. The bulky man spotted them before either could utter a word. "Ohh, getting a little nookie nookie?" He wiggled his hips suggestively, resulting in Cameron flipping him a middle finger.

"Quinn, have you seen Joci? She ran out on a perfectly good cake," Rayna asked from the window closest to the couple of interest.

"I'm coming, I'm coming," Joci called.

"Not yet, but soon enough," Cameron replied, lightly slapping her ass then jogging over to Quinn.

If she didn't love him so much, she might throw him back in jail. The man was a flirt, but hell, she loved every second of it. Watching the easy sway of her childhood crush's backside, Joci figured she could manage endless teasing if he was the ultimate prize. "Okay, Rayna, let's go back in."

"Yay! It's time for the piñata."

Joci's face screwed into a frown. "What the hell did you get one of those for? This is a baby shower, not a five-year-old's birthday party."

Rayna clapped her hands and squealed. "You're going to love it. Let's go!"

Glancing back to where Quinn and Cameron stood tossing back shots, Joci did her best to paste on a smile and returned to the mayhem inside.

***

Examining the newborn outfit, Cameron pursed his lips. "Are they really this small?" Being around kids wasn't common for him. The one experience with the mini adults was when his second cousin came back from Georgia with a newborn. Yet another reason he stayed clear of his screwed-up family tree.

"No freaking way," he muttered, turning it over. A small pawprint was sewn into the backside.

Joci's voice carried through the ducts along with the air conditioning. Since the impromptu baby shower and "dad party," as Quinn called it, the day before, all they'd done was go through the gifts. Some were useful, like the boxes of diapers, while others made him shudder.

"Butt paste." He read the ingredients. "Yeah, I'm just going to leave this right here." He tossed it to one of the dressers in the spare bedroom. Two cribs were set up side by side lengthwise. The nursery theme was zoo animals, and Joci's friends ran with it like a marathon. Teething giraffes, mobiles with lions, a hippopotamus swaddling blanket, and laundry hamper spotted with cheetahs were among his favorite from the haul. The entire room screamed "baby boy" from the darkening curtains with blue zebras to the brown monkeys stenciled on the wall above each crib.

"Sure hope they aren't wrong about the gender." He chuckled. If that were the case, he couldn't begin to imagine Joci's reaction. She was banking on two little boys. Not one item purchased could be taken as neutral. *She wants clones of Adrian.* His chest panged at the notion. It wasn't completely impossible either. The odds were in Adrian's favor in more ways than the child's physical attributes. He wouldn't let his mind wander to the other reason her ex-husband could prevail.

Pulling out a drawer and placing the newly laundered clothes inside, he grinned. Each one was color-coordinated by size. *Joci at her finest.* In honesty, he didn't mind the borderline obsessive-compulsive act. It made finding an outfit much easier. The organization also gave him something else to mull over while Joci showered. He'd promised to paint her toenails afterward, something about her not being able to reach her toes anymore. Smirking, he recalled the awkward way she twisted her body last night to unstrap her shoes. Her flustered face was well worth the angry glance he received when she heard his laughter. Almost overnight, her belly had popped, and she looked the part of an expectant mom of twins. He didn't mind giving back rubs, drawing bubble baths, or coming home to cold suppers. He had Joci. It was all that mattered.

A buzz from his pants pocket pulled him to the present. Dropping the pair of baby jeans, Cameron snagged his phone. A scowl rippled across his face.

Blocked: Pick out the outfit for when you bring them home yet?

Cameron: Who the hell is this?

Blocked: I put my choice in the second crib. The blue will bring out their eyes.

Heart racing, Cameron waited for the rest. It'd come. He just knew it.

Blocked: My eyes.

Cameron: Adrian, what the fuck are you doing?

Blocked: Reminding you that you aren't safe in your own home.

Cameron: Joci is here too, you dipshit.

Blocked: I'd never hurt her.

He didn't trust the miracle man for a millisecond. He hardly knew the guy, but from what he did know, Adrian would go to any lengths for Joci. He'd said as much at the cemetery. Stomach souring as the lull continued, Cameron gripped the phone tighter. The not so elusive warning from the other man had him on edge. This was *his* home, *his* town, *his* woman. He wasn't about to roll over and take the lumps.

Blocked: Better watch your back. My guys tend to be trigger-happy.

Cameron: I'll gladly meet you anywhere and settle this for good.

The conversation paused for a good ten minutes. His body temperature soared the longer Adrian remained unresponsive. *Maybe he got the hint.*

Blocked: I'll be in touch.

He wouldn't text again. Maybe from another number, but that one most definitely was a burner. If the attorney ran with the Mikkelsen crew, he'd picked up their habits as well. Keeping the same phone for longer than a week didn't bode well. The moment Joci left the next morning, he'd have Jerry's guys come over to sweep the house for bugs. If all Adrian did was put a couple of newborn outfits in cribs, Cameron would be surprised.

The melody of a popular Maroon 5 song drifted to him. He should tell her everything, but a little part of him wanted to figure it all out on his own so she'd never know what was truly going on. Joci popped her toweled head into the room, a grin on her face. She wore nothing but a pair of black leggings and a tank top, bra excluded. She didn't need one anyhow. He'd burn them all if she'd let him.

"Hey, babe. What're you doing?" She rested her chin

on the back of his shoulder, peeking over to see his actions. "Oh, putting clothes away. Very nice. Having fun yet?"

Cameron wanted to enjoy her carefree attitude. He craved to put the recent dialog with Adrian on the back burner and relish the sensation of Joci's lotion-slathered arms against his fingers. The irresistible trace of strawberry lotion laced with raspberry body spray filled his nostrils.

"Hey, you okay?" Joci wrapped her arms around his middle and pressed her lips to the tattoo on the back of his neck.

"Um, yeah, fine. Sorry, I was thinking about work stuff."

Her tongue darted out and traced the ink on his skin. "Want a distraction?"

What he wanted was a stiff drink, a cheap hit man, and a private island. Sliding in the drawer, he spun around. "Always, but can you do me a favor first?"

"Of course." She searched his eyes with her own beautiful hazel ones. "What is it?"

"Be careful." He pushed the towel off her hair, letting the chestnut strands flow down her chest. "Being part of Del Rossi is like having a target on my back. Unfortunately, it extends to you too."

Her brow bunched together. "Did something happen? Are you all right? What's going—"

He shouldn't have kissed her right then, but he did. Crushing his lips to hers was the sole resolution for the present. Feeling the scorching heat radiate from every pore in Joci surged him forward. With this woman in his arms, he could conquer the world. If she somehow slipped from him, he wouldn't survive. Not in the way he wanted to. "Just be careful, Joce. Stay clear of strange or new people." He nipped her top lip, her delighted shudder completely worth the act. "I can't tell you the details, but I have your best interest at heart."

"Okay. Sure." Her eyes slid from concerned to admiring, and he inwardly cursed. It wasn't the whole truth. It was what she needed to hear. Hell, it was what he needed to hear. If Adrian was becoming more brazen by the day, it'd take more than simple kisses to keep her safe.

CHAPTER NINE

Hanging up the phone, Joci bit the nail on her thumb. Her parents were ten minutes from Des Moines and they wanted to see her. She dipped her chin to view the bulge in front of her. *Crap.*

"Rayna, I have a problem."

"What is it?" The other woman appeared, heels long ago shoved under her desk thanks to only having one hearing that day. "Well?"

Joci ran her fingers through her straightened hair. "My parents are in town. They're going to meet me at Diner 7."

"God, I love that place. Their fudge milkshakes are to die for." Rayna pursed her lips when she took in Joci's face. "But you're not excited? Why?"

Standing, she slid into the black ballet slippers. *Much better.* "They don't exactly know I'm pregnant."

The smile on Rayna's face melted into a frown. "I'm sorry, what?"

Cringing, Joci nodded. "Yeah, we aren't very close anymore, and with all that happened in the last year with

Adrian and Cameron, I never got the nerve to tell them.”

Rayna whistled then bounced her hands together to create a visual bomb. “Holy hell, Joci. What’re you doing to do?”

Joci pulled her sweater over her shoulders, the fit more than snug. “There? Can you tell?”

“Can I tell you’re pregnant or can I tell you’re insane to think a cardigan would fool your parents?”

“Yeah, you’re right.” She tossed the blue sweater off and scratched her scalp. “I’m freaking out a little bit.”

“Maybe you should call Cameron. He should probably meet his future in-laws.” Rayna snapped her fingers. “You could say the kiddos are his! Not like they’ll see the boys for years if your history is any indicator.”

“Um, no. I can’t do that to him.” She chewed on her thumbnail. “Plus, knowing Adrian’s genes, they’ll have red hair. Can’t hide that.”

“Good point.” Rayna eyed the screen of her phone. “What have they been doing in Colorado anyway?”

Locking her desk drawer, Joci pondered Rayna’s question. The visits with Shar and Toby Dorous were far and in between since they moved to Colorado. “They grow and sell marijuana and travel the world like hippies to try new drugs.”

“At least it’s legal there,” her colleague conceded. “What’s your brother been up to anyway? I haven’t heard you talk about him in ages.”

“No clue.” Joci patted herself down, a recent coping mechanism when her life hit a road bump. Needless to say, her hands got plenty of use. "Okay, I'm just going to tell them the truth."

"You sure?" Her friend's brows knit together.

Joci's stomach churned. "No."

"Call your fiancé. Have him meet you there." Rayna ushered her to the front door. "It's not like he hasn't met them before."

Joci slipped on her prescription sunglasses when the blinding light met her gaze. "We were kids back then. He's a much different person now."

"Exactly. Your parents will love him." She wrinkled her nose. "Maybe. I mean, he was on trial for murder not yet a year ago."

"Not helping, Ray."

Shaking her head, Rayna pushed Joci out the door. "Sorry. Old habits. Have fun! Call me when you're done. I'm dying to know how your stud muffin crumbles when faced with hippie foe. Maybe you should give them a special brownie before they meet him."

Joci pleasantly flipped Rayna her middle finger. "Sarcastic as ever. How do men not fall at your feet?"

"They're size tens, no man wants to see that!" the other attorney shouted before the door closed behind her.

After climbing into the suave rental car, Joci dialed Cameron, the ringing resounding over the car's speakers.

"Hey, babe, what's up?" The mere sound of Cameron's voice calmed her shaky nerves. There was no equal in the entire world.

"Hey, I have a ginormous favor to ask," she started.

"Anything for you."

She chuckled and flipped on the blinker. "Can you meet me at Diner 7…." She paused and bit her lip before continuing. "To meet my parents?"

A breathless moment passed over the line as she waited for his response. "Yeah, of course I will. Whatever you need, I'm your guy." He muttered something to Quinn then returned to their conversation. "Quinn's going to have to drop me off, though, then pick me up after if it doesn't go late. We have a station meeting later I can't miss."

Relief washed over her. Going alone to dinner was one thing, but Cameron would help more than he knew. "Okay, no problem. Thanks."

Cameron chuckled, and the siren piped up in the background. "Don't say that yet. We'll be coming in hot."

"You always do." She hung up, the police siren tempting a headache. At the moment, she couldn't turn around and head for home, as badly as she wanted to do exactly that. A family reunion was in order. Too bad they hadn't called earlier. It would have been easier to explain.

***

Grasping the handle, Cameron peered in the busy diner and spotted Joci within seconds. From the hugs still being exchanged, he assumed she'd arrived not long ago. Her smile was shaky at best, and her strapless dress turned more than one male head in the restaurant. *Those things are God's gift to man.* Joci in dresses was his favorite. Thanks to her long legs, the burnt orange article rested halfway up her thigh. With the hormonal Iowa weather, the outfit was fitting for the warm autumn day.

Quinn beeped the horn once, shaking him from the stupor Joci's body put him in. *I'm one lucky son of a bitch.* He calmed the bubbles of nerves in his gut and stepped into the 50's themed restaurant. With long strides, he easily attained the cozy turquoise booth in the corner.

Spying him, Joci sprang to her feet and grabbed his hand. "And here he is."

Cameron tried not to react to the viselike strength, but offered a warm smile instead. Extending his free hand, he greeted, "Mr. and Mrs. Dorous. Great to see you again."

Joci's mom, a shorter blonde version of her daughter, waved aside his words as she stood. "Oh, please. It's Shar and nothing but hugs from here on in." She pulled him into her arms. "You're family now."

"Thanks, Shar." Cameron patted her back awkwardly. He wasn't one for hugs. Joci was the only person he made the exception for. Period.

Shar held him back and slid her eyes over him. "You're quite the looker, isn't he, Toby?"

When Joci's mom let go, her dad took over the bear hug. Cameron held in an *oomph* at the man's strength. He looked much scrawnier at first glance. "So long as he treats her well, I don't give a shit what he looks like," her dad joked.

Cameron was relieved when everyone resumed their seats and he slid in beside Joci. Her hand nervously rubbed his thigh.

"Now, how did you become a police officer?" Shar asked, ogling his uniform.

"And when did you move to Iowa?" Toby inquired.

Shar's voice took on a condemning tone. "Are you going to tell your mama about the watermelon you're smuggling, or will I have to guess?"

The last one was directed toward Joci, and Cameron was glad for the reprieve. His parents had never been this energetic about any part of his life. A peanut butter and jelly sandwich and pat on the head was the most he'd gotten from them as a kid. If memory served him, Joci and her parents were much closer when she was younger. *I wonder if something happened.* Surely, she would've told them about this all before now. He watched her closely. She was more nervous than she let on. Instantly, he wanted to know why she kept her life separate from her parents.

Joci took a sip from the sweating glass in front of her. "Sorry you had to find out like this. It all happened suddenly, and I didn't know how to tell you guys. Then when you e-mailed me about traveling around the world, I wasn't sure if you'd have time or the ability to discuss it. I just thought I'd have more time. I guess I got sidetracked with work and life." She let out a struggled laugh.

Ah. Cameron's brows rose, but he kept his eyes on the trio. He didn't think about others when he traveled with the mob, but then again, he also didn't have a child or two.

Toby and Shar exchanged a glance. "Don't you worry about it," her mother began. "Why, when your dad and I got together, we didn't leave the hostel for a month."

"Eww, Mom. I don't need to hear that."

Cameron swallowed a chuckle at the horrified expression

on his fiancée's face. He'd have the same if his mom admitted something along those lines.

"Plus, our Internet was sketchy in Cambodia," her dad added. "And we weren't exactly sober the whole time. But the baby is a shock," Toby included, flipping through the menu. His dark hair and matching eyes reminded Cameron where the other half of Joci's beauty came from.

The waiter collected their orders then disappeared.

"It's twins, actually. Both boys." Joci looked between her parents, worry etched on her brow.

The jaws of both dropped open. "Twins? Holy cow, Joci. That's wonderful news!" Shar shrieked, clearly eager to become a grandma twofold.

Toby rubbed the bald spot on top of his head. "Sheesh, maybe we should've visited more. You'll likely be president next time if we keep this up."

"It was a surprise to say the least," Joci admitted.

The server delivered four chocolate milkshakes and a basket of cheese curds before vanishing.

"I was going to give you these fertility beads, but I'd better be careful. You're liable to have triplets!" Shar shoved the bracelet toward her daughter anyhow.

Choking on the purple straw, Joci pulled away from the gift. Cameron rubbed her back, unsure how to react. He didn't recall her parents being this open, but then again, he was a kid when he knew them last. It was nerve-wracking nonetheless.

"Thanks, Mom. Maybe I'll give them to Rayna." She tossed the beads into her purse with the care she'd give a dead mouse.

Shar stirred the chocolatey treat. "Can we go ahead and assume Cameron's family has twins somewhere in the lineage?"

This time, Cameron sputtered on the ice cream. He'd expected Joci to smooth this all out before he got there. Bringing up her ex was inevitable now. *Can't go one day without saying his name.*

"That's not actually how it works, Mom. Genetics don't play into twins at all."

"Oh, I see," her mom said with a nod.

Joci dipped a battered cheese ball in ranch dressing. "And um, the babies are Adrian's, actually."

"What?" her parents hollered, bringing attention from all ends of the diner.

"Your ex-husband, Adrian?" Toby folded his arms, one navy tattoo on his forearm now visible.

Hearing the amazement in their voices, it struck Cameron how much they liked the redhead. *Hell, he probably called them on a weekly basis.*

Their plates of burgers and fries arrived, postponing the next set of truths.

"Yes, that Adrian." Joci snatched the ketchup bottle.

"The last time we spoke, I believe you mentioned avoiding him at all costs. I thought the two of you weren't speaking," Shar said, frowning.

The fry paused in front of Joci's mouth. "Well, we weren't. Things, got uh, complicated." She kept her eyes down. "We had a case together and one thing led to another…"

Shar's brows rose. "Oh, well, now that you're on sleeping terms, we must visit with Adrian while we're in town. I'm sure he's ecstatic about the babies."

"Mom, stop. It's not like that." She glared at her mother until the woman bit into a crisp fry. "Adrian died last spring."

More coughs and backslapping from the Dorouses erupted. If they kept it up, the restaurant owner would call an ambulance for lack of chewing at their table.

"He's dead? Why didn't you tell us?" Shar placed a hand over her chest, moisture springing to her eyes. "I'm so sorry, sweetie. Despite all that happened with the divorce, I know he meant a lot to you." Her green gaze slid to Cameron. "Oh, and the whole family."

Toby slurped his water. "He was a good man. I'm glad you have two little guys to remember him by. He'd be proud of that."

The way Joci pressed her lips together to combat tears tore at him. Suddenly Cameron craved a foamy beer washed down by a double shot of whiskey. *On repeat.*

"Thanks, me too." She dipped a french fry in cheese sauce. "He'll forever have a place in my heart, but we weren't supposed to be together." Joci cuddled up into Cameron's wide chest, fingers delicately tracing the gold badge. "I'm so blessed Cam and I reconnected." Her hazels meshed with his wary browns. "He's the real deal."

Her quick peck to his cheek reiterated their connection, and Cameron kissed the top of her head. For the moment, his heartbreak was quelled. "I couldn't agree more."

Shar wiped her face with the back of her palm. "You happy is all we want, Joci."

"Agreed. Now, let's eat before this grub gets cold," Toby directed, chomping on the burger.

The remainder of Cameron's time was spent listening to Joci speak with her parents. He didn't mind being left out one bit. Watching the flippant and free dialogue between the three intrigued him. In Ohio, he'd shared a few meals with the family, but he never grasped the closeness until now. Notwithstanding the lack of communication over the years, he marveled at their easy jabs and jokes from the past. It was something he could never share with his folks. Without a doubt, he never would either. God alone knew where they were, if they still breathed. Judging from the drug binges he'd witnessed as a youth, a cemetery was his first guess for their mailing address.

His phone buzzing drew his attention from the group. He skimmed the message then stuffed it back in his pocket. "Quinn's outside, Joce. I need to go or the captain will have my ass."

She squeezed his knee. "All right, no problem. Thank you for coming." Leaning in, she locked her lips with his, astonishing him so much that he remained frozen. "I'll show you my gratitude tonight, okay?" Her mouth lingered above his, but she kept another kiss at bay.

"Sounds like a plan." He stood and offered Toby and Shar a tilt of the head and polite smile. "It was great to see you again. I hope you can make it to the wedding."

"You're engaged?" Toby asked sharply.

Shar squealed like a teenager, and Toby's eyes grew to saucers.

"And there's my cue." He shot a sympathetic look to Joci as she dodged questions while he escaped. Finally outside, Cameron took a deep breath of autumn air. It smelled of rain and leaves. "Storm's coming," he predicted, climbing into the patrol car.

Quinn veered out of the parking lot. "How'd it go?"

He slumped further into the seat and exhaled loudly, pressing two fingers to the bridge of his nose.

"That right there is why I don't meet the parents." Quinn laughed.

Cameron cast a sideways leer to his partner. "Not yet, but just you wait. I'll be sure to help you out like you help me."

"Hey, whoa there, buddy. I provided the getaway vehicle. Has to count for something, right?"

"True." He smirked. "Yours will most likely be an ambulance, though, if your cockiness is any indicator. I'd slug ya if you dated my daughter."

"Hardy har har." Quinn punched his partner's arm. "Thanks for the vote of confidence."

"Aw, what're you nervous for? You've got a few years before it happens."

Quinn's grip on the steering wheel tightened along with his smooth-shaven jaw.

"Or do you?" Cameron jeered good-naturedly.

"I don't want to talk about it." He switched on the radio. "Tell me what happened."

Riling Quinn up tempted him, but Cameron decided against it. After all, he had an hour to endure with the man who appeared more preoccupied than even him.

***

"Joci, you should've called me. So much has happened since we saw you last. You're engaged? When did he pop the question? I mean, your ring is stupendous, but you've barely gotten to know him. Aren't you taking this all too fast? Have you met his parents? Are they even still alive? You know they were a weird bunch."

"We've known each other practically our whole lives, Mom." Ogling the cup of coffee on the table, Joci tuned out her mother's nonstop questions. It always ended this way. The Dorous family would joke and josh until the sun set, but once a secret spilled loose, no one was going anywhere.

"Toby, don't you have anything to say about all this?" her mom said.

Her dad stirred cream into his coffee. "Shar, she's an adult. She doesn't have to tell us every gritty detail about her life." He pointed his spoon toward Joci. "But I would like to know the whole story of how Adrian knocked you up."

Joci gritted her teeth. "He died, Dad. Plus, we were divorced. It was a drunk hookup that resulted in this." She opted not to divulge their extracurricular bedsheet events and patted her stomach comfortingly. "I don't regret it and neither did he. Adrian knew we weren't going to start over."

Her mom sighed. "Too bad. We liked him."

"Yeah, well, so did I once upon a time. But now I love Cameron. I hope you'll get on board instead of just saying you are, when in actuality you aren't." She shoved the empty plate to the side and wished it'd magically refill with the scrumptious sugar cookies. The babies needed more sustenance. Even the enormous meal hadn't been sufficient for the twins. *They're going to eat me out of house and home when they're teenagers.*

"Joci, we support you." Shar bit down on her lip. "But we're worried. Cameron's family history isn't the best. He lived with his aunt a lot, and his parents weren't great examples of a stable home."

"I know all this. I'm not drunk on love here." She scratched her ear. "We've discussed his past and the future we want together. You have no idea how much I know about him."

"But there's always something hidden," her dad pointed out.

Deciding it was best not to disclose the murder acquittal or the details behind Adrian's death, she nodded. "I don't disagree."

Silence surrounded them for a minute before her mom snapped her fingers. "Whatever happened to the nice police officer you told your cousin about? I think his name was Quinn or something."

Oh, my God, how did she find out about Quinn? Joci scrambled for a response. It shouldn't stun her that her visiting cousin had spread gossip last year, but it did anyhow. "Quinn was a fling, not that it's any of your business."

"Oh." Shar lifted the coffee cup. "Couldn't keep you satisfied, huh?"

"Mom!" Joci screeched, planting her face to the tabletop. "What *the* fresh hell?"

"What? I'm just saying, if your Quinn was doing his job right, you never would've felt the need to sleep with Adrian again," her mom noted.

Toby chuckled, but otherwise remained mute. It was just like her dad to stay out of such conversations. He'd sit and listen, sure, but participate? No chance in hell.

Lolling her neck up, Joci inhaled and placed both hands to the kicking twins. "For the millionth time, I'm not explaining my love life, Mother. Just as I don't ever, for the love of God, want to hear about yours."

"Now, now, you're missing out there," her dad chimed in. "Your mom's a—"

"Ew, ew, ew, Dad. Stop. Just stop. I never ever want to hear your stories, and I'm done with this interrogation." She got to her feet and checked her smartphone. "It's late and I need to get home. Cam should be back soon."

"Where are you living these days? Still the apartment downtown?" Toby asked, leaving a tip for the waitstaff.

"No. Cam and I bought a house." She pivoted to see her mom's reaction. The woman clammed her lips together and shrugged as if she didn't care. *Right.*

Toby squeezed her hand. "Wonderful. I bet you two enjoy suburbia."

They reached the front door and the bell clattered their exit. Her parents' silver Prius with a tie-dyed peace sign bumper sticker sat next to her rental Mercedes in the sparse parking lot. *Probably shut the place down.*

"Well, sweetie, it was wonderful to see you and Cameron. If you're ever in Colorado, give us a ring." Shar kissed both cheeks and hugged her daughter. "I doubt we'll stick around long tomorrow. Just on our way to the East Coast for the annual peace convention."

And they never bothered to stop here until this year. Curious. After her divorce, the Dorous crew had drifted apart in more ways than one. They dealt with the loss of a grandchild and son-in-law one way, and she had her own way of coping.

Joci wrapped her dad in her arms. "All right. Thanks for grabbing dinner with us. It was great to see you."

Catching her chin within his fingers, Toby searched Joci's eyes. "Whatever you do, be safe, sweet cheeks. We love you."

"Love you too." Joci waited until their environment-friendly car sputtered out of the lot to release a frazzled groan. "And that is why they visit once every five years," she mumbled, straightening her back. She was in desperate need of a massage. "And more cookies."

Slipping into the driver seat, she stuck in the key and frowned at the gas gauge. "Dammit." She spied a gas station up the road, and before she could rehash the night's event, Joci was swiping her card for the fill-up.

Leaning against the vehicle's side, she folded her arms over her chest as the gas pumped by itself. Shar's firing squad of questions and concerns resurfaced. It hadn't been so hard when they met Adrian, but for some reason, her parents had played devil's advocate tonight. "Why does she have to be so infuriating?"

"Who?"

"Motherfu—" She twirled around at the Irish lilt and spotted Derrick. The man seemed to be popping up wherever she went, and warning bells went off in her mind at his suspicious way of knowing her whereabouts. "You, uh, you scared the hell out of me."

Derrick held up a thirty-two-ounce cup, ice rumbling together as it shook. "Whoops. Sorry. I was walking by and thought I recognized you." His blue eyes dipped to her stomach. The act was almost tradition each time they ran into the other. "I see the babies are growing."

She instinctively rubbed the swell. "Um, yeah, they're good." She took a step closer to her car, unsure how to react to Derrick's friendliness. Cameron had warned her about new people, and these recent run-ins validated her fiancé's worry. She'd never before run into any of her clients, past or present, when she was out and about in town. As an attorney, the knowledge that someone could find her more than once sent her stomach in jumbles. *Surely it's a coincidence and he's not stalking you.* She glanced to Derrick. *Right?*

"Glad to hear it." He pointed to his car on the far side of the pumping stations. "I'll leave you to stew."

For a moment, she was relieved he didn't linger. Something about his presence unnerved her. Yet she needed to vent, and with Rayna off on a date with some guy and Cameron at work.... Joci wasn't sure why she didn't let him walk away. It was the safest option. She didn't know him, and Cameron had all but begged her to stay away from strangers. Still, her voice met her ears before she could hush it. "My mom."

He swiveled on his heels, eyebrow cocked. "What?"

"You asked who I was talking about."

"Oh, right." He retraced his steps until he was beside her. "Saw your mom tonight, huh? Was she being a pain like most parents?"

Flabbergasted at how easily she opened up to the almost stranger, Joci bobbed her head. "Yep. As usual. She couldn't let the past go."

He swirled the ice around in the cup. "Hmm, is that such a bad thing?"

"It is when the past is dead and you're trying to move on." Joci bit the inside of her cheek. She shouldn't be talking about any of this with Derrick. It was Cameron who should be helping her with her mom issues. She eyed him. *Maybe he's related to Adrian in some way. He does have the mannerisms of a Petosa. And a lot of them are from Ireland.* When Derrick didn't reply, she had to ask, "Are you related to any of the Petosas in Des Moines? Maybe a cousin."

The question seemed to catch him off guard. He shifted his weight and cleared his throat. "Uh, no. Not that I know of. My family is from Cork county in Ireland. I haven't been in the States long."

"Oh, okay. Sorry, you look like my ex-husband, so I had to ask." The waver in his voice made her think the exact opposite. *But why would he lie? It's not like he's Adrian raised from the dead.* She shoved that thought aside and glanced to the gas pump.

"I'll take that as a compliment then." Popping the straw into his mouth, Derrick took a sip. "Look, I only know part of your situation, but can I offer you some advice anyway?"

She pointed to him and rolled her eyes. "I brought you back to the conversation, so sure."

He offered the drink to her. "Want some? It's Powerade."

"Oh, no, thanks, I'm good."

Derrick laughed and pushed it closer to her. "It's not spiked, and you look like you could use some hydration. Please, I insist. If it'll make you feel better, you can have this one and I'll grab another one. Can't have pregnant women getting dehydrated."

The babies kicked from within as if begging for her to accept. Joci was awestruck when she took a drink. She mentally kicked herself for accepting something from a stranger. *Yum.* Telling herself it was only because she was thirsty and not because she'd lost her mind, her eyes dipped over him. The gray sweatpants and long-sleeved red workout shirt molded to him like a pair of gloves. *Double yum.* She shoved the cup back to him, suddenly aware of the idiotic thing she'd just done. *No, bad, Joci! Bad!*

"Don't be afraid of what other people think. It's your life, so live it the way you want." Derrick met her eyes and placed a hand on her stomach. "But be safe while doing it."

Maybe it was the sincere tint to his blue eyes or the familiar way he made her feel, as if their unexpected meeting was nothing out of the ordinary, but Joci's pulse accelerated. "Thanks. I will."

"Okay, Ms. Dorous, stay out of trouble." He winked.

"Or get in trouble, whatever's your fancy. I'd guess you're a spitfire in and out of the courtroom, but that's just me." He chuckled. "Let me know if you'd ever like to indulge."

"In what?" Heart thrumming in her ears now, she felt her cheeks burn at the suggestion. Surely he didn't mean what she thought he meant.

"Telling me your darkest desires, of course," he teased, then walked toward his car.

Joci didn't know how to react. After the car sped from view, she looked to the gas meter and saw it was full. "Damn, you need to stop running into him," she chided, climbing into the car. Out of all the day had brought, running into the curious redhead after a frustrating meeting with her parents wasn't what she imagined.

CHAPTER TEN

"Are all these people having babies?" Quinn asked with a shocked face.

Rayna and Joci cast condemning eyes to Quinn, who in his defense was entirely new to the birthing world.

"No, they're here for shits and giggles," Cameron inserted before either woman could utter a reprimand.

Quinn surveyed the group of twenty-five couples and shook his head. "Cool. I wonder how many were drunk hookups."

Joci's snigger intertwined with her friend's as the instructor clapped loud hands at the front of the room.

"All right, folks, welcome to birthing class 101," the middle-aged woman started. "I'm Vivian, and I'll be helping you along this wonderful journey over the next week."

"Snoozefest," the cops whispered simultaneously.

This time, Joci sent daggers to Cameron. She didn't care if Quinn wasn't involved. She'd never expected he and Rayna to volunteer to attend with them. It meant a lot to her, having supportive friends.

Squeezing her hand, Cameron offered a pitiful face. Her wish to be prepared for everything muddied the waters a bit. He was relentlessly devoted to her requests, but this one took more convincing. She couldn't blame him. Going to a pregnancy class wasn't where most men wanted to be.

"Okay, now, who do we have here? Two police officers. What lucky ladies. Are you all first-time parents?"

Whipping her head up, Joci forced a smile to her lips when she noticed the teacher in front of the four of them. "Um, yes," she replied for the group.

Vivian beamed when her eyes dipped to Joci's belly. "Let me guess, twins, correct?"

"Whoa, she's like the baby whisperer," Quinn commented, his face baffled.

Joci nodded. "Good guess."

"It's no guess, sweetheart. I have a knack for these things. I have a separate course on twins if you're interested." Vivian turned to the second couple and her eyebrows rose. "You must not be very far along yet, are you?"

Rayna sat speechless, as if she hadn't expected to be put on the spot. Her mouth flopped open and closed, no words emitting.

Taking the reins, Quinn wrapped an arm around her shoulders and smooched her cheek. "No, ma'am. I knocked her up a couple months ago." The crowd chuckled at his candor, while red crept up Rayna's neck and face.

"Wonderful. The gift of life is spectacular no matter when it occurs." Vivian patted Quinn's arm then continued her walkabout through the maze of chairs.

"What the hell, Levi?" Rayna grumbled in a hushed tone.

The use of Quinn's first name caught Joci off guard. She knew he had one, and even what it was, but they'd never used it. *Looks like somebody's getting chummy.* Catching her fiancé's gaze, she smirked.

"Levi, huh?" Cameron teased, jabbing Quinn's arm.

Instead of replying, the officer straightened his name pin and stared straight ahead. There was more to Rayna and Quinn than Joci knew. *Now if only she'll tell me.*

After the pleasantries of getting to know the expectant families passed, Vivian ventured to the stages of pregnancy. The expressions on Rayna's and Quinn's faces were priceless the more they digested the instructor's words. Joci was positive she had the same "oh, shit" look on her face.

Sneaking a glance at the man beside her, she noticed Cameron was distracted with his phone. The thing kept dinging until he put it on vibrate. Even after the switch, he didn't appear to be listening to the wisdom spewed by the woman sporting a gray french braid. He'd acted peculiar the day before, but she chalked it up to his dual employment. His Del Rossi meetings were more frequent these days, and he was less inclined to discuss details with her. In retrospect, she was grateful. Being privy to ghastly details wasn't something a criminal attorney, or anyone for that matter, should know.

When they got to the breathing techniques, Joci was certain Rayna was going to hyperventilate. Bouncing on giant red balls, the women leaned against their spouses as Vivian went over the different types of Lamaze.

Since she never went to any such classes with Adrian the first time around, Joci was determined not to muck it up this time. "I sound like an idiot."

Cameron snorted from behind her, but didn't comment.

"Bonbon, I think you're breathing too fast. It's Lamaze not La-crazy," Quinn pointed out in a voice much too sugary for the bulky man.

Glancing over to the faux couple, Joci held in a laugh when she witnessed Rayna plunge an elbow in Quinn's gut.

"Worth it," he managed, sucking in a quick breath.

Rayna turned toward her. "So, this is supposed to help with contractions?"

"That's what they say." Joci wiggled on the ball, slipping off balance. Cameron's arms caught her before she completely belly-flopped. She couldn't understand how people used these throughout labor. She'd skate off the thing in the first five minutes. "Thanks."

He nodded once, keeping his hands splayed on her hips.

Joci added, "But I think it's predominately to keep your mind focused on something other than the pain."

"Oh." Rayna slapped Quinn's fingers away when he tried to steady her. "Is the pain really that bad?"

Giggling, Joci took in Rayna's scared expression. "Do you want the truth or a half lie?"

"Hit me hard," her friend replied.

"That's what she said." Quinn snickered and was promptly swatted at by both women. He managed to duck back before the hands reached him.

Thinking over her labor debut, Joci scrunched her face.

"To be honest, it sucks. They liken it to being zapped with adrenaline while you push a watermelon out." She saw the white tint to Rayna's face and added, "Mine wasn't too bad, but with twins, I'm sure it won't be a cakewalk."

"Hmm, maybe children are better left to adults who have a higher pain threshold," Rayna muttered under her breath.

This got Quinn's attention. "You don't want kids?"

"You heard that? Jesus, you've got bat ears." Rayna jiggled on the birthing ball, ignoring the next instructions from the teacher. "I don't know, Quinn. It's a possibility. Oh, I know! Maybe I should be in the room with Joci during her delivery, then make my decision."

"Talk about a horrible idea right there," Quinn noted.

Joci rested against Cameron's chest as she watched the exchange next to them. The banter between her best friend and ex was entertaining. It was blatant Quinn harbored some feelings toward Rayna, but less obvious whether she reciprocated.

"They're cute together, even if they don't stop arguing," Joci whispered to the man behind her.

"Joci, don't do it," Cameron warned, the husky tenor of his voice skidding along the base of her neck. It sent her hormones into overdrive. She'd never tire of how something so normal could drive her wild.

Straining to face him, she tossed a wily smirk his way then pressed a kiss to his chin. "I don't know what you're talking about."

"Uh-huh, sure." He planted his lips on the side of her neck. "Please tell me we're almost done. The guy beside us ate Indian cuisine before he got here and, holy hell, I can smell the curry."

Resolving to corner either Rayna or Quinn later on to discuss their fatal attraction, Joci sat up straight, thankful for Cameron's embrace on her waist. Though he wasn't his normal self, she couldn't fault him for the discomfort he felt amid couples happy to bring their child into the world. Her belly swirled from the twins' aerobics. *It'd be different if these were his.* She believed it without a doubt.

The hour passed rather quickly; Vivian was a wizard with the varying questions and crude innuendos tossed around the class. By the end, Joci was ready to collapse in a giant bed of pillows and never leave.

"Come on, babe, let's get you home." Cameron pulled her off the bouncy ball and searched her face. "You look tired."

"Thanks, a woman loves hearing that," she teased, but couldn't disagree. After a busy day in depositions, she wouldn't argue with falling into bed and staying there until morning.

The four ambled out of Des Moines's community center. The parking lot cleared faster than fresh donuts at the local bakery. Three cars remained, all located beneath the light post near the street.

Joci yawned as she unlocked the doors then handed the keys over to Cameron. He'd ridden with Quinn from the station, so she'd have to drop him off in the morning. Not caring at the moment, she slumped in the passenger seat. Rayna's scream beckoned her out of the car, eyes wide open.

"What's wrong?" She toddled over to where her friend stood gawking at the ground. Peering to the pavement, Joci gasped. "What the hell is this?"

A gruesome sight met her gaze, and she couldn't help but gag. A gory carcass of a black crow was positioned five feet from the driver side of Joci's vehicle.

"La morte arriva per tutti noi," Cameron read aloud the words scrawled in blood.

"What language is it?" Rayna asked.

"Italian," Cameron said quietly.

"What does it mean?" Quinn inquired, his face pinched with worry.

Cameron let out a breath, his face a mixture of anger and terror. "Death comes to us all."

"Is this a warning?" Rayna asked, more than perturbed by the incident. Her eyes were dilated, and she held on to Quinn's arm like a vice.

Joci clutched Cameron's arm between hers, but he wrenched out of reach. Running both hands through his hair, he pulled at the waves until she was afraid he may pull them all out.

"I can't talk about it," he finally said.

Quinn's eye twitched, but he didn't fire back. Circling to Rayna, he slid a palm to the small of her back. "Come on, I'll follow you home to make sure you get there okay."

Rayna bobbed her head then gave Joci a quick hug before leaving.

Once they drove off the lot, Joci spoke. "It's Del Rossi business, isn't it?"

Rubbing his temples, he met her gaze. "Yeah."

"Who was this for? You? Me? It was next to my car." She rattled on, and he held up both hands.

"I don't know, Joci, okay?" he ground out just below a shout. "Just calm down and give me a minute to figure it out."

"How do you expect me to stay calm when it could've been meant for me?" she almost screamed.

"Look, it's for me, okay?" Cameron ran a hand through his hair. "I'm the one in a mob, not you. Anyone would know better than to mess with you."

Joci's brows furrowed, and she crossed her arms over her chest. His words slightly quieted her unease, but didn't extinguish it. "Is this why you were preoccupied with your phone tonight?"

"What? No."

Not believing him, Joci let out a huff and snatched the keys from his grip. "Figure this shit out and call an Uber." She opened the car door. "I'm going home."

She didn't give him the opportunity to talk his way out of it. Her stomach grumbled, and her muscles screamed for relief. The first stop on the way home would be Tasty Tacos, followed by a tepid bath to wash away the night's events.

***

"Stupid, stupid, stupid!" He cursed explicitly the longer he glared at the dead bird. Joci's departure didn't faze him. She didn't need to worry about it anyhow. It wouldn't end well for him if she started poking her nose in Del Rossi schemes.

"But this wasn't Del Rossi." Cameron checked his text messages as he waited for the Uber to pick him up. He called Jerry to get him up to date with the Mikkelsens' calling card. It wasn't pretty in any way, and the Italian phrase was a new touch, but it was them, no doubt about it. He'd been part of joint tasks with the Mikkelsens, and they tended to use the "bird of death," as they called it, as a way of reminding their enemy who would prevail.

It annoyed him that they chose to display the carcass anywhere near Joci. Normally, they'd smear the blood on their victim's car. It seemed the Danish mob kept better tabs on him than he'd presumed. They knew better than to touch Joci's vehicle. She was protected; he, on the other hand, was fair game despite his mob connections. Rivaling mobs were always trying to take out the competition, but this felt different. This was personal.

Hopping into the black sedan, Cameron greeted the driver and was grateful when he didn't try to chitchat. He'd have enough of that to deal with once he got home. His phone chimed a message from Quinn. Oh, and Quinn. He was pissed. If the roles were reversed, he would be too. Quinn cared for both Joci and Rayna, and someone was inches from harming them whether he realized it or not. *That'll be a fun conversation.* He rubbed his eyes and wished he had the next day off.

Jerry scoffed at the news. Such threats were a commonality for the drug lord. Del Rossi had men who handled such events. Cameron took little comfort in the fact that the mob would make certain the crow and accompanying words were scrubbed from the blacktop—after photos were taken, of course.

The car arrived much too soon for his liking. The apology he patched together wasn't nearly ready for Joci's wrath. Clicking on the Uber application on his phone, he paid the driver and exited the car without delay. Standing in the driveway, he let out a frazzled breath. The light on the front door shone blue with pride in support of police officers after a slew were gunned down in the past months. *She left it on at least. Maybe she's not pissed.*

He clutched the handle and took back the wishful thought. Locked. It usually wasn't when she knew he was on his way home. After the night's events, he was glad she opted to lock the doors instead. Until he got to the bottom of the incident, he was tempted to have a Del Rossi guy tail her for her protection. After digging out the key, he swung the door open and stepped inside. Her shoes were strewn across the floor as was her purse. *And shirt. And pants.* Any other scenario, he'd appreciate the trail of clothes. This one led to the master bathroom.

Kicking his shoes to the side, he dropped the keys on the side table and followed her lead in tossing aside clothes. He reached the open door to the bathroom and leaned an arm to the top of the entry as he took in his fiancée's situation. Amid bubbles to her neck, Joci lounged in the giant tub with a flour taco in each hand. His lips broke into a wide smile when she paused midbite to acknowledge his presence.

"Don't you dare judge," she mumbled between bites of shredded chicken and cheddar cheese.

"It never crossed my mind." He folded his arms and rested his spine to the doorway. Salsa slid down her right arm, but she didn't pay it any heed. Never would he have imagined tacos and bubbles to be a perfect combination. "I see you stopped by your favorite Mexican joint."

Joci licked her finger, hands empty once more. "I was hungry and pissy. Bad combo."

"About what happened—"

"I don't want to know," she interrupted, reaching for the bag of goodies. A cinnamon-covered churro made its debut before passing between her teeth. "I just want to eat my food, simmer in the bath, then go to bed."

Relief should have coursed through him, but all Cameron felt was a nagging shame. It was obvious who was behind the threat, though he doubted Adrian had a hand in the act himself. He definitely didn't deserve the cavalier way Joci was handling everything.

"Whether it was meant for me or you, I don't like it, Cam." Her soft words echoed in the bathroom, ringing true in his ears.

"Neither do I." He settled on the side of the tub. "But like I said earlier, it wasn't for you. I know it for a fact."

Joci dipped her hands in the water, bubbles frothing at her movements. "Is this how the next five years is going to be?" Her belly button popped out when she slipped further into the water.

"I sure hope not." His hand drifted to her torso and circled the swell of her belly, babes kicking from the other side. "For all our sakes."

Joci let out a frustrated moan and dunked beneath the water. When she came back up, he couldn't pry his gaze from the suds floating on her body. It held him captive. Such an innocent act brought emotions to the surface when nothing else could. The knowledge that someone would dare do her harm unnerved him. "I'll never let anyone hurt you." He met her troubled hazel eyes. "Any of you."

"Then what was—"

"The message was for me, Joce. I don't want you to worry about it." He kissed her soapy palm. "Please."

Ruby lips pressed together in contemplation while her face showed her resistance to such a request. "I'm going to worry about you until Del Rossi is no longer a name we utter in this house."

Leaning over, Cameron moved his hand up her body and swirled circles down her long neck. "And I love you for it."

Joci clasped his hand between hers and kissed the tattoo on his wrist. "If I stay in here much longer, I'll turn into a mermaid. Help me out, please."

He cocked his head and reviewed the spots where bubbles failed to hide her tender flesh from his sight. "I don't know. You'd make a fetching mermaid." He grinned at the slow blush on her cheeks.

The crimson spread to the rest of her body, a perfect color for the beauty. Gently grabbing her hands, Cameron pulled her upright, but wouldn't allow her to move. "Cam, the towel."

Fluttering his brown eyes down legs longer than he deserved and arms primed to grip the back of his neck, he swallowed hard. "God, you're gorgeous."

"I'm a manatee," she rebutted, motioning for the fluffy cloth behind him.

Fluidly, Cameron molded their lips together and wrapped the large bath sheet around her shoulders. "More like a man tease."

Joci rolled her eyes all the way to the ceiling, but a smile didn't leave her lips. "All right, smartass. Get me to bed and I'll show you just how much of a tease I am."

Knowing full well what would happen the moment her head hit the pillow, Cameron lifted her out of the tub and walked down the hallway. By the time he reached the bedroom, Joci was fast asleep, but he didn't mind one bit. Simply having her near was enough for him. It was a luxury he wasn't sure he'd have for much longer.

CHAPTER ELEVEN

"Looks like both li'l guys are perfect," the obstetrician advised, wiping jelly from Joci's stomach. "I'll print off the photos."

Cameron sat in silent awe. No matter how many times he saw the inside of Joci's womb, he'd never tire of it. There was a special sensation that filled his soul at the sight of two growing boys inside. Miraculous was the word, but he wasn't ever one to use it often. Leaning over, he pressed a kiss to her belly before the dress slid into place. When he glanced up, he was greeted with adoring expressions from the women in the room.

"Aw, you're going to be a good daddy," the doctor stated with confidence.

"I agree," Joci chimed in, beaming at him. She ruffled his curls and smirked when he simply closed his eyes.

As the physician slipped out of the room, Cameron fixed his hair and sat back. He couldn't comment on their praise. Not when the biological dad of the dynamic duo ambled the streets.

"Can you pick up my dry cleaning on your way home tonight?" Joci asked, scooching to the edge of the chair.

"Sure." He stood and took a step back, the domestication in their conversation irking him. This wasn't ever in his ten-year plan. Getting shot by drug dealers, sure, but simple Iowa life? No way. Helping her down, he gnawed on his thumbnail. "Do you have a late meeting?"

Joci slipped into the red flats that perfectly matched the color of her dress. Ever since her clothes stopped fitting normally, she opted for more dresses. He couldn't complain. Hell, he wouldn't complain. He loved them on her.

"Actually, yes. Derrick is bringing by a few documents he thinks will aid his case."

The name on her lips screeched him to a halt. "Derrick? As in the guy who saved you from the car fire, Derrick?"

"Yeah. Petosa sent him over. Just a minor moving violation and an interference charge." She sighed at the sonogram picture, her fingers grazing the tiny faces. "Why?"

Cameron felt the air leak from his lungs. He stabilized his body by gripping the nearby chair. Any part of breathing was labored, catapulting him into a frenzy. *Adrian made his move. Goddammit!*

"Are you all right? You're ghost white, Cam." Joci's hand on the small of his back jerked him into motion.

"When did he make the appointment with you?"

"About a week ago. Why? What's wrong?" Her eyes were a mossy hue today with speckles of brown. He could stare into those gorgeous things for eternity. "You're freaking me out."

Cameron looped his arm around her waist and pressed a kiss to her temple. Closing his eyes, he wished he'd gone to Jerry earlier. He'd thought he could handle this, but clearly he was wrong.

"I don't like the guy, Joce. I won't tell you what to do, but there's an attitude about him. It isn't right. He's dangerous."

Searching his face, Joci's frown eased. "I think you're onto something, but his case is practically resolved. I'll be fine. I promise."

He tried to hold it together, he really did, but he couldn't. "Joci, please let Rayna take over the rest of his case. You're not safe with him."

"What do you mean?" She placed her hands on her hips. "What aren't you telling me, Cameron Anthony?"

Toying with his badge, he inhaled through his mouth. "I can't tell you. I'm sorry. You just have to trust me. Being anywhere near Derrick is trouble waiting to happen." He left out the obvious part where Derrick wasn't who he pretended to be. Cameron couldn't give the redhead a chance to steal Joci. Sure, she loved him, but what if she loved Adrian more? The Del Rossis would protect Joci, and Cameron would make sure of it.

She narrowed her eyes, seeming to mull over his request. "Taking your word for it won't fly. You know that." She adjusted her glasses, and all Cameron wanted to do was fling them against the wall. "His hearing is coming up. After that, I won't take another case from him, okay?" She grabbed her purse, missing the twitch of her fiancé's brow. "Now, come on. I'm going to be late."

Reluctantly, Cameron followed her out of the exam room. His first stop after dropping Joci off would be Jerry's hotel. His mob boss's text message last night confirmed he was in town to check on his business ventures in Des Moines. Cameron was grateful the man appeared when he needed him most. He wasn't about to go down without a giant in his corner. Thankfully for him, he knew the ugliest one.

***

Declining a call from Quinn, Cameron silenced his phone as he stepped into Jerry's suite. With three rooms, it was the largest on the floor, but he expected no less from the man who now owned the hotel chain. According to the pompous Italian, his latest business deal with the hotel's previous owner would be a great deduction for his taxes.

"Adrian is alive," Cameron cut in when he could take the preening no longer.

The woman massaging Jerry's hands paused at the curt tone. Waving the tension-free limb, Jerry waited until she left the room to speak. "You have concrete proof? Not mere spittle this time? You know how I feel about rumors."

"I ran into him at the cemetery." Cameron's nose twitched at the memory. "The Mikkelsens did plastic surgery or something on him, but it's Adrian. He made it pretty clear." He decided not to mention the veiled threats he'd received. Text messages weren't Jerry's forte.

Jerry folded his fingers together over his protruding waist. "Hmm, interesting."

Cameron's blood ran hot at the complacent reply. He was going to have to spell it out for the gangster. "He's here for Joci, and you're protecting her. You're involved, Jer. I can't do this on my own. The police force thinks I'm straight, but you keep me crooked."

"Like a boss should." The older man smirked. "But you're right. The Del Rossi mob has Joci under their guard, so this involves us. My best men are searching for J.J., but for the time being, I need to meet with whomever is heading this up in Des Moines. The Mikkelsens don't leave their safe zone unless it's imperative."

Parting his lips to speak, Cameron was interrupted by a familiar mob member. The bald man made a beeline to their boss, whispered into his ear, then handed an envelope off before retreating through the door. In bated silence, he waited as Jerry scanned the envelope's contents.

A dark brown lock of hair fell out along with the letter. "Damn. This is old school," Jerry muttered, holding up the hair clipping.

Swallowing the bile rising in his throat, Cameron rushed to him. "Whose is it?"

Jerry read the note then passed it off. "Joci's."

Cameron's eyes burned through the neatly penned missive, crumpling the paper after completion. "That son of a bitch!"

"This lock of hair is yours, Del Rossi, the rest of Joci Dorous is now under Mikkelsen protection," Jerry quoted, eyeing the discarded note.

Hearing the words come to life was a punch to Cameron's gut. "It's because of the babies, isn't it?"

Pulling on his suit coat, the leader nodded. "Your little lady's in quite the pickle, Cameroni. You brought her to us and now a rival mob wants her." He stood, buttoning as he went along. "You sure you don't want to resort to giving her up and reconnecting with one of my sisters?"

"No," he replied with enough force to cause Jerry's eyebrows to shoot up. "You told me you desired for Joci to be part of Del Rossi as their attorney."

"Yes."

"Well, then in order to maintain the asset, we need to have her, not cut ties like a dinghy in rough waters," Cameron reminded.

Chuckling heartily, Jerry slapped Cameron's back. "Damn, this is why I could never bring myself to kill you." He nodded toward the door. "You're not a lug head. Plus, you have unmined riches in your special skills just waiting for me to discover."

They walked into the brightly lit hallway. The amount of guards at each corner reminded Cameron to keep his cool. His heart wanted to set this place on fire until he got his way, but his mind reminded him to play along with his boss. Getting his way wouldn't be easy. It was going to cost Joci's stake in a mob-free life. *I hope she loves me enough to forgive me.*

"Now, let's discuss how to make Ms. Dorous the official attorney for Del Rossi." Jerry stopped at the elevator. "With a face like hers, my men will do anything I tell them to if it means they get to spend quality time with her."

The sinking feeling in Cameron's abdomen dropped to

new depths as the mobster continued to rattle on about the perfect motivation Joci would be to his brood. Regrettably for him, she was all the incentive Cameron needed to continue a life in the mafia.

CHAPTER TWELVE

"Joci, are you here?" Quinn's voice boomed through the office.

"Jesus Christ!" She closed the file drawer and poked her head out the door. "Could you be any louder?"

The arrogant cop grinned knowingly when he saw her. "Honestly, yes, but you were always the screamer, so I let you have it."

Offering him an annoyed glare, she stomped down the hallway. He wasn't wrong, but he needn't remind her. "Yeah, yeah, hot stuff." She nodded to the papers in his hands. "What do you have?"

"Oh, this is cop shit for Rayna." He plopped the files on the empty reception desk. "This is what you want," he stated, pulling out a thumb drive.

"What'd you find?" she inquired, eyeing the flimsy thing. She almost didn't want to hear the answer. If it led where she assumed, it could mean a fight bigger than the one she and Cameron shared earlier at the doctor's office.

Quinn guided them to her desk. "Let's see, shall we?"

He took her seat and plugged in the USB.

Hovering at his side, Joci held her breath as it loaded, fidgeting. It wasn't typical for her to take the backseat to an investigation.

"Aw, come on. I won't bite," he noted, dragging her onto his lap. He let out a huff. "Damn, girl, you gained a bit of—"

Joci smacked the back of his head, interrupting his playful jab. "You try being pregnant."

"Nah, I'm good." He grinned and poked her side. "You still hit like a girl."

Ignoring him this time, she focused on the screen. The cursor spun, then a window popped up. Immediately, files loaded in front of them. "Holy shit, what is this?" She took over the control and clicked through the documents.

"Del Rossi," he murmured, his voice holding a chilling depth. "The mob's been running money through your investment accounts."

Joci gasped sharply and shook her head. "What? No, not possible." She swiveled her torso to Quinn and identified his serious expression. "How?"

Taking the helm, his hand guided the mouse over her fingers. "Right here." He hauled up a string of stock statements. It clearly showed money deposited under the guise of stocks being exchanged. The withdrawals to another account nearly startled her off the chair, and she was grateful for Quinn's sturdy hold on her waist.

Joci grimaced at the proof. "So, the stock investments weren't actually investments?"

"Nope. They were made to look like the account manager

was buying and selling stocks, but it was actually someone cooking the numbers. It's genius really. From the outside, it just looks like someone is good at investment stocks, but when you dig deeper, there's more to the story."

"Shit. I knew the guy was too good to be true. I mean, I'm clueless when it comes to stocks, which is why we hired the guy in the first place."

He leaned backward. "Who did you say handles your accounts again?"

Joci bit her tongue until the metallic taste of blood surfaced. "Somebody Cameron recommended." She hated herself in that instant. For months her legal, quite literally, work had aided a notorious mob ring. And at the helm was the man she loved. "I feel sick," she complained, shoving away from the desk.

Acting quick, Quinn grabbed the garbage can right as she bent down and emptied her stomach. "Hey, you're going to be okay." He rubbed her back in a comforting circular pattern.

"I don't know if I am," she replied, wiping her mouth. "I trusted him." Tears formed in her eyes, her gut heaving. "I never thought he'd use my business for the mob."

Quinn cradled her face in his hands. "You need to talk to him. Maybe he didn't know what Del Rossi was doing. He was a footman for the guy, not the leader."

Joci pondered this for a few seconds then smudged the tear as it ran down her face. "No. he would've known. He all but insisted I use the guy."

"Then maybe he has a good excuse. Del Rossi likes to

strongarm his men. I wouldn't be surprised if he held some dirt over Cameron's head to get you involved. It's how the crook works."

"It's more than possible." She sniffled, wondering what horrid thing Jerry dangled over her fiancé. His spotted past wasn't quite behind him, and wouldn't be for a few years. She knew it going in and loved him no matter what he did, but the fact that he used her business was a separate matter. Sure, she expected some involvement from the mob, but not in her law firm. The very thought of illegal activity under her firm's guise made her stomach roll. His reaction this morning at the doctor's office filtered her thoughts. *What if Derrick has something to do with this?*

Quinn let out a breath. No doubt, this information was difficult to swallow for the upstanding cop who nearly always did things according to the law. "While I don't condone anything about the mob or Cameron's continued affiliation, he's my friend and so are you. I probably shouldn't be surprised either, though. The mob doesn't just let people walk away without a catch."

"Are you going to tell anyone?" she asked, almost not wanting to hear the response. If Quinn ratted Cameron out to the police force, she'd lose Cameron forever.

"No." He shook his head. "I should, and you know I don't like to hide the truth, but I also know a few things about blackmail and how much he means to you."

Though she was curious as to what experience Quinn had with blackmail, Joci guessed it had to do with his past. They never talked about it, but if a mob was involved, it made sense why he had a weak spot for anyone affiliated with one. "Thanks, Quinn. I know it's not easy for you."

"Cam and I have more in common than I'd like to admit." He cleared his throat instead of continuing the thought, much to Joci's disappointment. The cop's backstory piqued her interest now more than ever.

"He's crazy in love with you, Joci. He wouldn't put you in danger if he could help it." Quinn squeezed her into a giant hug. "If you need more of my help, I'm always here for you. Never forget it."

Joci slouched against the cop, eased by the familiar body molding to her back. She'd figure out what Cameron got her into. He better start explaining and fast. A mobster's fiancée could only take being in the dark so long before the lies would destroy their relationship. She could handle it so long as he was honest with her. If recent events told her anything, the fault lines were cracking in her once stable trust to Cameron.

* * *

The courtroom buzzed with lawyers, deputies, and inmates as Cameron settled into an open spot against the wall. The row of police officers standing in the same stance made him inwardly smile. They all looked the same, whether sheriff's deputy or city cop. None wanted to be there, but they all had no choice in the manner. They were the arresting officers of the hearings' criminals, so they were required to be in attendance, lest the scoundrels get away.

Resting both thumbs on his belt, he listened to the

judge's ruling. A year ago, the situation was opposite. He was among the jailbirds and Quinn was standing behind him, waiting for a wrong move so he could pounce. In retrospect, he probably should've been nicer to the guy. *Oh well, we're friends now. Water under the bridge.* He eyed a deputy further down the line with a bloody nose, no doubt the result of a wily criminal. He couldn't judge, though, since his face was never far from a good bruise or two. To him, it was a badge of honor to be roughed up. Bearing scars and scratches for the uniform proved he wasn't the man from last year. He was a better version. *All thanks to Joci.*

The gavel echoed in the room, and the next officer scooted into place, creating a domino effect as men filled in the gaps along the back wall. Moving to the left, he rubbed shoulders with a man sliding into the small slit beside him. "What the—" His curse paused when he noticed Quinn's eyes held a harder gleam today.

"What's up, rookie? Catch any mobsters running around town?"

Cameron couldn't help but notice the tension in Quinn's voice. "What're you talking about?"

"Or maybe you're helping them ruin Des Moines."

"Quinn, what the fuck?" He jabbed his elbow into his partner's side when a fellow officer glanced at them.

Quinn brushed his hair to the side and pointed to Cameron's head, switching gears on the conversation. "Getting kind of lax with the hair, aren't you? Maybe you don't like being a cop anymore."

Cameron patted the perfectly gelled concoction of

curls, but couldn't ignore the blatant hostility. "It's within regulation, don't worry." He looked straight ahead. "Plus, my girl likes it and I've got to keep her happy or she might run away with some dick ex of hers."

"Who me? Nah, Joci likes mobsters apparently." Quinn's forced chuckle made Cameron wary of the man beside him. Something was up with Quinn, and he needed to find out what. The obvious mob references made his throat dry.

"Everything okay, Quinn?"

Quinn kept his eyes forward. "Why wouldn't it be? Not like I joined a mob."

Cameron clenched his jaw. "Okay, what's up with you? You keep talking about the mob." He reviewed the people beside them. "Probably not the best thing to do in a courtroom."

"Neither is lying to an officer of the law," Quinn seethed.

Turning slightly, Cameron lowered his voice. "What're you talking about?"

"I saw Joci earlier."

Cameron studied the defendant at the front of the room. "Yeah? Is she doing okay?"

Quinn cleared his throat and lowered his voice. "Yep, she's good."

"Glad to hear it."

The court attendant called for the next case, and Cameron knew there was more that Quinn wasn't telling him. By the time the attorneys shuffled off with their clients, he noticed his friend was sweating.

"The air conditioner broken above you or something?"

he asked, noting the bead of perspiration racing down Quinn's cheek.

Swiping at it, he rolled his shoulders. "You should know a few things."

"About...?"

Quinn leaned over and replied, "About Joci and Adrian."

Cameron already didn't like the sudden pitch in his stomach. "Well, then go ahead. What do I need to know?"

"Of course, you know they were married and lost a kid."

"Mm-hmm."

"Well, even after their divorce and when Joci and I were...." Quinn stalled, searching for an appropriate word.

"Screwing?" Cameron offered, annoyed by his own candor.

"Okay, yeah, screwing." He shoved a hand in his hair, anxiety scrawled over his face. "Well—"

"Just fucking say it, Quinn," he seethed.

Sliding to the left, Quinn divulged, "They were screwing too."

An exploding cannon to his balls wouldn't have hurt as much as those words. "What?"

Quinn checked their surroundings. "Just a couple times though. Mostly when she went drinking and I was on shift, which wasn't very often."

Dread spiraled through Cameron's pores. "How do you know?"

Cracking his neck, Quinn's face took on an uncomfortable expression. "One night, we were out and she confessed. I get it, obviously. I didn't want to let her go either, but there was something about Adrian she couldn't let go of."

"Why are you telling me this?" he asked. "I really don't need to hear it." Suddenly, the air constricted around him and breathing became perilous. He gripped the wall to remain upright. If Quinn's admission held any merit, it made perfect sense why Adrian was reluctant to loosen any hold over Joci. Up until Cameron's appearance, Adrian had skirted by with occasional sex sessions with Joci. *He was working his way back to her.*

Quinn squinted his green eyes. "Because I'm not the only one keeping secrets, Cam, and I know you have a doozy you need to tell me. I'm trying to clear the air, and I think you should too. We're supposed to be partners, but more importantly, friends."

Cameron sighed. The jig was up. Somehow, Quinn figured it out. It shouldn't surprise him. The man was good at his job, and that included keeping an eye out for Joci. "What do you know?"

"I know you aren't done with Del Rossi." Quinn offered a polite smile to the court attendant as she walked by them. "And that you put Joci at risk with the money laundering through her law firm."

"Dammit. How did you find out?" Cameron hoped Joci hadn't told Quinn. Hell, she wasn't supposed to know.

"Joce asked me to look into some weird investment transfers. As it turns out, it wasn't stocks being moved around, it was money." He paused. "For the mob, Cam. I followed the trail to a Del Rossi account in Chicago. What were you thinking?"

Cameron swallowed hard. Nobody was ever supposed to find out about the extracurricular activities of Alley and Dorous Law Firm. "Look, I didn't want to do it. Jerry didn't give me a choice. It was either funnel money through her firm or take over another business. I figured it was safer if we kept the mob shit in-house instead of involving more private citizens."

Quinn frowned. "It's Joci. As in the woman you love—"

"Yeah, and I needed to do this or Jerry wouldn't trust me," he cut in. "If Jerry doesn't trust me, then he has no use for me. You know what happens when you fail a mob. We've seen the bodies."

They fell silent while the judge harped on a defendant about taking responsibility for his actions. The irony wasn't lost to Cameron.

"How long?" Quinn asked. "How long have you been helping Del Rossi?"

Closing his eyes, Cameron pushed down the shame. "I never stopped, Quinn."

"But you got into the police academy," Quinn argued. "You have this new life."

"Yeah, and how do you think a guy with a criminal history got in?" He studied the tattoo on his hand. "Jerry helped me secure this job."

Quinn shook his head, disappointment evident on his face. "So, you're a dirty cop."

"I don't like to think so."

"Of course you don't, but it's what you are. Who you are." He folded his arms over his chest. "I can't believe I thought you changed."

"You probably don't give a shit, but I have changed." Cameron let out a breath. "I don't want to be a pawn, but my life depends on it."

His partner grunted and cracked his neck then focused on the hearing at the front of the room.

"What're you going to do, Quinn, now that you know my secret?" Cameron asked, every second he stood under Quinn's scorn sent his blood pressure higher. The possibility that his life as a cop could be over with one word from his best friend scared the hell out of him. It was always a gamble, but he couldn't handle a complete return to the mob. He liked the new life better.

"I don't know yet," Quinn admitted, turning his neck toward him. "I'm not a saint either, but you're on a whole different level."

"Yeah, I know."

The jailers brought in the next inmate, and the attorneys started talking. Two officers beside them moved toward the bench, leaving Quinn and Cameron alone for the moment. The urge to run and never look back tempted him, but he couldn't do it. He wouldn't. Joci meant too much for him to tuck tail and disappear.

Quinn grabbed his arm and moved them out of earshot of the new group of police officers who entered the room. Facing him, he poked Cameron's chest. "I won't say anything, but if this blows back on me, I'm throwing you under the bus."

"Understood." Cameron rubbed his lips. "But it won't, I

swear. You don't have to help me any more than you already do."

"If Joci's involved, I need to know," he insisted. "I might not be in love with her anymore, but I still love her."

Cameron had to commend the guy for being protective. Quinn was the type of friend everyone wanted. "Then you should know something since it involves her."

"Sure, shoot."

He took a breath and uttered the words he hated. "Adrian's alive."

"Ha ha, very funny." Quinn rolled his eyes. "And pigs fly."

"I'm deathly serious." He narrowed his eyes to slits. "Adrian's alive and he's coming for Joci."

Quinn slapped a palm to his mouth, eyes wide. "Holy shit, man! You have to tell her!"

"Are you fucking kidding me? Tell her?" He shook his head.

The crowd turned at his loud voice. "Sorry, Your Honor. Police business," he offered when the judge lowered his spectacles.

Once the courtroom was under control again, Cameron gripped Quinn's elbow. "I can't tell her. You can't tell her. No one can tell her." He let out a haggard breath. "I shouldn't have told you. I don't know. I just needed to tell someone before I burst, I guess."

Quinn's eyes dimmed the more he spoke. "Joci is one of my best friends, Cameron. You must tell her. This is huge. How long have you known?"

Cameron rolled back his shoulders. "Long enough."

Quinn smoothed his shirt. "And you're sure it's him? A lot of people might try to take over Adrian's identity just to screw with you."

"I wish I was joking. I truly do. It'd make my life a whole lot easier," Cameron admitted.

They maintained eye contact, each wondering what the other was thinking for a solid minute. Just when Cameron was about to include more juicy details, Quinn spoke.

"Okay, because we're partners and friends, I won't tell Joci." His lips fell to a flat line. "But you better confess before she gives birth to those babies."

Cameron nodded his understanding. He hadn't thought the man would agree without being bashed over the head first. *He really is the best friend.* Focusing on the hearings once more, his stomach soured at the knowledge of bringing Quinn into the inner circle of his charade. The last thing to divulge was his true mafia role. Glancing to the other cop, he decided today wasn't the best time. *One secret at a time. It's all we can handle.*

CHAPTER THIRTEEN

Turning the key in the lock, Joci let out a labored sigh. The fall sky was sprinkled with bright shades of orange, but she barely noticed. Her mind was too weighed with the amount of data she'd consumed. She should've gone home when Quinn left two hours earlier. At the very least, she should've confronted Cameron, but he was working double shifts this week. They'd be ships passing in the night until the weekend.

Joci stalled by her car. She didn't want to go to an empty house full of deceit. Sleep wouldn't find her even if she tried. Clearing her mind was what she needed. The neon sign a block away snagged her attention. Eyeing her shoes, she shrugged. "I can totally make it," she said aloud, taking off toward the coffee shop.

No flippant wind tousled her hair or made the stickiness dissipate from her brow. Instead, the pages of the file in her arms clung to her skin. Weather in Iowa was a bitch with its easy switch from cool temperatures to muggy days and stale nights. Normally, this season was her favorite. Now, the firecrackers shooting in the neighborhood forced her lips into a straight line. If she wouldn't have to talk to Cameron, she'd call Quinn and set him loose on juvenile delinquents with the illegal substances.

The scent of grills smoking up tasty meat beckoned her mouth to follow. The twins kicked furiously when she turned in the opposite direction, mentally making a note to stop and buy some protein. A bead of sweat drizzled down her back, reminding her how easy walking used to be without a basketball in her gut.

From her purse, the Destiny's Child ringtone went off. She wasn't about to talk to her friend either. "It'd probably help." Still, Joci didn't desire discussing anything except what size coffee her parched throat craved.

At last she reached the building, the scent of java lingering at the entrance. PerkULater's giant sign gleamed for miles around, and when she stepped inside, she reviewed the tables full of coffee drinkers. Mainstream coffee places were fine, but there was something to be said about hometown shops. The Midwestern charm couldn't be bottled no matter how hard big box stores tried.

Impatiently, she stood in line while a group of teenagers argued over what drink to order. The entourage with rainbow-assorted hair colors and equally eccentric tattoos made her dwell on the fiancé she was pissed with. He didn't know yet, of course, but she couldn't escape him no matter where she went.

Her feet barking and mind swirling, she glanced around the small building. The artsy décor with a mural of the Des

Moines skyscrapers splayed on one wall, the red tables clashing with the orange in the sunset. Skimming over the heads of hipsters and the sun-kissed skin beneath football jerseys, her eyes widened when she spotted one of her clients. In a corner booth on the far end of the café sat the man Cameron was zealously against her representing. *Oh my God, how is he here?* The notion that he could be stalking her crept into her mind. *No, he's a nice guy. He wouldn't do that.* Still, Cameron's warning came to mind.

Rubbing her lips together, Joci weighed the pros and cons of remaining in the line versus turning around and going back to the office. The babies suddenly awoke as if sensing her plight and urged her toward the front of the line. *I'll just grab a coffee then hightail it out of here. He'll never spot me.*

"Joci, is that you?" His Irish accent rang clear in her ears. Suddenly, she wasn't fond of the Emerald Isle and their way of speaking.

Well, damn, that didn't work. Biting her thumbnail, she turned around and met Derrick's gaze. Losing her place in the line, she cut across the linoleum hardwood floor and knocked on the tabletop. "Derrick, hi."

The slender yet muscular redhead put aside his book. "What're you doing here?"

"Oh, you know, I'm a coffee addict." She looked back to the line. It seemed to have doubled since he called her over. *Great.*

"Sit, please. You look bushed." Derrick pulled his coffee cup and empty plate out of the way. "You didn't walk here, did you?"

"I did." For a moment, she thought about refusing the offer. The twins somersaulted, sneaking under one of her ribs. She was more than ready for them to be born. Being tired was a constant battle, and it wouldn't hurt anything to sit for a spell. *Just five minutes then I'll leave.* Collapsing into the soft cushion, she let out a satisfied exhale. She pointed at the window. "But my office is within walking distance. Rayna and I come here almost daily." Pushing on one of the tiny feet, she grimaced. "Except it was a whole lot easier a few months ago."

Derrick chuckled at her antics and took a sip of what appeared to be coffee with cream. "What can I get you?"

"Oh, I'll get there. I just need a moment to rest." She jerked her thumb to the line. "And for the teenagers to make a decision for once in their lives."

"I knew a woman who had the same troubles." He stood before Joci could inquire. "You relax for a bit. I'll be back with something sure to please the little ones." He winked. "And you too."

She wanted to argue, but it was no use. The man was already halfway to the counter. Telling herself one cup of coffee with a client wouldn't hurt, she settled into the booth. Her protruding belly got in the way when she slouched and attempted to put her feet up on the opposite cushion. The act took more effort than she could muster, and she blew the hair out of her face, comfortable at last.

"You two better be worth all this," she scolded when the duo began more acrobatics. She watched Derrick at the counter. He was nonchalant, and the barista appeared to like him. Cameron's words came to mind, and she felt bad for not heeding his warning. *He doesn't seem so bad.* Derrick paid for the order. *Except he's somehow at your favorite coffee shop. This shit isn't common.* She gnawed on her bottom lip as worry consumed her thoughts. *Des Moines is small, but not this small. Maybe Cam was right and I shouldn't be here.* Before she could act on her feelings, Derrick returned.

"Ta-da! One iced decaf raspberry mocha latte," Derrick announced with bravado, setting the plastic cup in front of her.

Joci's mouth watered at the combination of her favorite drinks. She'd been cutting back on the sweets with the recent weight gain that made her doctor's eyebrows lift, but she wouldn't turn this down by a long shot. "Wow. Thank you." She took a sip and closed her eyes, the beverage hitting every spot she imagined it would. "Oh, God, it's so good." Clamping her lips on the straw, she hoped the phrase didn't sound as erotic as it did playing back in her mind.

The booth shifted slightly as Derrick slipped into his spot. Without opening her eyes, she imagined he was gawking at her spread out like a starfish in a coffee house. Well, she was pregnant, and caring about such things as propriety went out the window the instant maternity pants slid into her closet.

"Glad you're enjoying yourself," he said, laughter lining the deep voice. "I also rescued a double chocolate muffin away from the counter. Think you could help me eat it?"

At this, Joci's head whipped up and her eyes pried open. "You really are my savior," she murmured, ogling the enormous pastry. "This," she took a chunk of muffin, "is my all-time favorite type." She held up the snack, her mouth watering despite the fact that he somehow knew her favorite combination. It was too eerie to be a coincidence. "How'd you know?" she asked, pulling her phone out of her pocket. He sounded more and more like a stalker each time she ran into him. A select few people knew her favorite coffee shop treats. Rayna wasn't too far away and could jet over in case she needed help. The problem was Derrick didn't act like a stalker. It was the one and only reason she hadn't busted out of the booth and run for the door. Sure, he happened to guess what food she liked, but did that make him a stalker? Not exactly. Still, Joci was positive something was going on with the easygoing guy across the table. He knew too much about her for her to believe their run-ins were happenstance. She scooched toward the edge of the seat in case a swift getaway was needed.

Shrugging indifference, Derrick snipped off a hunk of muffin and brought it to his lips. His cheery blue eyes clouded. "My wife always liked adding a sugary muffin with her coffee when she was pregnant." He shook his head as if clearing his thoughts. "I thought it'd be a hit with you too. Plus, what woman doesn't like chocolate?"

"Oh." His explanation quieted the stalker alarm in her head. He wasn't following her and watching to see what she ordered. He was just trying to be nice. *I hope.* Joci choked down her drink when his hand paused at his mouth. She wasn't sure if pressing him was the right thing to do, but staring wasn't helping things either. He quickly wiped the forlorn expression from his face, saving her the conundrum. She had enough troubles for the night. Becoming a therapist on top of everything else wasn't in the cards.

"Now, why are you out this time of night at work?" He rolled his shoulders back, his posture perfect under the casual green polo. "I'm going out on a limb here and say you don't live around here or you wouldn't be at the office."

"I was working, but I found out some information about a former client that's keeping me from going to an empty house." She reviewed the café, noting the teenagers decided on a blended coffee concoction. "But my woes aren't what you want to hear." Taking a chocolate chip out of the muffin, she nodded. "Tell me about yourself. Do you live in the neighborhood?"

Catching her off guard, Derrick's hand boldly clasped over hers. Her brain told her to abandon ship at his forward act, but her body refused to obey. "I'd much rather hear about your bad day than discuss me. I'm nothing to brag about, believe me. Typical businessman."

Maybe it was the honesty in his eyes the color of the sky or her longing for company who wasn't hiding something that swayed Joci to reexamine their circumstances. She wasn't planning on it, but everything inside her ate her resolve. "My fiancé and I are about to have a massive fight," she explained, keeping it vague. "Depending on how it turns out, I may be a single mom after all." She twirled the straw between her free fingers, not bothering to withdraw the hand he held. "Good thing I'm not a divorce attorney, huh? I'd be my own number one client with the way I screw up my love life."

"Why do you say that?" he asked with a tilt of his head.

She scrunched her nose then met Derrick's inquisitive gaze. "Because even though I'm hopelessly in love with my fiancé, a part of me wishes my ex-husband was around."

The expression on his face was a mixture of amazement and disbelief. "But why?"

"So these little guys can know their dad." She reflexively rubbed her stomach.

His eyes turned reflective at her words. "Ah, that makes sense."

Her fingers snuck over to a stray morsel of muffin and she popped it into her mouth. "I guess some part of me wonders 'what if' a little too often where Adrian is involved. It's probably selfish of me."

Derrick polished off his coffee and squinted to the window. "And what would you do if Adrian was here? Would it make a difference to your relationship with your officer?"

The food in Joci's mouth settled to ash on her tongue. The way he asked those questions was uncomfortable. From anyone else, they would be friendly, but the way Derrick asked personal information sent a shiver down her spine

Studying his complexion, she was disappointed when he looked nothing like her ex except for his red hair. Rehashing her time with Adrian hadn't happened much since his funeral. Sure, she visited his grave, but had she actually pondered the possibility of choosing between Cameron and Adrian, Cameron would win every time.

"I don't think so. I made my decision, and I wouldn't change it." She slurped the iced delight.

Retrieving his hand, Derrick tapped two fingers to the tip of his nose. He maintained his perusal of the outside world as if the answer lay directly on the other side of the building. Finally, his neck twisted in her direction. "Ah, I see, but…," he began, then stopped himself. His eyes were glued to something behind her, so Joci craned her neck. Cameron's solid body filled the doorway of the shop, his face brooding contempt. He looked like the man she'd initially met in jail; his eyes the color of coffee midbrew.

"Your fiancé shows up at the most importune times," her client commented, his tone turning dark. "You sure he doesn't have a tracker on you?"

Joci swiveled in the booth as Cameron reached them.

"A uniform really does look good on you, Shearer," Derrick started with a smug smile. "But I prefer an orange jumpsuit over this."

"Wait, do you know each other?" she asked, glancing to Cameron. "From before Iowa? Why didn't you say anything at the hospital?" She was beyond confused now. There wasn't any other way Derrick would know about Cameron's life in and out of jail unless they were mob friends. That thought made her stomach queasy. Couple it with the fact that Derrick had inserted himself into her life on more than one occasion, Joci worried her bottom lip. Plus, if they knew each other before her car accident, surely Cameron would've mentioned it. *Well, he did tell me to stay away from him.* Neither man seemed to hear her since they continued on hurling angry words.

"Still an arrogant prick despite the opportunity. What a shock," Cameron shot back.

"And still going for someone out of your league," Derrick snarled. "Equally stellar."

The muscles on Cameron's tattooed arms rippled as he clenched his fists. Joci swung her eyes between them. Enemies was more suited to the duo. *What the hell?*

"I didn't think you had history with each other," she led, heartbeat thundering in her ears.

"We don't," Cameron quickly informed her.

Standing to his full height, Derrick lifted his brows. "I wouldn't say that." His attitude turned smug, a change from the man she'd started to learn about. "Cameron and I go way back. We fell for the same girl."

Specks of perspiration broke out over her forehead. Watching the men reminded her of the spat between Adrian and Cameron. If she didn't know better, she'd swear it was déjà vu. "Lovely, your past is back as projected," she grumbled. It made sense now why Cameron didn't mention their acquaintance, but not why Derrick didn't tell her. If Derrick wanted to create waves before today, it would've been easy. *Why wait until now?*

"No, it's not like—" her fiancé began, but then slammed his mouth shut when Derrick cut in.

"And you tend to lie as well, huh?" Derrick snorted. "Just what every girl wants."

The room suddenly felt as if it were closing in on Joci. She hated arguing except within the confines of a courtroom.

This brought up feelings she'd long buried. "I need air."

Neither man seemed to hear her. They were too busy trying to decide who had the biggest dick. Well, news flash, they were both being enormous pricks.

Joci hauled ass to the exit. She didn't dare look behind her. Cameron was fond of fighting, and being in full uniform wouldn't stop him if throttled too far. Picking up her tired feet, she made it to the office parking lot as the sound of running on pavement met her ears.

"Joce, wait!" Cameron called.

Smearing on her best pissed-off smolder, Joci pivoted in the direction the voice emitted. "Damn, I shouldn't have done that," she uttered, taking in the flawless way Cameron sprinted toward her. It shouldn't be sexy, but when she tilted her head to the left, all she could think was that *Baywatch* with tattoos would've made a much better show. If he was only wearing lifeguard shorts, she'd completely forget why she was mad.

"Dammit, really?" She groaned when her heart fluttered and her body told her to rip his uniform to shreds. Yeah, she was just going to blame her hormones from here on in.

Cameron stopped beside her, not out of breath in the least. His stamina was illustrious compared to all other men she knew. Even Quinn paled in the bedroom, and that was saying something. "Look, I'm sorry. I acted like an ass."

"Yeah, you did."

Running his fingers through his hair, he let out a frustrated groan. "But seeing you with *him*." He paused and shook his head. "He isn't who you think."

She kicked at a small rock. "Neither were you."

Fidgeting with his belt loops, Cameron shifted his boots. "I know, but it was different with me." He jammed a thumb over his shoulder. "That guy just wants to get under my skin and steal you away. He's being a tool."

"And you're not?"

His eyes took on an apologetic hue, but she stood her ground. They weren't even close to being done.

"Okay, okay, you're right." Cameron sighed in defeat.

The squeal of tires at the nearby stoplight filled the silence. Staring anywhere but his eyes wasn't the best idea, but it was all she formed at the moment. "When were you going to tell me about the money Del Rossi laundered through my investment accounts?" She perched her fists on her hips, the act harder with the bulge on her middle.

His face fell flat at her question, hands tightening on the belt. "Fuck."

"You knew," she stated with venom. "You son of a bitch!" she screamed, not caring that she scared the Labrador walking by with his owner.

"Joci, he told me it was going to be a one-time thing." He moved toward her, but she held up her palm. "If anything, you probably made a little money from it."

"Do *not* come near me."

Cameron's figure slammed to a halt. Rocking on his heels, he lowered his voice. "They were supposed to pull out after the transaction's completion."

Despite being royally peeved, she couldn't help but smirk at the different direction his statement could veer.

She straightened her face when he mirrored her. "It's the mob, Cam. Why would you take them at their word?" She yanked on the car door. "I don't know why I took you at yours." She didn't like witnessing his shoulders slump or the defeated expression overwhelm his magnificent face, but she climbed into the vehicle nevertheless.

Snagging the door, Cameron crowded the small space. "I screwed up, yes, but I had to do it. Jerry doesn't request things; he demands them. I'll fix this, I swear."

Clicking the seat belt into place, Joci tossed her purse into the empty passenger seat. "You know, I think I need a little space. I'm staying at Rayna's tonight."

"Joce." His fingers curled around the door and the conviction in his voice nearly crippled her resolve.

She couldn't look at him. If she did, she'd take it all back. "And maybe until I sort a few issues out."

"Goddammit, Joci. This is what he wants." Cameron slapped the top of the car, his face pinched in frustration.

"Who? Derrick? You said you didn't know him, which was obviously a lie. I don't know why you can't just tell me what happened between the two of you."

"Never mind." He stooped low and crouched beside the car. "Please, come home. Give me time to make this right." He reached for her hand then withdrew it. "I can't protect you when you're somewhere else."

Swallowing the tears on the verge of spilling, she shook her head and started the engine. "If I'm not around you, I don't even need to be protected."

The weight of her words forced him to fall backward on

the parking lot. Knees bent up with his tattoos splayed on the arms crossed over each other, he resembled a boy lost from the world.

Now clear of his frame, Joci shut the driver door and rolled onto the empty street. Unable to resist, her eyes checked the rearview mirror. He hadn't moved from his lonely spot, just sat there staring after her until she disappeared over the hill.

***

Cameron wasn't certain how long he stayed in the bent position. He was surprised he didn't morph into a fetal form to cope. Time fell away with each passing moment of her retreat. His chest constricted as the seams Joci's love had sewed slowly unraveled. The sun had dipped beyond the buildings when he heard a car horn behind him. He couldn't pry his line of sight from the horizon, though. If he kept staring, maybe, just maybe, she'd turn around and come back to him. He'd stay there all night if he knew it would be the end result.

"Shearer, what the hell are you doing sitting in an empty parking lot," Quinn questioned from the patrol SUV, judging from the engine's rumble. Before any response could be formed, his partner kept talking as if the world hadn't recently turned upside down. "You kinda resemble a hobo if hobos wore badges and carried guns. Damn, talk about scary right there. It'd make an awesome horror movie. Hobos with badges. No, hobos and confetti! You know, because bullets are the confetti." His voice dropped off. "Yo, are you alive?"

"She's gone."

"What? Who?" The door squeaked open and his burly form came into view. No matter the number of times they hit the gym together, how his friend didn't chub up with all the food he consumed was a mystery to Cameron.

"Joci. She knows about the Del Rossi money." He looked over to Quinn. "But you already knew that since you're the one who found it."

Quinn shrugged sheepishly. "I can't say no to Joce."

"I get it. She's staying at Rayna's for the foreseeable future." He lowered his gaze to the blacktop sprinkled with rocks and loose dirt. "I fucked it up." His throat swelled, the words tar on his tongue. "And I think I'm losing her."

"Whoa. And I thought two thugs with nine-irons were a bad day." Quinn sank down beside him. "I'm sorry, man. What're you going to do?"

It was all he'd thought about since she'd driven off. Every plan he formed pancaked almost as bad as him actually cooking pancakes. The mob was pulling his strings. If he attempted to cut them, he was a corpse within hours. Not to mention, he needed help with handling the Mikkelsen death sentence. His life was shifting in the worst possible direction, and the woman who kept him balanced was no longer talking to him.

Briskly rubbing his palms over his face, Cameron squinted at his friend. "Find a solution not involving my imminent death and win her back."

Quinn unsheathed his handgun and eyed it. "You didn't cheat on her, did you?" He offered a sideways scowl.

"Hell no! I'd never do anything to hurt Joci." He winced, his words ricocheting the truth. "Intentionally, that is."

Fondling the loaded weapon, his partner cocked it, but kept the barrel downward. "Good, because otherwise, I'd have to show you a little Iowa justice."

Cameron smirked at the hollow threat. Sure, Quinn may rough him up, but putting a bullet in him was out of the question. He was too pure for such an act. "If it helps me get Joci again, you can beat me 'til I'm bloody."

"Yeah, yeah. Don't tempt me." Quinn stood, grabbing Cameron's hand along with him. "Now, can we go to work? Double shifts are enough of a bitch without starting them late."

Seeing no other way around his current predicament, Cameron nodded and rode in silence as the two patrolled Des Moines's streets. To his relief, Quinn kept occupied by singing along to the radio and pulling over speeders. He couldn't ask for an easier night.

"Hey, you want to freak these kids out?" Quinn asked three hours into their shift.

Scanning the crowd of teenagers drinking out of whiskey bottles, he gave two thumbs up. "Sure, why not? It's not like we have anything better to do right now."

Quinn grinned and flipped on the siren. Bottles smashed on the pavement and the kids scurried into the darkness, much like Joci had hours earlier.

CHAPTER FOURTEEN

Thumbing through the deposition transcripts, Joci grumbled under her breath when the twins started their Olympic dives for the fourth time that day. Normally, their antics didn't bother her, but gasping in pain midway through a court hearing wasn't ideal. She highlighted a witness's lie contradicting the police report and smacked her lips loudly in the empty room.

Rehashing the day, she had to admit watching two sheriff's deputies scrambling over benches to make sure she wasn't dying had felt kind of nice after sleeping alone on Rayna's couch. Even her client tried to help despite the handcuffs. Rolling her shoulders back, Joci held her head high and took a cleansing breath. It didn't aid in clearing her wayward mind.

The boys tumbled, this time bouncing on her bladder. Pushing on the mass, she grunted when the normal solution did nothing to ease their pestering. "You guys need to stop hurting Mommy. I'm liable to name you something horrid like Chip and Dale if you keep it up."

More kicks met her scolding, resulting in light laughter filling the office. "Fine, but just to forewarn, you'll probably have names your daddy would've loved."

A peculiar sadness crept through her veins at the mention of Adrian. She rarely spoke aloud about him, particularly to the twins. Chastising herself, she pushed back the chair and cradled her swollen abdomen and bent down as close as possible. "He would be thrilled to have twins. Especially boys." Her eyes misted, blurring her vision. "And he'd insist you play every sport I let you. At least, it's what he said about your older brother." Her eyelids fluttered with tears. "I'll tell you about him someday."

Her steady voice seemed to calm the storm, so she continued. "Your dad, Adrian, had the most incredible laugh. It was one of those contagious ones." Her lips paused, recalling the sound.

She cleared the desktop, hoping her busy hands would distract from the moisture begging to escape her eyes. "He was as pale as a vampire, but his red hair was one of my favorite things. He kept it short. A lot like our time together."

Guilt nagged her heart the more she reminisced. "I should've spent more time with him. Hindsight is always twenty-twenty." Joci wiped a stray tear from her cheek and let out a shaky breath. "I hope one of you has his blue eyes." She closed her own, picturing Adrian. "They sucked me in the moment I met them. I never told him, but it was the real reason why he swayed me to his dad's law firm. Sure, the increased pay helped, but it was his magnetic eyes."

Her phone rang, interrupting her monologue until she

saw the caller ID. It was a police department number, which meant either Cameron or Quinn. Seeing how her fiancé was trying to get ahold of her, she opted against answering. The light on her phone lit up red. Disregarding the recent message, she stared at her belly button sticking up under the white shirt. She'd never imagined pregnancy would occur a second time, and the memories of the past scratched at the door along with that reminder.

The situation with Cameron weighed more on her the longer she stayed at Rayna's. She wasn't ready to face his deception. Half of him she knew, the wrongly charged man and the police officer part. The mafia player with a tainted past was the slice of him she didn't know completely. He rarely shared any of his past, and the little he did, left unanswered questions. There were many more skeletons in his closet begging to break free. With them would come a slew of enemies she didn't think she could handle if Cameron was keeping information from her. Obviously, he kept the money laundering a secret, so there could be more. It was the more she wasn't sure of. Secrets tended to build up if communication wasn't open.

Before she knew it, tissues and tears stained the wooden desk. Her shoulders hunched, clear vision no longer an option. All she wanted was Cameron's arms around her, as he whispered everything would work out.

"Joci, you ready to go to the doctor's appointment?" Quinn's masculine voice chimed from the front door. "I'm so looking forward to being your fill-in."

Stuffing a tissue up her nostril to stop the leak, she

quickly slid the rest of the evidence of her plight into the trash can. Her movements weren't fast enough for Quinn's long strides.

"Joce, we need to have a chat about cramming things up your nose. I don't think it's a good look for you," he teased, stepping closer. When he noticed her puffy eyes, his smile faded. "You okay?"

Joci plucked the tissue out and tossed it in the garbage. "I was talking to the babies about Adrian and things got real." Like a professional, she dabbed the mascara that had managed to make a getaway. "I miss him, Quinn. Not romantically or anything, just him. Is that weird?"

"Not at all." Dragging her into his embrace, the off-duty cop rested his head against the top of hers. "I'm sorry, Joci." His hand rubbed up and down her back, lulling her.

"Thanks, Quinn." Joci snuggled deeper into his chest, inhaling the comforting scent of his body. He was her true hero. He'd helped her through life post-divorce and amid grieving. *Why didn't I think about talking to him?* The loud drumming of his heart silently reminded her. *Oh, right, because he's best friends with Cam these days.*

She put distance between them and snatched her purse from its spot on the chair. "We better go. I don't like being late."

Quinn dug through his pockets until he found his keys. "Lead the way, miss. I'll even give you the official police escort."

"Um, no," she interjected. "Maybe low-key is the way to go today."

"Your loss." He shrugged then followed on her heels.

"Rayna, we'll meet you for dinner," Joci called, shutting the front door without bothering to hear the reply. Since moving into her friend's bachelorette pad, their relationship had both grown and faltered. One bathroom with two women was a huge no-no.

Overcast skies above mirrored Joci's mood as she stepped off the sidewalk. Reviewing the lot, she scratched her stomach. "Damn shea butter isn't working," she complained. With her expanding belly, she found her skin was ten times drier than normal. Finding relief was more difficult by the day.

"What?"

"Never mind." She squinted when she realized her car was on the opposite end of the large space. The recently washed patrol car stood out since it technically wasn't in a parking space. It became clear he planned on driving, and since her feet resembled baked bread, she relented. "Okay, fine, you drive."

Clapping with childlike glee, Quinn hurried to the back door and swung it open. When Joci reached him, she offered a mystified squint. "You don't think I'm sitting back there, do you?"

"Oops." He chuckled and opened the passenger door this time. "Old habits and all." He waited until she climbed in to add, "Plus, if I recall, you like the back seat."

Joci's mouth dropped open as the door shut gently. Opting to ignore his gentle jab from their past, she flipped through the radio stations once Quinn put the car into gear.

The ride to the doctor's office went without a hitch. Mild conversation about their days temporarily helped chase away her troubles.

When they arrived, a content smile played on her lips and laughter wasn't far from either of them. Quinn looped an arm around her waist, guiding her inside. After Joci checked in with the front desk, a nurse led them to an exam room.

"Aren't you the cutest couple ever?" the short nurse crooned, her face beaming.

"We're not—" Joci began, but a hand on her leg stopped her rejection.

"We're keeping things hush-hush," Quinn cut in with a devilish grin. "I don't want the dad to find out."

The nurse's brown eyes expanded until Joci was afraid they might pop out. Her mouth gaped like a fish sucking air, words inaudible.

"He's kidding," Joci admitted, shoving at him.

Quinn winked then pressed a kiss to her cheek. "Or am I?"

"Officer Quinn, nice to see you again," Dr. Miller greeted, stepping into the room.

"You know him?" the nurse asked, her face uneasy.

Dr. Miller nodded and grabbed the clipboard from the counter. "Yes. He was nice enough to give me a warning instead of a ticket." She flipped through the papers. "And he comes with Ms. Dorous every now and then."

As if to prove a point, Quinn hopped up on the bed beside Joci and gave her an awkward side hug. "Don't worry, we're not screwing anymore."

"And we're not screwing any less," Joci inserted, unable to help it, and Quinn howled with laughter. "Kidding. Totally kidding. He's not my type anymore."

"Said no one ever," Quinn added with a smirk.

The eyebrows of both the nurse and doctor shot up, though neither addressed the joke. "Alrighty then. Let's do an ultrasound really quick, then we'll finish with an exam."

Quinn retreated to the extra chair while the women prepared for the next set of events. Rolling up the gown she slipped into, Joci cringed when her eyes met the pasty skin beneath. She was normally golden tan during the summer months, and her previous stretch marks had been surgically removed. Now, the ones she bore looked angry at the additional load of a second baby.

"You're ravishing, Joci," Quinn softly reminded.

Sliding her gaze to him, she met his serious eyes. A sassy reply came to mind, but he was being entirely sincere in the compliment. She couldn't fault him for being both sweet and too good for her. "Thanks, Quinn."

He leaned forward and laced his hands together. "Anything for my girl."

Dr. Miller squirted the blue jelly on Joci's stomach, startling her out of the tender moment. "It's too bad he's merely a friend," she sang, eyeing him. "He's awful handsome."

Watching the monitor, Joci agreed in silence. Quinn was a catch, just not hers.

"Here's Baby A. He's a cute sprite." The doctor zoomed

in on the heartbeat, secure in its strength, then moved to the second blob. "And Baby B is grabbing his brother's hand. Aw, how adorable." She hit a few keys on the machine, checking the vitals of the babies.

Joci's heart lifted at the intimate sight. Never had a computer screen looked like heaven before this moment. "Best friends already."

"Hmm." Dr. Miller's brows knit together as she rolled the wand over the exposed stomach. "I'm a little concerned with Baby B's weight. He appears to be on the small side and his umbilical cord isn't in the greatest position."

Quinn gripped Joci's hand. "But he's going to be all right, isn't he?"

"He should be." The obstetrician examined a few more screenshots, then wiped off the jelly. "I want you to come each week from here on in, Joci, so I can follow his progress and his brother's. Multiple babies tend to have higher risks. I don't want anything to happen to your boys."

"Me either." She grasped Quinn until he coughed. It was then she noticed her nails were digging into his skin. "Oops, sorry." She relaxed her hold, but he made sure their hands remained united.

"Sit tight. I'll be back with the pictures." Dr. Miller and the nurse skirted the room, leaving a lingering sense of restlessness.

"She's being cautious. Don't overthink it." Quinn attempted to console.

Covering up, Joci nodded in agreement. Her first pregnancy had gone smoothly in every way, but this one kept her up at night. If she lost a baby, she was losing Adrian all over again, and she couldn't handle that. She swiftly changed back into the flowing peasant shirt and leggings while Quinn studied a magazine.

The police radio went off from his chest, its loud alarm startling her. "Officer 2754, please respond to dispatch for a 10-00," the clipped voice stated over the line.

Immediately, Quinn jumped to his feet, clutching the device. "2754 responding. Please advise officer number of 10-00."

With bated breath, Joci listened to the crackling on the other side. She was on the verge of learning all the police codes, but if Quinn's reaction told her anything, this code wasn't good.

"Officer 2828."

Quinn's sharp inhale set off warning bells. "Joci, we need to go." He grabbed her purse and yanked open the door.

"Who is it, Quinn?" she asked, slipping on her shoes.

Gripping the doorway, he offered her a solemn glance. "Cameron. He's been hit."

"What? Oh my God." Her mouth dried, and she couldn't remember walking down the hallways, Quinn talking to the nurse, or the drive to the hospital. One thought terrorized her the entire trip. *Not him too.*

***

"Ow, watch it!" Cameron complained when the disinfectant set in. The nurse in the emergency room picked at the wound, her hands shaking. "Just fucking leave it alone.

I'm fine." He shoved his body backward and stood up to leave. He was done with being babied. If he wanted that, he'd go home. His eye twitched, recalling home was empty still.

"Are you causing trouble again, Shearer?" Tad O'Brien chastised with a tinge of humor.

Turning on his heels, the cop leered at the tall paramedic who seemed to be at every crime scene in the metro. He was the hospital's best, so naturally the man was in high demand. Although, it made Cameron wary of the all-knowing EMT. No one was *that* good at their job.

"No, your resident," he jerked a thumb over his shoulder, "over there couldn't patch me up, so I'm going home."

Tad touched the area around the gash on the officer's forehead. "It doesn't look too bad, but you need stitches." He nodded to an open bed. "Come on, I'll fix you up."

With the reluctance of a cat getting bathed, Cameron obeyed the man clad in a dark blue uniform made from scrubs material. Tad owned the emergency room, catching the eye of each female and a few males in his wake. If he didn't know better, he'd guess the man was a doctor, not an EMT.

Returning with the necessary items, Tad shook them. "Boom! Your salvation is here."

"Shut up and do it already."

"That's what she said," the paramedic snickered, dimples popping in both cheeks.

Rolling his eyes, Cameron slumped on the rickety bed and waited as the other man prepared the needle and bandages.

Tad grabbed a disinfectant. "You wanna tell me how this happened?"

He crossed both arms over his chest, his muscles screaming at the act after a rambunctious afternoon. "Not particularly, no."

Wiping the bloodstream from Cameron's temple, Tad kept his vision glued to the job at hand. "I have a buddy over at the station. I could read the police report myself if I call in a favor. Up to you."

Gritting his teeth, Cameron let out a huff. "I walked into a drug deal gone bad and some guys attacked me. Happy now?"

"Not enough." When Cameron didn't offer more information, he grabbed his phone and dialed. "Hey, it's me, can you send me over the Shearer police report really quick? I want to make sure his wounds match up." Tad nodded and hung up. "On its way."

Cameron rolled his eyes. "Your girlfriend work dispatch or something?"

"Nope, my sister," the paramedic filled in with a cheery grin.

"Great." The peroxide in the wipe bubbled on the cut. Cameron didn't want to admit what happened, but he'd known Tad since joining the force. Plus, he already asked his sister to send it to him. Why they weren't friends was a wonder. *Must be the cop and paramedic thing.*

A ding from Tad's phone chimed and he opened the e-mail. "Let's see, it says here, 'following a complaint called in from a neighbor, underaged and drunk assailants tossed

bricks at Officer Shearer as he advanced on their position.'"
Tad tilted his head. "Want to fill in the blanks?"

Cameron winced when the man numbed his brow. "Not much else to say. Five idiots were drinking and smashing the bottles along First Avenue. Dispatch got the complaint, and I got the call. Didn't know there were drugs being sold until I got there and recognized the bags of cocaine."

"Wait, don't you usually have a partner?"

Cameron's eye twitched. "Yeah, but he had to take someone to the doctor."

"I see." The blond nodded, accepting this version of events. If he were on the other end, he'd press until the man broke. Noting the scrapes, bruises, and gashes on his arms, Cameron's version of the story left much to the imagination. Yeah, he came across drunk hoodlums, but omitted the part where they jumped him and took turns kicking and thumping him. It wasn't a pretty scene, but at least the kids didn't know about the hit out on him. These were just drunk high school dropouts who sold drugs on the side, and he'd walked in on one of their deals.

Tad snapped his fingers in front of Cameron's face. "Hey, you awake in there?"

Shaking his head, he noticed the needle. "What're you doing?"

"I was telling you to brace yourself. Sometimes the numbing agent doesn't take full effect the entire time." Not waiting, he dug in the needle, making swift work of the gash.

Gripping the edge of the bed, Cameron stared at the tiled

floor, willing himself to think about something else. All his mind wanted to dwell on was either Joci or the death threats. Neither one worked in his favor as of late, so he counted the small triangles in the floor's design.

"Who found you?"

"Another cop was doing his rounds. He saw me on the ground then raised holy hell." Cameron smirked. "I guess it's one way to get attention."

Tad finished off the knot and tied it. "Won't be pretty for a couple weeks, but you shouldn't have a scar." He took off his gloves and tossed them in the wastebasket. "You better thank your stars. Who knows what could've happened if things went differently today." He patted Cameron's shoulder. "You're a lucky guy."

Cameron harrumphed and buttoned his dirty shirt. His entire uniform was scuffed up, but before getting to the hospital, his fellow officer thought he needed CPR at one point, which caused further damage. "Not sure about that, but thanks for the patch."

"Need me to call anyone?" Tad offered.

His eye twitched again. *Damn thing!* Sleeping would help with the problem, but it wasn't something his mind would allow. Not with Joci at Rayna's and his life on the line each day the Mikkelsen hit remained active. All he did was toss and turn until he eventually gave up and went for a run. It was the same each day since she left. So far, it'd been twelve excruciating days. His body thanked him for the brutal workouts, his heart not so much. "No, I'm good. Thanks."

Standing, he saw a flash of brown hair whip around the curtain to the makeshift room before disappearing. The hue resembled Joci's, but she'd have no reason to be here at this time. *Unless something is wrong.* He mentally shook his head. Quinn would advise him if an emergency sprang up.

"See ya around, O'Brien." He waved at the EMT currently on the other end of a nurse's batting eyelashes. Rolling back his shoulders, Cameron winced at the pain. His muscles could handle a battering, but the emotional drain was another story.

Disregarding the pitiful looks from the ER staff, he hobbled to the exit, ready to be done with the day. Just as the automatic door slid open, a voice paused his action.

"Shearer, wait up!"

He knew this one well. Pulling out his sunglasses, Cameron stepped outside and away from the door. "What's up, partner?"

Quinn's frazzled hair and worried brow put him on edge. "What's up? Seriously?" He eyed his partner thoroughly. "Dispatch said you were hit."

Cameron raked a bruised hand through his hair, coming across new lumps along the way. "Officer Ramirez may have dramatized my circumstances. I'm fine."

"Damn Ramirez, he's always doing shit like that." The enlarged vein on Quinn's head started to minimize. "I can't believe I dragged Joci from her gyno appointment when you're barely scratched."

"Joci's here?" He immediately scoured every direction in hopes of spotting her.

"She was, but she couldn't take seeing you. I told her I'd check on you."

Moving toward the hospital again, he was stopped short when Quinn gripped his arm. Glaring at it, Cameron ground his teeth together. "Let go."

"No, let *her* go. When she saw you were okay, she went up to the birthing ward to have a look around."

Cameron whipped his arm back and massaged the base of his neck. "All right." He leaned against the red brick exterior of the building. "She and the babies were doing well, though, right?"

"Yeah, I think so. I don't understand all the mumbo jumbo the doctor said, but she did mention one of the boys was smaller. She's having Joci go in every week now until they come." Quinn turned down the radio as another call came across the static.

Guilt nagged Cameron's gut. He should be the one driving her to the appointments, not her ex. "Thanks for taking her. I'd go, but...."

"She'll come around. Women like their space to think shit over until they're blue in the face."

The two stood in silent agreement. The wind picked up, the scent of rain tickling Cameron's nostrils. It was more than fitting that, ever since Joci left, the weather had turned dreary—as if commanded by his emotions. "With all the shootings and beatings I've had lately, it's a good thing she's steered clear of me."

Clapping his friend's shoulder, Quinn jerked his head toward the parking lot. "Come on, let's get a drink. You sure as hell need one and so do I."

"What about Joci? Didn't you drive her?"

Rain began falling overhead, and Quinn pointed to the hospital. "Rayna's picking her up after she's done. Don't worry, I have it covered."

Deciding Joci was in good hands, he nodded once and set his legs into motion. If his life kept going along this path, he'd be dead before Joci made up her mind about their status. Blinking at moisture on his eyelashes, Cameron couldn't tell if it was a tear or a raindrop. Either way, he would toss back a few shots, despite the fact they wouldn't help either of his problems.

***

The rustle of hospital curtains drowned out the rest of what Cameron and the paramedic were talking about. Sighing with relief, Joci hurried out of the emergency room. *He's safe*. It was all she needed to know before making an escape.

"Did you find him?" Quinn asked as she pushed open the door to the waiting room.

She pushed up her glasses. "Yeah. He's a little bruised, but looks alive to me."

"Good, because I'm going to kill him for worrying me." He stood and gave her a quick hug. "Do you want to leave?"

"Actually, no." The disinfectant smell of the hospital swirled around her. It wasn't an aroma she cared for, but it was better than going to Rayna's quite yet. "I'm going to check out the birthing floor. You go ahead."

"I can't leave you here," he argued, the top button of his shirt popping open when he straightened his chest.

Joci had to admit he was more buff than Cameron, but somewhere along the way it had ceased to matter. Her eyes craved to see the tattoos on Cameron's body instead of the chiseled physique of the officer in front of her. It baffled her. She hadn't gone for the bad boys until she reconnected with Cameron.

"When I'm done, Rayna can pick me up." She offered him a smile. "Go rough him up a bit." She pressed a hand to his right bicep. "But not too much."

Quinn's sensational smile turned rogue. "Leaving that particular job to you?"

"We're not talking. You're fully aware."

Poking her side, he tilted his head disbelievingly in her direction. "Yes, and I think you're both being idiots."

"You don't know the whole story, Quinn," she reminded. "Somebody from Cam's past popped up the other day and it means he hasn't been truthful with me."

Quinn's brows rose, and he opened his mouth as if to say something, then cleared his throat. "Look, I hate to say it, but do you really want him to be 100 percent honest with you? I mean, sometimes your clothing choices are questionable."

"Be serious, Quinn." She rolled her eyes.

"I am, and I know you." He snatched her hands, convincing her to keep his gaze. "In two plus years, never have I seen your face light up like when Cameron's nearby. Don't get me wrong, he shouldn't have hurt you, but is this something you can work through?"

"Maybe." She rubbed her lips anxiously. "I hope so."

Quinn pecked her cheek in a brotherly fashion then set off down the hall. "Well, hurry up, woman. I've never been the best man in a wedding, and I want to throw a bachelor party off the chain."

Joci pasted on her best exasperated expression until he turned around and vanished from view. Quinn wasn't wrong. She was a different person thanks to knowing Cameron. She headed to the elevator and waited while the button lit up. All the men in her life transformed her in one way or another. For the present, she would focus on learning about all her body would go through thanks to the constantly moving twins.

An hour and too many maternity pamphlets later, Joci ambled through the hospital, unsure which way would guide her to an exit. "I shouldn't have gone up here," she muttered, passing a coffee cart. As tempting as a cup of joe was, she couldn't afford the energy associated with the one cup of caffeine a day. The memory of her first delivery had faded over time, but the recent visit brought all those memories to surface.

The hospital staff was friendly and informative. "Too informative." Now she was immensely up to date on what would go down in each part of her body when the time came to birth the boys.

"Who knew sex could lead to ungodly pain?" she mumbled, scowling at the brochure about contractions.

"But it's fun when you're having it," a low rumble insinuated.

Startled at the abrupt insertion to her musings, the array of booklets fumbled from her hands. They happily scattered along the shiny white floor.

"Sorry, I didn't mean to frighten you," he continued, finally in view.

Staring at the slender build and red hair, Joci swallowed hard as he stooped down to pick up the lost scoundrels. "Derrick," she breathed, the name chilling her lips as it passed through them. *How the hell did he know I was here? This is weird.*

Derrick stacked the papers into a neat pile but didn't pass them over. "Hey, Joci."

Bubbles of unease shot through her gut when his green eyes pinned both feet to the tile. "What, um, what're you doing in the maternity wing?" The fact that she'd run into Derrick once again outside of the office made Joci's nerves bundle. There was no plausible way this was a coincidence. She hadn't planned on being here. Hell, she'd never run into her neighbor at the grocery store, so how could she see Derrick numerous times and not think he was following her? She couldn't. *Maybe Cam was right.*

Perusing their surroundings, he chuckled. "This is the private practice wing." He grabbed her elbow gently, and she snapped it out of reach. "Are you lost?"

Joci reviewed the signs on the doors and frowned. "Dammit, I wasn't paying attention to where I was going." She turned around a few times, but nothing looked familiar.

He chuckled. "Need a little help?"

Two thoughts crossed her mind. She could accept

Derrick's help or she could steer toward one of the nurses and ask them for directions. Glancing at the nurse currently wearing vomit on her scrubs, Joci opted for the former. Sneaking a glance to Derrick, she swallowed hard. He was friendly enough and didn't look like a serial stalker, but then again, some of his behaviors were straight from a psychology textbook. Serial stalkers were normal people with abnormal obsessions. She offered him a small smile and hoped she was wrong about her inclinations. Surely, the issues between Derrick and Cameron weren't volatile enough to include bodily harm. "I better or I'll be sleeping here tonight."

Derrick's rich laugh brimmed all the way to the ceiling. The sound instantly settled the worry lining her brow. She could listen to such a melody any time of day and never tire of it. It was harrowing, the way it resembled Adrian's. Almost as if he was still alive just in someone else's body. *And a semi-stalker. Right, so reasonable, Joci.*

"I wanted to apologize for the other day," he started. "Your fiancé and I have history and I let my temper get the better of me."

"Oh, well, I don't know everything about him. Part of life, I guess." She wouldn't accept his apology. There was too much she didn't know to forgive the disruption. Walking in step with him, Joci studied his profile. No facial hair lined his jaw—curious, though not uncommon for men with pale hair. His appearance was too put together for someone with an obvious limp. The sleuth side of her spurred questions to surface. "What happened to your leg?"

"Ah, noticed that, did you?" He patted the appendage. "Car accident of sorts."

Her recent skim with death from the same cause softened her observation of him. "I'm sorry. Those can be horrible."

His hand instinctively grazed the left side of his chest. Rubbing it slightly, he bobbed his head. "You have no idea."

"Are you all right?" she asked, taking in the side he was massaging. "Chest pains aren't usually a good sign."

His lips took on an amused expression, and he waved at a passing doctor. "Don't worry about me. I got a smidge of shrapnel in my chest during the incident."

"Oh wow." Joci's eyes widened.

Derrick nodded. "The piece is too close to a few vital organs, so my surgeon won't operate until either it shifts or becomes a death sentence."

Empathy inundated her mind. She couldn't imagine living through a car accident only to have a shard of the memory forever inside, slowly killing her. Sucking in her cheeks, she realized she was surviving a similar fate as the man beside her. Which was worse, she didn't know. "Is that why you're here?"

Steering them clear of a group of nurses, he replied, "Not today. One of those yearly checkups my doctor insists on."

Maintaining a steady walk and trying to determine if he was being truthful didn't go as well as she'd hoped when she tripped on the floor's slight incline.

Derrick's arms were around her in a split second, molding to her with ease. "I got you."

Grasping how close his mouth was to hers, she craned

her neck out of reach and attempted to joke. "Clumsy was never in my vocabulary until I got knocked up."

His eyes skittered across her lips. "You look perfect to me."

The hushed words combined with the mild tilt of her body he held tighter than any stranger would, compelled her neck backward. "You're sweet, but I'm, uh, fine."

The tangy tones of his cologne overwhelmed her senses, catapulting her to when Adrian wore the same scent. Other than being a completely different man and on her short list of clients who stalked her, Derrick was as close to Adrian as she could get. *What the hell am I thinking? No! He's magically at the hospital the same day you are? Not possible, Dorous. Get it together before he throws you over his shoulder and stuffs you in the trunk of a car.*

As if remembering they were in a public place, Derrick righted them, but didn't lose his hold on her arm. "Where to, madam?"

"Rayna! Crap! I forgot to call her for a ride." Joci cursed in silence. She should've left with Quinn instead of taking a tour. Somehow between running away from Cameron and running into Derrick, her day's course had deviated to unknown territory.

"I can give you a lift," he suggested, keeping his focus locked on the elevator as they neared it.

Joci hit the button and heard the machine whir to life, doors opening ten seconds later. The unease in her body skyrocketed at his seemingly friendly offer. "Thanks, but no. I'll just send Rayna a quick text and wait in the lobby."

"Aw, come on, Joci. It's not a big deal." He motioned for her to enter.

"I couldn't impose. I probably live on the other side of town." The last thing she wanted was this guy to know where she lived. Des Moines was getting smaller the longer she stayed here talking to him. Stepping inside, she almost turned toward the stairs when she noticed no one else was present in the metal box. "You know, maybe I should get some exercise and take—"

The doors clamped shut and they lurched into motion, the first-floor button shining bright orange. Standing in silence, Joci did her best not to stare at Derrick. On the one hand, he was good-looking even with the jagged scars on his arms. *And on the other, he's a psycho.* She cleared her throat, hoping the same would be done to her rampant thoughts. The air between them electrified and made steady breathing impossible. *If I die in this elevator with the guy Cam told me to stay away from, Cam's going to kill me.* She smirked at the thought and quickly sent a text message to Rayna. There was no way she was getting in any vehicle with Derrick.

"This isn't how I wanted to do this, but I can't control myself anymore," Derrick's hoarse words lingered in the air. He punched the emergency stop button, the lights flickering to a red glow.

"Wha—" Joci clammed up when his fingers lightly grasped her shoulders, enticing her eyes to him.

"Joci, you're a gorgeous woman. From the little time I've spent with you, I crave more." Derrick searched her face, looking for encouragement.

"Don't touch me," she rejected, her heartbeat thumping in her ears. She moved out of his reach and panicked when he stepped closer. "Please, just stay away from me." She reached for the panel, but couldn't connect. Cameron's face swam across her eyes, and she cursed herself for not listening to his plea. Even if Cameron didn't tell her about how he knew Derrick or Del Rossi cooking her books, she should've trusted his instincts and stayed as far away from Derrick as possible.

He straightened her frames, and she swore her heart stopped beating. The guy wasn't listening to her nor was he any further away. Immediately, she wrapped her hands over her large stomach. Horror films flashed through her mind at the possibility that this guy would kill her and steal her babies. She met his gaze and found it calm—the complete opposite of how she felt. Without a doubt, he was a creep and she was his prey. "Stay the fuck away from me," she yelled, shoving at his chest.

"Right. Sorry." Derrick stepped backward. "Since the accident, I swore to be more forthright with my feelings. You deserve to hear how incredible you are every single day."

What the fuck? Who does this guy think he is? Her stomach rolled with a mixture of anxiety and stress, the twins surprisingly quiet. She shouldn't say another syllable. Remaining mute until the elevator settled on level ground was the safest move. If she made it out of there alive, she swore to never doubt Cameron's judgment again.

When she reached for the knob to resume their descent, Derrick swiped her hand away and her stomach dropped. The guy wasn't giving up, and she was stuck in a confined place. He could do anything to her and no one would know until it was too late. Pushing her against the unyielding metal wall, Derrick's lips collided with hers. Fear gripped her muscles and she couldn't move. The only thing going through her mind was how to escape. She'd attended several self-defense classes, but none of the teachings made it to her brain. She was motionless when all she wanted to do was scream. She shoved at Derrick's chest, and he stumbled backward. "What the hell are you doing?" Tears slid down her cheeks, but he didn't seem to care.

"Joci, you and I have more in common than you realize." He paused, as if trying to remember something.

She wiped her mouth then eyes and moved out of his reach. "The hell we do. I'm not a creep who stalks people then kisses them after they say to stay away."

Derrick held up his hands and advanced toward her. "I'm not a stalker." He sounded convincing enough even to her own ears, but she knew better.

"Yeah, okay, that's what every stalker says." She reached for the emergency button, but he slid his body in the way.

"I can't let you do that."

Joci yanked out her cell phone, heart sinking when no signal bars were available. *Shit.* Her knees shook at the seriousness in his voice. "Are you going to kill me?"

"What? No, I'd never do that." He grabbed her arm, but she yanked it away. They just kept going round and round the elevator. It was like a sick roller coaster she couldn't stop. "I care deeply for you."

Her brows furrowed together. "You have a funny way of showing me."

"Look, it wasn't supposed to happen like this. I never wanted you to be uncomfortable with me."

"Too late." She tried to control her erratic breathing. She ran her hands over her throat, anxious to be done with this situation. She couldn't reach the exit without him blocking her, and he didn't seem to want to change his mind about letting her leave.

"What's that?" he asked, pointing to her neck.

Joci's hands fumbled over the chain. "My necklace."

He moved closer and snatched the necklace out of her grip. "A class ring." He met her gaze. "And not yours either." He tilted his head to the right, as if trying to determine where he knew it from.

"N-no it was my ex-husband's." Seeing him distracted by the ring, she kicked his shin and elbowed his gut. Derrick reeled back in pain, giving her enough time to break free and hit the emergency knob. The elevator sprang to life, and within seconds, the double doors opened.

Joci rushed out of the elevator, heart racing. If she wasn't so pregnant, she'd run. Speed walking would have to do to get as many feet away from Derrick as possible.

"Joci, you can't hide from me." His confidence unnerved her.

"Who the hell are you?" she asked, glancing around for a security guard or someone else to get help from.

A sad smile spread over his face, the brilliant whiteness of his straight teeth nearly blinding her. "I can't tell you yet. You're upset and need more time."

Joci shook her head. "I'm never talking to you again. Stay away from me."

"Aw, Joci, you're cute. I'm never letting you out of my sight, even if you ask nicely." He jerked his head toward the exit. "I'll see you at our appointment next week. I'm looking forward to going over my defense."

She gripped her cell phone and dialed Rayna. Calling the police would've been better, but she needed to know Derrick's connection to Cameron before she got them involved. "I think I'll transfer your file to my partner for now on."

"No. I paid for you, and I'm going to get you, not some redhead," he said flatly.

Joci's nostrils flared, and she stepped closer to him. Lowering her voice, she warned, "Come near me again, and I'll get a restraining order."

He smirked. "What about the other part."

"What're you talking about?" She clenched her hand into a fist. "What other part?"

Derrick licked his bottom lip. "The kiss. Will you get a restraining order on me if I kiss you again?" He leaned over and tucked her hair behind her ear. "Because I know you enjoyed it."

Fury consumed Joci's body. Before she could stop to think, she swung her hand and slapped him across the side of his face. She didn't even feel bad when the sharp sound echoed in the hallway or when a nurse stopped talking to look their way. "You son of a bitch. If I see you ever again, I'll do more than ask a judge for a protective order."

Not put off by her slap, he laughed. "Like what? You'll ask your mob fiancé to take me out?"

All similarities between Derrick and Adrian flew out the window. Adrian would never treat her like this. He was an asshole, but not one who would endanger her. Straightening her shoulders, she gave him a side look. "Maybe I will."

Derrick narrowed his eyes. "Have it your way. Goodnight, Ms. Dorous."

On shaky legs, Joci waited until the lanky man disappeared from her sight. Cradling the swell of her babies, she plopped into one of the seats in the waiting area. Calming her pulse was harder than she expected. *Cam was right. Derrick's bad news. I should've listened to him.* Her phone dinged, and she read the text from Rayna. Cursing her friend's timing, she pushed out of the chair and hobbled toward the sliding doors. Once outside, she was grateful Rayna's car was waiting near the awning. Getting rained on after the day she'd just had would be the clincher to her dismal mood.

"Hey, thanks for coming to get me," she said, climbing inside.

Rayna flashed her a grin. "Anything for my roomie." Her brows furrowed when Joci didn't return the smile. "Hey, are you okay? You don't look so good."

"Not really, but I don't want to talk about it." Buckling the seat belt, Joci couldn't understand what happened in the hospital. Even though she wanted to tell someone about the elevator fiasco, she couldn't yet. She needed to figure out who Derrick was and why he was stalking her. Surely, an old rivalry with Cameron wasn't worth scaring her half to death. Then again, if Derrick was involved with a mob like she assumed, anything was possible.

CHAPTER FIFTEEN

Sloshing the melted ice cubes in the kitchen sink, Cameron rested his forearms against the steel tub. The Mikkelsen crew was getting gutsy. They tailed him wherever he went. He'd managed to lose the black sedan after ten minutes of intense driving, but still he checked out the curtains every so often to see if someone was sitting outside in the driveway. Whenever he looked, he spotted the two men Del Rossi had sent to prevent altercations. While he was grateful for the extra help, he couldn't handle his own home potentially being under fire at any given moment.

Cameron marched to the living room, a football game competing with the air conditioner for the noisiest sound. It was another crazy hot day in the fall, and he didn't think he'd ever get used to the mood swings from Iowa's weather patterns. His phone lit up with a message, but he was disappointed when it was Jerry, not Joci, on the other end. Deciding calling was a better use of his time, he dialed the one of two numbers he cared to memorize. "Any news on J.J.'s whereabouts?"

"And a good evening to you as well," Jerry replied with a cackle.

If Cameron's fists didn't ache from the last week on patrol, he'd slam them into his boss's gut. He didn't have time for games. He needed answers. *And Joci.* He desperately needed to hear her voice and kiss her soft lips. "My evening isn't going well, Jer."

Jerry clucked his tongue to his teeth. "Well, then it's a good thing I have news." He paused for the dramatic effect Cameron loathed in the man. "J.J. was spotted near the small airport in Ankeny two nights ago. He was on a private jet that was unloaded shortly after landing."

"He's running drugs," he put together. If narcotics were being streamed through a city fifteen miles north, they were already in the capital.

"I assumed as much, so I had my men follow him to a warehouse off Martin Luther King Jr. Parkway. I'd bet it's their main distribution center."

Picturing the street, Cameron muted the television. "It's the perfect spot. With the bus stop nearby and the road running all the way to Des Moines airport, J.J. will get plenty of business."

"A couple of my guys are staking the place out in case he makes a move detrimental to our plan." Jerry coughed over the line, losing his employee's interest.

Business first used to be Cameron's mantra. Not these days. Not when his heart might be ripped from his chest before he made amends with the woman who kept it beating.

"Any update on Adrian? I'm surprised he hasn't stolen

your lady yet."

That got Cameron's attention. He rubbed a tired hand over his brow. "Adrian's smart. He's biding his time. He said as much when I saw him." Sagging into the love seat currently missing the love, he half-heartedly followed the sports game. "He was chumming up to her last I knew, which isn't helping my situation at all."

"*A chi dai il dito si prende anche il braccio*," Jerry rattled off the old Italian proverb. It was one Cameron had heard on day one of his association with the tycoon. It was as true now as it was during any part of the Del Rossi mob boot camp.

"Give them a finger and they'll take an arm," Cameron regurgitated in English. "He'll take more than my arm if I give him the opening."

"Cameroni, I've known you long enough to be blunt. My life isn't filled with love because I chose this path."

"But I didn't choose it," Cameron argued.

"*Di preciso*," Jerry jumped in. "I accepted you in the mafia because you are a fighter and you get the job done no matter the price. I don't know what this fight will cost you, but the family will continue to have your back."

Cameron bit his lower lip. "Is this supposed to be psyching me up for something, because I'm not feeling the good vibes."

"No." Jerry laughed. "The opposite in fact. You need to decide how much trouble Joci is worth. Clearly Adrian pulled out all the stops to get her back in his bed, so what will you do?"

He sat in silence, the words wreaking mayhem on his emotions. If this question was presented a year ago, he wouldn't have budged for a woman. But Joci wasn't just any random hookup. She was the other half of his soul. He didn't buy into the whole soul mates bit, but she was as close as he'd ever get to it. Shaking his head briskly, he answered, "Joci is my everything."

"Then dig deep into the criminal side, son, you're going to need it."

Not liking the sound of the truth, Cameron hung up and rested his head on the cushion. Crossing the invisible line he'd set for himself wouldn't be easy if he dove back into Del Rossi full-time. It would take a whole lot of motivation if he ever wanted to return to the other side.

***

Eyeballing the tumbler of aged scotch slowly sweating on to the napkin, Joci bit down hard on her straw leading to a virgin margarita. "You're killing me," she complained when Rayna took a long sip of her favorite liquor.

Rayna flicked her auburn hair out of her eyes. "You told me to get it."

"I know, and now I hate you a little for it." Joci took another drink of her strawberry smoothie and perused the bar. It wasn't too busy, but happy hour specials started in ten minutes, so the place would pick up. "I haven't been here in forever," she confessed. The bar was one of two she used to work at. Some days she missed the upbeat crowds, though mostly she missed the stories from the patrons. They kept her occupied when life was messy. If she ever needed a distraction, it was now.

"Me either." Rayna waved at a fellow lawyer. "Be right back. I have a case with her tomorrow."

Joci watched her friend move to a corner booth, her mind spinning with the recent events. She'd pulled out a win for her client charged with possession of a controlled substance earlier in the day, hence the celebratory, though unsatisfying, trip to 69 Taps. The rush of adrenaline from her success coursed in her veins even now, maintaining her high.

Bobbing her leg up and down under the table, she clenched the straw tighter. Immediately following the judge's ruling, Joci's first instinct had been to call Cameron and share her victory. They weren't there yet. Hell, they weren't even texting each other. *No, I take it back. He texts me. I don't respond.* It wasn't that she didn't want to. Talking to him would solve the bulk of her heartache. She still hadn't told anyone about what happened in the elevator with Derrick. She tried to push it away and ignore the situation. It didn't work, especially when she'd wake up in a cold sweat after dreaming of the different paths the attack could've led to.

Rayna's boisterous laughter filled the hole-in-the-wall pub, and Joci smirked at her partner's antics. She'd been a lifesaver these last weeks. Thus far, their shared residence hadn't caused too many rifts in their relationship, though her welcome was dwindling.

Slurping the drink, Joci turned her mind to another subject. Winning cases caused a domino effect on her body.

It always did. After shoving a disposition up the State's ass, her skin tingled for a man's touch. It was easier when she and Adrian were together. He'd willingly sneak her pants off no matter the location. When they split up, she'd had Quinn to scratch the proverbial itch.

Crossing her legs, Joci licked her top lip. All she wanted was rough, primal sex with the man who'd worship each swell of her body. There was only one man who fit the bill: Cameron. She'd craved Cameron every single moment of the day since she hiked to Rayna's. It wasn't wrong, but she felt guilty when her fingers hovered over her cell phone on his phone number. She couldn't fuck then duck out with him. He owned too much of her essence to allow a one-time satisfaction. Once she felt his tattooed flesh mingled with the delicateness of hers, she'd forget his secretive acts.

Those feelings were foreign no matter how long she attempted to dissect them. The one concept she kept coming back to was that they had a predestined link. Rolling her eyes at the gibberish, Joci concentrated on the other patrons. A couple locals she recognized from when she bartended were chummed up with the barkeep, as if they owned their seats.

A flash of red hair caught her eye, but the woman sporting the long locks wasn't Derrick. Sloshing the straw up and down in the tall cup, Joci reflected over her week. After Rayna took over his case, she was grateful when they didn't have any communication. Cameron had a reason for not liking him, and he wasn't wrong either. Derrick was part of the reason she and Cameron had fought at the coffee shop. *I should've listened to Cam.* She shook her head. *I'm such an idiot sometimes.*

The side door opened, summoning her attention. Taking in the person who walked into the dim lighting, Joci beamed as she stood. "Jeremy Schroeder?"

The attractive man with a hairstyle rivaling a young Justin Bieber's met her gaze. "Joci Dorous, as I live and breathe." He crossed the floor and stopped when his brown eyes dipped to her stomach. "Well lookie here, somebody went and got fat," he teased.

She casually hugged him, smacking the back of his head as they disconnected. "Pregnant with twins, jerk face, not fat."

He pulled back and reviewed her. "Seriously? Twins? Damn, you look amazing for carrying two kids around. Gwen was enormous with one." His eyes grew wide. "Don't tell her I said that. She'll put me on diaper duty for a year."

Joci sat and Rayna's seat was filled by Jeremy. "Gwen, huh? You finally took the plunge and expressed your undying affection?"

Jeremy's face broke into a giddy smile. "Yeah. It happened in a messy donut and coma oriented sort of way, but she's officially my wife."

"We'll circle back to the coma and donut part, but I'm happy for you. And a baby too! You've made quite the honest woman out of her."

Jeremy waved at the bartender and within seconds, a tumbler of scotch was in Jeremy's hand. He took a sip and held up two fingers. "Technically, two. One's on the way."

"Wow, that's awesome."

"Thanks. I'm happy about it." He loosened the gold tie. "Still kicking ass in the criminal realm?"

"Of course. And you're somehow managing corporate USA?"

He nodded. "It pays well and I like it, so yeah."

Taking a bite of the strawberry garnishing her cup, Joci was glad they'd stopped by. She hadn't seen Jeremy in years. They'd gone to law school together, but ran in different circles. If he hadn't been so infatuated with Gwendolyn Smidt during study groups, Joci would've thrown her hat in the ring for the slightly nerdy but extremely striking man.

"I take it you moved on after Adrian's death?"

The babies started kicking her stomach and she giggled. "Yes and no. These rascals are Adrian's."

Jeremy's eyebrows shot up. "Really? Wow. I thought after the divorce and your...." He stopped.

"We worked closely toward the end of last year." She wiped her fingers on a napkin. "One thing leads to another, as you obviously know."

"I'm glad you have two someones to remember him by then." A phone rang from his jacket pocket. "Better get this. Gwen's due anytime."

Joci waved him on as he hopped up, sweetly speaking to his wife. Sighing at the lovestruck expression on his face, she wondered if Cameron ever wore the same when they spoke.

"Who's the guy?" Rayna inquired, returning to the table.

"Jeremy Schroeder. We went to Drake together and

hung out a few times."

Rayna adjusted her low-cut blouse. "I could get into the sexy vibe he has going."

"He's married." Her friend shrugged, so she added, "Happily. Very, very happily married."

"Aw, well damn. You need to steer me in the direction of your single hottie friends." A fresh drink appeared at their table, and Rayna made quick work of it. "Because I could use a friend with benefits."

"What about Quinn?" Joci suggested, snagging a chip from the recently delivered nachos. Carbs were her best friend as of late, a reminder Quinn tossed her way whenever they crossed paths.

The auburn beauty queen scrunched her nose. "Quinn? Nah. Girl code and all. It wouldn't be right."

Joci popped a jalapeño in her mouth. "Believe me when I say Quinn is all yours." She handed a chip loaded with cheese and two kinds of meat to her friend. "You have my nacho cheese blessing."

Accepting the gift, Rayna lunged it to her mouth. "We'll see," she mumbled between munches.

Jeremy returned as they stuffed another load of chips between their teeth. "Those look incredible," he stated, practically drooling at the nachos. "But I should head out. Guess who's picking up baby food? Yeah, me." He leaned down and gave Joci a hug. "I hope things work out with whoever your new guy is. He's lucky to be part of your life."

"Aww, oh my God, are you sure I can't steal you?"

Rayna gushed from the other side of the table.

Joci ignored her and nodded. "Thanks. You too."

He tossed a ten-dollar bill on the table. "We should all get together sometime and catch up with our spouses."

Joci bit her tongue. Discussing her situation with Cameron wasn't one she wanted to have with Jeremy or anyone else.

Jeremy smiled at a few more people as he skirted through the now booming tavern. "He's a dreamboat," Rayna sighed.

"You have no idea."

They finished their appetizers before ordering more. As the night went on, Joci discovered she had a new role in Rayna's life while pregnant: designated driver.

***

"I don't mean to be a drag, but do we have an expiration date on how long you're going to crash on my couch?" Rayna appeared in the doorway of Joci's office, distracting her from the probation stipulation she was drafting. "Should I go buy a bed for the spare room or what?"

Saving the document, Joci rolled her chair out from under the desk. Two weeks had gone by since the coffeehouse fiasco and not a word had been shared between her and Cameron. She commended him for giving her space, but secretly, she wished he'd bother her. "No, you can hold off swiping your new American Express card," she replied, pulling herself up. The consistent weight gain worried her yoga pants, but she was carrying twins, so the doctor wasn't concerned. Patting the playful duo, she sauntered to the printer and grabbed the papers there.

"Have you made a decision about when to confront him so you guys can be a disgustingly adorable couple again?" Rayna asked blocking the exit. Joci wouldn't be escaping this conversation no matter how badly she wanted to.

"Not exactly. I'm working on it."

"Two weeks, Joci. Seriously?" Rayna let out an annoyed huff. "Don't make me call in the big guns."

"Who? Quinn?" She snorted. "Pretty sure he's been tampered with."

"Hmm, you may be right." The younger attorney snapped her fingers. "I'll investigate."

Joci held in a chuckle until her friend cleared the room. She was suspiciously too eager to volunteer to spend time with the rugged police officer. Once upon a star, so would she.

Returning to the monitor, she opened the accounting file. Ever since their fight, Joci had stayed late several nights a week, pouring over the figures. Navigating the deposits, she pressed her lips together as she read the names out loud. The majority were well-known stocks, but there was a new deposit that was an outlier since she and Quinn met.

Expanding the screen, she scratched her nose. "Who are you?" She tapped the PC on the stock description "ADP." It was the name of a finance company in West Des Moines, so she'd never given it any thought before today. "Automatic data processing, right?" She couldn't be sure since she didn't think the accountant used that particular company. Curious, she opened the entry and reviewed a string of letter, numbers, and symbols in the description. "Hmm, this is odd." She clicked on the description and studied it. A distant memory surfaced from her years with Adrian. They used to joke about encryption codes and ways to send messages so no one else could see. "No way."

Linking over to a decryption website, she copied the line and waited for the computer to generate a response. Her hand tremored at the note jumping off the screen. Blinking until she was sure her eyelashes were going to fall off, Joci pinched her arm to be positive she wasn't hallucinating.

"I'm still here," she read aloud. Her voice wavered as she passed over the initials. "A.D.P. It isn't the company. I'm such an idiot. Adrian Derrick Petosa."

Her mouth fell open, and she gasped for air. "Oh. My. God," she repeated as if he'd appear. The real world crept into her the longer she sat there like a big mouth bass. "No, he would've made himself known." She lowered her gaze to the massive bulge under her shirt. "Wouldn't he?" The boys within didn't respond.

The landline rang, making her shriek. Seeing the caller ID as "anonymous," she felt her pulse skyrocket as she refused to answer. Too many instances it was a client calling collect from prison.

Patting her chest to slow her heart, a wayward thought crossed her brain. *At the hospital, Derrick didn't want to tell me who he was. What if he's…?* She couldn't finish the thought. It was a long shot and made her throat dry at the possibility, but she had to figure it out. Credible evidence was what she needed now. She hustled to Rayna's office and yanked out Derrick's red file and perused the police report. *It's not signed.* She studied the back then front and saw another string of letters, numbers, and symbols. *Why didn't I see this before?* It was in the section with the traffic violation code, but hadn't caught her attention until just then. Pasting the line into the computer, she didn't have to wait long for the phrase to pop up.

If you figured this out, know I love you no matter what.

Tears sprinted down her cheeks until they landed on the note. "Adrian. Oh God, Adrian." She fumbled for the phone and dialed the number in Derrick's folder. As it rang, her stomach balled into a giant knot. If what she believed was true, Derrick was Adrian and vice versa. Somehow his face was altered to disguise the fact. The numerous run-ins she'd feared were stalking drifted across her memory. *Not exactly the best way to let a girl know you're alive, dumbass.*

"You reached me. Leave a message," the voice mail answered, but she hung up instead of leaving her information. She wanted to believe it wasn't a farce, yet it meant Adrian had stayed distant for some reason.

"But why?" She reworked her time with Derrick—no, Adrian, maybe—and pressed her fingers to the bridge of her nose. "Cameron didn't like him. It makes sense if he knew. I thought he seemed familiar." She frowned. "Still, why would he act like a stalker and scare me instead of telling me who he was?" She didn't like the thought of Adrian changing so drastically, but then again, *if* it was Adrian and not some mob scheme, he wasn't the same. Showing up at all the places she was made sense. He knew her routine as well as she did. To him, it wasn't stalking. Hauling her purse out of the chair, Joci rushed to the door. She didn't know what the whole story was, but she needed to find out. And fast.

***

He wasn't expecting the fist to come flying, but it hit him straight in the nose. "Bastard," he griped, locking the perpetrator in a headlock. The man scurried free after elbowing Cameron in the groin. Any man would've done the same, but being on the other end of a good ballbuster wasn't the best part of any day. The criminal got a whole ten feet before Quinn tackled him. Hard, if the loud oomph from the man was any indicator.

Wiping his face, Cameron's anger boiled over at the sight of the guy who just wouldn't stay down. The two officers had been wrestling the ginormous man off and on since following up on a robbery call.

"Grab the stun gun. I have a feeling we'll need it," Quinn grunted, pinning the man under his knees.

Cameron snagged the weapon and held it at the ready. The night had been going great until they ran into this douche at sunup. Now as they neared the end of the shift, all he wanted to do was crawl into bed and spoon Joci until her alarm went off. But he couldn't do that with an empty bed. "All set," he remarked, so his partner pulled the burglar to his feet.

Quinn paraded their catch to the back of the car. "Got a nice couple of shiners," he commented, slamming the door.

Holstering the gun, Cameron glanced at his reflection in the car window. His face held a black right eye and bruising to the left side. Those plus the coinciding blood drops dotting his septum made Cameron resemble the man he was five years ago, a thug deep within the mob's grip. He ran a hand over his stubbly jaw and sighed. Life without Joci was returning to shit at a pace alarming even him. "We've had a rough couple of weeks," he said at last. "You're welcome, by the way, for taking the brunt of the lowlife's punches."

"More like you raced headfirst into every fight we encountered," Quinn scoffed. He radioed their location to dispatch then concluded, "I'm surprised the only stitches you needed were from the hooligans who jumped you."

Cameron folded his sunglasses. "Just trying to save your pretty face."

"Dick."

"Prick." Cameron smirked, an act which caused more pain than expected. He didn't want to recall the busted lip received the other day.

"You sure you're going to be all right?" Quinn asked. "You might want to get your face looked at. Maybe more stitches are in order."

Shrugging off his friend's warranted concern, he snuck behind the steering wheel. "I'll survive. A lot is on my plate. You know that."

Latching in beside him, Quinn guzzled from the water bottle. "Let's hit the station, then head home. I'm ready to sleep for two days." His neck rested against the headrest and he closed his eyes. "Maybe sneak in a little action if I can manage it."

Pressing on the gas, Cameron silently agreed. Sleep plus sex was the ultimate goal on his list for the upcoming days off. One he was certain he'd achieve, the other was up in the air.

Checking on Quinn, he noticed the man usually on his phone was halfway asleep. Cameron's heavy eyelids begged for slumber, but he wouldn't relent. The last few days, he'd spent kissing mafia ass after yelling at Jerry about J.J. and Adrian. The man was manageable when it came to finding the Mikkelsen stench, but less so when it came to aiding in a reckoning with Joci. The mob boss desired her as the counsel of record, contingent upon her acceptance, naturally. Then and only then would the man relent his disinterest. Cameron knew better than to take him at his word, yet their options dwindled the longer Adrian remained aloof.

The car eased down First Street, the station on the horizon. It should be a welcome sight, but all it did was twist the knife deeper in his gut. Playing both sides of the law wasn't easy or desirable. He'd made a deal with Del Rossi in the hospital, and he meant to keep his end of the bargain. In another few years, he'd be free and clear of it all. *Unless something else happens before then, that is.*

"Have you heard from her?"

Turning to his right, Cameron found Quinn with green eyes set straight ahead, the final stretch until a weekend luring the man awake. They hadn't broached the subject of the hazel-eyed attorney. "Um, no. I sent text messages at the beginning. She didn't respond, so I stopped." He pulled into the parking lot. "It's more of an in-person discussion anyhow."

The felon in the back seat smashed his head against the window, and Quinn blindly smacked the space behind him. Cameron would never get over criminals' belief that they could bash through the thick material that could withstand a bullet. Often the acts led to hospital visits prior to booking. It made for more paperwork, but was a bit humorous too.

"If I've learned anything about Joci, she leads with her emotions." Quinn picked at the scab on his forearm, a reminder from their arrest earlier in the week. "Hell, you would know. She juggled Adrian and me while you stole her heart." He gave Cameron a disgusted glare. "You're an asshole for that in case you weren't aware."

"Emotions, yeah. I'm not super with those." He blatantly skipped over the rest and shot his pal a grin. He may have revealed Adrian's ghost and Quinn dragged the mob details out of him, but he didn't want to talk about any of that right now. Part of him refused to accept the whole facial reconstruction bit. It'd be simple for Adrian to win her over if he sported war wounds.

"Well, you're about to figure it out in a hurry."

Knitting his brows together, he followed Quinn's wave to the other end. "Shit." He swung into an open parking spot, a lump growing in his throat.

"Good lucky, buddy. I'll book the drooling jackass." He patted Cameron's shoulder then stepped out of the car.

Following at a slower rate, Cameron observed the exchange between the exes.

"Hey, Joci. You're looking roly-poly these days," Quinn greeted with a bright smile.

Joci flashed a friendly grin to the retreating officer while Cameron scanned her. It seemed her belly had grown even more since last he held her. The dark circles beneath her eyes disturbed him. Judging from the flowing purple paisley button-up shirt and jeans, she wasn't on her way to work.

With stiff muscles, he moved in her direction. His heartbeat echoed in his ears. When at last he was in front of the pregnant enchantress, the sun crested behind her, blinding him in more ways than one. The comforting scent of coffee laced in strawberries made his mouth water and his hands itch to reach out for her.

"I haven't slept since I watched you drive away, Joce," he confided, barely above a whisper. "I was a complete idiot for getting you messed up with Del Rossi and not telling you about it."

Her brown hair was damp as though recently washed and held a hint of wave at the ends. The breeze wafted another fragrance his way and the cocoa on her skin tormented him. After she'd showered was one of his favorite times to sample her impeccable skin.

He searched her face but she focused on her pink slippers. She never wore those, so her normal shoes must be out of commission due to the swollen piggies. He cursed himself for not being there to rub her feet to lessen a small portion of her load. "I should've left Iowa and taken you away from all this." His voice cracked. "I should've done a lot of things different."

The top of her black-rimmed glasses came into view from behind her wispy hair. One nod was all she graced him with.

Gripping the back of his shoulder, Cameron refrained from letting a string of curses fly. She was stubborn, but he wouldn't love her any other way. "I don't know what else you want me to say." He paused. The corner of her mouth twitched into a tiny frown, momentarily bolstering his grit until she spoke.

"How long have you known Adrian is alive?" she asked.

Twenty pounds of regret socked him in the abdomen, and he took a backward step to steady himself. "You know?"

Joci snapped her eyes to him. "How long?" She stressed the syllables, grinding them into oblivion.

He let out a breath. "A while."

Massaging her temples, Joci groaned. "You thought I'd want him back."

"It crossed my mind, yeah," Cameron admitted.

A disappointed pout crossed her lips, and she fiercely shook her head. "You had doubts about my feelings for you."

"You did too," he barked, his soul ripping apart. He knew where their chat was leading. He'd been down this particular lane many times. The destination was always the same.

"You know what? I did for one stupid minute." She crossed her arms over her chest. "And then I realized that was ridiculous because I have an imperfect man who is perfect for me. What hurt was when you hid several crucial tidbits I have a right to know." She jerked her chin to her stomach. "*They* have a right to know."

Cameron held up his hands to thwart her attack. "You're right. I was wrong to keep so much from you, but, Joci, I was trying to help." She opened her mouth to argue, so he sped up his justification. He pointed to the distance. "That guy isn't Adrian. Not the same one you loved. Something happened when the bomb went off. You can't trust him."

Joci clenched her jaw. "I'm about ready to say fuck the both of you and take the next flight to Edinburgh."

"If it's what you want, I'll support you, but for the love of God, wait until we catch J.J. to travel the globe." His radio echoed a theft code, and he flipped the device off. Helping her escape him wasn't ideal, but he loved her enough to do it, if she truly desired to run.

"J.J.'s alive too?" Horror flashed on her features, and she instinctively cradled her stomach. Her eyes grew wide as the pieces seemed to fall into place. "Adrian's working for J.J., isn't he?"

Cameron cleared his throat. "Yep, he is. My guess is the Mikkelsen mob offered Adrian a trade of sorts since he orchestrated a hit on me."

"He did what?" Joci's face turned a lethal color, but she didn't move. "Why didn't you tell me?"

He took in her anxious brow, and pasted on a brave smile. "Because I'm supposed to keep you safe, not the other way around, babe."

"Is that what happened to your face? Did someone try to hurt you?" Joci asked, moving closer to him.

He rubbed the base of his neck and answered, "Somewhere along those lines, yeah."

A grimace covered her lips, whether worry or anger, he wasn't sure, but the tremor in her voice matched the one vibrating in his. Her nose scrunched ever so slightly, and he held in a groan. What he needed was a cold shower to erase the night's events. Instead, as the humidity rose between them, his body craved the opposite.

A squad car flashed their lights at them, and Cameron waved to the fellow officer getting off shift. "I won't pretend my heart isn't collapsing among the falling leaves, but I also won't rush you." He unbuttoned the top three buttons of his uniform and untucked the shirt. "You're worth waiting for now just as much as twenty years ago." He fished out his keys. "But I'd rather not be on the hook for another twenty years. There's too much life I want to live with you."

Though it pained him to leave the conversation undone, he turned toward the building. Halfway to the door, he heard Joci's demanding voice. It stopped him in his tracks, like every other time.

"Jerry will know how to fix this, won't he?" she asked.

He shrugged, not entirely wanting to answer, but he did anyway. "Possibly."

"Then take me to see the son of a bitch."

CHAPTER SIXTEEN

Calming her hysteria would've been simpler if Cameron didn't look so damned attractive. Sneaking a peek at him, Joci licked her dry lips at the way his hair tossed in the wind, thanks to the open car window. He'd shed his uniform at the station and sported a pair of deep blue cargo pants and a gray T-shirt with "police" scribbled in bold navy. Coupling his attire with the dark bruises on his arms, neck, and face with his vivid tattoos, her fingers itched to tear away the space between them and reassert their relationship. Yet she couldn't. *Adrian.* He was the mist who settled around her before she noticed.

Her goal for the morning was to harass Cameron until he broke about his mob involvement. She hadn't expected his meek yet firm plea for forgiveness. It was why she couldn't let him disappear into the sunrise. Her body ached to be near him in only the dirtiest of ways, but she'd settle for only the center console separating them. Not having his touch for two long weeks coiled her inner spring like no other. She needed even a simple embrace from Cameron to satisfy her these days. He was the most lethal drug, and her veins thirsted for him.

Her eyes disobeyed and slanted his direction. *Shit, bad idea.* With one arm lounged on the steering wheel of his Jeep, shirt plastered to the sculpted pecs, and the sun bouncing off his brown hair, Cameron epitomized every facet of her dream man. Even Adrian had paled the multitude of times she'd compared them at night when she lay awake with no one beside her. It was wrong, but she couldn't help it. Discovering that Adrian tricked her into believing he was Derrick then stalked her for months made her glad she told him to fuck off. Adrian wasn't the same guy anymore. There was something fundamentally wrong with him. Forgiving him for the fear he'd instilled wouldn't happen. At least not for years to come.

She fidgeted in the passenger seat of the brand new black Grand Cherokee, a gift from Jerry. Thrusting aside her enmity for the mobster, Joci interlaced her fingers together and fixed her gaze on the passing houses. If she didn't distract herself, she was liable to reach over and do something Cameron didn't deserve yet.

Forgiving him had occurred the instant he finished his little dialogue. *How could I not?* He wasn't perfect in any fashion, but he was the man she thought about most during the day and dreamt of during the lonely nights. She wasn't going to yank her heart out no matter what he did. Bandage it, yes, obliterate it, no.

The vehicle eased to a stop at an intersection, Cameron's dark eyes fixed on the traffic light. He exhaled loudly.

Staring at him, Joci remembered the incident with Derrick. *No, Adrian.* She wouldn't get used to that until the man acted more like the Adrian she knew. *I need to tell Cam.* Her stomach wasn't a fan of the thought, and she couldn't disagree. Their relationship, though old, was fragile. She wasn't certain how he'd react to the knowledge of her ex forcefully kissing her.

Joci crossed her ankles, affectionately referred to as cankles by Rayna. They pulled into a ritzy hotel parking lot and she shot him a leery look. Trusting Cameron would take time. They both needed to establish the bond between them again. She didn't want to be without him, yet being with him was perilous to her health as much as his.

"Maybe let me talk to Jerry first," Cameron instructed, retrieving the keys. "You're pissed and rightly so, but Jerry isn't a fan of being yelled at."

"What's he going to do, Cam? He already owns you," she growled, a teeny bit guilty of the tone. She scurried out of the car toward the beefy bodyguard at the entrance. It didn't take a rocket scientist to deduce someone important was nearby. The place was crawling with black-clad man-cakes.

"Joci," Cameron's voice held warning when she sailed through the invisible line beyond the guard.

She didn't stop but checked over her shoulder to see him speaking in hushed tones with the man. In all honesty, she was stunned the guy hadn't clotheslined her. Following the smell of fresh marinara sauce, Joci found the leader of the Del Rossi mafia in a private room off the kitchen. Hotel staff flitted about, dutiful in their attention to the chubby warlord. "Bernard, we need to chat," she announced, barreling into the room lit with candles.

The tubby man held up his fork and knit his eyebrows together. "No Jer-bear today, eh? Must be important." He pointed to the empty chair at the table. "Have a seat, Ms. Dorous."

"I'd rather stand." She huffed and tried to hide the fact that her lively jaunt in her condition had been foolish. Given the expression on the Italian's face, he knew it as well as she.

A hand on her lower back persuaded her otherwise. She hadn't noticed Jerry's security guard in the room until then. "He said sit."

Instead of fighting the short mobster with a gun tucked in his belt, Joci plopped into the seat.

Jerry held up a bowl of linguini. "Hungry?"

Who the hell eats pasta for breakfast? The twins flipped at the tantalizing aroma, but she refrained. "You used my law firm to launder money."

Setting down the food, he smirked. "This is why you and Cameroni are an ideal match. No bullshit, just business." He smirked toward the doorway. Curiosity won over and she followed his gaze. "Aren't I right?"

Cameron shoved his hands behind his back, posture pin straight. "Yes."

The difference in him astounded her. Here, Cameron was a submissive soldier to the enforcer. Frowning, she hated to see her malleable man as cozy as a board.

"We were new to Iowa, you see," Jerry continued. "And our accountant was in need of a business to ghost for a while." He dunked a breadstick lathered with garlic in a bowl of marinara. "He'll clear out your accounts within the day."

Astonished at the complacent explanation, Joci studied the bejeweled fingers of the man. "Oh, okay, thank you." She eyed Cameron, and he jerked his head toward the exit. His boss spoke up before either could move.

"I hear you found out about Adrian," Jerry said without preamble.

Nodding once, she waited for him to get to the point. The man liked to dance around conversations, whereas she'd rather see the gritty details up front and deal with them.

"What do you think about it?" the mobster asked.

Joci gathered her hair behind a shoulder. "I think I want proof it's him. Obviously, anyone can alter records when it comes to my business." She shot him a malicious smile. "I'm an attorney. I like evidence before I convict."

Chuckling low, the Italian patted her hand. "Believe me, when my bookkeeper saw the data entry from the other day, he was as baffled as you."

"What entry?" Cameron chimed in, his intonation beyond concerned.

"You haven't told him?" Jerry made a tsk sound with his teeth.

Immediately vexed, she glued her eyes to the pasta buffet. "We haven't talked much lately."

"Now, that is a disappointment." He clapped his hands,

and a man showed up with a laptop. "As to your proof, see for yourself, Ms. Dorous. We didn't tamper with the funds deposited by the elusive ADP."

Snatching the computer, she scoured the screen for traces of shenanigans. True to his word, the mob couldn't fiddle with the data if they tried.

Jerry continued, "We traced the funds to a Mikkelsen offshore account. Not a good start for your Adrian."

Closing the device, she shoved it on the table. "He's not my anything."

Jerry's grin broadened. "Good. I'm sure Cameron is happy to hear it too."

Deciding it was best to leave such a conversation to another time, she folded her hands over her stomach. Her taste in men veered all the way off the road. She was attracted to men prone to criminal activities. Every girl's dream.

"Since Adrian spilled the details of your relationship—" Jerry glanced between her and Cameron. "—whatever its status, Del Rossi's protection of you is compromised."

She raised an eyebrow. "Why?"

Lighting a cigar, the enforcer took a puff. "When we agreed to protect you last year during the whole J.J. incident, you entered an agreement where money—or a favor like using your business to move money—is exchanged to pay for our services. It's an old tradition, but always helped keep the family business going. Years ago, the founding Dons made a rule that if you were paying for our services, you couldn't be romantically involved with one of our members.

It's a death wish." He shrugged. "Most families don't abide by that rule since it was later removed. It appears the Mikkelsens made an exception for you."

"What about families of people in the mob. Don't they fall under the mob's protection?" Joci asked, trying to wrap her mind around the so-called rules.

Jerry smirked and tapped the side of his nose. "You're a quick one. It's a different type of protection if you have a family member in the mob. You don't pay dues. It's more of a family unit than a protection policy since you're family, whether by blood or not."

She nodded slowly. "Oh, I guess that makes sense."

He pointed a grubby finger at Cameron. "Now, your ex wants him dead for understandable reasons, but I never anticipated he'd join the Mikkelsen clan and they'd cast their own protection policy for you."

Joci's brain hurt from all the history and rules. Mafia traditions were as foreign as the groups themselves.

"Mostly for the twins, but the mother is included." Jerry chewed on his cigar. "Probably shouldn't smoke this around you, huh?" He shrugged and let a cloud of smoke float from his mouth.

"He wants my babies?" she put together. "Adrian wants to take them from me?" Her breath sped up, hyperventilation threatening.

"Yes, but we won't let him," the kingpin said, amazing them both. He squeezed her shoulder in a fatherly fashion. "You're a Del Rossi, Joci. If not from your upcoming nuptials to Cameron, but your livelihood. Your business is bound to ours whether you admit it or not. It's not a very substantial price when you think about it. Your safety for a little harmless money laundering. Not a big deal." He nodded once. "You've been under our protection even before you conceived those boys." He sauntered to the door and jiggled the handle. "Cameron, we scheduled a meeting for tonight with J.J. I want you there in mob affiliation this time around."

Cameron dipped his head in understanding. His employer grinned with enough cheese to drown a mouse. "Oh, and, Joci, you're beautiful when you're pregnant. I hope you and Cameroni will add to your bunch in the coming years." He winked at her then ducked out of the room.

Shoulders sagging, Cameron sighed, the sound echoing in the empty room. His brown eyes clashed with her distressed ones. "Do you see why I keep you in the dark?"

Sorting the details out, she absently stood. "Yeah, I get it. All of this is complicated. How is any of this possible?"

Cameron nodded toward the door. "That's a story for another day."

The blurry picture cleared for Joci in the silent moment, but she'd never thank the drug lord for the explanation. Inspecting Cameron beside her, a rush of emotion overwhelmed her. He looked more battered than she felt. Clearly, their short separation had sent him off the rails. That fact bolstered her feelings into actions. She didn't want his touch; she needed it to feel whole.

"I'm worn out. I think I'll head home." His voice broke the quiet. When she didn't respond, he moved for the door.

She beat him to it, hand covering the handle. "No. Wait." With everything that had happened recently, she needed reassurance. He alone could offer it. The languid way his eyes scanned her reminded Joci of when she met him at the jail. It sent shivers down her spine and longing through her veins. *Hormones, yep, blaming the hormones.*

Cocking his eyebrow, he studied her. "What's wrong?"

Shoving the unease swirling in her gut to the side, Joci turned the lock on the handle. "Don't think for a second I'm not pissed at you." Her eyes fluttered over his body, solid as ever. "But I'm horny as hell and all I want is you."

A devious smirk covered his cheeks, and he didn't hesitate before he clutched her ass. He didn't need to say a word. He spoke enough with the possessive way he pressed her into the door, making desertion impossible. It'd be background noise to the conversation their bodies created.

Within moments, Joci's fingers traveled up his shirt, worshipping at the divots the gym created. As her hands moved beneath his belt, she gasped when Cameron's mouth fastened to her neck. The intensity of his act reminded her of the first time he did it to her, when he was her client. He'd left a hickey then, and judging from the ministrations and solid grip he possessed on her body, he wasn't about to let her forget him. She panted when his fingers shoved aside her underwear. Mere breathing expended less energy than the throbbing between her legs. Cameron unbuttoned her shirt and slipped it off her shoulders; he moved aside her bra to allow his perusal of the peaked nipples beneath. Capturing one bud between his teeth, his tongue swirled, forcing new sounds to escape her mouth.

Threading her fingers through his short hair, she tugged roughly. His response was to lift her slipper-clad feet off the floor and thrust her back into the door. Yeah, angry sex was going to be hotter than hell.

***

Snaking his arm down Joci's bare back, Cameron's heart lightened as his fingers grazed her spine. She was asleep. Well, he guessed as much from the sound of even breaths. From his position on the other side of the mattress, he couldn't see if her captivating eyes were open or closed. Continuing the light strokes, a hopeful grin sprawled over his lips when he reviewed the day. As a couple, they'd indulged in primitive sex in the past, but what happened at the hotel made all other shagging seem juvenile.

Propping his head on his palm, Cameron traced the swell of Joci's hips. He'd missed the simple act of touching her skin. Not once did he think anyone else consumed her mind when their lips meshed in tune with their slick bodies. She was a complicated woman who sometimes lost her mind when it came to men she cared about, but it was why he strived to be the *only* one she loved. Joci wasn't the same callous attorney he'd met last year. Sure, she still kicked ass in the courtroom and enjoyed every victory, but she'd changed too. She doted on him both physically and emotionally until he swore she was a sorceress for making him love the simple things like cuddling on the couch and homemade pizza. He hadn't seen that side of her during his case. Each day he'd fallen deeper in love with her as she gradually opened up. He hoped it was his affection that had the sway over her, but he'd never really know unless they weren't together. He swallowed hard. And that wasn't something he ever wanted.

An afternoon breeze drifted through the open window and her skin pebbled. She'd made it abundantly clear he wasn't forgiven; those words had escaped her mouth along with a myriad of obscenities that would make a virgin blush into a deep grave.

He didn't blame her. Hell, he'd been dumbfounded when she insisted they go home after they caught their breaths on the hotel floor. Told, not asked. If she'd been wearing a dominatrix outfit, it still would've paled to the provocative demand.

After spending the remaining morning and better half of the afternoon locked within Joci's arms, he never wanted to wake up and face the world. Sleep was no longer on his mind. How could it be when he feared this would all be a dream when he awoke?

"You stopped," a muffled voice protested.

Placing a feathery soft kiss to her right shoulder, Cameron rolled her over. The adoring look in her eyes made him forget how to breathe. "I thought you were sleeping." His lips dallied down her arm until he traced her fingers with his tongue. "I'm glad you're not." He pushed her frazzled hair off her collarbone, which was littered with red marks left by his mouth. He could kiss her body all day and never tire of it. "We should—"

"No, please." Her index finger covered his mouth, tempting him to taste it. "Let me speak first."

He nodded slowly, but couldn't resist kissing her one more time as he pecked the finger.

"You wanted to ensure my safety." Her hand sidled to cup his jaw, instantly making him regret not shaving for the last week. It wasn't important with no one there to see him. Quinn didn't count in his mind. "With Del Rossi mixed up in our lives, I understand your delays. I'd do the same if the roles were reversed." Her thumb ran along his top lip. "But if you ever even think about lying to me again, I'll go primal on you." She traced his cheek. "And not the way I showed you earlier."

Chuckling, he snared her face in his grasp. "Then you forgive me?" He needed to hear her say it.

"I forgive you." Her hands toyed with the thick lock of hair over his forehead. "Can you forgive me?"

Out of all the requests she could make, he hadn't expected this one. "There's nothing to forgive."

Her nose scrunched. "But there is."

"Okay, what is it?" He held his breath, an overabundance of potential transgressions swamping him.

"Derri—er—Adrian kissed me," she admitted sheepishly.

Hazardously, he released the pent-up huff as the admission escaped her. "Ah."

"I didn't know who he was, I swear. He caught me off guard, and I couldn't stop it." She twirled a strand of her hair between two fingers as she continued. "It was horrible. I just wanted it to be over." Joci kept some distance between them, allowing the minimal space Cameron hadn't known he needed. "I'm sorry."

For a full minute, he studied the end of the bed and analyzed her declarations. The information that Adrian had dared touch her in such an intimate way that scared her made his blood thicken. Smashing the bastard's face, newly plastic as it may be, sounded too good to pass up. Although he wanted to do far worse than beat him. Her part of the story didn't bother him. Adrian's part on the other hand made him furious. The Cameron of three years ago would've punched Adrian to a bloody pulp.

Taking in her tormented face, tenderness swam through his body. He wasn't that miscreant anymore. Sure, he wanted to shatter Adrian with a jackhammer, but losing Joci…. Nah, he couldn't handle any existence without her in it. He avoided the notion at all costs, but she changed him for the better. Joci instilled a shred of light within the confines of his dark soul. She'd saved him, a fact he'd never forget.

"Aw, babe, I'm sorry. Did he hurt you?" he started.

Her bottom lip quivered, and her eyes dimmed. "Well…"

"God, Joci, are you serious?" He scanned her body for any physical wounds. "I'm going to make that motherfucker wish he was dead. Again."

"Cam, don't, please. I'm fine." She held a hand over his lips. "Truly, I am. I just thought you should know. I was worried about how you'd react. I didn't want you to think I'd kissed him on purpose or that I didn't love you."

Cameron closed his eyes. When he opened them again,

he saw Joci's worried brow. "I'm not upset with you over the kiss."

"You're not?"

"No, that's on him for being a dick and fucking with both of us. But I have another reason." The constricting pain from her retreat resonated in his chest once more. "I don't ever want your taillights to be the last thing I see of you, Joci."

Her head bobbed, face crinkled in regret. "I'm sorry. It was a bitch move on my part."

"*Amore mio*, you're my heart. I would do anything to harbor your love for me." He spoke the Italian words as if the language was his first. It just felt right in this setting. Not coerced or dictated for a purpose, simply a way to express himself when other words fell flat. "And I forgive you." Cameron snuck his hand into her left one, his eyes pinpointing the platinum band, and lightly kissed it. "So, you're still my fiancée, right? Because I doubt I can get my money back."

Joci studied the diamonds. "I could get more if I sold them a sob story. Anyone would help a single pregnant lady."

Tucking her carefully under his body, he kissed a trail on her neck, only stopping when she purred beneath him. "Not even remotely funny, Mrs. soon-to-be-Shearer."

She waggled her brows. "Hmm, not sure if I'm taking your name yet or not."

"How else will I hold back the guys hounding you?"

"True. All right, I'll give it another pass around the

noggin." She lightly dug her nails into his shoulders, her gaze drifting down his torso. "I have a little time to decide."

Cameron beamed at the ravishing woman in his embrace. "As long as you're mine, I don't care what your last name is."

Joci tipped her hips up and nipped his chin. "No matter what happens, I need you to know I love *you* and only want to be with *you*, Cameron Shearer."

The earnestness in her promise, coupled with the affectionate way she pulled him close, sent tremors straight to his soul. He truly desired to take her word for it, but they weren't a sure thing. Her baby daddy was alive and walking Iowa's streets. Anything could happen to change her interpretation of an ideal life and the man it incorporated. "Let's get a few winks. I need to meet Jerry at seven tonight." He nuzzled her nose with his. "And I'm coming off a double shift, which you made a lot longer."

"That's not the only thing a lot longer at the moment," she insinuated, catching his mouth in a passionate kiss.

Resisting temptation never hurt so bad. "Woman, you're going to kill me."

Wrapping her arms around his neck, Joci skidded her lips along his arms. "Might as well go out with a bang."

"Fuck, this is why I love you."

CHAPTER SEVENTEEN

Pacing the hollow tunnel, Cameron watched rain splatter into pools on the street. The damn sky had been full of cheery rays until he left Joci alone at the house. It was as if the universe knew he was headed for a clash of the mobs.

Scuffling his boots on loose concrete, he listened to Jerry's Italian banter with his bodyguard. They were discussing a new shipment from Chicago, but he stopped paying attention after that. Once he was done with this mess, he'd find enough money to buy his way out from under Del Rossi. Silently, he scoffed at his pipe dream. It wouldn't happen if Jerry fought back, so he needed to stay in the brute's good graces.

Eyeing the end of the bridge's underbelly, he saw two sets of headlights zoom into view. The windshield wipers blasted on high as two men stepped from the sleek SUVs. "Fuck," he mumbled, spying the cocky Danish prick, J.J. A mallet would be better suited on his face than the smirk currently there.

"Shearer, you're alive!" the Mikkelsens' head mobster

mocked. "What a pity. I thought someone would've clipped you for sure." J.J. stood twenty feet from him, hands resting on the gun tucked in his belt.

He cracked his neck. "A few tried, but no one wants to kill a cop."

"Yeah, good call on your profession." J.J. jerked his thumb to Adrian. "Most likely why this one didn't do it for the lawyer chick. She's got a cop fetish."

Cameron's eyes narrowed, and he was mildly put off when Adrian's did the same. "Keep it up, Jepsen, and we'll see which one of us is standing at the end."

Chortling darkly enough to scare a famished rat, J.J. shook his head. "Nah, I'd rather watch you two duke it out over a pretty piece of ass."

"Cut the shit, Jepsen I want to make this fast." Jerry spoke into the evening, his voice lined in annoyance. Time was money for the mogul, and he was losing more as the clock ticked.

A hint of panic crept onto J.J.'s face at the booming voice. He cleared his throat and smoothed his jacket. "The Mikkelsens want in on the Midwest, Bernard. Primarily Des Moines. We can't achieve it if the Del Rossis block our advance." He nodded to Adrian. "We've ensured the legal spectrum for settling in here, but since you hold more sway over the police department, we propose a joinder."

Clenching his jaw, Cameron swung his gaze to his boss. The man seemed to be mulling the prospective alliance.

"It wouldn't come cheap," the enforcer stated with a greedy grin.

"How much?" J.J. whipped out his phone and dialed. After listening to his employer, he hung up. "The Mikkelsens are willing to settle with a seventy-thirty percent stake on the business we accomplish within Des Moines city limits."

"City limits? Ha! No deal." Jerry thrummed his fingers together. "This state is mine. If you want a piece of the action, I need something to get me out of bed each morning. Thirty percent won't do it."

Cameron recognized the familiar glint in the Italian's eyes. This was a business transaction now. Jerry would sell his sister if the price was rosy enough.

J.J. scratched his nose. "All right, well sixty-forty is the best I can offer, but it extends to the entire state."

"Fifty-five-forty-five and it's a deal."

Cursing quietly, Cameron watched J.J. feign rejection before nodding.

"But it comes with strings attached," Jerry added, smearing the grin off the blond's face.

"I wouldn't expect it any other way," J.J. said with forced surprise.

J.J. and Jerry moved to the far right of the underpass, leaving Cameron alone with Adrian. The urge to bash the traitor until he was nothing but graffiti wall art overwhelmed him.

"How is she?" the attorney inquired, breaking the silence with the gravelly sound of his voice. It most assuredly wasn't the same, but there were too many similarities for it not to be Adrian.

Cameron shot him a judgmental glare. "Joci is happy

and safe with me."

Meandering to the bright graffiti on the bridge, Adrian nodded. "She found my notes, though?"

A pang of resentment filled his gut. Joci and Jerry had mentioned the coded messages from Adrian, but neither went into detail about what was said. "Sure."

Awkward turmoil lingered on the rain, and Cameron tried not to stare. This new version of Adrian was impressive. In his opinion, the man wasn't quite up to par with him, but he was a bit biased. "So, you kissed her, huh?" He finally voiced the horror rotating in his skull.

"Yeah." The redhead took a deep breath.

"And?"

"And what? She loved every moan-worthy minute of it. Want me to go into details?" Adrian sneered.

Cameron bit back a snarl at the man's haughty grin. The ass might as well have flicked a knife in his heart. Joci had told him what happened, and he believed her over Adrian's lies.

The hushed voices of Jerry and J.J. escalated, and they both glanced over in time for the guards to swarm.

"You need to talk to her." Cameron abhorred the words as soon as they left his lips. He didn't understand why he put it out there, except for the fact that Joci deserved closure with the redhead.

Adrian sniffed, his face amused. "You actually want to give me the opportunity to steal her heart?"

"You won't." He jutted his chin to the once powerful lawyer. "You're a different guy than the one she loved.

I've never changed. What you see is what you get. She knows it too."

"Yeah, you only became a crooked cop," Adrian heckled. "Bravo."

"And you got a new face."

A secretive smile flashed on the other man's cheeks. Cameron loathed it. "Your little stunt cost me a lot, Shearer, but you won't gain my family. Joci will see the truth soon enough."

"And how're you going to do that? You're dead to the world, Adrian." He shook his head. "I can't even imagine how you'll sort it all out. Your own father thinks you're dead. Does he even know you're alive yet?"

Adrian scowled. "That's none of your concern. As to the whole death part, it's a good thing my family is rich and I have mob connections, isn't it?"

Cameron's eye twitched at the insinuation that Adrian's fake death was just a mound of paperwork that could be solved with money and pressure. In his experience, it wasn't unlikely either. If J.J. planned to fake Adrian's death, he would've had a plan in place so that it wouldn't be impossible for the lawyer to make a few calls and have his life back.

Fed up with the obvious lack of honesty behind Adrian's warning, Cameron strode over to Jerry.

"Ah, just in time," J.J. crooned.

"What're you talking about?" He looked between the two of them, not liking the smile on J.J.'s face.

Jerry placed a solid hand on Cameron's stiff shoulder.

"The Mikkelsens took out an insurance policy."

Judging from the tone, already he wanted to be sick. "What is it?"

"It's not a what, but a who. We have Joci," the louse of a mobster concluded.

Rage filtered into worry then finished with a need for revenge. Succumbing to the latter, he spun around and connected a fist to Adrian's jaw.

"I didn't know," the smaller man insisted between blows.

Cameron paused long enough to see fury flash over Adrian's features when he looked at J.J.

"You never said anything about kidnapping her," he ground out, the sound as sticky as molasses.

"Surprise!" J.J. taunted, which set the crowd of men into disarray.

Amid the jabs and punches, Cameron felt a foreign object slide under his nails when his right fist hit Adrian. "You fucking bastard," he uttered in shock, glaring at the damning evidence strong enough to sway even Joci.

The sound of bullets tore the men away from each other and tires squealed as everyone moved toward the safety of their cars. This fight was far from over.

***

Nothing smelled more appealing than musty books as Joci leafed through an old law report. The glass-paneled ceiling let in the last strains of light despite the consistent rain.

Wheezing from the recent laborious trek, she acknowledged Cameron was right to worry. She wasn't quite the agile cat anymore, and this was just a visit to Des Moines's law library. Browsing the area, she didn't spy any Drake University students cramming before finals like she'd done years ago. The sole person roaming the shelves was the elderly, yet friendly, Gus who'd been here longer than some of the first editions.

She reread the same sentence three times before shoving the book regarding federal regulations to the side. Leaning back in the wooden chair, she tucked her hands behind her head and grinned at the spiral staircases leading to the cozy spots she may have visited with a guy or two. The hidden corners of the library were popular with young couples in search of a spot for a quickie.

Outside troubles paused whenever she stepped through those massive doors. Nothing else mattered except diving into the pages of a book. It was why she chose this location to lie low while Cameron was amid unfriendly forces. No one would look for her at a library.

Gus cleared his throat from one of the upper decks, and she spotted him peering across the expansive rows of shelving. Judging from the ancient grandfather clock on the wall, closing time was nigh.

Joci slipped her phone out from under a thick volume of constitutional debates. It was an odd way to unwind, but she couldn't help her vices. Reviewing the black screen, she exhaled and started stacking the books. Cameron was supposed to let her know when he was finished then pick her up. After the Uber ride comparable to her harrowing taxi trip in Venezuela, Joci didn't want a repeat. As much as she'd love to drive herself, Cameron asked her not to. With the recent events and newfound information, he thought switching up her routine would be a wise idea. She glanced at her stomach. Plus, her ever-expanding belly was in the way now more than ever.

Typing a speedy text to Quinn, she awaited a reply. If all else failed, he'd give her a ride home. Rayna was visiting a friend in the hospital, so she didn't want to bother her. If she was honest, Joci's mind had been consumed with Cameron over the last twelve hours. She hadn't responded to messages from Quinn or Rayna due to her hands being occupied with tattooed muscle.

Deciding to repay the librarian for all the times she failed to return the books to their places, Joci made her way to the allotted shelves with fully loaded arms. As she reached the first row of bookshelves, her phone chimed irritably on the wood desk. She was torn between answering it or completing her task. Going with the last choice, she carefully slid the law titles in their spots.

When her phone wouldn't cease, she walked to the end of the row and peeked around for Gus to see if he was wearing a scolding frown. The typically alert man was nowhere in sight to scold her for the phone's noise. At the resonance of a quiet thud, her stomach pitched. *Maybe he fell. He's getting up there in years.*

"Gus? Hello?" she called, shifting the hardcovers. No answer met her ears. The constant ringing of the cell phone motivated her to see who was calling.

Quickly, she sped through one row of racks, chucking

the books to a nearby table. Just when her purse came into view, someone grabbed her, pulling backward. Screaming, she lunged forward, only to have a thick, hairy hand drag her back. Fear flooding over her, Joci jabbed an elbow into the man's gut. The satisfying grunt from the assailant gave her enough time to break free and sprint toward the table.

Snagging the phone, she managed to find Cameron's number before thick hands clapped around her face. Biting at the fingers that oddly tasted too sweet, Joci's muffled cries ricocheted in the library, but the call never connected. Before she could wriggle free, her eyelids drooped, suddenly too sleepy to care what happened to her next.

***

The lack of response when he dialed Joci's number tore a new hole in Cameron's brittle heart. "She didn't answer." Balling his hand into a fist around the phone, he refrained from crushing it. Instead, he punched in Quinn's number.

"What's up?" the officer answered.

"They took Joci," he filled in, walking to the vehicle where Jerry waited.

"What are you talking about? Who took Joci?" Quinn's voice turned dark. "What did you do?"

Climbing in beside his employer, Cameron slammed the door, and the driver peeled out of the lot. "I don't have time to explain. I just need you to track her location and let me know where she is, okay?"

"Track her? With what? I'm guessing they didn't bring along her cell phone for easy tracing."

Crumpling a hand in his curls, he ground out the next words, each tasting of remorse. "Her ring. I put a tracker in the engagement ring. I don't have the receiver with me though. It's at home. I never expected to use it." A pregnant pause danced across the line, and Cameron closed his eyes. It wasn't something he'd ever wanted to admit to.

"Whoa, we'll circle back to that bombshell later, but it gives me a lead. Text me where it's at and I'll grab it on my way to the station. I'll call when she's safe." Quinn hung up.

Stuffing the Android into his pocket, he stared out the tinted window. He didn't want to ever lose Joci, but now he may be doubly screwed.

"I see you stole a line out of my handbook," Jerry congratulated. "I'm proud you picked up a few nuances from our time working together."

Cameron cast a sideways glance to the Italian. He wouldn't admit to anything, much less thank the man who'd taught him one too many illegal activities. His mind turned to the past with the Del Rossis. One kidnapping in particular haunted him. He shook his head, hoping it would help. It didn't. "Did you find Jepsen?" he growled, the car taking a sharp right turn. The other cars disappeared before anyone could see which direction J.J. and Adrian went.

Jerry dipped his head, the black hair not moving an inch thanks to the extensive gel. "My techs are on his trail, but they lost Adrian amid the gunfire." He studied the younger man. "But you knew that already."

"Yeah, he won't stay in the Mikkelsens' good graces if he's on his way to find Joci." Biting at his nails, Cameron worried about what'd happen if Adrian got to her first. "Drop me off here. I can't go with you to regroup." He perched on the front of the seat. "She needs me more."

Jerry signaled the driver and the car screeched to a halt. "I'm impressed. You *did* learn something from me. This is proof enough."

Cameron hopped out and paused. "Yeah, except unlike what you did with Bambi, I won't leave Joci to an unknown fate." He slammed the sleek door in Del Rossi's face, despite his mounting uncertainty.

CHAPTER EIGHTEEN

The steady drip of water startled Joci awake. Popping open her eyelids, she gasped at the stormy sky above her head through slits of a light blue awning. Scouring her surroundings, she recognized the blinking red light mellowing out the night air. No doubt about it, she was on the top of Des Moines's tallest business building. The new roof was halfway done on the pointed peak of the skyscraper. She'd noticed the building had closed the overlook on the top floor during the construction. *How did we get up here?* Scrambling, she whipped her head around at the scrape of movement. A dark form emerged from the shadows.

"My, my, aren't you pretty up close?" J.J. mocked. He hunkered down in front of her, gently sliding the back of his hand over her face. Joci turned from his touch, but he didn't pull away. "Even pregnant, you're gorgeous. I understand why he's infatuated with you. It's all he'd talk about for months. Annoying, really."

"Who?"

J.J. wiped a raindrop from his brow. "Adrian, of course.

Who else?"

"You've been with him this entire time?" Her throat seized, and the twins subsided their normal somersaults. She placed a protective grip around her stomach when one small kick reverberated.

"Most of it, yes. He went through hell, you know. His recovery was brutal." J.J. snickered and sat on a folding chair. "But he wouldn't give up. He'd spew the same nonsense day in and day out about the lovely woman he needed to get better for."

Regret tensed Joci's muscles. She should've been there to help with his recovery, friend or not. "I didn't know he was alive. The car blew up. What was I supposed to think?" she defended. "No one called me to share his survival or even e-mailed me with his whereabouts."

"Simmer down, darling. I don't give a shit, to be perfectly honest." He stuffed both hands in the pockets of his jacket and withdrew a flask. After taking a drink, he languidly perused her form. "But I do like the fire in your eyes when you're mad. If you were my type, I'd piss you off just to see the spark over and over again. It's addicting."

"What do you want?" she asked, fed up with the direction her kidnapper was going. The malicious glint in his gaze didn't ease the sinking feeling in her gut either. She thought about calling for help, but at their height, no one except birds would hear. Joci looked over the edge and her breath caught at the sight. The staggered terraces around the building were too far to jump to and live. At this time of night, none of the businesses in the tower were open either.

She was stuck whether she liked it or not.

J.J. stepped closer to her, the scent of liquor now prevalent on his breath. "I want your fiancé dead." He licked his lips. "But I'll settle for you if I must."

Swallowing the paralytic fear, she adjusted her glasses. "So, you kidnap me? What about Adrian? Isn't he involved in this little scheme?"

"Adrian? No, he isn't privy to this change of plans. My men were to spirit you to a safe location while we dealt with the Del Rossi situation." His cheek muscle jerked. "No, Adrian won't be happy with this bump at all."

"Cameron will come for me," she said defiantly.

Swigging from the flask again, he nodded. "I don't doubt it. He always comes for a woman in danger. It's disgustingly chivalrous of him."

A wave of shivers skidded across her skin. "This has happened before?"

J.J. grinned, the act almost cheerful. "Oh, yes. Cameron has a weak spot for pretty faces. I figured it out when we worked together."

"When was that?" Joci silently assessed her situation, hoping the captor would ramble and ignore any movements on her part.

She noticed the scaffolding nearby. If she could sneak over to one, she may be able to catch a ride to a safe distance. A breeze slammed against her, rattling the nearby roofing material. *Or not.* Still, plenty of tools were within arm's length if she could reach one and hit him with it.

"A few years ago, Cameron and I worked for Del Rossi

on a job." The blond didn't cease his story, though Joci had missed the first half of it.

Returning to the safety of the construction workers' hut, she sat on a solid brick mound and crossed her legs. The twins were sitting on her bladder, making the situation worse by the minute. *A bathroom would be good right about now.*

"Cameron fell in love with a girl." He paused and stared at the grime beneath his fingernails. "They were inseparable, but she got nabbed by a rival mob. Don't ask how or why. He was probably being a dumbass. It's the main reason women drop like flower petals around him."

Fidgeting on the makeshift seat, Joci decided she didn't like this story.

"Anyway, on the day our—" He coughed. "—heist was to go down, Cameron decided to save her instead of helping me." J.J. straightened his shoulders. "And I was the lucky one who was caught by the fuzz." He closed his eyes for a moment then flicked them to her. "I would've spent ten years behind bars if the Mikkelsens hadn't helped me out."

Standing, J.J. inched toward her. Enveloping her hands, he traced her face with his vile gaze. "My sole purpose since then has been to get revenge on the son of a bitch. It wasn't until you came around that I had any chance." He patted her stomach awkwardly. "Thanks, by the way."

Jerking out of reach, Joci almost toppled off the bricks. Her movement resulted in her arm connecting with a jagged piece of rebar sticking out. Blood pooled, but she didn't feel the pain. She was too distracted by the conversation.

"And you think involving Adrian helps your case?"

"Adrian was a happy accident in more ways than one. He has just as much a reason to hate your fiancé as I do. The hit on Cameron's life was a stretch, but it's incredible what blackmail will do for a man. Well, and a few other ways of coercion." He winked and pointed to her bump. "If I batted for your side and a woman like you was carrying my sons, I'd move heaven and earth to make damn certain she ended up with me."

"Part of this was Adrian's idea?" Alarm fizzled in her, the hair on her arms standing at attention.

"Not this, Joci. Never this," a cracked voice interrupted the looming tension.

Craning her neck, Joci felt her eyes grow wide as Adrian's tall form came into view. Bewilderment instantly registered when she caught sight of his face. It wasn't Derrick who stood near J.J. with balled fists and blazing blue eyes, it was Adrian. Completely and irrefutably Adrian Petosa with one small hitch: the left side of his face bore a jagged scar from eyebrow to chin. It wasn't deep, but it was bold enough to know something horrible happened to him.

"Oh my God, Adrian," she whispered, gradually coming to her feet. In all her hopes, she never anticipated him to truly be in front of her ever again. "I can't believe—how're you—your face—Derrick…. Son of a—" She couldn't sew together a full sentence if she tried—and she did. Numerous times. Nothing she uttered made sense, so she slammed her lips closed and waited for him to speak.

Adrian took in her form then glowered at her captor

when he noticed the blood streaking down her arm. "You weren't supposed to hurt her!"

"Yeah, well, you know better than to trust me." J.J. shrugged. "Keep her here. I'm going to look around to make sure no one followed him." He stepped into the drizzle, leaving them in minimal privacy.

Leaving five feet between them, Adrian's hand reluctantly traced his scar. "The Mikkelsens set me up with a face mask for the scar and visual effects makeup for the rest of me. It's really quite cool if I'm being honest. I had to use it on my arms too. Well, pretty much any part of me that you might see."

She let out a shaky breath. The scars on his arms were noticeable but were always muted before now. She could only imagine the pain those wounds caused. "But your voice—"

"I did the accent on my own. Not bad either if I do say so myself. I used a voice changer to make it deeper." He held up a small device and clicked the button. "Makes me sound like anyone," he informed, his voice distorted.

"And your eyes? They were green."

He nodded. "Colored contacts."

Joci swallowed the bile rising in her throat.

"This is after all the plastic surgery they could safely perform," he advised, as if reading her thoughts. "I found a few surgeons willing to do skin grafts, but I have to wait until I'm completely healed from the other procedures." He glanced toward where J.J. left, then back to her. "Honestly, I don't remember a lot of what happened."

"What do you mean?"

Adrian winced. "When I woke up, I didn't know how I'd gotten there or much else. The doctors said it was post-traumatic amnesia, but I think J.J. fucked with my mind somehow." His voice turned hoarse. "One minute I was fine and the next I did things I don't remember agreeing to."

Joci stood mute, her hands shaking, though she wasn't certain if it was from the cold or shock. If J.J. manipulated Adrian's memories, the way he'd acted the last few months would make more sense. "Why didn't you tell me who you were?" she asked, the words tasting bitter and angry.

Pain crossed Adrian's features. "I planned on it, but when I finally made up my mind, I saw you in the courthouse. Your face lit up when you talked to the court attendant about your recent engagement." His eyes dipped to her finger. "And for a minute, I thought about letting you go. You'd already mourned me, so entering your life again would cause more agony than anything."

Understanding crept into her heart at his tale. It would've been torture if the roles were reversed.

"But then one of J.J.'s contacts found out what Del Rossi and Cameron were doing and J.J. told me." His lips curled into a grimace. "How they were using you to their own gain right under your nose. You deserve better than that."

Adrian shuffled in front of her and reached for her hand. She wasn't sure why, but she allowed the touch. Shoving him away was what she should've done, but her mind needed tangible proof of his existence so much that it short-circuited her common sense.

"So, I asked the Mikkelsen mob for their help. It didn't go as I expected. Obviously."

His tale in the hospital about the shrapnel hit her hard. He'd all but told her who he was the same day he shook her core at his less-than-kosher elevator act. She just didn't put the pieces together.

A gust of wind ruffled his shirt, letting her catch sight of a hint of scarring on his chest. "But you were never to be put in harm's way. I wanted to show you Cameron's errant ways, nothing more." He looked away. "Well, I may have had a few selfish motives too."

Gaping at their perfectly meshed hands, reality swarmed to the present. "You stalked me, Adrian. I was scared for my life." She nodded to her stomach. "For their lives."

"Joce, I'm sorry. I was following you when the car accident happened. After seeing you in the hospital with him, I couldn't keep away. I know I didn't approach you correctly from then on, and I'm sorry. Once I fucked up, I had to keep on with the charade. It was J.J.'s idea to keep tabs on you. I didn't mean for it to turn so dark like it did."

She didn't stop to address his apology. She was too pissed. "Plus, you called for the hit on Cameron," she reminded, her voice stern. "You want him dead." She tugged her hands free. Even though J.J. admitted to forcing Adrian's hand, he was still an accomplice. "I can't forgive you for participating in it."

Adrian's hands tightened. "I swear to God, I didn't do that." He looked around for J.J., fear in his eyes. "I mean, I did, but I didn't want to. J.J. forced me to sign it. I just wanted you back." Tears formed in his eyes, and her heart momentarily ached for him. What hell had he been through? She wasn't sure she wanted to know.

"I don't believe you. After all the shit you did last year and how you worked with J.J. before… no, I can't trust you."

"Joci, you have to, please." His blue eyes burned brightly. "I explained what happened after Cameron's trial. I was indebted to the Mikkelsens. I couldn't just walk away." He leaned closer and kissed her forehead. "They were threatening your life and my dad's. You mean too much to me."

Her hair whirled around her face etched in disappointment. Even if she took Adrian at his word, there were too many variables now. He was involved in a mob and owed them his life. His web of lies was too large. She couldn't forgive him. Not yet at least. "I love Cameron and—"

"You love me more."

"Maybe once, but not any longer." She shook her head. "Not now." She stormed to the railing of the overlook, space the one thing she desperately needed, but couldn't attain it from the height. The information she'd gleaned in the last ten minutes rattled her emotions, but not as much as the response her body had to Adrian's touch. He didn't feel the same. Adrian would always be Derrick to her. He'd be the man who'd toyed with her for hollow reasons.

"Joci, you don't mean it." His arms swooped around her waist, twirling her to face him.

Inches from his lips, a wave of memories collided with her. Each instance they kissed popped into her mind like some sick movie reel. Every fight that ended in make-up sex stormed her, and she hated every second of it. The cases they worked on side by side swirled until they all enhanced her anger toward him.

"You died," she blurted, unable to keep the tears at bay. "I watched them put your casket in the mausoleum." She moved his palms to her stomach. "I carried your babies alone while you've been playing mobster. And for what, Adrian? To get revenge on Cameron because he's playing mobster too?"

"I wish I could remember everything, but I can't, and it's killing me." Adrian's eyes remained glued to her belly, hands slowly sliding along the swell. "I'm sorry for everything. I was wrong to keep my identity a secret and for treating you like I did."

"Damn straight." Running her fingers through her mangled mess of brown hair, she predicted he'd release her; he wouldn't send her into a tailspin by maintaining eye contact.

"I'm here now." His right hand cupped her jaw while his left gathered her as close as her stomach would allow. "For all of us. I'm not going to let my family go. Not ever."

The graveled tenderness in his voice catapulted Joci to the past when they were just like this before their first child's death. Adrian looked at her more intensely, as though he'd seen the devil and clawed his way out of hell to reach her, to hold her once more. It scared her more than anything. The last months were torture. She saw it in his gaze.

"Adrian, I'm glad you're alive, but…" She couldn't

complete the thought when his hypnotic blue eyes excavated old feelings she'd buried at his funeral. The good times abounded; nothing else dared interrupt them. Timidly, she propelled her hand up and traced the angry scar, heart sinking at each dent. He'd survived for her. She swept a red lock off his forehead. His hair was longer now. *Probably to hide his identity.* He was trying to protect her just as he'd done in their prior life. Damn, she had foolish men in her armada.

Biting her tongue to wake from this dream, Joci let out an unsteady breath when he didn't vanish from her arms. She needed space to wrap her mind around the revelations of the last few hours.

Just when she made up her mind to yell at him for the elevator scare, Adrian pressed her lips to his. Her gut pitched at their connection. He didn't taste like the Adrian she once loved. He plunged his fingers through her long locks and swallowed any resistance she could muster. It was like kissing an absolute stranger. He wasn't who she wanted. He'd done too much to their family to make even a kiss matter to her at all.

By the time he came up for air, her mind was a muddled haze about the man in front of her. Sure, she cared about him and was glad he was alive. He was the father of her children, but she didn't want to see him ever again. The pain he caused outweighed his resurrection.

"Please, Joci," he begged. "Let me take you from all this and give you the life you deserve. Let me love you." He glanced at their surroundings and lowered his voice. "I have a private plane waiting at the airport. If we leave now, we can make it somewhere tropical by morning."

"What about J.J.?"

An odd expression covered his face. It scared her more than anything. "You let me handle J.J. I have more than enough reasons to want him dead."

Still draped in Adrian's warmth, Joci's teeth chattered as his words digested. Believing him at his word would never happen again. "I… I…."

"Joci, we need to go!" a surprising voice demanded, shaking her out of Adrian's cloud.

Swiveling her neck, she spotted Quinn heading her direction, gun in hand. If he was here, he wasn't alone. Stuck between the two, Joci wrenched out of Adrian's grip and shuffled to the railing. She wasn't normally afraid of heights, but this situation created a new phobia for her.

"Kidnapper is a far cry from attorney," the cop stated, motioning for her.

"I didn't kidnap her or know about it," Adrian replied with a similar gesture.

"Yeah, right. You just asked contract killers to hunt down Cameron and put one between his eyes." Quinn's eyes turned as cold as stone. "Not cool, man. He's my partner and her fiancé."

Adrian chuckled, the sound distorted. "It's funny how the two of you get along fine after screwing Joci, but you and I never did. Maybe all three of you had some fun together," he insinuated. "Because I'd never be best friends with my girl's ex."

Joci watched in horror as Quinn went from caring officer of the law to full-out cop on the verge of kicking ass. "I think that's enough, Petosa. Drop your weapon and turn around."

It was then she noticed Adrian had a handgun pointed at Quinn. Nothing good could come from guns and babies. His earlier statement about wanting J.J. dead came back to her. Adrian would've killed her kidnapper if she'd agreed to go with him. She held her stomach, suddenly sick. The distant sound of police reinforcements and ambulance sirens drifted up from the street. The safety in the noise she took for granted made her decision that much easier. Swiftly crossing the invisible line between the men, she heard a disappointed groan from the redhead.

"You always choose wrong, Joci." Adrian's cold words slapped her more than the rain.

Gunshots peppered the balcony, sending her scurrying for shelter and hoping they all made it safely to ground level.

***

He'd witnessed the kiss. How could he miss it? Aliens in deep space could have seen the damn act of love. It all but mutilated his already lacerated heart. Gripping the gun with new motivation, Cameron wanted to pop two bullets through Adrian's throat for caressing Joci in such an intimate way. Still, he refrained when he saw her reaction. It wasn't a complete denial, though he couldn't hear any of their words. "Fuck! She has feelings for the asshole."

Nudging Quinn forward, Cameron crept around the main event in search of the slippery snake who'd directed the nab and grab. He ignored the conversation his partner was having with Adrian. He didn't want to hear it anyhow.

Rounding the bend toward where he last saw J.J., he narrowly ducked out of the way when a two-by-four swung in his direction. "Shit."

"Always prepared, aren't you?" J.J. harassed.

Whipping up his gun, Cameron lifted his brows. "When it comes to you, hell yes."

J.J. waved his hands to show no weapon in them. "Tut, tut, Officer. I'm unarmed."

"And I'm not a cop right now." He pushed the blond against a stack of metal sheets with his forearm. "You can't let this go, can you?"

"Nope. You're a traitor. Then and today," J.J. somehow managed to say with the left side of his face smashed to the materials. "Joci may as well learn before it's too late."

A slew of bullets zinged on the other end of the balcony that wrapped around the top of the skyscraper, momentarily distracting him. J.J. used the surprise to his advantage and punched Cameron's gut. Stumbling back, he coughed to catch his breath. Joci was in danger and there was nothing he could do about it.

The deadly click of a gun brought his head up fast. Not pausing to think, the training from the academy kicked in and he leapt into action. He chopped at J.J.'s wrist, disarming him, and tackled the Dane. The two rolled around, each vying for the perfect vantage to reach a weapon and trying not to roll too close to the edge of the balcony.

Cameron did his best to block out Joci's frantic voice,

but it got the better of him. Jamming a fist to J.J.'s skull, he crawled over to where his Glock rested in a puddle and fumbled with the handle. J.J. grappled for his ankle, but Cameron swiftly stood and pinned the man with the bottom of his boot.

"You're a disgrace to the mob!"

Glaring at the man under his foot, Cameron shook rain from his hair. "No, you made me choose love or the mob. I'll choose the same every time."

J.J. jerked a thumb in Joci's direction around the balcony. "Obviously, but this go round, the pretty lady may not choose you."

The veracity bashed Cameron hard, and his hold loosened enough for J.J. to roll out from under him and pull a gun from a holster at his ankle. He cocked it to Cameron's head.

"I hope you enjoyed your time with Joci because I'll make certain Adrian dies once you're gone. My use of the pawn has expired. She'll be left with no one, all thanks to you," J.J. taunted.

Gritting his teeth, Cameron tried to move, but the cold steel at his forehead halted the act. "Look, take me and do whatever the hell you want, but leave Joci out of our dispute. She doesn't deserve this."

J.J.'s laugh sent shivers down Cameron's spine. "You don't get it. I don't want you to have any happiness. You don't deserve any for what you've done."

Shock shot through Cameron's veins as fast as lightning. Wracking his brain, he recalled the only situation that could leave J.J. this aggravated. "This is about Bambi not Joci? Are you serious? I left to help Bambi because I loved her. That was years ago."

"I got caught, remember?" J.J. pushed the gun harder against his temple. "I spent years in prison while you galivanted as a free man. If you hadn't left, I wouldn't have been caught."

Cameron swallowed his resentment. "An old grudge over Bambi was why you grabbed Joci today and came after me in the first place last year?"

"Ding, ding! You destroyed my life. I had a family once too, and they left me because of my incarceration." J.J.'s breath washed down Cameron's collar, souring his stomach.

"Look, I'm sorry that happened, but—"

"You chose to screw me over with a woman. No bitch is worth leaving your comrades to rot in prison." His forehead rested on Cameron's face. "It was rather fun to watch you squirm this last year. Always wondering if you and your lawyer girlfriend would make it last or if you'd get caught doing mob business while on duty as a cop." He rolled his eyes. "Now that I've had my fun, you don't get to live anymore. Any last words?"

"You're sick," Cameron spit through the rain. "I'm sorry that shit happened to you, but Joci doesn't deserve this. I'm guessing you were the one with the Derrick ideas."

"Yep." He preened. "I even installed fun little mind bombs in Adrian's memories."

Cameron scowled, already not liking the abrupt turn. "What're you talking about?"

J.J. wiped his face. "Oh, I tinkered with Adrian's memories a bit. I left his hatred for you in there because, hell, why not? But he can't recall a lot of what happened between he and Joci after the divorce. He's still in love with her, you know? She was the one thing that got him through the surgeries. And even when I'd smack him around a bit. He'd call for her in his sleep. It's sweet, truly."

Cameron closed his eyes tight. Even if he survived this skirmish, his love with Joci would always be compromised.

He laughed at the look on Cameron's face. "It's amazing what money can buy. Did you know you can suppress memories?" Cameron swallowed hard as J.J. continued. "Oh, don't worry, I left the best memories to resurface when he comes across keywords in the future. They're normal words too like "baby" and so forth, so it should be anytime." He straightened his shoulders. "Then, once he gets all his memories back, Adrian will be dead-set on claiming Joci again. And the best part is, even if I go to prison—which I never plan on doing ever again—my diabolical revenge plan will work long after I'm gone. If you somehow survive this bullet, you'll never be safe." He looked off toward the capital building. "Just imagine it. Cameron Shearer always wondering if today will be the day Joci and Adrian gallop away toward the sunset. It's genius."

The severity of J.J.'s backup plan stuck in Cameron's heart like a dagger. He should've known better. Nothing was ever easy for him. But he couldn't give up. He'd figure out a way to help Adrian and not lose Joci at the same time. *Well, if I live long enough.*

"It's not too late," Cameron said. "You can just walk away. I won't come after you, I swear."

Turning the gun sideways, J.J. let out a huff. "Hmm, nah, I'm a psychopath according to the prison shrink, so the only way to get over your betrayal is to step over your dead body."

There was no arguing any longer. He'd had a good life. Well, the last year at least. The rest was shit in comparison. Any time with Joci was the best he could ever imagine. Bracing himself for the inevitable, Cameron clamped his eyes shut and pictured Joci. He didn't want anyone else in his thoughts if he was to die. *Quinn has her. She's safe.* It was enough.

When a loud pop erupted in his eardrum, he waited for the blowback. After a second, he pried one eye open then the other. To his right, J.J.'s mouth gaped and a perfect hole in his chest bubbled blood. Turning his head, Cameron muffled a cry when he spotted Joci with a gun aimed at J.J.

"Shit. I think I killed him," she voiced, eyes bulging wide.

The body beside him collapsed against an opening in the railing where the construction workers cut to allow for a scaffolding. Cameron reached for J.J.'s hand, but his limp body fell through the hole and landed on the terrace below them. If J.J. hadn't been dead already, he was after such a swan dive.

Rushing to her, Cameron wrapped Joci in his arms. "It's okay. He's gone," he repeated for his sake as much as hers. He hauled her at arm's length and gripped her face in his bloody hands. Smiling down at her, he heard the gun thud to the ground. "You just saved my ass."

"Yeah. I think I did." Raindrops splashed her eyes, black streaks of mascara trickling down her face.

Hugging her tight, Cameron breathed in the intoxicating berry scent of her perfume. Never had anything felt so right. The world was in his embrace despite a jolt to its revolution. "Joci, I—"

"Please just shut up and kiss me."

Not one to argue, he tilted her face to his and engulfed her lips with enough passion to make them forget the rain.

"Joce, we'll need you to come down to the office for your statement," Quinn broke into their reunion.

Joci reluctantly pulled away. "Oh, yeah, right." She stared at the recently fired weapon in Quinn's hand. "It was self-defense and—"

"Hey, hey, calm down." Quinn rubbed her back reassuringly. "I saw what happened. You don't need to go all lawyer on me."

She smirked. "What can I say? It's my job."

Quinn glanced around. "Have either of you seen Adrian?"

Tucking Joci behind him, Cameron surveyed the construction zone. One too many shadows could harbor a jealous lawyer.

"No need to search. I'm here," the man announced from the tent structure. His gun was securely tucked in his waistband, though he looked far from compliant.

Joci's breathing picked up, the warmth spreading worry across Cameron's neck. A kidnapping followed by a shooting and her three most recent lovers on one roof would leave him breathless too.

"You'll need to come with me," Quinn advised, holding up a pair of handcuffs.

Adrian shook his head. "I didn't do anything you can prove."

Quinn took giant steps toward the scarred man, causing guns to be drawn simultaneously. The outcome wasn't encouraging, no matter who pulled the trigger. "Come on, Petosa. I like you, but you've done shady shit."

"So has he." Adrian nodded to Cameron. "Arrest him too and put us in the same cell. We'll see who makes it out this time around."

Cameron's hand stiffened at the threat. Without a doubt, he could obliterate the attorney, but it would hurt Joci in the process.

Quinn eyed his partner. "True. You'll both be questioned, but he's not the one with a gun aimed at me, so drop it."

Moving toward the two men, Cameron spoke. "Let's all toss our guns in the middle and call it a night. I don't want any trouble."

"The fuck you don't," Adrian growled. "You started this all."

"I started this?" Cameron's finger itched to pull the trigger. "The hell I did. You're the one who—"

A cry of anguish cut off the filthy response on Cameron's lips. All three men swung around to see Joci clutching her stomach, her back hunched. "I think my water broke," she said, eyes wide.

A moment of silence drifted among the steady raindrops. Each man glanced between the other before Quinn asked, "Are you sure it's not the rain?"

She shot him a glare that'd shame a priest. "Pretty damn sure rain doesn't fall up my pants, dumbass," she ground out, gripping a box next to her, knuckles white.

Cameron's feet refused to move. He checked Quinn's and Adrian's reactions, and it seemed he wasn't the only one scared witless. "She's in labor. Joci's having the babies."

CHAPTER NINETEEN

With each labored breath, Joci clung to Quinn's forearm as if it were a lifeline. The contraction subsided, but not before she caught sight of the faces of all the men crammed in the ambulance. It was humorous, really, the amount of masculinity in the vehicle, yet she was the one handling enough pain to thwart them all. Any other time, she would've suggested they just drive to the hospital, but since reinforcing police cars and an ambulance arrived on the scene by the time they reached the ground level, she was grateful for the paramedic escort. There was no way Cameron, Quinn, or Adrian would've driven safely.

"I thought there was a rule about passengers," she joked to the same EMT who'd helped her after the accident.

Tad checked her pulse for the twentieth time then nodded. "There is, but Quinn and I go way back." He eyed Cameron and Adrian. "Plus, it looks like there's a weird story here and I really don't want to know what freaky stuff the four of you do. Hell, I'd be surprised if you even knew who the dad was."

"Tad, shut the fuck up before I make you," Cameron growled. The paramedic smirked but stopped talking nonetheless.

Joci lifted a puzzled brow to Quinn, but he merely patted her belly in awkward response. This wasn't the first time someone had made the wrong assumption, but she was surprised Quinn didn't correct him.

"Yep, you know me. Always knocking up beautiful lawyers after orgies." Quinn coughed.

If they hadn't pulled into the hospital bay at the same moment, Joci was positive Adrian would have wiped Quinn's boyish grin clear off his face. His face was dark red and not just because he was squished in the seat beside Cameron.

"Adrian," she murmured, and he released his fist then bobbed his head. She couldn't count the number of times she'd wished him alive, but actually having him two feet from her was surreal. She couldn't believe her eyes even in that moment. He was alive and within an arm's grasp.

Two nurses and a doctor opened the ambulance doors, ushering everyone out before pulling the gurney last.

"Whoa, you're having twins, aren't you?" a nurse questioned, taking in Joci's stomach.

"Either that or I have one giant baby," Joci said, her body seizing in pain.

"And how far apart are the contractions?" the short woman in scrubs asked.

"Three minutes," Cameron informed her.

The doctor nodded as they pushed through the ER doors.

"For the initial exam, we just want the father present. Which of you is the father?"

The entourage screeched to a stop at the double doors leading to initial exam rooms. It was comical, the way each man glanced at the other as if to challenge whoever spoke first. In a sense, they were all fathers to the twins. Adrian fathered them, Cameron cared for her and them, and Quinn was always around as a helping hand if needed.

"Do they not know?" the nurse asked, her eyes brimming with intrigue. It'd make a fabulous gossip for the hospital if indeed it were the case.

Joci pushed up on her elbows. "Adrian," she educated, and heard the collective exhale from those surrounding her. "I think," she couldn't help but add with a sly smile. The reactions to her joke were well worth the following contraction. "But seriously, it's Adrian," she whispered despite the new onslaught of pain.

The doctor and nurses exchanged a look before shuttling them through the doors. She felt a tinge of regret when Cameron's reflection bounced back in the glass. He deserved to be with her more than anyone, but it was unlikely Adrian or the nurse would agree to his presence even if she insisted on it. She could argue for Cameron to be with her, but in her current state of pain, she didn't want the extra drama the request would include. All she wanted was to get the babies checked out to make sure they were okay.

When they reached a crisp white room, the nurses made quick history of Joci's clothes before sliding a gown over her shoulders. It was a relief to be out of the damp articles.

"I paged obstetrics, so they should be here soon to see if you're ready to be admitted or not," the ER doctor stated before he and the nurse cleared the space. The last nurse pulled the cloth curtain in place behind them, giving a reassuring grin to the couple within.

Codes rang through the speaker system as Joci sat under the starched sheet. The contractions subsided for the moment, but her stomach fluttered from nerves all the same. Peeking over to Adrian, she couldn't help but stare. His clothes were soaked and clung to him in the most audacious way, informing her of the changes he'd been through in the last months. The ugly scars crawled down his arms and disappeared beneath his shirt.

"You still have your sense of humor, so the pain must be tolerable." He spoke at last, though the coarseness of his voice bespoke agony.

"Sorry, it kinda slipped out."

Adrian cleared his throat and pulled at his wet shirt. "It's fine." His eyes grazed her torso before meeting her face. "You're the Joci I fell in love with, and that's what's important."

"Adrian, I—"

"Alrighty, folks. I'm Dr. Dahl. Your regular doctor, Dr. Miller, is in surgery right now, so I'll be taking over. Now, what do we have here?" the obstetrician greeted, whisking the curtain to the side.

Joci held in a giggle at the man who looked like he was ripped out of an episode of *Grey's Anatomy*. She smirked. *Hot doctors in Iowa? Yes, please.*

"She's in labor," Adrian's words fell flat when the doctor nodded and grabbed Joci's chart.

"Yes, I see that. Looks like you're prone to blood loss, is that correct, Mrs. Dorous?"

She nodded. "It's Miss and yes."

Adrian groped the sheet. "What do you mean?" He ducked into her line of vision when she didn't respond. "You've had problems with the boys?"

"Actually, yeah, but you'd know that if you'd made yourself available before this week." She didn't care that she sounded bitchy anymore. She was still deciding if she even wanted him around her. After what he'd done the last months, she was ready to go back to a time when Adrian was a fond memory, not an active ghost.

The doctor snickered and rustled his stethoscope. "Burn," he coughed before pressing the cold metal to her chest.

"Seriously?" Adrian bit out, annoyed.

Scribbling on the chart, Dr. Dahl gave her a pointed look. "If you don't want him here, I can have him removed," he suggested, the light brown of his eyes reminding her of Cameron.

Observing the red tint creeping up Adrian's neck, she shook her head. "No, he's fine for now. Thanks."

Dr. Dahl nodded. "Okie doke. I'm gonna duck under the sheet really quick if you don't mind."

Moving to the head of the bed, Adrian laced her hand with his. "I'm sorry, Joci. It was wrong to stay away. I regret all that I've done to make you worry. I'll spend the rest of our lives making up for my absence if you let me." He knelt, causing her more pressure than what the young doctor was causing in her nether regions. "Don't marry him." He paused and kissed her palm. "Please. I can't handle watching our boys grow up bouncing between two homes. And I definitely can't take you being in love with him."

Joci squirmed from the discomfort, but didn't speak. She wanted to hear everything he had to say first. She owed him at least that. It wouldn't make any difference relationship-wise, but he deserved to be heard.

"It's always been you and me. Now more than ever, I know it's true." He wet his lips, steadying his hold when the doctor went under for round two. "I want to pick up where we left off. We could be happy again, Joci. So incredibly happy together." Adrian stood and left a kiss on her cheek. "Don't break my heart. Not again."

Her emotions and hormones scattered, she wasn't certain if she could reply. He was her first true love and the father of the two bundles of pain edging through her uterus. At the same time, Adrian had skipped out on life in the name of vengeance and made her life hell instead of the exact opposite.

"Well, I'm a little concerned with what I see," Dr. Dahl informed them, popping his head out from under the white sheet. He tossed his gloves in the trash then pointed to Adrian. "But good job on the plea, dude. Nothing like putting a woman in the worst possible spot when her body's trying to expel twins. Classic wedding story."

Adrian bristled, whereas Joci snorted at the man's

candor. She was quickly liking this Dahl fellow. "What's the problem?" she asked, skirting the intentional jab at Adrian.

Dr. Dahl's brow furrowed together when he scanned her medical records. "You're just at thirty-seven weeks and the boys are busting down the door. I can safely deliver, but both babies are breech from what I felt. I'm afraid the cords may be cutting off circulation."

As if the machines understood his apprehension, angry lights and loud buzzers went off. Tightness rippled through Joci's abdomen, and suddenly breathing felt like climbing Everest.

"Joci?" Adrian gripped her shoulders, terror scrawled on his face. "What's happening? She's turning purple."

The next moments passed in a blur. She heard Adrian and Dr. Dahl argue over the bleep of the monitors, then saw three nurses rush into the space before the bed started moving on its own. What she didn't expect was for her mind to go blank and her body to curl into convulsions.

***

A puffy bag of potato chips teetered in the vending machine despite Quinn's constant banging on the glass. Cameron didn't know how his partner could think about food at a time like this, but then again, Quinn's future didn't hinge on Joci anymore.

Tapping his fingers together, he watched the ER doors, willing them to open. The flickering red lights and subsequent codes yelled across the floor set him on edge. His desire to be beside Joci outweighed any other wish he could imagine.

"She's going to be fine," Quinn commented, sticking his hand in the machine when the bag wouldn't budge.

"I hope you're right. I've never been around someone in labor. I don't know what to expect." He pushed his fingers through his messy hair. "I want to be there with her, but I'd have to knock Adrian out first."

"Ha, I'll pay to see that," his friend said, holding up the bag of chips, victorious at last.

The double doors burst open and Cameron jumped to his feet when he saw Adrian stumble through, his shirt covered with blood. "What the hell happened?" he demanded, advancing on the man.

Adrian's face was a mix of shock and distress, never a good combination. "She was fine, I swear. Then she started seizing." He took a gulp of air. "And then there was blood. God, so much blood. I couldn't help her."

A cold sweat broke over Cameron's face, shivers running along his spine. "Where is she?" He attempted to look through the tiny window leading to the rooms, but saw nothing.

Adrian slumped to the floor, hands covering his face. "She's going to die, and it's all my fault."

Starting to frantically pace, Cameron scowled at the other man. "No, it's not. This shit happens. She'll be fine. The doctors are prepared for this stuff."

"Where is she now?" Quinn repeated the question Adrian failed to answer the first time.

"They took her into surgery. They told me I couldn't be

in there. Why would they say that unless it's bad?" Adrian sniffled. "I should've come back to help her."

"Yes, you should have," Cameron snapped. He was done hiding his wrath. If Joci did indeed die while trying to give birth to Adrian's spawn, he was going to kill the attorney, his fate be damned. His fingers itched to throttle the heap of a man, but it was then that Cameron realized just how much Adrian loved Joci. The proud shoulders of the Petosa heir shook silently. Should the circumstances be flipped, he'd do the same thing. He wouldn't cease until Joci was his and their babies were safe from any force, including the mob. The knowledge hit him solidly in the groin.

Sinking onto the floor beside Adrian, Cameron propped his arms on his knees. "Our feud won't stop so long as we're in opposite mobs."

Adrian's head pricked up at the words. "And because you want my wife."

Ignoring the stray tears on the attorney's cheeks and the title of the woman they loved, he nodded. "Yeah, Joci is the other big part of our issue. Are you planning on staying with the Mikkelsens?"

Adrian wiped his nose. "No. I was done with them the minute they took Joci and fucked with me for the last I don't know how many months."

A slight weight lifted from Cameron's shoulders. "Good, then we may have a future."

"Well, I don't ever see us being best friends," Adrian said through bleary blue eyes.

Cameron shook his head, the wet hair flinging droplets

on his hands. "Hell no. But we need to at least be civil around each other. I'm not going anywhere. The sooner you figure that out, the better it'll be."

Adrian wiped his nose. "I can't make any promises, but for Joci's sake I'll try."

Getting up on wobbly legs, Cameron helped the other man stand. "Good, because I wasn't taking no for an answer."

They reached the chairs in the waiting area, Quinn already perched in one. When Adrian moved toward the nurses' station, the cop nudged his friend. "What in the hell are you doing?"

"What's best for Joci and her kids. If we can even pretend to get along, it helps everyone." Cameron rolled up his sleeves and grimaced at the ink displaying Joci's initials. It wasn't her idea, but she'd forever be engrained in his heart as well as his skin. "Even if it kills me."

"Really? Well, you're a better man than me." Quinn's voice took on an admiring tone. "She needs stability." He nodded toward Adrian. "If we work together, we can offer it."

"But the Mikkelsens—"

"He's done with them," Cameron interrupted. He didn't want to tell Quinn about J.J.'s failsafe. For all he knew, the dead man was bluffing. "And he has enough money to buy his way out. It's something I can't guarantee even if I groveled."

"All right, but I still think you're an idiot." Quinn grunted, and nodded toward Adrian. "If he gets even a glimmer of hope from Joci, he'll take you out of the picture completely."

"He can try," Cameron replied.

Adrian retreated to an opposite chair. No words passed between the three men as they awaited news of the woman they all loved in one form or another.

Twenty minutes passed into an hour. Rayna stopped by the waiting room, though her attention lay solely on Quinn. It suited Cameron just fine, since he wasn't up to chatting. He'd had enough of that when she used to visit him in the Petosa jail cell. Adrian managed to sleep for half an hour before waking with a jolt, sweat dripping on his face. *Serves him right.*

Cameron passed up the food offered by Rayna and Quinn when they returned from the cafeteria. How they could eat was beyond him. His clothes, once drenched in cold rain, gripped him uncomfortably. A fresh set of pants and a shirt would be a godsend, but all he could manage was to stand in front of the hand dryer in the men's bathroom to aid in the residual feeling of a damp and bleak future.

Finally, Cameron caught the stature of a weary doctor heading their way. All members of Joci's family stood at the same time, a collective breath held in anticipation. A surgical mask hung loosely around the man's neck as he approached. Scanning the three men, he scratched his head, reviewing them closely. "Uh, okay, Adrian, right?" He pointed to the correct man and was given a head bob.

"Is she—" Adrian began.

"What's her status?" Quinn interrupted, all business.

"Can I see her?" Rayna jumped in.

"Let's start over. I'm Dr. Dahl for those of you who didn't know, and I'm Joci's doctor for the evening." He eyed Quinn but then turned to Cameron. "And you're Cameron, right?"

Palms bathed in sweat, he nodded once. "Yes."

"Okay, great." Dr. Dahl shifted on his white shoes booted in miniature scrubs. "Joci is in recovery. Her blood pressure skyrocketed for some reason, which caused the seizure. The eclampsia came on fast, but we got it under control. She lost a substantial amount of blood." His gaze shifted from one person to the next. "Did she endure any abrupt distress or surprise before she came in?"

Quinn cast judgment-filled eyes at Cameron then Adrian before he spoke. "You could say that."

"Ah, okay. That explains it. We had to perform an emergency C-section for the twins. They're both fine, but one's premature."

"Wait, what?" Rayna cut in. "She's eight months pregnant."

The doctor struggled through the next words. "Well, after delivery, we discovered an anomaly, which is why I need both of you gentlemen to come with me."

If Cameron thought the possibility of Joci's death was bad, he wasn't prepared for the onslaught of nerves skydiving in him as he and Adrian traded apprehensive glances before trailing the doctor.

Every hallway seemed longer than the next. His mind spun out of control at each turn. At long last they reached a paneled glass wall.

Dr. Dahl stopped in front of the nursery window and pointed at two babies in neighboring bassinets. "I want to preface that both babies are healthy. We put the smaller of the two in the neonatal crib to monitor him. Despite being a bit younger than the redheaded guy, he's developed enough to breathe on his own."

"Wait, what? How is one younger?" Adrian asked.

The doctor turned toward them. "It's a bit complicated, but those are your sons."

"What?" both said at once.

Not understanding the reason for his inclusion, Cameron's eyes swung to the cradle. A sneaking suspicion spun his mind out of whack. "Oh my God. This isn't possible, is it?"

The notably smaller baby was in a hooded crib with what looked like a heater at the top, while the baby in the clear bassinet beside him slept soundly. The newborns couldn't look more different. The boy on the right displayed light-blond hair and blond eyebrows, whereas the one on the left sported a tuft of dark hair.

"What the hell is this? Some sick joke?" Adrian ground out. "They're just fraternal twins."

"Uh, well, while they are fraternal, we didn't have any concern as to the paternity until their blood panels came back." Dr. Dahl handed him a printed sheet. "These are their blood tests. Joci's blood type is O. She said yours, is AB, Adrian. Is that right?"

Adrian nodded. "Yeah, that's right."

"Okay, great. Baby on the right has the blood type of A.

It's one of two types that you and Joci can produce, the other being B." Dr. Dahl scratched his head. "The problem arose when we tested the baby on the left. His blood type is O, the same as Joci."

Cameron started to piece together the reasoning. "So, the baby on the left couldn't be Adrian's because of the blood type?"

"That's correct," the man informed. "When we asked Joci what your blood type was, Cameron, she didn't know, but did tell us that you donate blood on a regular basis." He paused and handed him another piece of paper. "If you sign this, it will give me permission to open your file with the blood bank and see if you're a match to the baby."

Swallowing, Cameron grabbed the form and pen from the doctor. If Adrian and Joci couldn't create an O baby with their blood types, he could. Another thought crossed his mind and rattled his bones. "What about Quinn?" he asked, scribbling his signature. He couldn't help but notice his hand shook when he passed the clipboard back to the doctor.

"What?" Both Adrian and Dr. Dahl said at once.

He cringed, not wanting to even voice the other possibility. "Joce slept with all three of us in the last nine months. How do you know one of these babies isn't his?"

Adrian's face turned red then white then red again. "Fuck."

"Well, I didn't see that coming. Joci only mentioned the two of you. Um, I guess we'll have to do a DNA test then." Dr. Dahl scratched his neck. "I'll go grab him too.

Stay put." He paused and turned around. "By chance, do you know your blood type? With Joci's O type, the baby's blood type is possible with a parent with A, B, or O. I'm sorry, Adrian, it isn't available with yours."

"O. My blood type is O," Cameron said, looking over to Adrian.

"It just had to be, didn't it?" Adrian glowered, then returned to stare at the newborns. "I'd rather have Quinn be the dad than you," he said, after the doctor nearly ran down the hallway.

Ignoring, Adrian's statement, Cameron brushed his hands over his face. Too many scenarios crossed his mind. It was a complete possibility that he wasn't one of the baby's dads after all. He watched the dark-haired baby yawn and cuddle into his blanket. A dull ache crept to his forehead. Obviously, he and Joci weren't together when she slept with Adrian and Quinn, but somehow the possibility that Quinn was the dad to one of the babies felt like a vise around his heart.

"Guys, what's going on?" Quinn asked as he and the doctor arrived at the nursery.

Dr. Dahl cleared his throat and took a step back. "Thanks to newly discovered evidence, at least one of you is the father to those twins."

"Ha ha very funny." Quinn snorted. "But seriously, why am I here?"

Cameron clenched his jaw and met Quinn's confused green eyes. "You slept with Joci."

"Yeah, like nine—" He paused, and the smile vanished

from his face. "Wait, you don't think...." Realization dawned on his face. "Holy shit."

"It's a possibility that one of the babies is yours or even both of them depending on your blood type," Dr. Dahl filled in, when neither Adrian nor Cameron replied. "We'll need to take a sample from each of you to test the paternity of the boys."

Quinn slowly shook his head, eyes wide. "Sure of course. Whatever you need."

"Okay, I have to ask before we even go into questioning paternity." Adrian took a breath then yelled at the doctor, "How is this possible? How could two of us father the twins?"

"Well, there are two options here. The first being, only one of you is the father. Easy enough. The second is called superfetation. I read about it in medical school, but have never seen it. If two of you are the father, this is the first case in Iowa." The doctor grinned a little too brightly. "It'd be incredible. One for the books. Don't be shocked if medical journalists and news anchors want an interview. I'm not a believer in miracles, but this is as close as you get."

Quinn held up his hand. "All right, calm down, Doc. We don't know if that's what happened here."

"And *how* did it happen?" The words spewed out of Adrian's mouth like lava.

"Oh, well, superfetation occurs when a woman is pregnant and she ovulates again a bit later then becomes impregnated a second time. Science is marvelous, is it not?" The doctor lifted his eyebrows. "I've heard of threesomes gone awry for the cause of reported births as these." He kept rattling on scientific words and phrases, but the sound was lost to the open hallway.

Cameron wasn't expecting the right jab to his jaw moments after the doctor finished his explanation. The small trickle of blood from his lip tasted tangy compared to the other sensations coursing in his body.

"You slept with her right after I died? Real classy," Adrian growled, his muscles ready for action.

Quinn jumped in between them. "Calm down, Adrian. We don't know what happened yet."

"Wait, what? You died? I'm confused." Dr. Dahl pursed his lips together and waited, but was answered with scowls from the potential fathers. "I do think we should hurry with the paternity test so all of you can move forward with life."

"You're right, we should wait to see the results," Adrian ground out. A light seemed to turn on in the man. The shaky truce they'd called in the waiting area was replaced with hatred. "This is all your fault, Shearer. She would've been mine again if you hadn't made an appearance."

"What are you talking about, Adrian?" He pointed to Quinn, pissed he was the only object of the redhead's fury. "He slept with Joci before either of us." Rubbing his chin, Cameron resisted socking Adrian in return. "I'm the last one here, so the probability that I fathered one of those kids is slim to none." He shook his head, not believing the turn of events.

Adrian ran a trembling hand over his face then eyed the newborns. "Of course this happens to me. Everything I did was for nothing. I fucked it all up."

Dr. Dahl stepped in at that moment. "Let's get the blood for the DNA tests really quick, okay?" He led them toward an empty room and grabbed three new needles and tubes. "The test could take up to twelve weeks to—"

"Are you fucking kidding me?" Adrian said, rolling up his sleeve and sitting on the bed. "I can't even find out if I'm a dad for four months?"

Quinn exchanged glances with him. Suddenly, Cameron wasn't sure how to feel. His gut pitched at the whole situation.

"I'll see if we can rush the DNA results," Dr. Dahl said softly. "The blood test is easy. I'll get the blood types back within minutes." He capped the blood into the vial then replicated the act on Quinn and finally Cameron.

Adrian glared at Quinn then Cameron before he sped down the hall. "I need some air. I'll be back in a few minutes."

"No problem," Dr. Dahl said, walking the other direction. "I'll be back in about five. Hang tight."

Cameron watched Adrian's pissed thrust at the double doors to the stairwell. It was a lot to take in no matter which side they were on. For now, he'd let Adrian have some space. They could figure it all out after the news digested and the results were in.

Cameron leaned his forehead against the window, not caring about the smudge he left.

"This is a super weird day," Quinn said quietly, standing beside him.

"Yep. We should all go talk to Joci after we get our blood types back. From the sounds of it, she doesn't know about any of this." His heart tugged at the sight of the two babies. No matter what, he'd be there for the boys, even if he wasn't a biological father.

Letting out a breath, Quinn turned around and shook his head. "I always thought we were careful."

Cameron pried his eyes away from the adorable twins and looked at his friend. This abrupt news had Quinn nervous. He'd never seen his partner even relatively nervous before. "It'll all work out."

"Yeah, one way or another."

They stood by the nursery window until Adrian and Dr. Dahl returned. The pinched expression on the doctor's face didn't ease Cameron's mind at all.

"Let's go in here to chat," Dr. Dahl suggested, leading them to a small doctor's office. He sat and motioned toward the empty seats. The three men exchanged glances, but no one took up the offer. "Okay, let's just dive right in." He pulled out three sheets of paper and pushed them toward the trio. "Cameron, your blood type is O. Adrian, yours is AB. Quinn, yours is AB as well."

"So what's this mean?" Cameron asked when silence simmered in the room.

Dr. Dahl frowned. "It means, you, Cameron, are the father of the baby with dark hair."

"And the other baby?" Quinn asked, his face pale.

"The baby with blond hair could be either yours or Adrian's." The doctor shook his head. "I'm sorry, that's just how the blood types work. The paternity test will give us the full answer." He paused. "But there is good news. I spoke to a lab tech buddy of mine and he's rushing the DNA test. It should be back later this week."

Cameron's knees knocked together as the words digested. He was a dad. He ran his hands through his hair. *Holy shit, I'm a dad.* It didn't feel real. Hell, it probably never would. He never expected one of Joci's babies were his. Glancing up, he studied Quinn. The man's face was plastered in panic, but his sturdy body hadn't moved. The doctor's news didn't help him or Adrian today. In fact, it probably made things worse.

Shaking his head, Adrian closed his eyes. When he snapped them open, the fiery blue gaze was glued to Cameron. "Son of a bitch."

"Look, I never—" Cameron began.

"Adrian, stop." Quinn cut in, glaring at the Adrian. "We all love Joci in our own way. The judging needs to stop since we all knew what we were doing. Once the DNA tests come back, we can figure this all out. As a family." He smirked. "We may be the most dysfunctional family, but those babies deserve the best from us. Blaming each other won't give them that."

Adrian stuffed his hands in his pockets and left the room without another word. His heavy footsteps disappeared down the hall. Cameron couldn't even imagine what he was going through. Quinn asked the doctor a few more questions. He couldn't imagine what Quinn was going through either.

"I'm going to go talk to Joci," Cameron said, breaking

into the conversation.

"Good idea. She'll take the news better from you." Quinn returned to grilling the doctor while Cameron headed toward Joci's recovery room. His pulse accelerated the closer he got. *I sure hope she doesn't freak out.*

***

Hushed men's voices summoned Joci out of the second nap of the long evening. Her entire body ached as though she'd run a marathon, but she was determined to see who else was in the room. Cracking her eyelids open, a warmth spread down to her toes when she spotted Cameron's head bent over a pamphlet. It was nice to wake up and see him near her this time around in the hospital. He looked amazing despite a swollen jaw, stitches, and bruising. When they were kids, he'd always sported one goose egg or another, but now the wounds affirmed he was the man she adored. Her heart jumped when a sliver of his hair toppled over his forehead. She didn't bother to greet the other man, Dr. Dahl, since he was on his way out. She'd have time to chat with him later no doubt.

Cameron tossed the booklet to the table after turning the last page, then glanced in her direction. It was cataclysmic in only the best way when his brown eyes meshed with her hazels.

"Hey," he greeted, his voice wavering as he moved to the side of the bed. Carefully, he laced her hand within his rough ones.

"Hey, yourself," she managed, tears forming. There wasn't

any good reason for them other than happiness, and she didn't bother to hide them.

Studying every inch of her face, he opened his mouth to speak, but nothing came out. He was in as much shock as her. More so, if his expression meant anything.

"So—" she started, but he held up his hand.

"Let me first." His eyes dropped to the floor then back to her. "Dr. Dahl had us take blood and DNA tests."

She nodded. The man had told her as much after the twins' blood types came back different than expected. "Okay."

"All of us." She quirked up an eyebrow, so he continued. "Including Quinn."

"What? Why?" Joci stopped herself before she could sputter off more questions. The reality slammed into her at full speed. "Oh my God." Suddenly, she was cold. Very cold.

Cameron scratched the inside of his tattooed arm. "Yeah, so that was interesting."

"And did you find out anything?" Her insides cringed at the past. While she didn't regret sleeping with Quinn, Adrian, or Cameron, the paternity fiasco was unfortunate.

"Adrian and Quinn have the same blood type, so we won't know which of them is the dad to Baby A." He squeezed her hand. "And I'm the dad to Baby B."

"You are? How do you feel about that? Are you mad?" she asked, nervous for his response. She knew Cameron was the father when the blood test came back different than the other baby. Quinn never even came to mind. While she didn't doubt Adrian was the other baby's dad, she still wanted the concrete evidence.

Tenderly, Cameron pressed his lips to her own.

"For having a son?" He settled closer to her. "Hell no. It's the greatest news I could ever hear." His hair flopped into his eyes, and she reached up to swipe it away.

"Honest? Because it's not very conventional."

His deep chuckle vibrated through his chest and echoed against her arm. "Nothing about us is conventional, Joce. It's why I love you." His face shadowed. "But I understand if it's all too complicated for you."

"Cam—"

"I mean, it's a lot to take in. Twins from two dads, my occupation, Adrian's apparent new occupation…."

"Cameron—"

"Hello! Time for a checkup." A nurse with flamingo scrubs interrupted the couple as she swung the door closed. She was clueless that she'd stepped into a conversation Joci urgently needed to complete.

The woman scurried about with her tasks, but Joci kept her focus on Cameron as he put distance between them. He didn't look nervous about anything, which calmed her moment of insanity when the doctor told her the twins weren't exactly twins in the normal sense. Hell, she thought the doctor was joking at first. The "scientific wonder," as the hospital staff called it, still made her wonder how it happened.

Mud clung to his dark wash jeans, and the casual tee and zip-up hoodie were a shade darker thanks to the night's events. Dark bags hung beneath his eyes, and another day's growth shadowed his jaw. A fresh cut on his lip made her wonder when he'd gotten it. Her fingers itched to feel the coarse hair on the length of her body. She didn't know how he was still awake. He'd just come off a double shift before he left to meet with Del Rossi after their reunion.

"Everything looks normal. I'll see you in an hour," the pretty brunette announced, sailing out.

Once they were completely alone and the latch on the door clicked, Joci parted her lips to finish, but he beat her to it. "Where did you learn how to shoot?"

Smirking, Joci twisted her hands in the bedding. "Quinn taught me."

His surprised expression made her stomach jolt. "Why? When?"

He remained an arm's length away, but she reached for him nonetheless. After struggling, she huffed and narrowed her eyes. "Because I needed to know how to protect myself if my husband was going to be in the mob for the foreseeable future."

He touched the back of his neck, his question stilling her heart. "And after the recent events, which mob does your soon-to-be husband work for?" His gaze lowered, almost afraid to seek the answer.

Joci tried to hold back a laugh. Why he ever thought she'd miraculously have a change of heart in a few short hours was beyond her. He always second-guessed her decision, almost as if he thought himself unworthy. Well, she wouldn't let him believe it any longer. No other man was Cameron. He was all she wanted. "You're a dumbass."

Cameron's head whipped up, his face distorted with frantic hope. "Excuse me?"

"You were one when we were nine years old and you're a class act right this minute." Softening her voice, Joci succeeded in snaring his hand and tugging until he was flush to the bed. "I love you, Cameron, and despite the recent revelations about my sons, you are the man I want by my side, kicking mob ass or not. You're it." She shrugged. "Although I think I handled myself pretty damn well for a lawyer from Iowa."

In one smooth move, Cameron cupped her face and firmly kissed her lips. When he pulled away at last, Joci swore she saw stars hover over his head, but the hospital medicines were quite strong too. "You are badass, Joce. I'll be your shotgun rider forever. Especially, if you keep up the gangster attitude," he teased, gently stroking her chin. "But I'm good with defense attorney too."

Heart swelling with joy, she pecked his nose and tilted his forehead to meet hers. "If you go behind my back another time, I'll make sure you walk lopsided," she joshed, though only somewhat.

"I swear you and our son are all I'm concerned about from this point forward. Jerry can go fuck himself for all I care." He eased onto the bed and tucked her in the crook of his arm. "While you were in labor Adrian and I chatted. We're going to try and get along. I don't know if he's the other dad or not, but you don't deserve constant fighting."

"Oh, Cam, thank you."

"Anything for you." Cameron pressed his lips to her temple. His touch instantly set her at ease.

"It's not going to be easy. I for one am having a difficult time wrapping my head around all that Adrian did and didn't do. It's hard to decipher between what J.J. orchestrated and forced Adrian to do and what he actually wanted to do." She shook her head. "We all need to talk before we leave the hospital."

Cameron held her a little tighter. "Yeah, I think you're right."

Resting her head on his shoulder, Joci closed her eyes and inhaled. The bleach and medicine stench paled compared to the comforting fragrance of Cameron. It was the first smell when she woke and the last she ever wanted to pass through her nostrils. "I'm glad you're here." She tilted her neck so she could see his face. "Even if neither of these boys were yours, I need you with me. You're my Captain Smartass and Mr. Infallible. I only desire you. The sooner you get it through your thick skull, the better." Smiling, she ruffled his hair.

Gripping her hand, Cameron pressed his lips to the back before settling it over his heart. "Even though your superhero names are debatable, I'm relieved to hear you say so." His eyes scanned hers. "Because whenever I picture my life without you, a little piece of my heart breaks." He tapped her hand. "It's done it a few times lately."

Joci rubbed his chest with reassurance. "Well, no more. I'll glue the other shards together for you."

"You already have."

They snuggled in quiet contentment, the sounds outside the door mere distractions. "You probably have no clue what to name your son, but do you have any ideas?" she asked, her entire being sleepy.

"I'm afraid the name game is going to have to wait," Quinn informed them solemnly from the doorway with a doctor and nurse at his side.

Cameron sat up swiftly, the dread etched on his face perfectly matching his partner's. "Why? What's wrong?"

Eyeing the new parents, Quinn took a breath and frowned. "It's Adrian. He's gone, and he left a note."

***

Nothing could describe the intensity of emotion flowing through Cameron as he and Quinn sprinted to the hospital security room. He'd left a distraught Joci as soon as the words settled around them. Rayna was on her way, his one solace for abandoning his fiancée. "Do you know where he went? Did he say anything?"

Joci had made it clear that while she wasn't happy with Adrian, she also didn't want him gone for good. Cameron would do anything to make sure that never happened. As much as he detested Adrian and what he'd done, Cameron loved Joci more.

Cameron shoved his way to the monitors and scanned the footage. Somehow Adrian had slipped into the nursery. Clenching his teeth, he watched as the redhead kissed the blond-haired infant before leaving a note taped to the crib. Cameron's stomach plummeted at the contents. He studied the words and frowned. *I destroyed everything. I'm sorry.*

Though the note didn't specify what action Adrian was going to take, nobody liked the possibilities. "Can you follow his movements through the hospital?" Cameron asked. He knew Adrian was unstable after what J.J. told him, but he didn't expect this. *What if there's a suicide word that J.J. added?* He didn't like the thought of that, but he couldn't cross it off.

The guard in an off-white shirt clicked through the cameras, and they watched Adrian maze through the hallways until they lost him to a stairwell void of surveillance.

Slapping Quinn's shoulder, Cameron started off toward the stairs. "The roof! He's on the roof." He didn't wait for the other man, just ran in the direction his heart pulled him.

In record time, Quinn caught up and they took the steps two at a time, attaining the final door to the rooftop helipad within minutes. Bursting through the door, Cameron's stomach leapt to his throat when he spotted Adrian. He stood at the edge of the helipad, looking down at the busy Des Moines streets, back straight, face unreadable. Soft strains of orange encompassed the horizon, announcing a new day.

"Cameron, let me—" Quinn whispered, but Cameron barreled forward.

"You don't have to do this." His voice sounded foreign to his ears, so he cleared his throat. "We can be a family. All of us."

Adrian checked over his shoulder, his sad laugh disintegrating the hope for a civil interaction. "That's bullshit and you know it. Nothing can save my relationship with Joci, so why should I stick around and watch you have a second happily ever after?" His blue gaze turned cold. "It'll kill me."

Staying as close to Adrian as possible, Cameron's hands shook. "You might think that now, but it's not true. Joci doesn't deserve this, Adrian."

Adrian shook his head. "I fucked up too much. I just wanted to make Joci love me again. I can't even think about how horrible it all was. I'm sorry."

"You need help, Adrian." Cameron shuffled nearer, resulting in Adrian moving in the opposite direction. Heart sinking lower, he held up both hands and retreated. Talking the attorney down wasn't helping the situation. He was the wrong person for the job.

"Hey, hold on there," Quinn said in a calm voice. He tapped his friend's shoulder, tagging him out of the negotiation.

Accepting this as the best chance, Cameron moved backward. In silence, he watched Quinn's deliberate steps toward Adrian.

"Adrian, you've been through a ton of shit this year. It makes sense that you're hurting. I would be too if it were me." Quinn planted his feet. "I mean, hell, I wasn't expecting to take a paternity test today."

The attorney's blue eyes flashed malice. "There should've never been a question as to the babies' father. I'm the one who loved her."

Quinn sighed and clasped his hands behind him, fingers touching the handgun nestled against his spine. "No, we all did. Just at different times.”

Adrian’s face slackened. “I know.”

“You and Cam talked earlier about working things out between the two of you. No matter if you’re the dad or I am, we all have to get along.” Quinn pointed to Cameron. “He’s not going anywhere, and neither am I.”

“I was gone while Joci carried the babies, and when I came back, I might not even be the father of one was. I guess that’s karma for you.”

The cop shuffled a foot closer, tactics ever changing. “Have you seen Joci yet? She’d want to see you despite all that’s happened. You know how she is. She wouldn’t want you to run away or, worse, leave forever.”

“I can’t face her,” Adrian mumbled. “It’s too painful.”

Quinn harrumphed and shook his head. “If I was in love with her, I’d be on my hands and knees praying to whatever immortal being up there that Joci forgave me for being a dumbass these last few months. It’s not too late to mend those fences and be friends again. I know she’d say the same.”

The bitterness on Adrian’s face lessened at the cop’s deep voice. Hell, even Cameron’s nerves settled. No wonder Joci liked this guy. He could calm a cobra.

“But—”

“And if it’s about who Joci’s with, believe me, I didn’t think I could get over the fact of Joci being with either of you.” Quinn smirked. “I mean, she was a busy girl last year, but it’s why we all love her.” He met his partner’s eyes, right cheek twitching. “But when I saw her with Cameron, it clicked. Joci's going to love whoever the hell she wants. Controlling her is idiotic. It just pushes her away, doesn't it? You might hope you'll have a future with her if Cameron's out of the picture, but deep down, you know it's not true," Quinn said.

Completely facing them now, Adrian stared at the helicopter beside him where a paramedic was loading gear inside. Regret washed over his features as he digested Quinn's statements. "Dammit, you're right." He ran his fingers through his hair. "I just get so confused. Sometimes, I wonder if my memories are real or if the Mikkelsens fucked with them."

Quinn frowned. "What do you mean?"

Adrian sighed. "I was in a coma for a week. They told me I had amnesia when I woke up. Over the next few months, I had dreams of memories, but I couldn't determine if they were real or made up." He watched the traffic below. "The only constant was Joci. Everyone else was a blur. I really don't remember much of what happened after our divorce. It's all fuzzy. I remember bits and pieces, like how Cameron was our client and how she fell in love with him." He swallowed and stared at Cameron. "I keep fucking up when it comes to Joci."

Cameron exchanged a glance with Quinn. The possibility that J.J. messed with Adrian while he was comatose sounded just like what J.J. said. Something bad happened to Adrian while he was under Mikkelsen protection.

"All right, well, then you need to stay near Joci." Quinn cleared his throat. "And maybe see a few doctors and therapists who aren't taking bribes from mobsters."

Adrian shifted on his feet and cast one last look over the roof's edge before moving toward the safety of the roof. "Yeah, I guess I should." He looked like he was going to add more but shook his head instead.

"You're doing the right thing, Adrian," Quinn reaffirmed.

"I know." He took a deep breath. "But I can't see Joci yet. And as much as I want to know if that baby is mine, I need time to think about all this." He waved his wallet at the pilot in the helicopter and made his way toward the bird. "I need to sort out what happened when J.J. held me hostage. Until then, I'm not fit for anyone."

Before Quinn or Cameron could stop him, Adrian hopped inside as the blades started to turn. Quinn and Cameron exchanged a glance, but hunkered down to shield themselves from the wind.

"Don't worry, guys. I'll be back. I just don't know when," the redhead shouted before closing the door. The bird lifted off the top of the building and whirled into the distance.

"Shit!" Quinn cursed. "I didn't see that coming."

"Forget it. I don't think he knew what he was doing up here either." He nodded toward the chopper, now in the distance. "I doubt he would've jumped. Adrian is a lot of things, but never that."

"Think he'll come back like he said?" Quinn asked.

Cameron squinted his eyes. "My gut says yes. Adrian may be struggling through things, but he'll do the right thing."

Quinn snorted. "Well, we wouldn't want to second-guess your rookie gut." He lightly punched his friend's arm. "Come on, I think we both deserve a drink after the last day."

They reached the door and Cameron opened it. "I couldn't agree more."

CHAPTER TWENTY

Joci wasn't sure why she ever thought having two newborns at once would make life easier. She grimaced at the pile of clean laundry on the bed, the curtain showing the late December snow outside. After three weeks in the neonatal intensive care unit at the hospital, Levi and Brett came home, eager to keep their parents as zombies. Indeed, Adrian Petosa was proven to be the father of the baby with blond hair that'd since turned orange in the weeks since his birth. It only made sense to name the baby after his paternal grandfather, since Adrian was nowhere to be found. To say Quinn was relieved would be putting it lightly. She chuckled to herself when the results came in. While Quinn was ready to accept his responsibility had the test come back with different DNA, he was rather ecstatic to be out of mandatory diaper duty.

Pushing her hair over to one side, Joci listened to the quiet, an unusual event in the house most days. "You got them to sleep again?" she groaned, padding to the doorway.

The vision that met her gaze made her mild

disappointment for being unable to hush the boys vanish. In the recliner, Cameron lay shirtless with both boys asleep on his chest. His eye-catching tattoos against the tender skin of the babies stole her breath. His eyes were closed, and he was cupping the kiddos gently under their diapers. With a contented trace of a smile, he looked the epitome of a proud dad.

Joci tiptoed closer and pressed her lips together. Except for the messy hair, he'd pass for a model without a doubt. Not wanting to disturb the precious slumber, she snapped a photo with her phone, ensuring the flash was off. It'd be forever engrained in her memory, but having the proof of innocence mingled with mobster beginnings was a necessity.

Putting off the mound of baby clothes, Joci snuck into the kitchen and caught sight of clouds moving in from the west. The crystal blue of the sky instantly reminded her of baby Brett, then his father. Adrian hadn't uttered a word to them since the hospital. He'd vanished along with any prospect of a relationship between him and his son. Though painful, it was for the best. As was the decision to give Cameron's last name to Brett. Cameron was his father, biological or not. Adrian wasn't in his best mind, and she guessed the Mikkelsen mob had something to do with the change in him. She held out a glimmer of hope that someday he'd get his act together and be prepared to be a dad. Until then, she was thankful Cameron was around for her and their boys.

A grunt from the living room made her pop her head around the corner. Little Levi scrunched his nose, ready to cry, but when Cameron snuggled him close, the baby returned to dreams of endless milk. She couldn't resist a satisfied smile. Cameron went above and beyond for his boys. Not once had he pushed the light-haired Brett aside, despite having a different father. This was their family, as dysfunctional as it may be. He accepted it with ease, never wavering once.

Her phone lit up with a new message from Rayna, forcing her to tear her gaze from the man she couldn't wait to be with for all time. Maternity leave ended today, and her partner was more than ready for the triumphant return. She sent a reply, regretting taking a mere three months off. Criminals didn't cease their ways for her absence and neither would she stop in her zealous representation of them.

Out of the corner of her eye, she noticed the Des Moines Register from the week before lying open to the obituary page. Brett Petosa's photo stared at her, and an unexpected tear fell from her eye. The funeral had been last week, and she was grateful he'd gotten the opportunity to meet his grandson and namesake before succumbing to a heart attack. A ring full of keys sat beside the article, a constant reminder of her newfound responsibility. Brett had left Petosa Law Firm to her. Well, she and Adrian were co-owners, but the latter was all but dead, just like earlier this year. Brett never got around to updating his Last Will and Testament and didn't even know his son lived. Plus, any of his shares were passed down to Adrian's heir pursuant to the Will, which meant she oversaw the whole place.

Sighing, Joci's unease about what to do with Brett's

legacy made catching a plane to Aruba tempting. Controlling not one but two law firms wasn't what she'd had in mind when she attended law school. She'd sell the Petosa Law Firm, but she wasn't sure when yet. If she let go of the firm, she was also releasing her last hold to Adrian. With a baby identical to the man she once couldn't live without, it was easier said than done.

"Uh, Joci, he's doing it again."

Returning to the cozy room, Joci covered her laugh when she saw Levi suckling on Cameron's nipple. Carefully nabbing the now bigger of the two boys, she settled him in the crook of her arm. "Now, now, Levi, that's *my* job, not Daddy's," she playfully scolded, running her fingers through his thin, wavy hair. The twins couldn't be more different if they tried.

"You're incredible with them."

Joci lowered her eyes to Cameron's. "You're not bad yourself."

He offered a languid smile and stood, Brett stowed in his right arm. By the time he secured his bundle to the crib, Levi was zonked.

Once the nursery door was closed, both parents let out a quiet sigh. Neither boy would sleep without the other next to him. It was adorably innocent given their genesis. Someday she'd have to explain everything, but for now, she was glad for a moment's reprieve from constant crying.

Grabbing her hand, Cameron led her away from the master bedroom, his index finger to his lips until they reached the kitchen. Once safe from the loads of laundry and pacifiers, he hoisted her up on the counter and thoroughly kissed her.

"What was that for?" she asked, coming up for air. Her eyes grazed along his body, hands pleading to follow suit.

"You're the best thing I could ever dream of," he confessed, tracing her lips. "Your love—" He paused, his brown eyes melding to hers. "—it's exonerated me of every crime I've committed. You never gave up on me no matter what shit I did. I'm the luckiest son of a bitch alive."

Wrapping her legs around his hips, Joci pulled him to her. His eyes transmitted more affection than she ever knew possible in a man. It wasn't a passing fling or infatuation between them. She accepted it as truth from day one of their reunification.

"This is real, Cam. But if it ends up being a dream, please don't ever wake me up."

Nibbling at the crease of her lips, he nodded. "I promise it's not." His hands snaked up the front of her shirt. "But if it was, I think I'd have a six-pack on top of my six-pack, don't you?"

Bursting with love, Joci let out a gleeful laugh, which Cameron instantly inhaled with his lips. She'd made the right decision not once, but twice when it came to Cameron Shearer. Their future was sealed nearly as tight as the way he held her in that very moment. Nothing would rip them apart if she could help it.

A chorus of cries echoed through the small house, bursting their precoital bubble. When she wrenched her face from him, Cameron shook his head. "No, ma'am." He tossed her shirt to the floor, his hungry gaze demolishing each curve of her body. "I've heard letting babies cry it out is for the best sometimes."

Gasping when his lips touched the top of her breast, Joci raked her fingers in his hair. "All right, but just for a few minutes."

Cameron's teeth nipped at her breast. "Yeah, okay, but I'm going to need more than a few minutes." He whipped his head up and nestled her face between his tattooed hands. "Because I'm not even close to being done with you, Joci."

Searching the honest depths of his lust-rimmed eyes, Joci sighed at the hitch in his words. "I think I can live with that," she replied, fastening her lips to him. She never wanted to stop when it involved Cameron. From the way he ripped off her pants, it seemed he was in full agreement.

***

With a fresh pressed black suit coat and matching pants, Joci stepped into the elevator, purple heels first. The morning thus far was eventful yet droll. Meeting with clients and lawyers drained any ounce of energy her coffee provided. Rayna greeted her with a hug big enough to overtake Texas, but Joci appreciated the effort.

Beside her, the stylish auburn flipped through the file of their newest client, a man alleged to have robbed a bank at gunpoint. He made bail, thanks to his Del Rossi backing, and awaited them once the elevator doors sprung wide.

Immediately, Rayna flashed the fortysomething mobster a flirtatious grin. She whisked him aside before Joci heard the equally devious remark, if his low whistle hinted at anything. It appeared her partner didn't mind their less-than-kosher clients. Time and money had changed a lot for their firm. Rayna took to the vices as any eager lawyer would: with enough spunk to overtake the world and change the devil's heart. It wouldn't surprise Joci if her partner fancied a Del Rossi man herself, though she had hoped Rayna and Quinn would amount to something other than philandering coworkers.

Deciding to chat with the county attorney prior to the hearing, Joci ducked into the bustling courtroom. Inmates sat on the front bench while public defenders littered the open seats. Nothing looked out of the norm for Monday morning at the Polk County courthouse. The court attendant waved to her. Joci bobbed her head, but opted to stay near the rear since Judge Hiller was on a rant about discretionary discovery.

Thumbing through the police report, she held in the first-day jitters. It was like being fresh out of law school all over again. The hum of the court reporter's machine and click of computer screens downplayed the hushed tones of family members in the gallery. If the stench from the criminals wasn't enough to send you packing, the scowl on Judge Hiller's face sealed the deal.

Finally, Rayna and their client entered the room and sat behind the jailers, their heads ducked together in conversation. She thought about sneaking over to their position, but decided against it when the public defender's voice squeaked up an octave. When Rayna's face broke into a wide grin, Joci rolled her eyes. *Looks like someone got a head start on meeting our new clients.*

Jerry Del Rossi had made certain she had plenty of clientele when she returned from maternity leave. It was something she was both grateful and spiteful for. The man had ulterior motives, but hadn't posed them yet. Eventually, he'd make his desires known. For the time being, she and Rayna would enjoy a consistent payload, despite the lingering mafia appearances.

After the judge wiped his brow and took a sip of water, Joci made her move toward the attorney tables. She cast a glance to the opposing counsel, but couldn't tell among the group which one was assigned to the upcoming case. The judge mumbled under his breath about common decency and she stifled a laugh.

The attendant called out their case number and Joci stood, the rest of her assembly at her side within seconds of the loud announcement. Swirls of anxiety filled her gut as she clicked her heels together and offered the judge a kind nod.

"Ms. Dorous, have you chatted with your co-counsel regarding a plea offer?" the aged man asked, all nicety gone long before this hearing. "He arrived early to get a jump on the hearing."

"What? My partner is—" Swiveling toward the other table, the words on Joci's lips dissipated when she met the eyes of the man speaking to the county attorney. She blinked several times, her mascara clumping the faster she tried.

From beside her, she heard Rayna gasp out loud. "Holy

mother of…," her partner began.

Joci couldn't tear her eyes from his dark blue suit and matching pinstripe tie. Every inch of the man was how she'd known him, right down to the haircut. There wasn't a question in her mind of who stood mere feet from her. "Adrian."

In full court glory, Adrian Petosa grinned at her. His scar, still prevalent, cast him in an audacious manner, as if he'd crawled out of hell and held the mutilations to prove it.

"Hey, Joci. Miss me?"

"Sweet mother of mercy," Rayna whispered.

"I'll take it as a no, then," the judge grumped.

Gaping like a fish, Joci's neck took on bobblehead tendencies. "No…. What're you…? Why…? How…?" She couldn't complete a sentence. Not with him staring at her. Not without pinching herself to wake from this dream.

"Mr. Petosa, do the court a favor and fill Ms. Dorous in on my recent rulings regarding discovery and plea offers."

Joci couldn't breathe the more she stared at Adrian. He sounded sexier than what should be allowed for any man on the planet. His lean body beckoned her to remain in the same room until he broke the spell he conjured over her.

"Don't worry, Your Honor. My partner and I have quite a bit to catch up on." He cocked his head to the right, his determined blue eyes attached to the hazel hue of hers. His took a step closer and lowered his voice so the exchange could only be heard by the two of them. "But I can't promise all my tactics will be legal."

***

Switching off the siren, Cameron looked up the license plate of the sleek red Rolls Royce Phantom. He'd clocked the vehicle going fifty miles over the posted speed limit. Though on a side road, he wasn't about ready to let a snobby rich guy get away with dangerous driving in his town. "You wanna join me? I'll bet he tries to bribe his way out of this one," he suggested to his partner.

Quinn's envious green eyes lit up. "Hell yeah! You take the driver, I'll see if he's toting a babe around with him."

After calling in their location to dispatch, the officers jumped out of the patrol car and made their way through the swirling snowflakes to the perpetrator.

Knocking on the tinted window, Cameron waited for the glass to slide down. Even behind the diamond-encrusted Cartier sunglasses, he recognized the bright blood-orange lipstick and curved smile. The low-cut, long-sleeved designer dress accented the white Chanel satchel sitting on her lap. Only one person would be flashy enough to pair all these elements together.

"Hello, handsome," the woman purred, pushing her sunglasses on top of her long, platinum blonde hair. She rolled down the passenger side window and nodded to Quinn. "Care for a ride, Officer?"

No fucking way. Cameron swayed in utter shock, unable to rip his eyes from the sight before him. He'd been positive this greedy woman was out of his life. He'd forked over enough money to keep their breakup final.

"Bambi." The way her name slipped off his tongue tasted too much like her Chanel perfume currently surrounding both of them.

"Ah, so you do remember my name." She beamed, tapping her manicured nails on the steering wheel.

When Quinn obnoxiously coughed, Cameron snapped out of her trance. "What the hell are you doing here?"

Bambi fluttered her thick eyelashes coyly. "Why, to see you, Cameroni. I've missed you."

"The feeling isn't mutual," he ground out.

The depth of her chuckle caught him off guard. He was too used to the airy one from Joci. This sound hurled him backward in time to places he never wanted to think of ever again.

"Not yet, no, but I'd bet my villa in Tuscany that you'll change your mind." She glanced to Quinn. "Give us a moment, will ya, hon?"

Quinn raised his eyebrows but glanced to him. Nodding once, Cameron waited until his partner was out of earshot to speak.

"Get the fuck out of my city, Bambi." He ripped off his sunglasses and stared into her china-blue eyes. At one point, they'd held him captive. Now they were thorns shredding his flesh. Gripping the windowsill with one hand, he shook his other index finger. "I'm not touching whatever shit you brought to Iowa with a ten-foot pole, got it?"

Too perfect to be real, her nose scrunched up at his threat. Bambi captured his finger and pressed a kiss to it, her rosy lipstick smearing along the appendage. "You sure about that? Because I've been chatting with my brothers as of late. They informed me of some stolen money used for my European getaway. They were curious how you got your hands on all that cash. I wonder if it was from the heist you supposedly couldn't finish."

Cameron's throat dried, already aware of the next sentence. He'd thought he hid it better. No, he *knew* he covered his tracks. If she'd found out, it meant someone told her.

"You sent me away, sweetheart." Her lips slid into a pout. "That's not very nice, *mi amore*. What will I tell the children?"

"We broke up. I made sure you had plenty of money to keep you satisfied and away from me. And you don't have any kids," he growled, still trying to piece together how in the hell Bambi wasn't in prison or dead. The last he saw her, she was halfway to one of the two. She'd tricked him into a scheme, and it cost him dearly back then. He wasn't about to replicate the past.

The blonde batted her eyelashes. "Don't I?"

"Cut the shit, Bambi. You and I both know we don't have anything in common anymore, much less children." He was done with her antics, though his stomach warned him she wasn't nearly finished.

She chortled. "Yeah, you're right. I hate kids, but it'd be funny if we had one, wouldn't it?"

"Not in the least." Cameron ignored the backhanded tease, using every ounce of willpower in his arsenal. She knew how to get under his skin, but this time he wouldn't allow it. He'd be strong.

Bambi picked at her cuticle. "I hear you have a son.

Congrats, big daddy."

Shit! Dammit, Jerry. His boss was the biggest blabbermouth sometimes. He didn't react. How could he with his blood frozen?

She pressed a finger to her lips. "I wonder how that pretty fiancée of yours would react to your mobster ex-girlfriend coming to town to rekindle a romance."

He clenched his jaw until he swore it'd break. "Leave Joci out of this," he cautioned. The holstered gun on his leg was becoming more and more tempting as their conversation continued.

"I won't touch a hair on her mama head if you play nice," Bambi said with a small grin.

"What do you want?" It was always something with Del Rossi's best conman. She could siphon money from monks if she had enough time, and she had. It had been her greatest achievement when they were a couple. All these years later, he was certain she'd added to her resume.

"I have a job, *amore*, and I require your unique set of talents." Bambi met his scowl. "It'll be like old times, except maybe you won't run from me."

"You turned the mob against me when we broke up. Your brothers nearly killed me." She shrugged as if it didn't matter. Well, for her, it truly didn't. Bambi could get away with murder and no one would care. In fact, it would only make her stronger.

"Water under the bridge," she purred. "My brothers are willing to let you out of your contract if you do this one last gig."

Cameron didn't like her nonnegotiable proposal. It wasn't a request. This was a mandated mob job. He couldn't refuse unless he was dead. She knew it; he knew it; hell, the entire Del Rossi network knew it. Even if it meant getting out of the mob for good, he may be leaving it in a casket instead of walking away.

Leaning into the car, he wrapped his hand around her wrist and squeezed. "Let me make a few things perfectly clear, Bambi: I wish you were dead, the past isn't coming back to bite my ass, and the sole reason I'm forced to go along with your scheme is because if I don't, your brother will kill the only woman I'll ever love."

Her eyes clouded, but she didn't speak. He liked her better this way anyhow. Releasing her, he stepped back and rested his hands on the thick holster. "Got it?"

Bambi revved the engine and slipped her sunglasses into place. "Got it." She grinned. "Oh, and, Cam?"

"What?" he ground out.

Bambi blew him a kiss. "You should know better than anyone that no one stays away long when you're in the mob."

The expensive vehicle squealed off the side of the road and over the hill while he watched it disappear. The thudding in Cameron's chest intensified as reality crumbled around all sides. He'd dug his way out of Bambi's manipulative dungeon and sworn he'd never return. As it turned out, all of his efforts were for naught. His past had returned, and she wore a color only the devil would commend.

Be on the look out for book three,

CREDENCE.

ACKNOWLEDGMENTS

Thank you to my incredible publisher, Hot Tree Publishing. These lovely ladies provide an encouraging atmosphere, and I'm beyond grateful to be part of their tribe. Endless thanks to the editors, beta readers, cover designers, and each person who helped *Exonerated with Love* come to life.

Lastly, I'm blessed to be involved with writers and authors who challenge me to never give up on my stories.

ABOUT THE AUTHOR

Skye McNeil began writing at the age of seventeen and has been lost in a love affair ever since. During the day, she moonlights as a paralegal at a law firm favoring criminal law.

Skye enjoys writing romantic comedies and cozy mysteries novels that leave readers wanting more and falling in love over and over. She writes contemporary and historical novels ranging from sweet and sassy to steamy and sultry. Her constant writing companions are two cats and two dogs. When she's not writing, Skye enjoys spending time with family, photography, volleyball, traveling, and curling up with a cup of coffee and reading.

Skye love to connect with her readers.

FACEBOOK: WWW.FACEBOOK.COM/SkyesTheLimitWriting

WEBSITE: WWW.SKYEMCNEIL.COM

TWITTER: HTTPS://TWITTER.COM/SKYE_MCNEIL7

INSTAGRAM: WWW.INSTAGRAM.COM/MCNEILSKYE

ABOUT THE PUBLISHER

Hot Tree Publishing opened its doors in 2015 with an aspiration to bring quality fiction to the world of readers. With the initial focus on romance and a wide spread of romance sub-genres, they envision opening up to alternative genres in the near future.

Firmly seated in the industry as a leading editing provider to independent authors and small publishing houses, Hot Tree Publishing is the sister company to Hot Tree Editing, founded in 2012. Having established in-house editing and promotions, plus having a well-respected market presence, Hot Tree Publishing endeavors to be a leader in bringing quality stories to the world of readers.

Interested in discovering more amazing reads brought to you by Hot Tree Publishing? Head over to the website for more:

WWW.HOTTREEPUBLISHING.COM

www.ingramcontent.com/pod-product-compliance
Lightning Source LLC
Chambersburg PA
CBHW032209180726
48284CB00001B/251